THE END OF THE
WORLD IN BRESLAU

THE END OF THE WORLD IN BRESLAU

Marek Krajewski

Translated from the Polish by
Danusia Stok

MACLEHOSE PRESS
QUERCUS · LONDON

First published in Great Britain in 2009 by

MacLehose Press
an imprint of Quercus
21 Bloomsbury Square
London WC1A 2NS

Originally published in Poland as *Koniec świata w Breslau*
by Wydawnictwo W.A.B. Co Ltd, 2006

A CIP catalogue reference for this book
is available from the British Library

ISBN 978 1 906694 06 7 (HB)
ISBN 978 1 906694 07 4 (TPB)

2   4   6   8   10   9   7   5   3   1

Designed and typeset in Octavian by Patty Rennie

Printed and bound in England by Clays Ltd, St Ives plc

THE END OF THE
WORLD IN BRESLAU

NEW YORK, SUNDAY, NOVEMBER 20TH, 1960
TEN O'CLOCK IN THE EVENING

The black cab-driver, James Mynors, increased the speed of his wipers. Two arms greedily gathered large flakes of snow from the windscreen. The wipers worked as a singular metronome which accentuated the rhythm of Chuck Berry's rock'n'roll hit, "Maybellene", flowing from the radio. Mynors' hands danced on the steering wheel, nonchalantly pushed and pulled the gear stick, and slapped his knees and thighs. The song made not the slightest impression on the glum passenger who, with one cheek pressed against the cold window, moved the newspaper he was holding this way and that so as to catch the light from passing street lamps and shop windows. When Mynors turned the volume up to maximum, the passenger shifted to the centre of the back seat. The eyes of the two men met in the rear-view mirror.

"Turn it down and stop jumping about at the wheel," the passenger said with a strong German accent. His gloomy, bloated face, shaded beneath the rim of his old-fashioned hat, took on a malicious expression. "We're not in Africa, on some banana plantation."

"Motherfucking racist." Mynors' words were drowned out by the happy chorus; he turned the volume down and drove into a side street of pseudo-Victorian, one-storeyed houses. There was not much light here. The passenger carefully folded his paper and slipped it into the inside pocket of his coat.

"There, on the corner," he muttered, trying to see through the dirty curtain of snow and rain. The car drew up at the place indicated. The passenger grunted his disapproval, opened the door and sank his shoes into the muddy slush. He unfurled his umbrella and, panting heavily, approached the driver's window.

"Please wait for me."

Mynors rubbed his index finger against his thumb in response and lowered the window a little. The passenger pulled a banknote from his wallet and slipped it into the driver's hand. A merry voice distorted by a peculiar accent came from behind the window:

"You can walk back, you old Hitlerite."

With a contemptuous and controlled skid of its rear wheels, the cab waltzed on the slippery road and sped away. The driver lowered his window – Chuck Berry played at full volume in the quiet street.

The man slowly climbed the steps to the small porch, stamped his snow-covered shoes and pressed the bell. The door opened almost immediately. In the doorway stood a young priest wearing thick, tortoise-shell glasses and sporting a Chuck Berry hairstyle.

"Mr Herbert Anwaldt?" asked the priest.

"That's me. Good evening," panted Anwaldt in annoyance as he watched the cab turn the corner. "How am I supposed to get home now?"

"Father Tony Cupaiuolo from St Stanislaus' Parish," Chuck Berry introduced himself. "I was the one who telephoned you. Please come in."

The familiar click of the lock, the familiar parlour filled with books and the lamp with its green lampshade. Missing were only the familiar smell of cigars and the familiar host. The troubled Father Cupaiuolo hung Anwaldt's sodden coat and hat by the door and clumsily shook off the sticky spittle of snow from his umbrella. Instead of the smell of Cuban cigars, Anwaldt's nostrils drew in the sharp odour of medication, the pitiful stench of a bedpan, the penetrating smell of death.

"Your friend is dying," the priest declared.

Anwaldt inhaled a deep gulp of nicotine. From a bedroom on the first floor emerged a young nurse. With apparent revulsion, she carried the enamel containers that the sick man had filled a moment earlier. She glanced at Anwaldt. He sensed immediately that she felt the same towards him as to the bedpan she held out in front of her.

"Do not smoke in here, please." Heartfelt indignation almost burst the buttons of the housecoat that tightly hugged her breasts. Anwaldt, counting on just such an effect, inhaled even deeper.

"Mr Anwaldt, your friend is dying of lung cancer," Father Cupaiuolo whispered reproachfully. "Smoking tobacco in his house is ill-advised."

The nurse went into the bathroom, so Anwaldt decided to abandon his smoking and threw the cigarette into the fireplace. He looked at the priest expectantly.

"My dear sir, your friend's nurse telephoned me today asking for the last rites for the sick man." Father Cupaiuolo drew in his breath and gathered his confidence. "As I'm sure you know, the sacrament of confession is one of them. When I sat down beside him, ready to hear his sins and bless him on his last journey, Mr Mock told me he had one terrible sin on his conscience which he would not confess until you were here. He will confess only after he has spoken to you. You come practically every morning – I could have waited with confession until tomorrow, but he insists I hear it today. *Salus aegroti suprema lex*,[†] and for a priest too. Go to him now. He will explain everything." Father Cupaiuolo looked at his watch. "Please don't worry about the cab. I fear you will not be going home today."

† The well-being of the sick is the first priority.

3

Anwaldt made his way upstairs but, halfway up, he turned back. Father Cupaiuolo watched in surprise as Anwaldt approached the hat-stand and pulled a newspaper from his coat pocket. Tilting his head, the priest read the German title. "What can *Süddeutsche* mean?" He pondered for a moment and let his memory flick through the small exercise book he had once filled with German vocabulary – "*Deutsche* means German, but *süd*? What does that mean?"

The priest put aside these musings on the German language and, as Anwaldt reached the top of the stairs, returned to the problems of his Puerto Rican parishioners. The sound of retching and gurgling sanitary appliances came from the bathroom. Anwaldt pushed open the bedroom door a crack. A streak of light severed the bed in two. Mock's head was resting on the summit of a mountain of white pillows. Next to the bed stood a drip and a bedside table cluttered with medicines. Slender little bottles with parchment-like hoods stood alongside squat jars full of pills. Mock lifted a hand perforated by needles and aimed an ironic smile at Anwaldt.

"See what a malicious old man I am. As if it wasn't enough that you were here this morning, I call for you in the evening too." The hiss of Mock's breath fell a tone deeper. "But I'm sure you'll forgive me when I say I wanted to show off my new nurse. She alternates with the one you see here every morning. What do you think of her? She finished nursing school a week ago. Her name is Eva."

"Worthy of the name." Anwaldt made himself comfortable in the armchair. "She would tempt many a man with her apples of paradise."

Mock's laughter whistled for a long time. The flaccid skin across his cheekbones tautened. Beams of car headlights glided across the bedroom walls and briefly drew from the semi-darkness a framed map of a city encircled by a broad, mangled ribbon of river.

"What brought the biblical comparison to mind?" Mock looked intently at Anwaldt. "The priest, no doubt."

4

Silence descended. Sister Eva choked and spluttered in the bathroom.

Anwaldt hesitated, nervously twisting his fingers, then spread out the newspaper.

"Listen, I wanted to read something to you . . ." Anwaldt began to search for his glasses and instead found his cigarette-case. Remembering it was forbidden to smoke, he put it away again.

"Don't read me anything, and go ahead and smoke. Smoke here, Herbert, go ahead and fucking smoke, one after another, and hear my confession," Mock caught his breath. "I told you about my first wife, Sophie, remember? This is going to be about her . . ."

"Exactly . . . I wanted . . ." Anwaldt said, and stopped. Mock was whispering something to himself and did not hear him. Anwaldt strained his ears.

"Thirty years ago, it was a Sunday too, and snow stuck to the windows just like it does today."

BRESLAU, SUNDAY, NOVEMBER 27TH, 1927
TWO O'CLOCK IN THE AFTERNOON

Snow, swept along by gusts of wind, stuck to the windowpanes. Mock stood at the window looking out at Nicolaistrasse, covered in tyre tracks that criss-crossed the snow and mud. The clock on the Town Hall struck two. Mock lit his first cigarette of the day. His hangover returned with another wave of nausea. Images of the previous night teemed before his eyes: the theatre-variété and the three inebriated policemen – Commissioner Ebners, with his bowler slipping back to the crown of his head; Counsellor Domagalla smoking his twentieth Sultan cigar; and he himself, Counsellor Mock, pulling at the crimson velvet curtain which separated their discreet alcove from the rest of the room; the owner of Hotel Restaurant Residenz with a servile smile bringing them pot-bellied

5

tankards on the house; the cabby trying to calm Mock as he forced an open bottle of schnapps into his hand; his twenty-five-year-old wife, Sophie, waiting for him in the bedroom, throwing back her hair, spreading her legs and looking stern as he rolls in, dead drunk. Mock calmly extinguished his cigarette in the horseshoe-shaped ashtray. He glanced fleetingly at the waiter coming into the parlour.

Heinz Rast, a waiter from Schweidnitzer Keller, was carrying plates and dishes. Placing them on the table, he cast an eye over the gathering. Franz Mock he already knew; overawed, he had approached Rast's boss, Max Kluge, a few days earlier to order a grand dinner in honour of his brother. With Rast himself he had not been so humble, and had argued over every pfennig as they sorted out the menu. Today the waiter had also met his wife, Irmgard Mock, a dispirited woman with gentle eyes who took the enormous thermoses of food from him and stood them on the coal cooker.

"The corned brawn with caraway is excellent. Speciality of the house, cold, in aspic," the waiter commended, unable to conceal his admiration for the shapely blonde with dreamy, slightly absent eyes who casually passed a crystal cigarette-holder to the college boy sitting next to her. The boy dug out the smoking cigarette end from the holder and turned to the stocky, dark-haired man of over forty standing at the window:

"Uncle Eberhard, please come to the table. The hors d'oeuvres are served."

The dark-haired man kissed the dreamy-eyed young woman on the hand and sat down next to her. Franz and Irmgard sat opposite them. The college boy was planted awkwardly at the head of the table. Rast, hastened by a gesture from Franz, hurried into the kitchen and brought in five stout bottles of beer with E. HAASE engraved on their porcelain caps. He opened three and poured beer into the narrow tankards. Then he settled down in the kitchen and, through the closed door, listened to the conversation at the table.

"You shouldn't have spent so much on this grand dinner. Irmgard is such a good cook – her dishes could be the boast of Schweidnitzer Keller," – a calm bass voice, the sucking in of beer froth and a sigh of relief.

"We couldn't let a lady like Sophie eat our Sunday black pudding and sauerkraut. Here we have something that is eaten in higher . . . society," – a nervous baritone, stammering at every word. "Thank you for finally agreeing to come and visit us. It is an honour for a simple foreman."

"I assure you, Franz, I've seen ladies lick the grease off bowls," – a melodious, quiet and almost childish voice. "Although I come from an aristocratic family, I rid myself of class prejudice when I was at the Conservatory . . ." – a note of impatience. "Besides, I don't understand this 'finally'. As far as I know, nobody's ever invited me here before."

"Erwin, you're taking your final school exams this year," – the bass voice, the crackle of a match, smoke exhaled through nostrils. "What are your plans for the future?"

Rast stirred the bouillon and filled the soup dishes. On a large platter he arranged some asparagus and poured over it some melted butter. He opened the door, carried all this into the room and announced merrily:

"And here is something hot: bouillon with egg yolk and asparagus."

Eberhard put out his cigarette. His nephew studied the Trebnitzer embroidery of the tablecloth and said slowly and emphatically:

"I want to study German at university."

"Ah, interesting," Eberhard poured spoonfuls of the bouillon into his mouth with evident satisfaction. "I remember you wanted to be a police-man not long ago."

"That was before I discovered Heine's poetry."

As Rast reached for the plate of aspic to take it away, Franz Mock grabbed the waiter by the wrist and sliced off a sizeable piece of brawn with his fork.

"I've paid for it so I'll eat it," Franz Mock's face grew pale and he made

7

Rast think of a drunkard who, in one movement, had turned a table upside down in his restaurant. "I know a simple foreman on the railways cannot be a role model for his son . . . But I've told you so many times — be a railway engineer; you'll earn lots of money, go to Zoppot every year . . . But you won't listen to me and insist on studying some Jew . . . "

"Papa, I'm a poet," Erwin cracked his knuckles nervously. "I want to do the thing that I love . . ."

Irmgard signalled to Rast to leave the room. Rast grabbed the plate with what remained of the aspic, but Franz Mock held his hand back once again.

"'I love, I love . . .'" Bits of meat and spittle landed on the Trebnitzer tablecloth. "Are you some sort of queer, or what? Poets are all queers, or dirty Jews. And what sort of poems do you write? They're all about stars and machines. Why don't you write a love poem to a woman? I know, I know . . . That new German tutor of yours . . . He's the one who's trying to turn you into a queer . . ."

"Franz, stop, or you'll remember this for a very long time." Irmgard's eyes threw daggers first at her husband, then at the waiter. The latter tore the dish with the remainder of brawn from Franz Mock's hand and hurried into the kitchen. He melted some butter in a huge frying pan and arranged slices of potato on top of it. He stood a pot of mutton in thick sauce on another hob. Silence descended in the dining-room. It was broken by the voice of a spoilt child:

"Ebi, you were interested in Latin literature yourself once. You wanted to be a professor. Does that make you a homosexual?"

Rast carried in a tray with the next course.

"Ladies and gentlemen, mutton in herb sauce, roast potatoes, celery salad and sour cherry compote." Rast efficiently gathered up the plates, hastened by Irmgard's angry eyes. He repaired to the kitchen and glued his ear to the door: nothing but the penetrating clatter of knives and forks.

"My dear," — a calm voice — "Surely you would know that better than anyone."

"Uncle Ebi, what is wrong with studying literature?" — the uneasy tenor rising occasionally to a falsetto — "Explain to my father that there's nothing wrong with it. You of all people know how many sublime moments poetry can give us, what ecstasies it imparts . . . You studied Horace yourself and you wrote an article about him in Latin . . . Our Latin scholar, Rector Piechotta, values those comments of yours a great deal . . ."

"I think," — the hiss of gas from a bottle being opened accompanied the hoarse voice, strained by the dozens of cigarettes smoked the previous day — "that education and the career one pursues do not always go hand in hand, as you can see in my case . . ."

"Stop, Ebi, and speak like a normal human being," — a suppressed burp. "You left behind all that nonsense and chose to work as a policeman. Get to the point: what is best for the boy — poet or railway engineer?"

"Go on, tell us," the child indulged herself. "We're all waiting for a solution to this interesting dilemma."

"Engineer." A mouthful was gulped down loudly.

Rast sprang away as Erwin all but demolished the door as he fled the room. The boy thrust a cap onto his head, wrenched on his somewhat too tight coat and ran into the street.

"Here is the dessert, ladies and gentlemen: Silesian poppy cake." Rast served cake and coffee. As he removed the untouched chops from in front of Sophie's bust, he noticed that her hand holding the cigarette-case was shaking. He looked at her and understood that this would not be the end to this unpleasant dinner.

"It is interesting, I have known my husband for two years and today is the first time I do not recognize him." A faint flush appeared on Sophie's cheeks. "Where is that plebeian strength of yours, Eberhard, which makes criminals flee from you and once enthralled me so? Today it ran out when you should have defended that sensitive boy. When we're at home you sneer at technocrats, at people whose horizons are limited to financial gain, but when we're here you put a railwayman above a poet? It is a pity your refined brother cannot see you reading Horace, or witness how moved you are by *The Sorrows of Young Werther*. Criminal Counsellor Mock falls asleep in his armchair, in the safe halo of his lamp, and onto his round belly, bloated with beer and pork knuckle, slips a school edition of Horace's *Odes*; a school edition with a little dictionary because this eminent Latin stylist can no longer remember his vocabulary."

"Shut your trap," Eberhard Mock said quietly.

"You pig!" Sophie suddenly got up from the table.

Mock watched with melancholy as his wife ran from the room, then listened to the clatter of her shoes on the stairs. He lit a cigarette and smiled at Franz.

"What is the name of Erwin's teacher? We'll check, maybe he really is a queer?"

BRESLAU, THAT SAME NOVEMBER 27TH, 1927
MIDNIGHT

Mock staggered out of the Savoy restaurant on Tauentzienplatz. The bellboy ran out after him and handed him his hat, which Mock did not put on, instead allowing the wet flakes of snow to settle on his sweat-dampened hair. Beneath the windows of Sänger's restaurant swayed a lone drunk, interrupting his involuntary movements only to whistle for passing cabs. The bellboy's whistles were evidently more persuasive because in a moment an old and patched droschka stopped beside Mock. The drunkard lurched towards it but Mock was closer. He threw a fifty-pfennig piece to the boy and collapsed into the seat, almost squashing a delicate human being.

"Forgive me, sir, but you got in so quickly I didn't have time to inform you that I already have a passenger. I'm cabby Bombosch, and this is my daughter, Rosemarie. This is my last run and we're on our way home." The cabby jovially twisted his bristling whiskers. "She is so tiny that the gentleman will not find himself too cramped. She is still so young . . ."

Mock observed the triangular face of his travelling companion. Enormous naïve eyes, a toque with a veil, and a coat. The girl might have been eighteen; she had slender hands, blue from the cold, and re-soled shoes with holes in them. All this Mock took in by the light of the street lamps located around the Museum of Silesian Antiquities.

Rosemarie watched the vast edifice of the museum slip past on the right-hand side of the street. Mock counted out loud the bars and restaurants on Sonnenplatz, Gräbschenerstrasse and Rehdigerstrasse, and announced the results of his findings to Rosemarie with genuine pleasure.

The carriage stopped outside a splendid tenement on Rehdigerplatz, where Mock and his wife Sophie occupied a five-room apartment on the second floor. Mock scrambled out of the droschka and threw the driver the first crumpled banknote he pulled from his coat pocket.

"Use the change to buy your daughter some shoes and gloves," he hiccoughed loudly and, without hearing the cabby's joyous thanks, stretched his shoulders wide, lowered his head and made as if to charge at the tenement door.

Fortunately for Mock's head, the caretaker of the tenement was not asleep and managed to open the door in time. Mock hugged him effusively and, in no particular hurry, began his arduous expedition up the stairs, tumbling against the Scylla of the banister and the Charybdis of the wall, threatened by a Cerberus who, wailing and barking, was thrashing about in the vestibule of Hades behind some closed door. Mock, detained neither by the siren song of the servant who tried to take his coat

11

and hat, nor by the wild delight of his old dog, Argos, reached the Ithaca of his bedroom where the faithful Penelope was waiting for him in her muslin dressing gown and high-heeled slippers.

Mock smiled at the pensive Sophie whose head was leaning against the backrest of the chaise-longue adjacent to their turned-down bed. Sophie stretched herself a little and the muslin of her dressing gown clung to her generous breasts. Mock took this to mean only one thing and feverishly began to undress. As he struggled with the cord of his long johns, Sophie sighed:

"Where were you?"

"In a tavern."

"With whom?"

"I met two friends, the same as yesterday – Ebners and Domagalla."

Sophie stood up and slipped beneath the eiderdown. Mock, somewhat surprised, did the same and snuggled close to his wife's back. He squeezed his hand under her arm with difficulty and greedily spread his fingers over one soft breast.

"I know you want to apologize to me. I know that perfectly well. Carry on being proud and hard and don't say a word. I forgive your behaviour at Franz's. I forgive your coming back late. You wanted a drink, you were annoyed," she said in a monotonous voice, staring into the mirror of the dressing table opposite the bed. "You say you were with friends. I know you're not lying. You certainly haven't been with a woman." She propped herself up on one elbow and looked into the eyes of her reflection. "You wouldn't manage it with a woman in the state you're in. You've had no fire in you lately. You're simply feeble in bed."

"I can do it right now. I can hold you down. You'll be begging me to stop," Mock's cheeks were burning; with one hand he tore at the muslin of the dressing gown, with the other, at the cotton of his long johns. "Today is the day our child will finally be conceived."

12

Sophie turned to her husband and, touching his lips with hers, spoke with the voice of a sleepy child:

"I waited for you yesterday – you were with friends. I waited for you today – again you were with friends, and now you want to fuck?"

Mock adored it when she was vulgar. He ripped his long johns in his excitement. Sophie leaned against the wall. From beneath her nightdress appeared two narrow pink feet. Mock began to stroke and kiss them. Sophie slipped her fingers into her husband's thick hair and pulled his head back.

"You want to fuck?" she repeated the question.

Mock closed his eyes and nodded. Sophie drew her legs towards her and planted both feet on her husband's ribcage. She straightened them abruptly and pushed him off the bed.

"Fuck with your friends," he heard his wife whisper as he fell onto the rough carpet.

BRESLAU, MONDAY, NOVEMBER 28TH, 1927
TWO O'CLOCK IN THE MORNING

Mock woke up at the desk in his study. His right hand was covered with clots of blood. In the lamplight stood a bottle of Rhein Spätburgunder and a half-filled glass. He scrutinized his hand. Stuck to the dry, brownish clumps of blood were a few fair hairs. Mock went to the kitchen, holding up his torn long johns. He washed his hands meticulously in the cast-iron washbasin. Then he poured some water into an enamel mug and drank, listening to the sounds coming from the courtyard: a metallic creaking of springs. He looked out of the window. Cabby Bombosch had put a nose-bag over his horse's head and was stroking its nape. The carriage shook and bounced on its suspension. Rosemarie was earning the money for a new coat.

Mock opened his eyes and listened for a while to the persistent calls of milkmen. The coldness of the morning penetrated his body, squeezed as it was into an armchair. He opened his mouth with difficulty and ran his parched tongue over the sandpaper of his palate. Since no position in the armchair was less than painful, Mock decided to stand up. He wrapped himself in his dressing gown and padded down the sandstone floor of the hall in his bare feet. Argos the dog expressed his usual morning delirium, not shared to any degree by his master. In the bathroom, Mock dipped his toothbrush into a box of Phönix powder and began his oral ablutions. The result was such that to the acidic-alcoholic effluvium was added an acrid aftertaste of cement. Mock furiously spat the grey paste into the basin and soaped his huge badger brush with Peri shaving cream. The razor was an object he should have used that day only under close supervision. A sharp prick, and he realized he had cut himself. The small trickle of blood was very light, much lighter than the blood which had poured from Sophie's nose the previous night. Mock studied his reflection.

"How is it that I can look you boldly in the eye?" He wiped his face dry and patted it with Welzel eau-de-cologne. "Because nothing happened yesterday. Besides, I remember nothing."

Their servant, Marta Goczoll, was busy in the kitchen while her husband, the butler Adalbert, stood straight as an arrow, holding more than a dozen ties in one hand and a hanger with a suit and white shirt in the other. Mock dressed hurriedly and tied a deep-red tie around his neck. Marta tucked its fat knot under the wings of his collar. Mock just managed to squeeze his swollen feet into his shoes – freshly polished by Adalbert – threw his pale, cashmere coat over his shoulders, donned his hat and left the apartment. On the landing, a large Pomeranian began to fawn on him. Mock stroked the dog. Its owner, the lawyer Patschkowsky, looked with contempt at his neighbour from whom, as every day, emanated a smell of alcohol and eau-de-cologne.

"There was a terrible noise coming from your apartment last night. My wife couldn't get to sleep until morning," Patschkowsky drawled.

"I was training the dog," Mock mumbled.

"Your wife, more likely," Patschkowsky's pince-nez glinted in the yellow light of the hallway lamp. "You think you're allowed to do anything, don't you? That dog of yours wailed with a human voice."

"Some animals speak with a human voice a month before Christmas Eve." Mock felt the urge to throw his neighbour down the stairs.

"Is that so?" Patschkowsky raised his eyebrows in surprise.

"I'm talking to one of them even now."

The lawyer stood as if turned to stone, staring for a moment into Mock's bloodshot eyes. Then he walked slowly downstairs, plucking up the courage to offer one last witty "Is that so?"

Mock turned back to his apartment. Finding that the door to the bedroom was locked from the inside, he reeled into the kitchen. Adalbert and Marta were sitting anxiously at the table.

"You haven't eaten any breakfast, sir. I've made scrambled eggs with chanterelle mushrooms." Marta revealed the gaps in her teeth.

"Enjoy it yourselves," Mock smiled effusively. "I wanted to wish you a good day. May it be as good as last night. You slept well, did you?"

"Yes, sir." It seemed to Adalbert that he could still hear Sophie's dreadful screams and the dull scratching of the dog's paws against the closed bedroom door.

Mock left the apartment, squeezing his eyes shut and gritting his teeth.

Criminal Sergeant Kurt Smolorz was one of the finest employees of the Breslau Police Praesidium. His brutality was cursed by villains and his laconic reports praised by his bosses. One of his superiors valued yet another of his virtues above all others — his perspicacity. Smolorz demonstrated this virtue very clearly that morning — twice. First, when he walked into Mock's office with its dark wood panelling and saw the red impression of Mock's signet ring on its owner's forehead, a clear sign that the Counsellor had been resting his tired brow on it. He did not report right away the terrible crime committed in the Griffins tenement on Ring where, by order of Criminal Director Heinrich Mühlhaus, he and his boss were to present themselves without delay. He knew that Mock was in no condition to understand anything just then.

"I'll wait for you in the car, Counsellor sir," Smolorz said, and left to bring the new black Adler up to the gate of the Praesidium. This was not the only reason the Sergeant had taken his leave so swiftly. Mock discovered another when, cursing, he rolled into the passenger seat and saw Smolorz's red-haired hand holding out a bottle of milk. Mock opened it and greedily took a few gulps. He was now ready to hear the story. Smolorz turned on the ignition.

"The Griffins tenement, eight o'clock this morning," Smolorz spoke just as he wrote his reports. "Shoemaker Rohmig couldn't stand the smell in his workshop and knocked down a wall. Behind it was a corpse."

It was not far from the Police Praesidium at Schuhbrücke to Ring. Mock drank the last drops of milk as Smolorz parked the Adler outside the Lottery Bookmakers on Nicolaistrasse. In the inner courtyard of the Griffins tenement, outside the shoemaker's workshop, stood a uniformed policeman who saluted as they approached. Next to him was a whiskered consumptive who bore the weight of his heavy leather apron with heroic effort, and a stout woman who could not accept the fact that there was no bench in the dirty yard. Every few seconds, magnesium lit up the wretched room filled with the odour of old shoes, rotten with sweat, and bone glue. When Mock and Smolorz walked in they detected another smell, one well known to them and unique in its nature. A counter, sticky with glue, divided the workshop in two. Two walls were lined with cellar shelves on which stood rows of shoes. There was a small window and a door in the third, and from the fourth wafted that familiar stench. An opening of roughly one metre by one metre had been knocked through this wall. The police photographer, Ehlers, was kneeling in front of it, poking his lens into the dark recess. Mock held his nose and peered in. From the darkness of the small niche, his torch picked out a hairless skull covered with decomposing skin. The hands and feet had been tied to hooks on the far side of the recess. The Counsellor looked at the corpse's face once again and discerned a fat maggot trying to worm its way into the film that covered one eye. He quickly stepped out of the workshop, removed his coat, threw it to the uniformed policeman and, legs astride, leaned his hands on the outside wall. Smolorz, hearing the sounds coming from his boss, reproached himself for failing to anticipate the combined effects of a hangover, a bottle of milk and a disintegrating corpse. From his trouser pocket, Mock pulled out a handkerchief on which Sophie had embroidered his initials and wiped his mouth. He turned his face to the sky and greedily swallowed drops of falling rain.

"Take the pick-axe," he told the uniformed policeman, "and bring the wall down so we can get the body out. Smolorz, tie a handkerchief around your mouth and nose and search the recess and the dead man's pockets, and you, Ehlers, do what you can to help Smolorz."

Mock pulled on his coat, adjusted his hat and cast his eye around the yard.

"And who are you?" he said, aiming a brilliant smile at the stout lady who was shifting from one leg to the other.

17

"Ernst Rohmig, master shoemaker," the consumptive eagerly introduced himself without being asked. He hunched his shoulders to adjust his leather armour.

"The tenement administrator," the lady huffed. Cheap dye flaked from her greasy hair which was wrapped around curlers. "Get on with it, sir. Do you think I can stand around for ever worrying about the extra money I'm going to have to pay someone to clean up the wall you've fouled? Now, please introduce yourself! I am Mathilde Kühn, the owner's plenipotentiary, and you are?"

"Eberhard Mock, ladies' prize-fighter," muttered the Criminal Counsellor, turning abruptly and squeezing himself once more into the little room. "Ehlers, tidy up here and gather anything that might be of importance. Smolorz, question these people."

Mock trotted off to the tenement lobby, passing Smolorz who was huddled under an umbrella with those he was questioning, trying to avoid venom on the one hand and bacilli of tuberculosis on the other. At the entrance door Mock greeted Doctor Lasarius from the police mortuary, followed slowly by two men carrying a stretcher.

Mock stood outside the building and distractedly watched the traffic in the street, already busy at this hour. A couple were so engrossed in each other they did not notice him. The young man accidentally jostled the Counsellor and immediately apologized, politely removing his hat. The girl glanced at Mock and instantly turned away her face, which was ashen with tiredness. The night's rocking in the droschka had obviously disagreed with Rosemarie.

Mock looked about and quickly strode off towards Apelt florists. In the made-up eyes of the plump flower girl, he detected a flicker of interest. He ordered a basket of fifty tea roses and asked for it to be delivered to "Sophie Mock, Rehdigerplatz 2". On a cream-coloured card, which he requested be attached to the bouquet, he wrote in his beautiful script:

18

"Never again, Eberhard", and then he paid and left the flower girl alone with her mounting curiosity.

A newspaper boy got under his feet. Mock dismissed him, pressing a few pfennigs into his hand and then, wielding a newspaper under his arm, cut diagonally across the western side of Ring. A moment later he was sitting in the Adler, smoking his first cigarette of the day and waiting for Smolorz and Ehlers. He passed the time reading the *Breslauer Neueste Nachrichten*. On one of the announcement pages, his eye was caught by an unusual illustration. A mandala, the wheel of change, was drawn around a gloomy old man with his finger pointing upwards. "Spiritual father, Prince Alexei von Orloff, proves that the end of the world is nigh. The next revolution of the Wheel of History is now taking place – crimes and cataclysms dating back centuries are recurring. We invite you to a lecture held by the sage from the Sepulchrum Mundi. Sunday, November 27th, Grünstrasse 14–16." Mock lowered the window and flicked his cigarette end straight at the approaching Smolorz. The latter shook the ash from his coat and climbed into the car, passing over Mock's apologies in silence. Into the back clambered Ehlers, weighed down by his tripod, and Criminal Assistant Gustav Meinerer, the fingerprint expert.

"Rohmig has been renting his workshop for a month now: from 24th October, to be exact." Smolorz opened his police notebook. "From July to the end of October, according to the old bag, the workshop was empty. Anyone could have broken in. The caretaker is often drunk and asleep instead of keeping watch. He's disappeared somewhere now. Probably recovering from a hangover. The shoemaker complained about the stink from the beginning. His brother-in-law, a mason, had told him about a joke masons play if they don't get paid properly. They set an egg into the wall. And it stinks. Rohmig thought there was an egg behind his wall, and he decided to get rid of it this morning. He knocked down the wall with a pick-axe. And that's it."

"What did you find?" asked Mock.

"This." From a brown envelope, Smolorz extracted a wallet of crocodile leather and handed it to Mock.

Mock examined the wallet. It contained an identity card in the name of Emil Gelfrert – born February 17th, 1876, musician, bachelor, living at Friedrich-Wilhelm-Strasse 21 – a notebook with addresses and telephone numbers, a receipt from a laundry in the same name, a card for the Municipal Library, a few tram tickets and a postcard from Riesengebirge with the words: "To my sweet, best wishes from the mountains, Anna, Hirschberg, July 3rd, 1925."

"Is that all?" Mock asked, as the men from the mortuary carried "sweet" to the hearse parked nearby.

"No, there was this too. Someone had pinned it to his waistcoat." With his tweezers, Smolorz held up a page from a universal calendar dated September 12th, 1927. No writing, simply an ordinary page from a calendar, which some unfortunate people – those who monitor the passing time, that is – tear off each day. The page was pierced by a small safety pin.

"No fingerprints," Meinerer added. "Doctor Lasarius estimates the date of the murder as being in August or September."

"Smolorz, we're going to Friedrich-Wilhelm-Strasse, to the musician's apartment." With some relief, Mock became aware of pangs of hunger. His body was ready for a beer and a roll with paprika dripping. "Maybe we shall meet the faithful Anna there, waiting patiently with her needlework for her artist's return from the Philharmonia?"

BRESLAU, THAT SAME NOVEMBER 28TH, 1927
TEN O'CLOCK IN THE MORNING

Elisabeth Pflüger undressed slowly, arranging her clothes neatly on a chair. She unfastened her stockings from her suspenders. Sophie Mock admired her narrow, white hands as they slowly rolled down the smooth stockings. Elisabeth removed the suspender belt, then slipped off her silk knickers. She was completely naked. In the slender fingers of her left hand she held a small silver case; in her right dangled an engraved spoon with a long handle. She dipped the spoon into the case and held it close to Sophie's face.

"It's very good cocoa," she whispered. Sophie inhaled through her nostrils, shuddered and ran her fingers over her velvety, slightly reddened nose.

"Cover your face with a veil," Elisabeth said. "You'll hide the bruise and you can stay incognito. You don't have to show your face to anyone. Everything you do will be entirely of your own free will. Or you can just watch. And you can leave at any moment. Those are the rules."

Elisabeth took her friend's hand and opened the door that led from the boudoir to the Moorish bedroom. Sophie stood somewhat helpless, holding the basket of tea roses in her free hand. On the bed, under a yellow canopy, sat a naked young man drinking an infusion. The room smelled of mint. Elisabeth approached the man and took the empty cup from him. From a jug nearby she poured herself a cupful.

"It's mint," she told Sophie. "A drink called Venus."

The drink was clearly beginning to take effect on the man.

"Remember," Elisabeth said, pretending not to see this and blowing into her cup. "You can leave any time you like. The boudoir leads straight out to the staircase."

Sophie did not go anywhere.

BRESLAU, THAT SAME NOVEMBER 28TH, 1927
ELEVEN O'CLOCK IN THE MORNING

Gelfrert had occupied a small room in the garret of a sumptuous tenement at Friedrich-Wilhelm-Strasse 21. Apart from a stool, a basin, a mirror, a clothes stand and an iron bed, the room contained only empty bottles of Guttentag alpine herb liqueur, neatly arranged beneath the window. On the sill stood a few books and a case containing a French horn.

"He had a delicate palate," Ehlers remarked, spreading his tripod.

Mock gave his men the appropriate instructions, went downstairs, crossed the street and made his way towards Königsplatz. It had stopped raining and the sun had come out, accentuating the bright sign of Grengel's Inn. A moment later, Mock was devouring a much-needed pork-lard roll, washing down the hot taste of paprika with a beer. He drank the last drops with relief and experienced a faint dizziness. He tossed some small change to the sympathetic bulldog who was drying tankards behind the bar, and shut himself in the telephone booth. It took him a while to remember his own number. Adalbert picked up after the first ring.

"Good day, is the mistress at home?" Mock enounced the syllables slowly.

"Unfortunately, Counsellor, Mrs Sophie left an hour ago," Adalbert spoke quickly; he knew his master would want to be told everything without having to ask. "She went shopping with Miss Pflüger shortly after some roses were delivered to her. She took the basket with her."

Mock hung up the receiver and left the bar. His men were back in the Adler, filling the car with cigarette smoke. He joined them.

"Gelfrert had a fiancée once, a large blonde of about thirty. She used to visit him with a two-year-old boy," Smolorz recounted his questioning of the caretaker. "An unmarried woman with a child. The caretaker hasn't seen her for quite some time. Gelfrert worked in some orchestra and visited pupils. Gave piano lessons. He had been in a bad way recently. He drank. Nobody visited him. Neighbours complained he left shit in the crapper after he used it. Nothing more from the caretaker."

"We found a request form from the Municipal Library." Ehlers held a piece of printed paper under Mock's nose. "September 10th, Gelfrert returned a book entitled *Antiquitates Silesiacae*. The library gave him a receipt confirming the book's return."

"So he was still alive on September 10th. Taking Doctor Lasarius' reckonings into account, our musician was walled in at the shoemaker's workshop in the Griffins yard between 10th and 30th September."

"Someone lured him there, or dragged him when he was unconscious," Smolorz opened the window to let in a breath of air.

"Then he was gagged and tied to the hook on the far wall of the recess, so that he wouldn't thrash around and knock down the newly erected wall," added Mock. "One thing interests me: wasn't our Bluebeard afraid that the following day a new tenant might move in and discover a wall had just been built or, worse still, hear inarticulate sounds uttered by the victim, despite the gag?"

The men did not say anything. Mock thought about another tankard of beer, then spread himself out on the passenger seat and turned to the policemen in the back. His hat, tipped back to the crown of his head, gave him a rakish appearance.

"Smolorz, you're to drag that drunken caretaker of the Griffins from his underground lair and question him. Then check for the deceased in our files, as well as all the acquaintances in his notebook. You, Ehlers, are to research Gelfrert's past. Where he was born, his religion and so on. Then question those acquaintances of his who live in Breslau. I want a report the day after tomorrow at noon sharp."

"And what am I to do?" Meinerer asked. Mock thought for a moment. Meinerer was ambitious and vindictive. Once, he had confided to Ehlers over a schnapps that he did not understand why Mock favoured a dunder-head like Smolorz. Meinerer had not realized that to criticize good-natured Smolorz was an offence difficult to wipe out in Mock's eyes. From that moment onwards, Meinerer had encountered numerous obstacles on his career path.

"You, Meinerer, I want to assign you an entirely different task. I suspect my nephew has fallen in with some bad company. You're to follow him for two weeks, every day. Erwin Mock, nineteen years old, lives at Nicolaistrasse 20, attends Matthiasgymnasium." Pretending not to see the disappointment on Meinerer's face, Mock climbed out of the car. "I'll go on foot – there's something important I have to do."

He strode briskly in the direction of Grengel's Inn.

"Counsellor sir, Counsellor, please wait," he heard Meinerer's voice behind him. He turned to wait for his subordinate with an indifferent expression.

"That assistant of yours, Smolorz, he's a bit taciturn," Meinerer was triumphant. "He didn't tell you there was a universal calendar hanging on the wall, the kind you tear the pages out of. Do you know which page had been torn out last?"

"12th September?" Meinerer nodded as Mock looked at him with approval. "The one the murderer attached to the victim's waistcoat with a pin? Do you have the calendar with you?"

"Here it is." Meinerer brightened and handed Mock yet another brown envelope.

"Good work," Mock said, and slipped it into his coat pocket. "I'll take care of it; I'll check whether the page on the waistcoat comes from this very calendar."

Then he looked at his silent subordinate with amusement and quite unexpectedly patted him on the shoulder.

"Go and follow Erwin, Meinerer. My nephew is more important to me than all the walled- and unwalled-in corpses in this city."

The agreeable bulldog kept leaving his place behind the bar to refill the stove. He smiled pleasantly as he did so, nodding in agreement to everything Mock said. Accepting his interlocutor's anti-American and anti-Soviet views, he did not utter a single word throughout.

Mock downed his third beer of the day and decided to move on to something stronger. Not in the habit of drinking alone, he ordered two glasses of juniper schnapps and pushed one towards the barman, the only other person in the room. The barman grasped the glass in his dirty fingers and emptied it in one go.

Into the tavern stepped a short travelling salesman bearing a box of goods.

"Kind gentlemen, Solingen knives cut everything – even nails and hooks," he began his sales pitch.

"This is a tavern. Either order something or clear out," snarled the bulldog, proving he could speak after all.

The salesman reached into his pocket and, not finding a single pfennig, began to retreat.

"Hey!" Mock came to life. "I'm standing this gentleman a drink. Another juniper schnapps for us, if you please."

The salesman took off his coat, stood his box on the ground and sat down next to Mock. The barman did his duty. A moment later, only the wet marks left by two glasses remained on the faux-marble countertop.

"They really are excellent knives," the salesman returned to his original theme. "You can cut an onion with them quickly and efficiently, or bread, sausages, or" – here the little fellow winked at Mock – "shred your mother-in-law!"

Nobody laughed, not even the joker himself. Mock paid for another round of schnapps and leaned over to his companion.

25

"I'm not buying anything from you. But tell me how your business is going, how people treat you and so on. I'm a writer – I'm interested in all sorts of stories," Mock was telling the truth, for he frequently wrote character profiles of people with whom he came in contact. Many a Breslauer would have been prepared to pay a fine sum for the information contained in these "lives of famous men".

"I'll tell you a story – about how these knives cut iron." The salesman was genuinely rapturous.

"But nobody's going to be cutting iron with them," yelled the barman angrily. "Who needs knives like that? These scoundrels come in here, trying to force on me something I don't need. You're lucky this gentleman's bought you a drink or I'd kick you out."

The travelling salesman looked dejected. Mock stood up, put on his coat and approached the barman.

"And I say you might find these knives useful," he said.

The salesman now blushed with satisfaction.

"And what for, may I ask?" the barman said, bewildered.

"You can use them to commit hara-kiri." Seeing the barman did not appear to understand, Mock added, "Or dig the dirt from under your fingernails."

The agreeable bulldog stopped being agreeable.

The weather was even less agreeable. A strong wind tore at the droschkas on Wachtplatz, slashing them with sleet. Mock held on to his hat, jumped into a droschka and asked to be taken to Rehdigerplatz 2. The cabby licked his pencil and slowly wrote down the address in his greasy notebook. He pressed his antiquated top hat onto his head and shouted at the horse. Mock felt the moment had come when alcohol is at its most cajoling and deceptive: one bursts with euphoria and yet at the same time feels sober, thinks clearly, and does not stammer and or sway. *Knock back another*, prompts a demon. Mock noticed a rose on a short

26

stem in the corner of the droschka. He reached for it and froze: a tea rose, somewhat withered. He looked around for a card with "Never again, Eberhard" neatly written on it, but found nothing. He clapped the cabby on the shoulder in a friendly gesture.

"Hey, coachman, it's nice here in your droschka. You've even got flowers."

The cabby shouted something back which was drowned by the wind and the noise of a tram sliding along the busy road near Freiburg Station. To the cabby's surprise, Mock climbed up next to him.

"Do you always decorate your carriage with flowers?" he slurred, pretending to be more drunk than he was. "I like it. I'd pay well for a journey like this."

"I had two lady customers today with a basket of roses. One must have fallen out," the cabby said politely.

"Stop this carriage," Mock thrust his identity card under the surprised coachman's nose. The droschka turned to the right, blocking the entrance to the inner yard of the station buildings on Siebenhufenerstrasse. "From where to where did you take these women?" Mock had sobered up completely and began his questioning.

"To Kleinburg. Where from? The same place as we're going now – Rehdigerplatz."

"Do you have the exact address of the place in Kleinburg?"

"Yes. I have to square up with my boss." The cabby took out his grubby notebook and, licking his fingers, struggled with the pages as they flapped about in the wind. "Yes, Eichenallee in Kleinburg."

"What did the women look like?"

Mock was quickly noting down the address in his book.

"One was dark-haired, the other blonde. They were wearing veils. Fine women."

27

Mock was woken by joyful, childlike cries. He switched on his bedside lamp, rubbed his eyes, smoothed down his hair and gazed around the bedroom as if in search of the children who had disturbed the unsettled sleep that followed his starchy, greasy and viscous lunch. He looked through the window into the darkness: the first snow was falling, and children had come out to play in the yard of the Jewish Communal School. Hearing Sophie's voice, he took off his quilted smoking-jacket and trousers of thick, grey wool, and dressed again in his suit, tie and leather shoes bright with polish. He looked in the mirror and examined his face and his eyes, underpinned with two-tiered balconies, and reached for the jug of unsweetened mint tea, which Adalbert had advised him that day was the best antidote to over-indulgence. He patted some eau-de-cologne onto his somewhat wilted cheeks and, jug in hand, walked into the hall where he met Marta bearing the coffee service. He followed the servant into the parlour. Sophie was sitting at the table in an azure dress. Contrary to the prevailing fashion, her white-blonde hair reached down to her shoulders and was so thick it could barely be contained by the blue hairband. Her green eyes – fractionally too small – lent her face a resolute and somewhat ironic expression. "A whore's eyes," Mock had thought when, introduced to her at a carnival ball at the Regierungsbezirk Schlesien a couple of years earlier, he had forced himself with difficulty to raise his eyes higher than her full breasts. Now Sophie's eyes were those of a tormented, tired and disillusioned woman. The bruise around one of them was a shade darker than the pale arches of her blue eye-shadow. Mock stood in the doorway, trying not to look her in the face. He contemplated the innate elegance of her movements: as she coyly tipped the milk jug and admired the milk breaking up the black of the coffee; as she carefully raised the fragile cup to her lips; as she turned the knob of the radio a little impatiently in search of her beloved Beethoven. Mock sat at the table and gazed at Sophie.

"Never again," he said emphatically. "Forgive me."

"Never again what?" Sophie slowly ran her index finger up and down the handle of the milk jug. "Never again what? Alcohol? Violence? Attempted rape? Pretending in front of your brother that you are a real man who keeps his woman at heel?"

"Yes. Never again – any of it." In order to avoid looking at Sophie, Mock stared at a painting, a present he had given her for her twenty-fourth birthday. It depicted a subtle landscape by Eugene Spiro and bore the artist's dedication: "Many happy returns to melancholic Sophie".

"You're forty-four. Do you think you're able to change?" There was not a trace of melancholy in Sophie's eyes.

"We will never change if we carry on being alone, just the two of us." Mock was pleased Sophie was speaking to him at all. He poured himself some mint tea and took a sandalwood box out of the sideboard. The metallic sound of cigar clippers and the grating of a match. Mock tried to chase away the very last mists of his hangover with the tea and the aroma of a Przedecki cigar. "We'll both change when there are three of us, when you finally have a baby."

"I've been longing for a baby ever since we got married." Sophie ran her finger over the spout of the milk jug. Then she got up and, with a faint sigh, huddled next to the stove. Mock went to her and fell to his knees. He pressed his head against her belly and whispered: "You give yourself to me every night, and you will conceive. You'll see, every night." Sophie did not return his embrace. Mock felt her belly undulating. He got to his feet and gazed into her eyes, which in laughter had become even smaller than usual.

"Even if you drank whole tankfuls of mint tea, you wouldn't be able to

29

possess me every day." Sophie wiped tears of laughter from beneath her black eye.

"What, does mint increase virility?" he said.

"Apparently," she said, still laughing.

Mock went back to his cigar. An enormous circle of smoke drifted down to the deep-pile carpet.

"How do you know?" he asked suddenly.

"I read it somewhere." Sophie stopped laughing.

"Where?"

"A book in your library."

"One by Galen, perhaps?" Mock, as a would-be philologist of Classics, possessed nearly all the editions of ancient writers.

"I can't remember."

"It must have been Galen."

"Possibly." Sophie sat down and turned her cup in its saucer. Anger flashed in her eyes. "What do you think you're doing? Not only do you mistreat me physically, but now you're trying to torment me mentally as well?"

"I'm sorry," Mock said humbly. "I only want to clear the air. Where were you today?"

"I don't want questions or mistrust." Sophie screwed a cigarette into her crystal holder and accepted a light from her husband. "Which is why I'm going to tell you about my day as if I were talking to a husband who is changing for the better and is curious to know how his dear wife's day has been, and not to some furiously jealous investigator. As you know, Elisabeth and I are soon to appear in an Advent concert. She came to see me this morning, not long after you sent the roses. We took a droschka to Eichenallee, to Baron von Hagenstahl's who is paying for and organizing the concert. We needed his blessing to hire the Concert Hall on Gartenstrasse. We made a detour on the way and I left the roses at the church of

Corpus Christi – I was furious with you and didn't want the flowers. Then Elisabeth and I rehearsed. I had dinner at her apartment. That's all. And now excuse me for a minute. I'm tired and Marta has prepared a bath for me. I'll be back in a while."

Sophie finished her coffee and left the parlour. Mock peered into the hall and saw her close the bathroom door behind her. He went quickly to the telephone, dialled Smolorz's number and issued a brief command into the receiver.

Sophie sat naked on the edge of her bath and wondered who Eberhard was calling. The water had turned pink with Hager rose bath salts, thanks to which – the travelling salesman had claimed – "pain is diminished and tiredness disappears". Sophie did not remove her make-up. She knew her husband liked a woman to wear make-up, especially in the bedroom. With the tips of her fingers she could already feel the fresh, stiff linen and sense Eberhard's closeness. She submerged herself in the half-filled bath and contentedly contemplated the wall tiles showing a happy wanderer on his way somewhere carrying a small bundle on a stick. All of a sudden she bit her lip. The bath salts eased the subtle pain in her lower belly and her memory of that morning.

"It was only revenge," she whispered to the wanderer. "If I had not taken my revenge, I would not be able to forgive him. As it is, we're starting from scratch today. We're going to be together every night."

Argos began to bark. Sophie heard the murmur of comings and goings in the hall, a familiar masculine voice and then the slamming of a door. Shaking with nerves, she climbed out of the bath.

"Marta, who has arrived?" she called through the door.

"The master has left with Criminal Sergeant Smolorz," the servant called back. Sophie angrily washed away her make-up.

31

Mock and Smolorz sat in the Adler, parked outside the apartment on Rehdigerplatz. The windows and roof of the car were soon shrouded in a blanket of snow. Mock was silent because he was overwhelmed by jealousy; Smolorz, because it was in keeping with his nature.

"What did you find out?" Mock asked finally.

"The caretaker was drunk. He didn't know Gelfrert. Gelfrert was a Nazi . . ."

"I'm not talking about Gelfrert." Mock kindled his cigarette to a bright tip. "I'm talking about the church."

"Nobody brought flowers to the church today."

Mock studied the windows of his bedroom; the light had just gone out.

"Smolorz, you're on a new case." In times of great agitation, Mock addressed his subordinate using the familiar form of "you". "I want to know everything there is to know about a certain Baron von Hagenstahl in Eichenallee. You're to stop work on Gelfrert's case. I'll take care of it myself. Apart from that, you're not to leave my wife for a minute. You don't need to hide especially. She doesn't know you except by name and voice. Report to me every evening at eight, at Grajeck's restaurant on Gräbschenerstrasse." Mock lit another cigarette. "Listen, Smolorz, today my wife told me she read something about the use of mint in Galen. In my library. I do indeed have Kühn's edition of Galen's work there, a parallel text in Greek and Latin. But my wife doesn't know either of these languages."

Smolorz looked at his boss in bewilderment, unable to understand what he was talking about. But he did not ask any questions.

And that is what Mock valued in him most.

Mock swallowed and, for the first time in many days, felt no burning sensation in his gullet, nor any post-alcoholic protests from his stomach. Only a slight thirst reminded him that not all the liquids he had consumed the previous day had been as innocent as fresh milk, which gave off a reassuring bovine warmth, and which he was drinking now. He set the mug down, went from the dining-room to the hall and stood in front of the large mirror. The mist of eau-de-cologne, which he had dispersed with the help of a pear-shaped rubber atomizer, was settling on his cheeks. At that moment the door to the bedroom opened a fraction and Mock spied Sophie's long fingers on its handle. He stopped spraying the spicy scent over his face and with a swift move grabbed the handle to prevent the door from being closed again. Sophie did not struggle with him. She sat down at her immense dressing table with its two-winged mirror and, with a faint hiss of impatience, began to remove the morning tangles from her hair with a bone comb. Fair strands fell diagonally across her face, covering the black eye.

"Do you think I'm going to sleep in my study every night?" he asked in a raised voice. "That you're going to lock yourself away in the bedroom?"

Sophie did not even look at him. Mock pulled himself together and cleared his throat, returning his voice to the timbre which pleased his wife: soft but resolute, amiable without being sentimental.

"I had to go out for a while. Smolorz had something important for me."

He thought he could detect a trace of interest in Sophie's eyes, around which greyish circles indicated a lack of sleep. He approached her and delicately rested his hands on her shoulders, amazed as he always was by their fragility. Sophie abruptly shook herself free and Mock folded his arms over his belly.

"I know, I know . . . You had forgiven me. You were magnanimous. I shouldn't have gone off anywhere. Not even for a moment. I should have spent every minute of the evening with you. And it should have been the first of many such nights, our nights, so that you can conceive. And I went out. For a short while. That's the kind of work I do."

The phone rang in the hall.

"No doubt that's them calling me again now." Mock gazed anxiously into his wife's half-closed eyes. "A summons, a corpse perhaps . . ."

Sophie heard her husband's receding footsteps and voice in the hall:

"Yes, I understand, Taschenstrasse 23–24, third-floor apartment."

The clatter of the receiver, footsteps, hands on her shoulders again, a closely shaven, somewhat damp cheek against hers.

"We'll talk this evening," he whispered. "I'll be off now. I'm needed."

"Not by me. Go," Sophie said, proving that she was still able to utter a sound. She went to the window and watched the snowflakes flying by. Mock's head began to ache. Laboriously he mulled over the amount of alcohol he had consumed the previous day; certainly not enough to induce this sudden hangover, which now gripped him. His cheeks burned, and small pendulums struck rhythmically in his temples.

"You slut." He wanted to sound dispassionate. "Are you trying to provoke me? You like getting your face slapped, don't you?"

Sophie stared at the light dance of snowflakes.

BRESLAU, THAT SAME NOVEMBER 29TH, 1927
HALF PAST SEVEN IN THE MORNING

Mock had never seen a quartered man before. He had not realized that the muscles in the neck press tightly on three sides against a stiff wind pipe, which is itself segmented into four, that human joints contain a yellow, sticky liquid, and that bone gives off a fearful odour when sawn in two.

34

He had never before seen severed fingers floating in a tub full of blood, a wide-open ribcage, flesh scraped from shins to reveal the tibia, or a shattered ball-and-socket knee joint split by a steel chisel. Mock had never seen a quartered man before. Until now.

He also saw several streams of blood, coagulated now, on the walls, blood-stained floorboards, a chamber pot protruding from under the bed, tangled, dirty linen, soot-covered chairs and a greasy kitchen stove. He noticed a Liebes pocket diary lying on the table, open at November 17th, with two streaks of blood crossing over the date. Nor did he fail to register Ehlers' ashen face or the flushed cheeks of his superior, Criminal Director Heinrich Mühlhaus.

The usually kind-hearted face of the latter was now contorted in a derisive smile which, as Mock knew, heralded immense agitation. Mühlhaus pressed his stiff bowler onto his forehead and indicated with a movement of the head that Ehlers should leave the room. When the photographer had relieved his superiors of the sight of his pained face, Mühlhaus fixed his eyes on Mock's chest. This evasion of Mock's eyes did not portend anything good.

"A macabre murder, Mock, is it not?" he asked in a quiet voice.

"Indeed, Criminal Director."

"Does my presence not surprise you, Mock?"

"Indeed it does, Criminal Director."

"Yet it shouldn't." Mühlhaus pulled a pipe from his pocket and began to fill it. Mock lit a cigarette. The intense taste of his Bergmann Privat smothered the stench of chopped limbs.

"I had to come, Mock," Mühlhaus went on, "because I don't see your men here. Neither Smolorz nor Meinerer. After all, somebody besides you has to be at the scene of such a dreadful crime. Somebody has to help you perform your duty. Especially when you've got a hangover."

Mühlhaus blew out a thick swirl of smoke and drew near to Mock, carefully avoiding the tub of fingers whose nails were covered in dirty, coagulated blood. He stood so close to Mock that the latter felt the heat from his pipe, shuttered as it was with a metal lid.

"You've been drinking for a good number of days now," Mühlhaus continued in a dispassionate tone. "You're making some peculiar decisions. You've detailed your men off to other cases. And what cases are these? More important, perhaps, than two macabre murders?" Mühlhaus, sucking energetically, tried to re-kindle the tobacco before it went out. "What is more important right now than the walled-in musician Gelfrert or Honnefelder, the unemployed locksmith's apprentice, who has been hacked to pieces?"

Mock opened his mouth in mute astonishment, provoking a malicious smile on Mühlhaus' face.

"Yes. I've done the work. I know who the deceased was." Mühlhaus sucked on his extinguished pipe. "Someone had to do it. Why not the Chief of the Criminal Department?"

"Criminal Director . . ."

"Silence, Mock!" Mühlhaus shouted. "Silence! The constable on duty who took down the report this morning found neither Smolorz nor Meinerer. It's a good thing he found the hung-over Counsellor Eberhard Mock. Listen to me, Mock. I'm not interested in your private investigations. Your job is to find the perpetrators of these two crimes. That is what this city wants; that is also what your friends and mine want. If I discover one more time that instead of working you have gone for a beer, I'll have a word with those men of rigid moral principles to whom you owe your promotion and I'll tell them a story about a wife-beating alcoholic. As you see," he added calmly, "there is nothing I don't know."

Mock carefully stamped out his cigarette and thought about the Horus Lodge Masons who had helped him in his career; he thought too about the subordinate Meinerer who, feeling himself undervalued, had poured out his troubles to Mühlhaus; and about loyal Smolorz, now hiding in a droschka staring fixedly at the door of the tenement on Rehdigerplatz, his eyes watering in the wind; and about the young painter, Jakob Mühlhaus, who, thrown out of the house by his morally impeccable father, sought happiness in the company of other male artists.

"If you know everything, Criminal Director," Mock said, tapping another cigarette against the bottom of his cigarette-case, "then I should very much like to hear about the locksmith's apprentice Honnefelder before he encountered the embittered and frustrated woodcutter.

"That woodcutter," Mühlhaus smiled sourly, "judging by his love of calendars, must also be rather a good mason."

BRESLAU, THAT SAME NOVEMBER 29TH, 1927
TEN O'CLOCK IN THE MORNING

It had become warmer and melting snow had begun to course down the streets. Dirty clumps slid off the roof of the droschka as Sophie and Elisabeth Pflüger climbed in. Both women were wearing furs, and their faces were hidden by veils.

"Menzelstrasse 49, please," Elisabeth instructed the cabby, then turned to Sophie. "Do you feel like more of the same today?"

Sophie did not say anything as the mournful tones of Mahler's 3rd Symphony resounded in her head. She came to moments later when Elisabeth snuggled up to her.

"Oh, please, not today." Sophie was clearly upset, still thinking about her husband. "Do you know what that cad said to me this morning? That I provoke him on purpose to get slapped across the face. That I must like it! He thinks I'm a pervert!"

"And is he entirely wrong?" Elisabeth rested her head on Sophie's

37

shoulder and watched wet lumps of snow as they fell from the branching chestnut trees next to the school on Yorckstrasse. "Are you not a little pervertette?

"Stop." Sophie resolutely moved away from her friend. "How dare he treat me like that? Spending day in day out with corpses has deranged him in some way. One day he beats me up, the next he pleads for forgiveness, and then, when I forgive him, he leaves me alone for the evening and begs forgiveness again the following day, and when I'm on the point of forgiving him, he coarsely insults me. What am I to do with the lout?"

"Take your revenge," Elisabeth said sweetly as she watched a tram grating its way along Gabitzstrasse. "You said yourself that it helps and makes it easier for you to put up with the humiliation. Revenge is the delight of goddesses."

"Yes, but he humiliates me every day." Sophie observed a poor wretch as he heaved a double-shafted cart to the municipal stoneyard on Menzel-strasse. "Am I to take my revenge on him every day? If so, vengeance will become routine."

"Then your revenge will have to get harsher and harsher, and become ever more painful."

"But he can take even that away from me. He was highly suspicious yesterday when I carelessly mentioned something about a mint infusion."

"If he deprives you of the possibility of revenge," Elisabeth said seriously, tapping the cabby lightly on the shoulder with her umbrella, "you'll be all alone with your humiliation. Completely alone." The droschka stopped outside Elisabeth's house.

Sophie began to cry. Elisabeth helped her friend out of the droschka and put an arm around her waist. As they went through the gate, they met with the friendly and anxious gaze of the caretaker, Hans Gurwitsch.

Five minutes later, the caretaker bestowed the same gaze upon the stocky, red-haired man who, with the help of a ten-mark note, was trying to draw information from him about Miss Elisabeth Pflüger and the company she keeps.

BRESLAU, THAT SAME NOVEMBER 29TH, 1927
TWO O'CLOCK IN THE AFTERNOON

Bischofskeller on Bischofstrasse was alive and busy. The front room was crowded with corpulent warehouse owners greedily swallowing huge dumplings garnished with hard, fried crackling. Before Mock had time to work out whether the dumplings constituted a main course or merely a side dish, the polite waiter Max clicked his heels, smoothed down his pomaded whiskers and, with a starched white napkin, brushed away the invisible remains of a feast enjoyed by some other merchants who, in polishing off the spongy dough and hard crackling, had set their digestive tracts a difficult task only moments earlier. Mock decided to take the risk too and ordered the same dumplings to go with his roast pork and thickened white cabbage, to Max's evident approval. Without needing to be asked, the waiter stood a tankard of Schweidnitzer beer in front of the Criminal Counsellor, as well as a shot of schnapps and a dish of chicken in aspic garnished with a halo of pickled mushrooms. Mock stabbed a trembling gelatine square with his fork and bit into the crispy crust of a roll. A drop of vinegar, trickling off the cap of a boletus edulis, seasoned the bland chicken. Next, he knocked back the tankard and with pure pleasure washed away the stubborn aftertaste of nicotine. True to the maxim *primum edere deinde philosophari*,† he thought neither of Sophie nor of the investigation, and got to work on the dumplings drenched in sauce and the thick slices of roast meat.

Before long Mock sat smoking a cigarette, an empty glass and a wet tankard with froth dripping down its sides in front of him. He reached for

† Eat first, then philosophize.

a napkin, wiped his lips, pulled a notebook from the inside pocket of his jacket and began to fill it with nervy, slanting writing.

"Two macabre crimes. One murderer?" he wrote. In his mind he answered his own question in the affirmative. The fundamental argument supporting this hypothesis was neither the cruelty of both crimes nor the degenerate extravagance of the murderer, but his attachment to dates, his desire to mark the day of the crime in a calendar, his attempt to write his deed down in history. As Mock had been informed by Doctor Fritz Berger, Head of Evidence Archives and an expert in forensic science, the page found on Gelfrert dated September 12th, 1927, had been torn from the victim's wall calendar. Doctor Lasarius had suggested that this might have been the date of Gelfrert's death. A pocket diary had been found that day in the room of Berthold Honnefelder, a twenty-two-year-old unemployed locksmith; the murderer had scored through the date November 17th with the victim's blood. Doctor Lasarius had no doubts whatsoever that this was when Honnefelder had died. "And so two men, both sadistically murdered, are found," thought Mock, as if explaining to an imaginary opponent in his mind. "Next to each, the date of death is found marked in a calendar. If, on the scene of two equally elaborate murders, a rose, a page from the Bible or from a calendar has been left, then the perpetrator of both is one and the same person."

Mock gratefully accepted a slice of apple cake, a coffee and a glass of cocoa liqueur from Max. There was nothing in the preliminary reports and findings to link the walled-in alcoholic and virtuoso French horn player, supporter of the Brown Shirts and amateur historian, with the quartered teetotal communist activist. Nothing, that is, apart from the date of death, clearly and eagerly given by the murderer. "The murderer wants to tell us: 'I killed him on precisely this day. Not a day earlier, nor later. Right then'," Mock thought, swallowing the delicious cake with its duvet of whipped cream. "Let us therefore assume that the victim is incidental; only the day on which he died is not incidental. Question: why is it not incidental? Why does the murderer kill on some days and not on others? Perhaps he is simply waiting for a favourable opportunity: when it becomes possible, for example, to convey a bound man past a drunken caretaker to his place of execution. And then, triumphantly, he leaves a note as if to say: 'Today is a big day. Today I was successful.' But to all intents and purposes, an opportunity presents itself at every step. One can kill on any day, stick a page from a calendar onto the victim's forehead, wall him in somewhere or chop him up. And if that opportunity is not out of the ordinary, then is it worth proudly proclaiming to the world when it took place?"

Mock carefully wrote his thoughts down in his notebook and realized he had arrived once more at his starting point. He was not, however, depressed. He knew he had clarified the field of his search and was ready to conduct the investigation. He felt the excitement of a hunter who, in the clear, brisk, fresh air, loads his double-barrelled shotgun and buckles on his cartridge belt. "Old Mühlhaus was wrong," he thought. "We don't need many men on this. Smolorz and Meinerer can carry on with the cases I have assigned to them."

This thought pleased him so much that, after the sweet liqueur, he ordered a glass of dry red wine. Instead of bringing it to his table, however, Max produced a telephone. The voice of Counsellor Herbert Domagalla from the Vice Department grated in the receiver:

"Eberhard, come over to the 'chocolatier' straight away. I'm here with Ebners and Völlinger. We can play a couple of rounds of bridge."

Mock concluded that he would be able to return to the point of departure equally well the next day and decided to have his dry wine at Schaal's chocolate shop instead.

41

Winter sun flooded the white parlour. Its walls flaunted white-painted panelling; the white varnish of the furniture glistened, the white upholstery tempted with its softness; the white-glazed grand piano elegantly raised its wing. This whiteness was broken by the cream tapestries that hung on the wall, and by the unnatural flush on Sophie's cheeks as she passionately struck the keyboard, transforming the piano into a percussion instrument. Elisabeth's violin sobbed and squeaked, attempting – in vain – to break through the piano's crescendo. The bare branch of a maple tree, thrashed by the wind, beat an accompaniment against the window-pane, down which trickled pitiful remnants of snow. They also trickled down caretaker Gurwitsch's inadequately wiped shoes as, having let himself in through the front door with his key, he unceremoniously and without knocking opened the door to the parlour. With relief the women interrupted their playing and rubbed their chilled fingers. A small, dirty coal-caddy on wheels rolled across the white parquet. The caretaker opened the stove door and poured in a few generous shovelfuls of coal. He then stood straight as an arrow and looked expectantly at Elisabeth, who felt a headache coming on when she saw the muddy patches left by his boots. The violinist reached for her purse, handed Gurwitsch half a mark and politely thanked him. The recipient clearly did not intend to leave.

"I realize, Miss Pflüger," the tenement's most important occupant smiled cordially, "that half a mark is enough for bringing in the coal. That's what I always get," he explained to Sophie, "when Miss Pflüger has given her servants the day off. But today," he looked at Elisabeth again, "I deserve more."

"And why is that, my good man?" Sophie, irritated by this banter, stood up from the piano.

"Because today . . ." Gurwitsch turned up his walrus moustache and glanced lecherously at Miss Pflüger's friend. "Because today I could have revealed many truths about Miss Pflüger, but instead I told a pack of lies."

"How dare you!" Sophie's affected tone had no effect on Elisabeth, who quickly asked:

"You lied? To whom? Who was asking about me?"

Gurwitsch folded his arms over his protruding belly and twiddled his thumbs. As he did so he winked knowingly at Sophie, gradually infuriating her with his impertinence. Elisabeth reached for her purse once more, and Gurwitsch's willingness to continue the conversation returned.

"The plain-clothes policeman who came after you arrived this morning, that's who."

"And what did you tell him?" Elisabeth said.

"He wanted to know who comes to see Miss Pflüger, whether men visit, whether they spend the night, whether Miss Pflüger drinks or snorts snow, what state she comes home in and at what time. He also asked about the other lady. Whether she visits Miss Pflüger frequently, and whether there are any men with her." The caretaker smiled at the five-mark note Elisabeth had rolled into a narrow straw. "And I said that Miss Pflüger is an extremely respectable lady who is sometimes visited by her mother."

Gurwitsch held out his hand for the money, astounded by his own perspicacity and intelligence, thanks to which he had earned a week's worth of vouchers for the canteen.

"Wait," Sophie said, taking the rolled-up note from her friend's fingers. "How do we know all this isn't a lie, that our good man really did see someone, and if it's true he was questioned by a policeman, then how do we know that is what he told him and not something entirely different?"

"I am not lying, madam," Gurwitsch raised his voice. "I know that ferret. He once locked me up at the police station even though I wasn't all that drunk. I know him. He's called Bednorz or Ceglorz. That's what the other policemen called him."

"Smolorz, perhaps?" Sophie suddenly grew pale, losing a great deal in the eyes of the caretaker who favoured large, rosy women.

"Yes, indeed, Smolorz, Smolorz," the caretaker said, quickly slipping the money into his canvas trousers.

BRESLAU, THAT SAME NOVEMBER 29TH, 1927
HALF PAST THREE IN THE AFTERNOON

Three men occupied a large table in the window of Schaal's chocolatier at the corner of a block in the centre of Ring. This was where, having just bought their sweet delicacies, Schaal's customers generally gave free rein to their greed, and Mock's cohorts were doing just that – washing down sugary specialities with coffee and smoking excessively. Schaal had congratulated himself on having such important customers, and when one of them had complained about the lack of a skat club in the neighbourhood, he proposed that they play in his shop. The card-players greeted the proposal with delight, and ever since had played bridge or skat over chocolate and liqueurs while the owner rubbed his hands. And so it was now. Counsellor Herbert Domagalla, an old friend of Mock's and Head of the Vice Department – that is, Department II of the Police Praesidium – executed a dovetail shuffle and the cards fell into an orderly pile. Commissioner Klaus Ebners, a Sipo official,[†] concertinaed the cards from one hand to the other. Only the astrologer and clairvoyant Helmut Völlinger – derided by many, but whose exceptional abilities were sought by practically every policeman – was not shuffling or cutting cards. His

† Sicherheitspolizei – Security Police.

hands were busy turning the stem of a large wine glass around its axis, and his eyes were fixed on the window that gave on to the western side of Ring.

Mock greeted his friends effusively, hung up his coat and hat on a modern hat-stand, and took his place at the green baize table. A moment later he was presented with a glass of nut liqueur, and thirteen cards lay in front of him, dealt by the efficient hand of Völlinger, his partner in the first rubber.

"One spade," began Völlinger. Ebners, sitting to the right of Mock, politely called "no bid" while Mock, seeing four spades in his own hand plus the ace and jack of hearts, raised his partner's bid to four spades. Domagalla's "no bid" brought the bidding to an end. Ebners led with a trump. Völlinger quickly drew trumps, finessed with Mock's jack of hearts, and then laid down his cards.

"As a reward for allowing me that brilliant finesse, I'll give you the expert advice you asked for." Völlinger pushed a dark-blue envelope decorated with the stamp H. VÖLLINGER — ASTROLOGICAL SERVICES AND CONSULTATIONS towards Mock.

"Thank you," Mock smiled, "for the praise and the expertise."

Völlinger did not respond; he stared out of the window and drummed his fingers uneasily on the green felt of the card-table. Mock stashed the envelope in his briefcase alongside the material evidence from both crimes and the cardboard folder containing his subordinates' reports. Ebners quickly dealt. A moment later he had to do so again when Völlinger picked up two of Domagalla's cards, mistaking them for his own.

Three "no bids".

"Two no trumps," Völlinger said. There was a murmur of authentic admiration.

"I haven't had cards for a bid like that in ages. All I can say to such a challenge is 'no bid'," Ebners sighed.

Mock studied his three kings and jack of spades. "Six no trumps," he said, provoking a loud double on his left. After two "no bids" Mock redoubled, and that was the end of the bidding.

Ebners led with a low spade and Domagalla took the trick with the king. "Why didn't Völlinger take it?" thought Mock. "Could it be he hasn't got an ace?" Domagalla slapped down the ace of spades. After taking the trick he nonchalantly threw down the queen of spades. Mock closed his eyes and did not reopen them until the end of the hand.

"Four down," Ebners summed up. "Why, for the love of God, didn't you say 'no bid' with the queen of diamonds? If you had played her early, you might have won control."

Völlinger glanced again at the window.

"I'm sorry, Mock," he said quietly. "I shouldn't be playing here."

"Why not?" Domagalla asked ironically. "Cosmic fluids flowing through here, are there?"

"You know nothing about these things, Domagalla. So be quiet."

"We can change places," Ebners suggested.

"I don't mean my position at the table. I mean this café."

"What are you talking about, Völlinger?" Domagalla began shuffling the cards. "We've played at Schaal's often enough."

"But usually in the back." Völlinger pulled at his stiff, rounded collar and loosened his tie.

"I'm your partner today, Völlinger." Mock lit a Hawaiian cigar. "I have no intention of losing vast amounts of money just because you're out of sorts. Have you got a hangover or something? Herbert," he turned to Domagalla, "you invited me here. Maybe you thought it would be a brilliant idea," – he mimicked Domagalla's falsetto – "'We'll give Mock an ailing partner and then share the money between the three of us.' Is that it? You wanted to play with 'an ass', and the ass today was to be me." He looked under the table. "Maybe that's where I left my ears!"

Ebners and Domagalla burst out laughing, whereas Völlinger was a long way from sharing his friends' mirth.

"That is a serious accusation," he hissed. "Are you accusing me of cheating?"

"Do calm down, my dear Völlinger." Mock turned the ashtray, fastened as it was to the table, towards him. "That was only the second hand. It must have been a slip of the tongue. You should have opened one no trump, not two."

"If we go on playing here I'm going to make even bigger mistakes. Since you have made these accusations against me, albeit jokingly, I owe you an explanation. It's because of that house opposite. We've played here before, true enough, but in the back room. I couldn't see that house from there."

Mock looked out of the window and felt a peculiar stabbing in his diaphragm. Through the rain washing down the pane, he saw the Griffins tenement. Silence descended. Deep down, not one of Völlinger's partners made light of his premonitions and trances. It was very often as a result of these that their investigations were brought to a successful conclusion.

"Völlinger, please, tell me more about the building and why it makes you so uneasy?" Mock had grown visibly pale. "I'm conducting an investigation into a murder committed right behind it."

"I read about it in the paper," Völlinger said, getting to his feet. "Forgive me, gentlemen, but I cannot stay here a moment longer."

Völlinger bowed and went to the cloakroom.

"Too bad." After his visit that morning to a certain young lady who had a substantial file in his own department's archives, Domagalla was unusually understanding. "We'll find a fourth soon enough."

"You'll have to find a third and a fourth," Mock said and hurried after Völlinger, seen off by Ebners' abuse.

The astrologer was no longer in the café. Mock opened his wallet, pressed a coin into Schaal's hand, took his coat and hat from him and ran into the street. A gusty wind sluiced sharp needles of rain. The Counsellor unfurled his umbrella, but did not enjoy the protection it offered for long. The wind tore at it and, bending the wire spokes, turned it inside out. A man in a pale overcoat was struggling with the same problem. It was Völlinger. Mock ran to him.

"I really have to talk to you," Mock shouted over the din of a tram turning the corner. "Let's go somewhere where you can't see that cursed building. There's a little bar here," he pointed to a passage, sheltered by an arched vault, that lead to Stockgasse.

Escaping from the wind that raged in the narrow streets around the Town Hall, they entered a tavern at Stockgasse 10 bearing the sign PETRUSKE GASTWIRT. The place was filled to the rafters with students, carters, thieves and an assortment of petty thugs who swiftly made themselves scarce at the sight of Mock. What counted to Mock at that moment was not how they knew him, but the fact that they had freed up a table. He occupied it with Völlinger and nodded to a gloomy waiter, who clearly considered his job to be some kind of divine retribution. The sourpuss stood two large glasses of *glühwein* in front of them and retreated behind the bar, fixing his tormented eyes on an enormous jar of a cloudy suspension in which there swam herrings, gherkins and other hard-to-identify snacks.

"My dear Mock," Völlinger took a draught of the clove speciality with obvious pleasure. "I have given you my expert astrological opinion. Analysing your and your wife's cosmograms, I have marked out several dates for the possible conception of an heir. The first of these is in a few days' time."

"I thank you very much," Mock said. "But let's get back to bridge and the Griffins tenement . . ."

"I assure you I would never . . ." Völlinger could not get himself to utter the word "cheat". "I wouldn't dare . . ."

"Enough," Mock interrupted him. "Tell me about your fears regarding the Griffins tenement."

"I first saw it in a photograph." Völlinger's eyes skimmed over the pictures on the walls whose subjects were about as obvious as the contents of the jar. "I had just passed my school-leaving exams and was on my way to study medicine in Breslau. Since I had never been to the city before, I wanted to find out more about it. In a shop in Lauban, I was looking through a photographic album called *The Old City of Breslau* when I came across the Griffins tenement. I felt a rush of deadly fear and closed the book. I had experienced déjà vu; I realized I had often seen that building in a terrible nightmare. In this recurring dream I would be running up a staircase, away from someone. I would get outside onto the roof, look down, and see what appeared to be enormous white birds, and then I would get dizzy. I wouldn't fall, but the dizziness would turn into a pain in my head which then usually woke me up. So when I saw the photograph I felt such searing fear that I even abandoned the idea of studying in this city. As you know, I studied in Leipzig and Berlin. I did, however, spend my final two terms in Breslau because it is closest to Lauban, where my deceased father, God bless him, suffered his last days in dreadful agony. One evening I was waiting for a droschka with some friends after leaving Lamla wine bar. I was rather tipsy, but I will never forget the acute fear I experienced when I realized we were standing outside that accursed building. My friends quickly caught on to my phobias and began to play practical jokes on me. They would engross me in conversation then lead me up to the building, or they would send me postcards of it . . . I tried to fight these fears with self-hypnosis. In vain. That's it, Counsellor. I'm simply frightened of that tenement."

Völlinger drank the last drops of his wine and began to struggle with his umbrella. Mock realized that the question he wanted to ask might compromise his intelligence, but he could not stop himself.

"Can you explain your fear regarding the building?" he asked, expecting a gibe from the astrologer, or an expression of regret, or, at best, a repetition of his words about the futility of self-hypnosis. But what he heard astounded him.

"Yes, I can explain it with metempsychosis, a migration of souls. My soul had probably been trapped in the body of a man who had fallen from that tenement. My nightmares were the memories of a previous incarnation."

Völlinger put on his hat and began to button up his coat.

"Surely you're having me on, Völlinger." Mock's tone was as friendly as a factory siren calling in workers for the first shift. "I don't know much about reincarnation but I know perfectly well when someone is trying to skirt around an issue. In the summer, I think it was July, we played bridge at Schaal's. You and I, and two of your acquaintances – a journalist and a schoolteacher. That day we sat at the same table as today, by the window, and you didn't have a single anxiety attack. I remember precisely that contract of three no trumps which you made by outwitting our opponents. You didn't have any clubs in your hand and, after a rather friendly opening lead, you played precisely a club from dummy. The opponents fell for it and – not wanting to lose a high card under one of yours – played low, and let us beat them hollow. Do you remember that excellent psychological ruse?"

"You're right," Völlinger agreed, troubled. He removed his bowler and began to fan himself with it. "Indeed . . . Do you know what? Perhaps I was so engrossed in the game I didn't look out of the window . . . I simply . . ."

"You simply wanted to make an ass of me today, Völlinger," Mock smiled in derision. "And after we've known each other for so long, all our grand slams together, all our undertricks . . ."

"Believe me, please!" the astrologer cried out. "I'm not lying, I'm not inventing excuses *ex post*! Let's send for Ebners and Domagalla and play here, at this table. You'll see, I'll play without making serious mistakes. I don't know, damn it, why I wasn't frightened of the building in July and today I was . . . why I couldn't see the difference between a picture card and a plain card. Perhaps it's because I'm more on edge in the autumn – I grow melancholic . . ."

Without waiting for a response from Mock, Völlinger got up, nodded to him, opened the bar door and went out into the gale, rain and fog that shrouded the melancholy city.

BRESLAU, THAT SAME NOVEMBER 29TH, 1927
FIVE O'CLOCK IN THE AFTERNOON

Wisps of cigarette smoke turned slowly in the beam of light cast by the projector. First, a caption appeared on the screen: "The execution of Russian spies", then an image of a row of people in white Russian shirts. All had their hands tied. They were running, legs jerking in the accelerated speed of old film. Soldiers in spiked helmets moved just as quickly, pushing the prisoners with their rifle butts towards a low thatched cottage. The prisoners did not even have time to line up along its wall before the smoke of gunfire bloomed. None of the men who had been shot fell on his face or back. All folded over like puppets whose strings had suddenly been cut. Then there was a close-up: a soldier approached one of the murdered men, lifted his head and popped a lit cigarette into his mouth.

The young, dark-haired man comfortably sprawled in front of the projector burst out laughing. The bearded old man sitting next to him did not follow suit.

"It makes you laugh, doesn't it, Baron?" the old man said.

"And does it not you, Prince?" The Baron stared intently at the corpse's shot-through eye socket. "Maybe because the dead men were your countrymen. If so, I apologize."

"You're wrong," replied the Prince. "This is yet another crime which has already been committed once. I'm showing it to you, Baron, to convince you . . ."

"I don't believe in your theory. It simply amuses me. Your films amuse me too. I'm not bored, thanks to you . . . And you," the Baron turned to a third man who was earnestly watching the screen, pressing his bony fingers together as hard as he could, "and you, Doctor, do you, as an eminent historian, believe in this theory? Can you add any arguments to support it?"

"Like you, Baron, my attitude is emotional," retorted the man. "You it amuses, me it horrifies. I'm no historian now, I'm a disciple . . ."

These lovers of the silent screen did not notice the quiet footsteps muffled by the thick carpet. The Baron started when he saw the telephone in front of his nose; one enormous hand wielded the cradle, the other the receiver.

"Hello?" the Baron accentuated the second syllable. The projector stopped clattering, switched off by the man with huge hands, and now a woman's voice could be heard in the receiver. Though not clearly enough for a brain relaxed by sophisticated distractions to register everything fully.

"Could you repeat that, please," he grunted. "Kurt Smolorz, right? Please, don't worry about anything."

He replaced the receiver and looked expectantly at the bald head and enormous moustache of the athlete dressed in wrestler's attire.

"Did you hear that, Moritz? Police Officer Kurt Smolorz – stocky, well built, reddish hair."

"I heard everything, Baron sir," reported Moritz. "And I know what to do."

The troubled barman of Petruske's tavern placed a plate of thick, fried bacon slices in front of Mock. When Mock pointed to his empty tankard, the barman assumed an expression of someone greatly put upon. Mock decided to torment him even further by ordering some bread and horse-radish. An existential agony swept across the barman's features.

Mock observed the effects of alcohol and anger in the eyes of the wretchedly dressed drunks crowding the tables and walls. The most genial person in the place seemed to be the blind accordionist playing a sentimental tune. Had he not been blind, he would have been glaring at Mock just as amicably as the builders, carters, cabbies and bandits crammed into the bar.

Mock tore his eyes away from his brothers in alcoholic misery, and set about his food. First he decorated the slices of bacon with mounds of horseradish, then, using a knife, pressed it into a hot mush after which, with a faint sigh, he devoured the smoked and roasted meat followed by slices of dark, wholemeal bread. He washed down the strong taste of meat and horseradish with Haas beer.

Scanning the bar with bloodshot eyes, he listened to the swearing and cursing. Foremost in this were unemployed workers, embittered at the whole world. All of a sudden a butcher joined in their laments to complain about capitalist exploiters who undervalued his rare ability to decapitate a cow with one blow.

Mock had a revelation: the supper had not been unpalatable because it consisted of foul and badly prepared food, but because his mouth was acidic with the indigestion of an unfulfilled duty. The statement by the unemployed butcher had been as effective as a chiding from Mühlhaus: it was a sign and reminder.

He spat the bitterness that filled his mouth onto the dirt floor, pulled out his police notebook and fountain pen, and got down to work, unconcerned by his slight inebriation or by the regular customers who no longer had any doubts as to the profession of this elegant, stocky man with thick, dark, wavy hair.

Mock looked at the notes he had begun to make in the Bischofskeller. He read: "Let us therefore assume that the victim is incidental; only the day on which he died is not incidental. Question: why is it not incidental? Why does the murderer kill on some days and not on others?"

"These crimes are not incidental because they have been committed on precisely these and not other days," he whispered to himself. "Nothing is incidental. The fact that I met Sophie at a ball at the Regierungsbezirk, the fact that we still have no children." He thought of Völlinger's expertise. "According to astrologers, chance does not exist. Völlinger, even though he doesn't know why he is more frightened of the building in autumn than in summer, is sure of one thing: it is not down to chance. Place and time are the necessary elements in Völlinger's phobias because the tenement terrifies him sometimes more, sometimes less. Nor is Völlinger himself a chance entity – he is a clairvoyant, a sleepwalker, a man who picks up signs that are imperceptible to others."

Mock sensed that the long-awaited moment of revelation was near at hand; that he – like Descartes – was about to experience his philosophical night and philosophical dawn when, after silent, choking darkness, everything suddenly appears in the bright glow of the obvious. "In Völlinger's view of the world, these three elements – man, place and time – are not incidental, they are necessary," he quickly noted in his book. "Can my case, the Gelfrert–Honnefelder affair, have only one essential element: time? The victims have nothing in common with each other: a member of Hitler's party with a communist, a refined musician with a locksmith, a lover of history with an illiterate! This much I know from my men and from Mühlhaus. So that person, the victim of the crime is – at

54

this stage in the investigation – an irrelevant element. If we assume that the murderer is not deceiving us, we can be certain that the date is essential because the murderer himself has drawn our attention to it."

An arm in a dirty oversleeve stood in front of him the tankard of beer he had ordered. Mock turned to a new page in his notebook and instantly filled it with three words: "And the place? And the place? And the place? And the place? And the place?"

"Cannot be incidental," Mock said to the *Weltschmerz*-afflicted barman. "Damn it, the places where the murders occurred cannot be incidental."

BRESLAU, THAT SAME NOVEMBER 29TH, 1927
EIGHT O'CLOCK IN THE EVENING

Grajeck's restaurant on Gräbschenerstrasse in no way resembled the Petruske tavern. It was a dependable and decent venue that was usually filled with work-tired citizens and work-tired prostitutes. At this relatively early hour, the daughters of Corinth were not yet tired but fresh, sweetly scented, full of hope and plans for the future. Two of them were sorely disappointed by Mock and Smolorz who, scorning their charms, were involved in a discussion at a window table on which stood two snifters of cognac. One of the rebuffed prostitutes sat nearby and attempted to eavesdrop on the men's conversation.

Mock listened as Smolorz spoke:

"From nine until two, your wife was at Elisabeth Pflüger's. They played music. The caretaker of the tenement, a certain Gurwitsch, paid them a visit. We've got files on him. He deals in snow. I locked him up once for being drunk. I'm not sure if he recognized me. From what he says, Pflüger is a virtuous Susanna. No men visit her, only her mother sometimes. From three to eight, your wife was back at home, playing more music. That's how she spent her day."

"I don't suppose you had time to find anything out about Baron von Hagenstahl."

"I didn't, but my cousin Willy did." Mock silently congratulated himself for having once recommended the unemployed miner, Wilhelm Smolorz, as a constable on the Old Town beat. "Baron Philipp von Hagenstahl is rich." Smolorz glanced at his notebook. "He has a manor on Eichenallee in Kleinburg, a villa in Karlowitz near An der Kloster-mauer, some land near Strehlen and a stableful of racehorses which often win at Hartlieb. He organizes charity balls. Bachelor. Doctor of philoso-phy. He has a practically impeccable reputation, marred only by a former circus artist, Moritz Strzelczyk, who was deported to Poland two years ago but has returned. Quite a brute. Suspected of murder. He's always at von Hagenstahl's side. We have a statement from a certain whore who was beaten up by Strzelczyk. He broke her fingers. But the following day the accusation was withdrawn."

They fell silent, thinking about von Hagenstahl's constant companion and how they could make life difficult for him. That evening, however, Moritz Strzelczyk was not at the side of his master. He was standing outside the convent and church of St Elisabeth on Gräbschenerstrasse, watching the illuminated windows of Grajeck's restaurant.

BRESLAU, WEDNESDAY, NOVEMBER 30TH, 1927
NINE O'CLOCK IN THE MORNING

Sophie stretched lazily, gazing out of the bedroom window. The arthritic old woman living in the annexe stepped out of the tenement. On her protruding belly rested an enormous wooden pastry-board fitted with little ledges around its sides to prevent its contents from slipping off. A complicated system of sackcloth belts around her neck and shoulders held the board in a horizontal position. Underneath a none-too-clean tablecloth cooled doughnuts dusted with icing sugar. She shuffled off towards Rehdigerstrasse, touting her home-baked produce. Nobody paid her any attention. Sick old men, riddled with gout, dragged their feet; petty drunks counted their pfennigs; cabbies scattered sand over horse manure. Nobody wanted to eat her doughnuts.

The sun hit the window, sparkling in droplets, traces of the night's rain. Dirty reminders of the early winter snow persisted on the pavements. Sophie hummed the sentimental tango "Ich hab' dich einmal geküsst"† and went into the hall. Marta was at the market, Adalbert was shovelling coal into the cellar, Argos was napping by the door. Sophie could not help surrendering to the beauty of that dreamy morning. She still felt her husband's morning kisses and violent caresses, her lips still tasted the crisp crust of the roll from Frömel's, and her smooth skin was glowing from the agreeable warmth of her rose bath. Deciding to share her euphoria with Elisabeth, she sat down in the armchair in the hall and dialled her friend's number. She was looking forward to a long, prattling chat.

"Hello?" answered Elisabeth's impatient voice.

"Good morning, darling, I wanted to tell you how good I feel." Sophie took a deep breath. "Eberhard behaved like a young groom on his wedding night this morning. He was shy, and hugged me so passionately, as if it were the last time. He was strong and even a little brutal, if you know what I mean . . ."

"Good," sighed Elisabeth. "Long may it last. I fear it might be just another peak, darling, and you'll find yourself in a dark abyss once more."

"The darkest of abysses are nothing compared to such peaks," Sophie said dreamily. "Besides, Ebi promised me something today. He's going to stop drinking and said he would spend the evenings with me. He's not going to be away from me for a moment. I hope he keeps his word."

† "Once I kissed you".

"You know, dearest, when you find yourself at your lowest ebb, you can count on me. Remember, if that young newly-wed ever humiliates you again, I am at your disposal. You can call me any time, whether you're happy or sad."

"Thank you, Elisabeth. If he treats me badly, I'll meet up with you and the Baron. I'll take my revenge. When I have revenge I feel clean inside; my heart is so innocent then that I cannot be angry with him any more, and I forgive him," Sophie laughed quietly. "Just think, all those disgraceful things we got up to have made me a paragon of Christian mercy. Without them I'd be a spiteful, frustrated and repressed *Hausfrau* . . ."

"I'm glad you look upon it as therapy. Oh, it's terrible, Sophie, but I'd like to repeat what we did at the Baron's one day . . . . . ." Elisabeth's voice cracked. "Meaning I don't want things to work out for you and your husband . . . Oh, it's terrible . . ."

"Please, stop!"

"I can't stop," Elisabeth began to cry. "Because now if I say anything bad about Eberhard you'll think I'm lying to you, that all I'm thinking about is repeating what we did on Monday. But how can I say nothing when I know the hurt that is being done to you . . . Besides, you're being dishonest with me. You were offended yesterday, hurt when my caretaker said Smolorz was spying on us, and today you give yourself to your husband . . . So you don't need any therapy!"

"Then you don't have to have any scruples." Sophie was getting a headache from her friend's reasoning. She felt a mounting anger. "I don't know what you mean. Are you picking holes because today I am happy while you're constantly unhappy and have nobody to make you feel good and safe? Besides, as far as I remember, Smolorz was asking about you and your lovers, not me. So I can't be angry with Eberhard for spying on me because I cannot be certain that he is."

"You're wrong if you think Eberhard isn't having you followed,"

58

Elisabeth shouted. "He met that man Smolorz in a restaurant yesterday evening. The Baron told me so."

"And so what if he did," Sophie said derisively. "Smolorz is his subordinate. He can meet him whenever he likes."

"You don't understand anything! Listen to me carefully: Moritz paid a certain woman in that restaurant to eavesdrop. She didn't hear much, but she did remember one thing. Do you know what that side-kick kept repeating? Do you want to know?"

"Yes," Sophie said, growing worried. "I do."

"That man said the words 'your wife' several times," Elisabeth almost choked she was so upset. "Do you understand? They were talking about you. Smolorz was following you and he was reporting on what he discovered yesterday."

Sophie also choked and put the receiver down on the table. The early morning was just as beautiful as it had been a moment earlier: Argos slept as peacefully as before, the sun had not stopped shining for a second, only Sophie no longer felt the benefits of her amorous awakening, the taste of the crispy roll or the redemptive effects of her hot bath. She raised the receiver to her ear.

"Are you meeting the Baron today?" she asked calmly.

"Yes. Moritz is coming for me in half an hour." Elisabeth, too, had calmed down. "We're going swimming."

"I like swimming," whispered Sophie.

BRESLAU, THAT SAME NOVEMBER 30TH, 1927
A QUARTER TO TEN IN THE MORNING

The arthritic old woman was losing all hope of selling her *spécialités de la maison*. Quite unnecessarily, for from a black Adler parked by the curb emerged a hand with two fingers outstretched. The old woman beamed

59

and handed two doughnuts to Kurt Smolorz. The Criminal Sergeant paid, then unscrewed his thermos and poured himself a little coffee which was good enough to kill the yeasty aftertaste of the under-baked doughnuts.

Smolorz chewed more slowly when he saw a sandy Mercedes draw up outside Mock's tenement and Elisabeth Pflüger leap out. He admired the graceful sway of her hips as she disappeared through the entrance, miraculously avoiding a collision with the doorframe. A moment later the two friends – one happy, the other sad and pensive – filled the interior of the Mercedes with the scent of their perfume. At the wheel, Baron von Hagenstahl raised Sophie's hand to his lips and fired the engine. Without the slightest regret, Smolorz deposited his half-eaten doughnut on the passenger seat as the Baron rapidly pulled away into the traffic of Rehdigerstrasse. Smolorz stayed a while, unable to join the flow. Finally he spied a small gap, roared the engine's cylinders and almost ran into a terrified horse which then launched itself, together with its shaft, onto the pavement. Smolorz, laughing as the furious coachman directed a lash of his whip at the Adler's roof, accelerated again, turned right into Gräbschenerstrasse and drove under the railway viaduct. Beyond the droschkas and delivery wagons, he caught a glimpse of the rear of the sandy Mercedes as it passed the crossroads with Hohenzollernstrasse. The traffic policeman stopped a line of vehicles coming from the viaduct, among them the Adler. Feverishly, Smolorz began to calculate how he might be able to gain ground on the Mercedes. He counted on the Baron turning right into Sonnenplatz, and decided to drive past Busch Circus to catch up with it somewhere near the Concert Hall on Gartenstrasse. This proved unnecessary, however: the Mercedes stopped at the corner of Gräbschenerstrasse and Zietenstrasse.

The policeman gave the go-ahead. Smolorz moved forward slowly. The Baron got back into his car, slipping a box of cigars into his coat pocket.

Smolorz braked and found himself right behind the spare wheel in its sand-coloured cover. At Sonnenplatz, he allowed an old Daimler to squeeze in between himself and the Mercedes. The latter accelerated sharply on Neue-Graupner-Strasse, turned right and drove alongside the Old Town moat. Smolorz divided his attention between the Mercedes and the massive building site of the Police Praesidium under construction on Schweidnitzer Stadtgraben. Just before Wertheim's department store, Baron von Hagenstahl turned left, and then right at the church of Corpus Christi. Passing the merchants' club, he stopped outside the baths on Zwingerstrasse. Smolorz braked suddenly and pulled into a driveway. He slammed the car door, ran a hundred metres and, panting heavily, hid behind the hedge of a playground. Through the bare branches he observed the entrance to the large building housing the baths, into which Baron von Hagenstahl had disappeared with Sophie Mock and Elisabeth Pflüger a moment earlier. Smolorz entered the vestibule and looked around. It was empty. The uniformed ticket collector was vigilant and briskly approached him, saying:

"Pool number one has been hired out privately. Until twelve. Pool number two will soon be occupied by pupils from the Realgymnasium. Perhaps you would like a steam bath?"

Smolorz turned and left. It was cold. The paving stones on Zwingerstrasse were damp. A column of schoolboys, walking in pairs, was approaching from the direction of Liebichshöhe, with an upright man who looked like a sports teacher at its rear. The schoolboys marched up to the entrance and went in, disrupting their fine formation. Smolorz approached the teacher and showed him his Breslau Police Praesidium identification card.

"I'm coming in with you," he said. The teacher showed no surprise.

A few minutes later Smolorz was being crushed in the men's changing-room belonging to pool number two. Leaving his coat, hat and

61

umbrella, he climbed the stairs, looking out for the ticket collector who was just explaining to a fellow with the neck of an ox where he would find the changing-room for the steam baths. Smolorz hurried along a gallery decorated with little columns and arrived at the double door leading to pool number one. It was locked. He took out a picklock and put it to use. Soon he found himself in the public gallery. Leaning over a little, he surveyed the pool but could not distinguish Sophie Mock or Elisabeth Pflüger among the naked nymphs frolicking in the water. He climbed a few steps and looked around. The gallery ran the length of the pool. On his right-hand side stretched a row of doors leading to changing-rooms, on his left a barrier to prevent people from falling into the water. At the end of the gallery was an exercise studio from which drifted the sound of a piano and a violin. Smolorz was drawn to this room in particular because he had caught a glimpse through the doorway of the naked bodies of the two artistes. To get to the exercise studio without being noticed would require a miracle; if he made his way along the gallery, he would be in full view of those rehearsing in the studio and the swimmers in the pool. He decided to hide in the public gallery and wait for his chief's wife to appear.

Unfortunately this, too, proved impossible. His way back was blocked by a bald, moustachioed giant, whose hand almost entirely concealed the barrel of a pre-war Luger. Smolorz cursed his own stupidity. He had given no thought as to why the Baron had been driving the car himself, and where his chauffeur had disappeared to.

"I'm from the police," the Sergeant said very slowly. "I'm now going to take my identification out of my pocket."

"You're not going to take anything out, my friend," the giant smiled gently. "Go straight to that exercise studio. Only be careful not to fall into the pool. You could easily drown. Especially if you're weighed down with lead."

62

Smolorz did not move. He was sure the bald man would not risk a shoot-out.

"I'm from the police," he repeated. "My boss knows I'm here."

The giant made a sudden move. Smolorz saw a huge hand spread out on his waistcoat and felt a strong shove. He fell onto the cold tiles of the gallery. The assailant kicked, and Smolorz felt himself slide across the floor tiles towards the exercise studio. He tried to get up, to grab the barrier or the changing-room door, but after another kick in the crotch he could not. Both hands were clasped around his abused testicles. The giant was still swinging his legs at him. Smolorz rolled like a bowling ball along the track marked out by the barrier and the changing-room wall. When he had been kicked as far as the studio, he admitted he had been right: the bald man had not risked a shoot-out in a place where shots could ricochet.

BRESLAU, THAT SAME NOVEMBER 30TH, 1927
NOON

Mock left by the side door of the Breslau Construction Archives on Rossmarkt and stretched so hard his joints creaked. He stood on the pavement of the narrow street and stared in irritation at the deep puddles slashed by sharp sheets of rain.

He unfurled his umbrella and jumped through the traffic on Schlossstrasse, soiling his newly polished winter shoes with mud. He cursed the vain hope for snow and winter, and glanced at his watch. Hunger had reminded him that it was lunchtime, which irritated him even more. He insulted the whole world out loud as he walked on along the eastern facade of Blücherplatz towards Ring, moving with the fast flow of passers-by who were holding on to their hats or being tossed about among the stalls, catching the wind in the sails of their umbrellas. When he stepped onto Schmiedebrücke the wind became less trying. Mock turned into Ursulinenstrasse and went through the doors of the Police Praesidium.

Panting heavily, he climbed the wide stairs to the third floor where two offices were located behind a glass partition wall: Mühlhaus' and his own. The pale-faced trainee secretary, Ernst von Stetten, jumped up in deference at the sight of Mock.

"Has there been anything?" he asked, hanging up his sodden garments in the outer office.

"Ehlers left the photographs for you, Counsellor. Apart from that, there's nothing new," replied von Stetten as he slotted Mock's umbrella into the brass-rimmed aperture of a dark, wooden stand.

"Nothing new, nothing new," mimicked Mock once he had gone into his office. "Nothing new in the investigation either. I haven't moved an inch in the Gelfrert–Honnefelder case."

Mock lit a cigar and summed up his morning working through dusty old construction documents: diagrams of sanitary installations; unrealized plans for lifts to carry people and coal; dry explications by architects and engineers. In three hours he had not found anything that would prove useful in furthering his investigation. The worst thing in all this was that Mock did not really know what he was looking for.

"What are you going to tell Mühlhaus," he said to himself, annoyed, "when he asks what you did today?"

To that question the answer was simple: he had looked through every document concerning the scenes of both crimes; he had acquainted himself with the plans of all the floors, including cellars and attics; he had learned what had previously been on the sites of the two tenements, how the foundations were layered one on top of the other, and who had sold the land and building sites, and to whom. Mühlhaus might ask a far worse question: why? He would then hear a complicated, philosophical exposition on the three elements: person-time-place. The victims are incidental, the time is not. And so only the place remains to be investigated. It cannot be incidental. "Something has to link both places," is the answer Mühlhaus would hear. "But even though I've been through the Construction Archives I still don't know what it is." It was easy for Mock to imagine Mühlhaus' sarcastic laugh. Just then he remembered that the Criminal Director was at a conference with Police President Kleibömer, and it was highly unlikely he would be back that day to ask this difficult question.

The Criminal Counsellor breathed a sigh of relief and, with the iron handle which ran along the frame, opened the small window. He then removed his jacket, loosened his stiff collar, sat down at his desk and began to type non-existent words on his new Olympia, random combinations of letters. Mock thought best to the accompaniment of a regular tapping of keys. On the paper appeared five-letter words. Five taps – a space. Five taps – a space. Ernst von Stetten knew that for as long as the typewriter played out that particular rhythm, Mock was not available to anyone save his beautiful wife, Sophie, and old Mühlhaus.

It lasted a long time. The secretary chased away a few clients, lied to a few more, and politely apologized to others. Just as the University church struck two, von Stetten heard a sheet of paper being rolled out from the platen of the exhausted typewriter. Then there was silence.

"The old man has been thinking and he's come up with something," he concluded.

His conclusion was correct. Mock sat among scattered pages covered in even lines of type, dipped his nib in a large inkpot and wrote on the back of one of the pages in small black letters: "You investigated the murder sites from the point of view of construction. That was a mistake. What explanation could there possibly be in plans and designs? What is important is the history of the building, not the history of the pipes, bricks, cellars, cement, repairs and renovations. What is important is

65

the history of the people who live there, and of those who lived there in the past."

"So, am I now to study the family trees of people living there? When Aunt Truda met Uncle Jörg?" he asked himself.

A moment later, he launched himself once again at the inkpot and the sheets of paper gleaming with fresh ink. "Why would anyone kill so brutally on a given day? Only on that one particular day? Because that day is important to him. Perhaps he is taking his revenge for something that happened on that day? What could that person be taking revenge for? Something bad that happened to him. What could that person be taking revenge for in such a sadistic way? Something terrible that happened to him."

There was a knock at the door.

"Wait one moment please!" shouted Mock and began to write. "Where can one learn about truly terrible things?" he scrawled. "In a police file." The nib snapped. Von Stetten knocked again. Mock muttered furiously when he saw splashes of ink settle on his shirt cuff. The secretary took the mutter to be an invitation for him to enter.

"Your wife is on the phone, sir." Von Stetten knew this would bring a smile to his chief's lips, and he was not mistaken.

Mock picked up the telephone and heard Sophie's sweet voice:

"Good morning, darling,"

"Good morning. Where are you calling from?"

"Home. I wanted to remind you about the charity concert this evening. It starts at eight. I'll go along earlier with Elisabeth. We still have one Beethoven piece we need to practise. We're playing right at the beginning."

"Good. Thank you for reminding me. Have you had lunch yet? What has Marta prepared for today?"

"I ate at Elisabeth's. We practised all morning. Marta didn't cook lunch today. You told her this morning you'd have something in town."

"That's fine. I forgot."

"That's all." Mock detected hesitation in Sophie's voice. "You know, I've got dreadful stage-fright . . ."

"Don't worry. I'm keeping my fingers crossed for you."

"You're talking so clearly and simply . . . So assuredly . . ."

Mock did not reply. Visions of that morning's rapture appeared before his eyes. He felt thrilled and filled with a sudden wave of happiness.

"I know, I know, darling, I ought to go," he heard Sophie say.

"Yes, Sophie. Yes, my darling," he said softly. "I've got something urgent to see to. We'll see each other at the concert."

Mock replaced the receiver. A second later he picked it up again. He thought he could hear Sophie's sighs of that morning through the monotonous dialling tone. He shook off the memories, fastened his collar and tightened his tie.

"Von Stetten!" he shouted. "Come here, please!"

The pale-faced secretary entered without a sound. In his hand was a notebook and he stood awaiting his orders.

"Note this down," Mock said, wrapping his hands behind his neck. "One. For several days – as of today – I am going to have to work in our archives until late. Please write an appropriate form and give it to Kluxen, the building administrator. Scheier the archivist is to bring me the spare key to the archives as soon as possible, so that I can work there day and night. You'll find a sample of a form among the documents relating to the Lebersweiler case of December 25th. Two. Tomorrow, at eight in the morning, Kleinfeld and Reinert, Mühlhaus' trusted men, are to be here. They're to work in the archives alongside me. Please ask for our chief's permission in the morning. I'm sure he won't mind, but *pro forma* . . . Three. Pass two messages on to my servant, Adalbert. The mink stole I ordered earlier is to be collected from Beck's, and my tailcoat from the launderette on Topfkram. He's to have them here by seven. Four. Buy me something to eat and bring it to the archives. I'm going there now. That is all."

Mock stepped into a cab on Blücherplatz and asked to be taken to the Concert Hall on Gartenstrasse. The cabby was far from delighted by such a short run, and so did not even attempt to amuse his passenger with conversation. Besides, it would have been pointless. Mock, squeezed into a tight tailcoat and irritated by the negligible results of his archival research, was just as averse to holding a conversation as his cicerone. Even the unmistakable onslaught of winter did little to improve his mood. Staring at the roof of the Municipal Theatre as it swelled with snow, he turned the results of his quest over in his mind. There were approximately a thousand files in the police records that related to murders. Mock had looked through close to a hundred of them. The work was tedious and futile. No police archivist had ever anticipated someone wanting to search for toponyms in the card index, and the files were not indexed by town or street. Apart from an index of surnames, which had been put together only recently by archivists appointed for the purpose, there was no aid for anyone exploring the files. So Mock had to read through the records, hoping to come across the address Ring 2 or Taschenstrasse 23–24, and find the date of some crime which may have recurred in a later year. Only once did he hit upon the tenement where Gelfrert had lived. The files reported the case of a paedophile who had raped an eight-year-old girl in a cellar on Cat's Alley in May. The pervert had lived on the ground floor of Friedrich-Wilhelm-Strasse 21, which meant he had been Gelfrert's neighbour. Mock had found nothing else.

Now, as he travelled across the snow-covered town, Mock was prey to violent emotions. He was annoyed at his own inquisitiveness, which had fixed his attentions on past crimes and misfortunes; he had studied them with such commitment that he kept forgetting about the Gelfrert–Honnefelder case. He cursed himself for the thousandth time that day for having started off from some pseudo-philosophical, deterministic assumptions, basing his entire case on the singular analysis of what is incidental and what necessary. He was furious at himself for conducting an investigation in which the object of his search was not clearly defined. In addition, the sentence of fifteen years' imprisonment handed down to the paedophile by the Prussian judicial system gave him no peace. There was one more reason for his irritation: not one drop of alcohol had passed his lips that day.

In this state of mind, it is not surprising that he gave not a pfennig above his fare to the taciturn cabby when they stopped on Gartenstrasse opposite the Concert Hall. Above the entrance hung a huge sign, CHARITY ADVENT CONCERT. Bearing the box with Sophie's present under his arm, Mock entered the enormous vestibule of the magnificent building designed recently by Hans Poelzig. He left his outer garments and the present in the cloakroom, then made towards the double doors where a spruced-up ticket collector was arguing with somebody.

"You haven't got a personal invitation!" shouted the ticket collector. "Please leave!"

"So you don't want my money?" Mock recognized Smolorz's voice. "Isn't it just as good as everyone else's? Maybe I should leave it with you so you can go for a beer? Maybe you don't like the fact that I'm not wearing a tailcoat?"

Mock hurried over to Smolorz and took him by the arm.

"This gentleman does not trust you." Mock, unexpectedly amused by the situation, threw a derisive look at the ticket collector. "And quite right too. Judging by your mug you were given schnapps at school, not cod-liver oil."

Mock drew Smolorz aside, paying no heed to the astounded attendants.

"So, what's new?" he asked.

"Everything's alright. The morning at Miss Pflüger's. Then at home, at your place. Both of them. They rehearsed all the time," mumbled Smolorz.

"Thank you, Smolorz," Mock said, looking benevolently at his subordinate. "Less than two weeks to go. Put up with it. Then, as a reward for your good work, you get a week's unofficial leave. Just before Christmas. You're done for the day."

Smolorz tipped his hat and, dragging his feet, made towards the exit which shimmered with snow-white, starched shirt-fronts, sequins, Chinese fans and coloured feathers. Mock pulled out his invitation and stood in the queue behind a thin lady wielding a lorgnette in one hand and a long cigarette-holder with a smoking cigarette in the other. The ticket collectors did not demand to see her invitation, but instead lowered their chins to their chests as a mark of their respect.

"Oh, whom do I see?" exclaimed the lady. "Is that really you, Marquis? Oh, what an honour!" The affected lady turned to the people behind her in order to share her wonderful discovery with them. Her attention was riveted by Mock.

"It's unimaginable, my dear sir," the lady said, mistakenly holding the cigarette-holder to her eye instead of the lorgnette. "The ticket collector at today's concert is the Marquis Georges de Leschamps-Brieux himself!"

Clearly miffed that her information had made such little impression on the Counsellor, she floated towards the foyer, blowing smoke like a steam-engine while Georges, who had been accused of drinking schnapps at school, glanced contemptuously at Mock's invitation.

"And did that troublemaker who tried to get in without an invitation hand his contribution over to you, Your Excellency, Criminal Counsellor?" Georges slowly read the titles on the invitation.

"Yes, because I'm a teetotaller," retorted Mock, and walked past the displeased Marquis.

BRESLAU, THAT SAME NOVEMBER 30TH, 1927
NINE O'CLOCK IN THE EVENING

The charity concert was drawing to a close. Sophie, delighted by the ovations, the absence of alcohol on her husband's breath and the admiration expressed by the cream of Breslau society during the interval, slipped a glove down one arm and allowed Eberhard's dry, strong fingers to stroke the smooth skin of her hand.

Mock closed his eyes and recollected Sophie's performance, her unaffected calm at the piano, her restrained elegance with no show of exaltation or wild tossings of her head. He admired not so much his wife's playing as the outline of her body set off by the tight black dress. He was enchanted by Sophie's profile: the proud swell of her bun, the gentle concave of her neck, the fragility of her shoulders, the twin roundness of her buttocks. He was bursting with masculine pride. During the interval, he looked down his nose at the other men and walked round and round his wife as if to say: "Don't come near – I'm marking my territory."

The last chords of Debussy's *L'après-midi d'un faune* were played out. Applause thundered. Mock, instead of looking at the bowing musicians, admired the grace with which Sophie brought her hands together to clap, raising them high above her head. He whispered a few words in her ear and left the auditorium. He hastened to the cloakroom, collected his wife's fur coat and toque along with his coat and hat, and laid them on the counter. He opened the box with the mink stole and slipped it inside the

71

sleeve of Sophie's perfumed coat. Then he put on his coat and waited, with Sophie's slung over his arm. A moment later she appeared at his side. She thrust out her substantial breasts and slid her arms into the sleeves of the coat he held out to her.

"That's not my fur," she said in fright, removing the stole from her sleeve. "Ebi, the attendant has made a mistake. He's given you somebody else's fur. I didn't have a stole."

"It is your fur," Mock said with the expression of a schoolboy who has just tipped drawing-pins onto the chair of a teacher he dislikes. "And your stole."

"Thank you, my love." Sophie held out her hand to be kissed.

Mock put an arm round her waist and led her out of the Concert Hall. He looked about and caught sight of the parked Adler. Slamming the door behind Sophie, he settled himself in the driver's seat. Sophie stroked the stole with the tips of her fingers. Mock embraced his wife, kissing her passionately. She returned the kiss, then moved away and burst into uncontrollable laughter.

"It's wonderful what you said to Leschamps-Brieux," she cried with amusement. "And what's more, you hit the nail on the head. He really does drink a lot . . . That's all Breslau is going to be talking about now . . . Nothing but your *bon mot* . . . 'Georges drank schnapps at nursery school instead of cod-liver oil . . .' People were already laughing about it in the foyer."

Mock, losing his self-control, squeezed Sophie so tight that he could feel her dainty ear through the soft stole.

"Come on, let's do it in the car," he whispered.

"Are you crazy? It's too cold," she panted softly in his ear. "Let's go home. I'll make it special for you."

With difficulty the car pulled away from its wet and sticky bed of snow. Mock drove very slowly along Höfchenstrasse, trailing behind a mighty cart from which a man in a greatcoat was pouring sand onto the road. Mock did not overtake until just before the crossroads with Moritzstrasse, and then gliding along Augustastrasse, where the snow was packed down by horses' hooves, he arrived safely at Rehdigerplatz.

It had stopped snowing. Mock jumped out of the car and opened the passenger door. His wife timidly plunged her slippered foot into the glistening, cold powder, and then quickly withdrew it into the car.

"I'll bring you some shoes, my darling." Mock ran up the steps of the tenement, but instead of going in he turned and went back to the car. He opened the door and squatted. Sliding one arm under Sophie's knees, he wrapped the other round her back. Sophie laughed, embracing him around the neck. Mock took a deep breath and lifted his wife. He tottered under her weight and stood catching his balance a while with his legs astride. Then he carried Sophie to the entrance and stood her on the step beside the sign that read BEWARE OF THE DOG. He shut the car doors and returned to drown himself for a moment in the soft fur, pressing Sophie's delicate body against cream-coloured tiles as her strong thighs wound themselves around his hips and the smooth stole around his neck.

All of a sudden the light came on and Doctor Patschkowsky's dog began to bark. Mr and Mrs Mock climbed to the second floor, shocking the lawyer who was on his way out with the dog: she was just pulling her dress down over her hips, while he smoothed his hair and pulled the stole from his neck.

Marta opened the door to them and, seeing their mood, left immediately for the servants' quarters from which Adalbert's snoring could already be heard.

Mock and Sophie rolled into the bedroom, bodies clinging. The surprised dog was initially pleased, then, seeing what he thought was a fight, growled. Sophie closed the door on him, pushed her husband onto the divan and began to undo the numerous buttons of his outfit.

She began with his coat. Then his hat went gliding towards the door. Next came his trousers.

At that moment, the telephone rang.

"Marta will take it," said Sophie. "She knows what we're up to, she'll say we're not at home." The telephone kept ringing. Marta did not pick it up.

"Nothing can be more important than you right now," whispered Mock. "I'll deal with whoever's calling."

He stood up, went into the hall and lifted the receiver without saying a word.

"Good evening. Counsellor Mock, please," said an unfamiliar voice.

"Speaking," muttered Mock.

"Counsellor, my name is Willibald Hönness, from the casino at the Four Seasons Hotel." Mock recognized the voice of one of his informers, distorted though it was by the telephone. "There's a drunken young man here. He's losing a lot at roulette. He told me his name was Erwin Mock, said he was your nephew. On that account, he was given credit. If he continues to play like this, it's going to end badly. It looks as though he's losing money he hasn't got."

"Listen, Hönness," Mock said, taking his gun from the wall cabinet and slipping it into the inside pocket of his coat, "do something to stop him from winning. If the worst comes to the worst, knock him out. I'll be right there."

Mock went into the bedroom and reached for his hat which was on the floor, arousing much excitement in the dog.

"I'll be back soon. Erwin's in great danger."

Sophie was taking off her dress. A streak of mascara ran down her cheek.

"Don't bother to come back." Her voice did not sound as if she had been crying.

74

Willibald Hönness, an attendant at the Four Seasons Hotel casino at Gartenstrasse 66–70, had obeyed Mock's instructions yet had managed to eliminate Erwin from the game without the use of violence. He had simply spiked Erwin's beer with a substance that induced violent vomiting. So when Mock burst into the casino with his coat billowing behind him and ran into the men's toilets on the directions of a porter and an ape-like doorman, the young man was kneeling beside a toilet bowl with his head cradled in Hönness' caring hands. This sight reassured Mock a little. He lit a cigarette and asked at which table Erwin had been playing.

"Table four, uncle," came the answer from the depths of the bowl.

"I'll be right back," Mock said, thrusting a ten-mark note into Hönness' pocket. He left the toilets and approached the doorman who was standing next to an enormous fountain in the hall between two enormous palm trees. There was no more fitting place for the ape, who fixed his small eyes on Mock.

"I'd like to see the manager," Mock said, instinctively reaching for his identification. But he checked himself; he did not want to reveal all his cards yet. "My name is Eberhard Mock. Where would I find him?"

"Complaints are dealt with at the tables. You should have called the boss from there," muttered the doorman. "Come back tomorrow after three."

"I'm here on a different matter. A very important matter," Mock said, and resorted to a method sure to calm his nerves, that of mentally reciting Horace's *"Exegi monumentum"*.[†] Beneath the low vault of the doorman's skull, a small brain was strenuously at work. When Mock got to the well-known line *"non omnis moriar"*,[‡] the doorman said:

[†] "I have erected a monument . . ."
[‡] "Not all of me will die."

"Tell me what it's about. I'll pass it on to the boss – maybe he'll see you . . ."

"You're not going to pass anything on to him," said Mock, "because you'd have to repeat ten words and that goes far beyond your capabilities."

"Fuck off. Right now," the doorman glowered, clenching his fists. He was on the verge of thumping his bulging chest with them.

Mock recited to himself the famous ode about the immortality of the muses' chosen one. Suddenly he got stuck and no longer knew who it was who had climbed the Capitol in silence: was it the priest or the Vestal? At the same time he turned abruptly and delivered his first blow from a half-spin. The astonished doorman grabbed his chin and lost his balance. That was enough for Mock. He bent down, gripped his opponent by the ankles and pulled him forwards. A spray of water indicated where the doorman, deprived of the support of his short limbs, had found himself. Water over-flowed from the fountain, pouring onto the red carpet as the doorman thrashed about helplessly in the marble basin. He tried to push himself up with his hands. The waterfall poured over his white shirt and blinded him. Mock, mentally analysing subsequent lines from Horace about the roaring Aufidus River, donned a knuckle-duster and aimed another blow at the doorman's chin. The ape's elbow slipped on the bottom of the fountain and his head fell back into the bubbling whirlpool. Mock threw his coat aside, grabbed him once again by the ankles and, with a mighty heave, dragged him out of the water. The ape's head thumped against the stone rim of the fountain before his body landed on the soft carpet. Mock leaned one hand against a palm tree and set about kicking the prostrate man. Unnecessarily: the doorman was already unconscious.

Mock looked with irritation at the drenched sleeves of his jacket and his blood-stained trouser legs. He realized he was holding an extin-guished cigarette end between his lips. Spitting it into the fountain, he scrutinized the casino guests who had left the gaming-room and were now staring at the unconscious doorman in horror. Their sentiments were shared by the porter who, without waiting to be asked, said:

"The manager's office is on the first floor. Room 104."

Room 104 looked a little too small for the hefty, fat body topped with a bald head, which sat sprawled in an armchair, carefully inspecting its croupiers' reports. Norbert Risse's stature evoked indescribable joy among restaurateurs and tailors: ten-course meals and the bales of material used to make his elegant clothes allowed representatives of both professions to forget, at least for a while, their everyday material concerns.

Mock's profession was entirely different, so the sight of Risse did not arouse much enthusiasm in him. He was not interested in the casino manager's silk cravat, his quilted dressing gown, and least of all in the set of Chinese porcelain that stood on the coffee table and the listless parrot which knew only sign language.

"My name is Eberhard Mock," he said. "Criminal Counsellor Eberhard Mock. I am a suppliant, a humble suppliant."

Risse studied Mock's sodden clothes as the latter stood shuffling from one foot to the other. He picked up the telephone and listened for a moment to the hasty and garbled report. He turned pale, replaced the receiver and offered his guest an armchair.

"Humble perhaps, but somewhat impatient," Risse remarked. "What can I do for you, Counsellor?"

"My nephew, Erwin Mock, lost a sum of money in your casino this evening. I'd like to know how much," Mock said, rolling a cigarette between his fingers. "My further requests depend on that."

Risse pushed a Chinese porcelain container full of blue-striped cigarettes towards Mock. Mock lit one and stared at the beautiful coffee service. The delicate design of bamboo shoots weaving around the cups, pot and sugar-bowl reminded him of his old, passing fascination with the Orient. The steam that emanated from the pot was inviting.

"Your nephew was out of luck today. He lost a thousand marks. He took on credit for them, saying he was a relative of yours. We only grant credit when we're sure it will be paid back the following day, at the latest."

"Card debts are debts of honour." Mock turned his hat in his fingers. "I don't know whether I can repay it by tomorrow. I would be grateful if you would grant us an extension." He thought of having to pay Beck for the stole. "I'll settle my nephew's debt the day after tomorrow."

"We are renowned, Counsellor," Risse said, his cheeks and double-chin undulating, "for not allowing our clients to defer repayment of debts. This ruthlessness is our trump. Our clients stand eye to eye with their fate, a challenge with an illusory opponent, if you prefer, and they know that this opponent is hard and uncompromising. He must be faced with an open visor. Last week, Prince Hermann III von Kaunitz borrowed a certain sum from us which he soon lost. We lend money only once. Von Kaunitz was here on a Saturday, and on Sundays the banks and cheque administration are closed. *A conto*, he had to leave some family jewellery with us. And what does your nephew have to leave? It is a good thing you appeared when you did. My men can be very ruthless with insolvent clients."

"Aren't you going to offer me some coffee?" Mock said, no longer reciting Horace in his mind. "I'll have to think over this sales patter of yours."

Risse huffed. He neither said nor did anything. Mock poured himself some coffee and went to the window.

"I wouldn't dare break such sacred principles," he said. "You, Risse, will simply lend me the sum. Privately. As to a good friend. And I'll give it back to you during the week and never forget your friendly gesture."

"I would very much like to be a good friend of yours, Counsellor," smiled Risse. "But as yet I am not."

Mock slowly drank his coffee and strolled about the room. His attention was caught by a Japanese painting of fighting samurais.

"Do you know what happens when I carry out a search?" he asked. "I'm very exacting. If there is something I cannot find, I get annoyed, and I have to off-load my reaction accordingly. And do you know how? I simply demolish. Destroy."

Mock approached the table and picked up the pot of coffee. He poured himself a small amount and added sugar.

"And just at this moment I'm very annoyed," he said, holding his cup in one hand and the pot of coffee in the other.

"But this isn't a search," Risse observed intelligently.

Mock shattered the cup against the tiled stove. Risse's expression changed, but he sat quite still. Mock trampled the shards of the cup with his heels, turning them to crunching grains.

"I'll bring you a backdated search warrant tomorrow," he said, taking a wide swing. "Can you bear the tension, Risse? Are you going to allow this coffee pot to be destroyed?"

Risse pressed a button under his desk. When he saw this, Mock threw the coffee pot against the wall; black streams of coffee flowed down to the floor. Next he pulled out a flick-knife and leaped towards the painting. He positioned the point of the blade at one of the samurai's eyes. Three attendants burst into the office. Risse wiped away the tears trickling down the folds of his face and gestured for the men to leave. Then he began to write out a cheque.

BRESLAU, THAT SAME NOVEMBER 30TH, 1927
HALF PAST TEN IN THE EVENING

The Adler stopped on Nicolaistrasse outside the tenement in which Franz Mock lived. Erwin was feeling better; he was almost sober, but his gullet was exploding with drunken hiccoughs.

"Uncle," he hiccoughed, "I'm sorry. I'll pay you back. Thank you for coming to my rescue. I had to get some money to help someone. Someone who's in real trouble."

"Go home and don't tell your father," Mock muttered.

"But," – something was not giving Erwin any peace – "you could have asked . . . hic . . . the man who helped me where the boss' room is. You didn't have to lay into that . . . hic . . . doorman in the fountain."

Mock said nothing.

"I understand," said Erwin. "You had to . . . hic . . . hit someone. I understand you perfectly."

Mock revved the engine. Erwin climbed out.

The Adler glided slowly through the snow-covered city. The man behind the wheel knew that when he returned to his sleeping house he would find the bedroom door locked and the mink stole on the front door handle. He was wrong. The stole was lying on the doormat.

BRESLAU, THURSDAY, DECEMBER 1ST, 1927
EIGHT O'CLOCK IN THE MORNING

The police archives were located in the Police Praesidium basement at Schuhbrücke 49. A broad window up near the ceiling gave onto a cobbled courtyard. Officers Eduard Reinert and Heinz Kleinfeld, for reasons unexplained, had not switched on the electric light and sat with their chins resting on their hands. They could hear horses snorting, snow being cleared, handcuffs clanging on a detained prisoner and the occasional cursing of a screw. Suddenly a new sound was added: the drone of a car engine. A car door slammed and snow crunched underfoot. Through the dark window appeared first some trousers and, a moment later, Mock's face. A minute later the Criminal Counsellor, emanating two smells, was standing before the policemen. One smell, that of stale alcohol, spoke of a night spent in the company of a bottle; the second – eau-de-cologne –

testified to an unsuccessful attempt to kill the first. Reinert, gifted with an extraordinary sense of smell, picked up another scent too – a lady's perfume. Reinert pictured Mock drunk in the arms of a high-class call girl. This image did not correspond to the truth. The alleged *rex vivendi*[†] had spent the night with a bottle of schnapps, wrapped in a mink stole permeated with the delicate scent of Tosca perfume.

The Counsellor switched on the light and greeted the two policemen who officially reported to Mühlhaus. They were clever, discreet and taciturn inspectors whom Mühlhaus employed for special assignments. The assignment with which Mock now presented them required, above all, patience and doggedness.

"I know, gentlemen," he began like a university lecturer, although his schnapps-baritone was more suggestive of extra-curricular pastimes, "that I would offend you if I asked you to work through years of files in search of two addresses without giving you my reasons."

Mock lit a cigar and pulled the plate-sized ashtray nearer to him. He waited for a reaction from his listeners. There was none. This pleased him greatly.

"You have doubtless heard about the Gelfrert–Honnefelder case. Both men were murdered with some ingenuity: Gelfrert was tied to hooks in the small recess of a shoemaker's shop, and then walled in. Honnefelder, on the other hand, was quartered in his own apartment. Gelfrert was a lonely musician who abused alcohol, a member of Hitler's party. Honnefelder was an unemployed locksmith and active communist. Everything set them apart: their age, their education and social status, and their political views. Yet something linked them, which the murderer himself told us about. To Gelfrert's waistcoat he pinned a piece of paper with a date, September 12th of this year. That page came from Gelfrert's wall calendar, which is why Doctor Lasarius is inclined to believe this was when he

† King of living.

81

was killed. The murderer visited Gelfrert's room, tore the page from the calendar, then led him – or somehow lured him – to the shoemaker's shop, where he rendered him unconscious and walled him in alive. All we know about the circumstances of Honnefelder's death is what I have already told you. Again the murderer left a clue: on the table was a pocket diary with the date November 17th marked. Doctor Lasarius is certain that was when Honnefelder was killed. You have no doubts I take it, gentlemen, that both murders were committed by the same person."

Kleinfeld and Reinert had no doubts.

"So you can see," Mock continued, not noticing that Mühlhaus was standing in the door listening to his arguments, "the beast is telling us: this, and only this, is the day on which I killed. I interpret it thus: this is when I killed because only then *could* I kill. 'Could' here does not mean 'was in a state to' but 'only then did the circumstances allow me to do so'. What circumstances? That is the question we must answer." Mock extinguished his cigar and bowed to Mühlhaus. "Gentlemen, it is not the characters of the victims that connect the two murders – they are probably innocent – it is only the perpetrator. We would have nothing to go on if it weren't for the signs given to us by the murderer himself. However, if we were to analyse the dates of these crimes inside out, if we were to juggle them and add up the numbers, we wouldn't move the case forward one iota. It occurred to me that these murders might be a reminder of something that happened on these days and in those months, but earlier, in years gone by. The murderer might be telling us to dig out some old investigation that may have resulted in an erroneous conclusion or was simply hushed up. This, of course, took place in these places, exactly at these addresses. So for the addresses of the crimes, look in the files. If you manage to find a mention of them, then record exactly what it relates to. We are interested in what happened there and, above all, when it happened! And we have to find all this out here."

Mock glanced at Mühlhaus who, lost in thought, had approached the wall lined with shelves behind wooden blinds. He ran his hand along them.

"Both of you completed a classical education, and so you are acquainted with the various declensions. We have the qualifying declensions of location, time, cause, condition and affirmation. We are interested in the first three. We won't find the answers unless we examine the time and place. Do you have any questions?"

"Counsellor," said Kleinfeld. "You mentioned some addresses. We'd like to have them, please."

BRESLAU, THURSDAY, DECEMBER 1ST, 1927
TEN O'CLOCK IN THE MORNING

The somewhat regular row of tenements on Grünstrasse between Palmstrasse and Vorwerkstrasse was abruptly broken by a gap as broad and as deep as a tenement. This recess was partially filled by a small one-storeyed building separated from the street by a two-metre wall with a gate in between two turrets. The rear of the building appeared to be stuck on to the back of the huge tenement whose frontage gave on to the yard of the nearest block of houses. This peculiar construction had two small windows on the ground and first floors, and an enormous set of doors above which hung the sign MONISTISCHE GEMEINDE IN BRESLAU.[†] Breslau's Monists, apart from being convinced of the spiritual and material unity of world and man, preached the need for a natural education for the young, non-religious morality, pacifism and a sympathy for socialism, and were linked to various other sects and groups, including the Breslau Society of Parapsychic Research.

The building had interested the secret police for a long time, and

† Monistic Community of Breslau

83

especially the small department devoted to religious and para-religious movements which reported directly to Commissioner Klaus Ebners. His men had not been able to obtain much information about the mysterious building, and so had contented themselves with adding a note about it to the files of a known parapsychologist and clairvoyant, Theodor Weinpfordt, founder of the Breslau Society of Parapsychic Research. This note conveyed that the building was guarded by four men on a rota, working in pairs. Apart from them, the place was visited twice a month by a great throng of people who stayed between five and twenty hours, spending their time – in line with the society's principles – engaged in spiritualist séances. Occasionally, open lectures were held on subjects relating to occultism and astrology. Ebners' officials had noted something rather surprising in the files. Their informers had told them that those visiting the building were sometimes accompanied by children. The policemen assumed that the society's members were introducing the children into the mysteries of the secret arts, and once he had familiarized himself with his men's reports, Ebners resolved to ensure that the children were not being led there for any ignoble purposes. His suspicions were heightened when it turned out that the children were exclusively girls from an orphanage whose director was a member of the society. After a thorough investigation, it was established that the girls were being subjected to hypnosis by qualified doctors, and were coming to no harm. Ebners happily set aside the case of the building on Grünstrasse and went back to spying on communists and Hitlerites; his secretary duly copied out the files and transferred them to the Vice Department. Its chief, Criminal Counsellor Herbert Domagalla, had not noticed anything untoward in the society's work, and got on with his day-to-day affairs, that is, the mass recruitment of informers among prostitutes. The girls from the orphanage continued to visit the house on Grünstrasse.

And they were there now. Dressed in long, white robes they stood as if hypnotized or intoxicated around an enormous divan on which there reclined three women. Only a little light fell from the small window and reflected off the empty, white-painted walls of the lecture hall, from which all chairs had been removed. The morning light of winter fused with the warm glow of a multitude of candles placed irregularly throughout the hall. On the podium behind the lectern stood a bearded old man, naked, quietly reading from a small book bound in white leather. Two stoves emitted quivering waves of hot air.

Over the naked bodies of the women the girls scattered white flower petals which slid down their smooth skin and fell with a faint rustle onto the stiff sheets. Some of the petals came to rest on the mounds and hollows of their bodies. One of the women, fair-haired, lay motionless, while the other two – one dark, one red-haired – performed a number of actions that bore witness to their great skill in the field of *ars amandi*. When the dark-haired woman decided that the motionless blonde was quite ready for the next stage, she stopped what she was doing, restrained her red-haired colleague's zeal, and nodded to the old man in encouragement. He was not long to respond.

BRESLAU, THAT SAME DECEMBER 1ST, 1927
HALF PAST TEN IN THE MORNING

Mock's skull was exploding. An excess of tobacco and black coffee, an unnecessary bottle of schnapps the previous day, an unnecessary two bottles of beer that morning, tense nerves, a pile of files, his marriage in ruins, the slanting calligraphy on the reports, the interminable skimming through paragraphs in search of words ending in *-strasse*, the dirty ribbons holding the files together, the necrosis of feelings, the dust blowing about, a sense of helplessness and the futile research in the archives – all this had clouded the acuity of Mock's mind, who only a few hours earlier had been showing off in front of Reinert and Kleinfeld with his precise grammar of the investigation.

He squeezed his temples in an attempt to prevent his skull from bursting with the dull, persistent pain. Resigned, he tore his hands from his head and took the cradle and receiver that Scheier, the archivist, was holding out to him.

"Good morning, Counsellor, this is Meinerer . . ."

"Where are you?"

"Outside Matthiasgymnasium; but Counsellor . . ."

"You're to get here as soon as possible."

Mock replaced the receiver, stood up from the table with difficulty and switched off the light. Reinert gave him a vacant look, while Kleinfeld repeatedly licked a dirty finger. Mock dragged himself upstairs to his office. He arrived ten minutes later, having whiled away a fair amount of time paying nature her dues. Angrily, he assailed the door to his office. The panels in the glazed door clattered, Meinerer jumped to his feet and von Stetten gave him a look as if to say "the old man's very angry".

Mock waved him aside and went into the office, letting Meinerer through the door first. The latter had not taken two steps before he felt a heavy blow on the back of his neck. He flew forward so violently that he tumbled to the floor. He got up immediately and sat down opposite Mock, who was already at his desk, glaring at him furiously.

"That's for my nephew, Erwin," Mock said sweetly. "You were to follow him day and night. And? And last night my nephew nearly gambled everything away in the casino, on credit. He got himself into considerable danger since he didn't have anything to pledge. Why didn't you tell me?"

Mock leaned over his desk and reached out an arm. A loud, burning slap resounded off Meinerer's cheek. The latter retreated and no longer looked at his assailant with fury.

"Listen to me, Meinerer," Mock said, his tone still sweet. "You're bright enough for me not to have to waste my breath telling you about certain individuals from this establishment whose careers I successfully cut short – even though I like them more than I do you. So I'll be brief: if you bungle it one more time, you'll be transferred to the Vice Department where you'll spend your time persuading old whores to have regular check-ups for venereal disease. Apart from that, another exciting activity awaits you there: blackmailing pimps. And they're not easy to blackmail – you can't pin anything on them. All the whores keep their mouths shut about any weaknesses their bosses might have. So you'll taunt each other and take the abuse that's thrown at you day in, day out. And the results will be miserable. Reprimands, one after another . . . My friend Herbert Domagalla won't take pity on you. And that's it, Meinerer. That'll be where you end up. You'll accept a position as constable on the Ring beat with relief, anything so as not to have to face the stench, the decomposition and the syphilis."

"What do you want me to do?" asked Meinerer. His voice betrayed no emotion, which worried Mock.

"You're to continue tailing my nephew. From the moment he walks out of the school gates." Mock pulled a fob watch from his waistcoat and looked down. He felt small explosions in his temples. "But now it's only eleven, so you've still got some time. Go to Counsellor Domagalla and get me something in Vice on the boss of the Four Seasons Hotel casino, Norbert Risse. Well, what is it? Go and see what your future department looks like."

BRESLAU, THAT SAME DECEMBER 1ST, 1927
NOON

The old man gave one last amorous sigh. Sophie cried out loudly, hoarsely. She squeezed her eyes shut and lay like that for some minutes. She was relieved, freed from the old man's weight. She heard the shuffle of his bare feet. Without opening her eyes, she stroked her neck where his coarse beard had left an itchy red mark. The divan rocked beneath the pressure of Baron von Hagenstahl's muscular body as it transferred its kinetic energy to the red-haired street-walker and, through her, to Elisabeth's body which lay at the bottom of this complicated pyramid.

Sophie opened her eyes. Two little girls were standing by the bed, their eyes now clear, with no trace of intoxication or hypnotic trance. At that moment, the Baron slapped the red-haired prostitute across the face. A bright red patch appeared on her cheek. Von Hagenstahl took another swing at her. The girls shuddered, their eyes filling with tears. Helpless and horrified, they clutched white rose petals in their little fists.

"Are we to go on scattering them?" one of them asked.

Sophie burst into tears.

BRESLAU, THAT SAME DECEMBER 1ST, 1927
TWO O'CLOCK IN THE AFTERNOON

"And?" Mock asked.

Heinz Kleinfeld wiped his pince-nez and looked at Mock with tired, myopic eyes. His gaze exuded shrewdness, melancholy and Talmudic wisdom.

Eduard Reinert interrupted his reading of the files and rested his chin on one hand. His expression did not give much away. Neither of the policemen needed to answer Mock's question; the Criminal Counsellor already knew the results of their archival search.

"Go and get something to eat, and come back in an hour," said Mock, arranging the files he had looked through in an even pile. For the next few moments he occupied himself with his hair, which stubbornly entangled itself in the teeth of his bone comb. He was in no hurry to go anywhere, even though a few minutes earlier Mühlhaus had telephoned to say he wanted to see him immediately. He spruced himself up, left the archives and began the tedious journey up stairs and down corridors. He did everything he could to delay the meeting with his chief: he stubbed out long-extinguished cigarette ends with the toe of his shoe, looked out for acquaintances with whom to chat, passed no spittoon without putting it to use. He was in no rush to face the sight of an enraged Mühlhaus and a conversation during which they would have to broach certain unavoidable topics.

Mühlhaus was indeed furious. His arms were stretched wide across his desk, his fat fingers drumming a monotonous rhythm on its dark-green surface. His jaws were locked in icy anger, his lips pursed around the mouthpiece of his pipe. Ribbons of smoke escaped through his teeth and nostrils. He was quite simply seething.

Mock sat opposite his chief and began to fill the enormous horseshoe-shaped ashtray.

"A messenger is going to knock on your door tomorrow, Mock," Mühlhaus' voice shook with emotion, "bringing you a summons to an extraordinary sitting of the Horus Lodge. Do you know what the second point on the agenda will be? 'The matter of expelling Eberhard Mock from the Lodge'. Exactly that. I've proposed it and I'm going to present it. Perhaps you still remember that I'm Secretary of the Lodge?"

He fell silent and studied Mock. Apart from weariness, he could discern nothing in his face.

"And the reason for my expulsion?" Mock extinguished his cigarette, grinding it into the bottom of the ashtray.

"Committing a criminal offence." To calm himself, Mühlhaus had begun to twist a small skewer into his pipe. "The police would expel you for the same thing. You've brought it upon yourself."

"And what offence have I committed?" asked Mock.

"Are you just pretending to be an idiot?" Mühlhaus refrained from shouting this at the top of his voice. "Yesterday, in front of ten witnesses, you beat up a casino employee, Werner Kahl. And you used a knuckle-duster. Kahl has only just regained consciousness. Then you destroyed valuable Chinese porcelain belonging to the casino manager, Norbert Risse, with the intention of forcing him to defer your nephew's debt. This was witnessed by three men, and the crime has been reported to the officer on duty. An accusation of assault and destruction of extremely valuable property will soon be drawn up. You will then stand before a court and your chances are minimal. The Lodge anticipates the facts and removes potential criminals from its circle. The President of Police will suspend you from your duties. And then we shall say our goodbyes."

"Criminal Director . . ." Mock fell silent after uttering this official title, and for a while he listened to the sounds coming through the window: a tram bell on Schuhbrücke; the squelch of thawing snow; the clapping of horses' hooves on wet cobblestones; the shuffling of students' feet as they hurried to their lectures. "Surely not everything has been fore-judged. That doorman abused and attacked me first. I was only defending myself. My nephew and a certain Willibald Hönness, an employee of the casino, will attest to that. I wouldn't trust Risse. He offered me coffee and I broke a cup. And now I see he has lodged a complaint that I smashed his entire Chinese coffee service. I'm surprised he didn't mention the rape I committed on his parrot."

Mühlhaus raised his arms and with all his strength thumped his fists against the desk. The inkwell jumped, the penholder rolled across the surface, sand scattered from the old sand-box.

"To hell with you!" he roared. "I want to hear from you what happened! And you, instead of an explanation, are fobbing me off with some miserable joke about a parrot. Tomorrow I am to be summoned before our President of Police. When he asks me how you justify all this, I'll reply that you defended yourself with the statement: 'I wouldn't trust Risse.'"

"The only justification I have is loyalty to my family ties," said Mock. "My nephew is my blood, and there's a great deal I'd do for that. Beyond that, I have nothing with which to justify myself."

"That's what I'll tell the old man tomorrow: the call of family blood," Mühlhaus said sarcastically. He had calmed down and lit his pipe, piercing his subordinate with two slits for eyes. Mock felt sorry for him. He surveyed the bald head criss-crossed by wisps of hair, the long beard as if from the nineteenth century, the sausage-like fingers nervously fiddling with his pipe. He knew that Mühlhaus would go home that evening after his customary Thursday session of skat, that his thin wife, who had been growing old with him for the past quarter of a century, would greet him with his dinner, that they would talk about everything but their son, Jakob, who had left behind him a cold, empty room.

"Criminal Director, you really shouldn't believe anything Risse says. The casino manager is a homosexual mixed up in the 'four sailors' affair. What is his word against mine?"

"In normal circumstances, nothing. But you went too far, Mock, and acted out a real-life western before numerous witnesses. I happen to know that Risse is preparing for an interview today with the *Breslauer Neueste Nachrichten*. I fear that even our President lacks the power to defend you and withhold such sensational material from the press."

"There is someone who could." Mock still held on to the hope that he would not have to share with Mühlhaus the information he had received from Meinerer. "And that's Criminal Director Heinrich Mühlhaus."

"Really?" Mühlhaus raised his eyebrows so high that his monocle fell out. "Perhaps you're right. But I don't want to help you. I've had enough of you, Mock."

Mock was familiar with the various tones of Mühlhaus' voice. This one was new to him — it was characterized by sarcasm, disdain and deliberation. It could mean that his boss had made his final decision. Mock had no choice but to use his ultimate argument.

"Will you really do nothing and let Risse walk out, triumphant? Allow the triumph of a homosexual patron of artists, who love him with their whole hearts and bodies? Among them a young painter who goes by the pseudonym of Giacoppo Rogodomi."

Mühlhaus turned to the window, presenting Mock with his hunched and rounded back. Both knew this was the pseudonym used by Jakob Mühlhaus, Heinrich's prodigal son. Minutes passed. Rain beat against the windowpane, a police siren wailed, the bells pealed at the church of St Matthias.

"Criminal Counsellor," Mühlhaus did not turn away from the window, "there will be no extraordinary sitting of the Horus Lodge."

BRESLAU, THAT SAME DECEMBER 1ST, 1927
HALF PAST SEVEN IN THE EVENING

A light frost was settling under a cloudless, starry sky. Cobblestones were covered with a layer of thin icing. Mock climbed into the Adler and drove out of the Police Praesidium courtyard. He greeted the porter who shut the gate, and turned left at the Two Poles tenement into Schmiedebrücke. A hunched coalman was leading his thin horse by its bridle; it dragged its hooves with such great effort that the coal wagon it was pulling had blocked the street, forcing Mock to slow down. The Criminal Counsellor's brain was empty and sterile rendered thus by hundreds of pieces of useless information from the police files, by dozens of names and reports of criminality, abuse and despair. He could not put his mind to anything and was not even angry with the coalman. He pressed his foot lightly on the accelerator and, in the glow of neon lights and shop displays, watched the passers-by. An enraged dandy in a bowler hat emerged from Noack's drinking den and tried to explain something to a weeping, pregnant girl. The light cast by the windows of Messow & Waldschmidt's department store illuminated two postmen arguing vehemently about the city's topography. The immense corpulence of one testified to the fact that his knowledge might be rather theoretical, derived from persistent journeys made by his finger across a map. From a gate adjacent to the preserves shop rolled a drunken medical student or obstetrician lugging a doctor's bag so large that, apart from his medicines and surgical instruments, it could also have contained his entire professional ethics.

With relief Mock overtook the consumptive coalman, then turned right and, with a roar of his engine, sped along the north side of Ring. He glanced over his left shoulder and caught sight of Mrs Sommé, the wife of one of the jeweller brothers.

"At this hour?" He was surprised, and then suddenly remembered something. He stopped the car, got out, crossed the busy street and made his way briskly towards the shop.

"Good evening, Mrs Sommé," he called. "I see you're still open. I'd like to see the necklace I spoke to your husband about, the one with the rubies."

"Certainly, Counsellor," Mrs Sommé said, displaying her pink gums in an alluring smile. "I didn't think you would be coming. Here it is — I've got the necklace ready in a maroon case. I think it will suit your wife beautifully. It goes so well with green eyes . . ."

They went into the shop. Leaning over the counter, Mrs Sommé handed Mock the necklace. His eyes swept over her thirty-something, shapely figure and then he pored over the piece. A stream of words and sighs flowed from the lips of the jeweller's wife at his side, flooding his mind with cascades of clear syllables, but a moment later they were joined by another sound. He listened intently; from the back room came the sound of a man's happy voice singing Otto Reutter's "*Wie reizend sind die Frauen*".†

" . . . it is so rare. A woman who is so loved must be very happy," prattled Mrs Sommé. "Oh, you always think of your wife, you're so hard-working, so concerned about our safety . . ."

Mrs Sommé's words reminded Mock that recently he had been concerned with his nephew's safety, and that the money with which he was about to buy Sophie's necklace was to have covered Erwin's gambling debts. He also remembered that there was no need for him to buy the necklace that day; that Völlinger had calculated the day on which they would conceive to be the following one. It was then that he would take his wife in his arms, and she would be wearing nothing but rubies . . . He tipped his hat, promised to buy the necklace the next day, and mumbled an apology to the jeweller's wife as she continued:

" . . . if only all married couples were like you two . . ."

He left the shop, deep in thought as to how he would obtain the money for the necklace.

BRESLAU, THAT SAME DECEMBER 1ST, 1927
A QUARTER TO EIGHT IN THE EVENING

Elisabeth Pflüger was practising the first violin part of Schubert's 'Death and the Maiden' when her servant quietly slipped into the parlour and, next to a vase of white chrysanthemums, placed a scented envelope with the monogram S. M. Elisabeth interrupted her playing, seized the envelope and, drawing her slender legs up beneath her, made herself comfortable on the chaise-longue. With trembling hands she lost herself in reading the cornflower-blue pages covered in rounded writing.

---

† "How delightful women are."

Dear Elisabeth,

I know that what I write may make you cry. I also know how devoted you are to me. Yet I cannot allow this noble feeling that unites us to be the death of my marital happiness.

My darling, do not blame yourself for anything. Nobody forced me to take part in the meetings with the Baron that give you so much joy. I took part in them of my own free will, and of my own free will I relinquish them. Yes, my sweet, I have to leave your circle, but that does not mean this letter to you is goodbye. What unites us will endure, and neither human anger nor envy will destroy it, because what can set at variance two priestesses who serve only one mistress — Art? It is in her silent temple that we experience spiritual rapture. Our friendship will remain unchanged, and the number of our meetings will simply be reduced by those we have spent with the Baron.

It would be dishonest of me not to give you the reasons for my parting company with the Baron's group. As you know, the meetings cleansed me spiritually. I am too proud to allow Eberhard to humiliate me. And every moment he spends without me — apart from those engaged in professional duties — is a humiliation. Every second he willingly deserts me is for me the cruellest of insults. He also humiliates me when he reproaches me, beats me, accuses me of being barren, or when, overcome with desire, he begs me for love. Spiritual blows are the worst, the cruellest and the most painful. But, my love, you know I cannot live without him, without his bitterness, his cynicism, his plebeian strength, his lyricism and his despair. If that were taken away from me, I would have no reason to live.

Darling, you know our meetings with the Baron were, for me, an antidote to the harm Eberhard subjected me to. After my humiliations there came our meetings, and with them a heavenly revenge. Then, purified and innocent, as if cleansed in a spring fount, I would throw myself at Eberhard and give myself to him, longing for the conception that was to change our lives. There was no conception and there were no changes. Then, desperate, Eberhard would begin his alcoholic rantings with his own demons, after which he would debase me, presenting yet another reason for revenge. I would phone you and you – so wonderfully debauched – would return to me my former innocence.

This rhythm has been broken. This morning I experienced a moment of dread in that awful, empty house when I looked into the eyes of a little girl who had emerged from hypnosis and was watching your highest ecstasies with terror. That little orphan standing at our bed was depraved in a most hideous manner, for she saw something she will never forget to her dying day. I am totally convinced of this, since I myself was a witness to such an act committed by my parents, and their bestiality tore asunder the most sensitive strings of my soul. The saddest thing is that the orphan looked with unimaginable dread and helplessness into my eyes, the eyes of a woman who could be her mother – bah! – who would like to have been her mother. Today I was not purified, today I cannot give myself to Eberhard for all the riches in the world. Instead of revenge, I have plunged myself into the depths of despair. I am evil and dirty. I do not know what can purify me. Perhaps death alone.

That is all, my love. I end this sad letter and embrace you, wishing you happiness.

Yours,

Sophie

The usual evening lull reigned in Grajeck's restaurant. Ladies of the night fixed their eyes in vain on the hard-working citizens who, in turn, drowned their eyes in perspiring tankards of beer. One man was doing so for the tenth time that day – Criminal Sergeant Kurt Smolorz. He smiled wryly when he caught sight of his chief, awakening in Mock vague suspicions as to his subordinate's sobriety. The golden beverage worked wonders for Smolorz's facial expressions, but not for the rather poor formulations of his tongue.

"As usual," the sergeant tried to speak clearly. "Ten till two: Miss Pflüger, music. After two, home."

"As usual, you say," Mock said sullenly, accepting a glass of cognac and a coffee from the waiter. "But something isn't 'as usual', and that's the condition you're in. When did you start drinking again?"

"A few days ago."

"What happened? You haven't been drinking since the 'four sailors' case."

"Nothing."

"Any problems?"

"No."

"What have you been drinking?"

"Beer."

"How many?"

"Five."

"You're sitting here drinking instead of keeping an eye on my wife?"

"Sorry, Counsellor, but I'd drop in for a beer then go back and watch the window. Your window. That ended up being five beers."

In the next room, a customer had made his way to the piano. His playing hinted at his profession – he was a butcher. From force of habit, he played as if he were hacking up carcasses on the keyboard.

Deep in thought, Mock blew out smoke rings. He knew his subordinate well; five beers would not be enough to bring a smile to his gloomy face. And there was no doubt the grimace Smolorz had produced on his arrival had been a smile. He must, therefore, have drunk more. Smolorz got to his feet, put on his hat and bowed as politely as he could.

"With that bow of yours, you could take part in a school performance," muttered Mock, without shaking Smolorz's hand as he usually did. Watching as his sergeant's angular figure made its way out, Mock wondered why his subordinate had broken his vow of abstinence, and why he had lied about the amount of alcohol he had consumed. He stood up, approached the bar and raised a finger to call the rather mature barmaid. The latter spun willingly on her heel and gestured to Mock's empty glass.

"No, thank you," he said, placing a five-mark coin on the counter, which hastened the barmaid and quickened the heartbeats of the lonely girls who sat about. "There's something I want to know."

"Yes?" The barmaid carefully slipped the coin between her breasts. A safe and comfortable hiding-place.

"That man I was talking to, how long has he been sitting here and how many beers has he had?" Mock asked softly.

"He's been here since three, drank four large beers," the barmaid answered just as softly.

"Did he go out at any point?"

"No. I don't think he felt like going out. He looked all broken up."

"How can you tell?"

"I can't explain. After twenty years working behind bars I can recognize customers who drink to forget." The barmaid was not lying. She may not have known much, but she knew everything there was to know about men. "Your friend pretends to be hard and uncouth, but he's completely soft on the inside."

Mock, not waiting for a psychological dissection of his own character, looked into her wise and arrogant eyes, tipped his hat, paid for the cognac and stepped into the street. "Even he's lying to me," he thought. "Even Smolorz, who owes me so much. Sophie could have been up to anything while he's been drinking."

Light flakes of snow were falling to the ground. Mock got into his Adler and drove towards Rehdigerplatz, a hundred metres away. He was exploding with fury; a violent rhythm pulsated in his veins and arteries, and the pressure of his blood pressed onto his cranium. He stopped outside his house and opened the car window. The frosty air and snow that blew in cooled his emotions for a while. He recalled the previous evening: the passion on the staircase; rescuing Erwin; the mink stole lying on the doormat; the bedroom pitilessly locked; the burning schnapps trickling down to his stomach. "I'll spend tonight cuddled up to Sophie," he thought. "We'll just lie next to each other. An excess of alcohol might not be to my advantage today – tomorrow I'll be full of virile strength, and I'll give her the necklace. Is it definitely tomorrow?"

He reached into his briefcase for astrologer Völlinger's chart and turned it towards the bluish glow of the gas-light. He skimmed through the cosmograms and personality profiles of both Mr and Mrs Mock, and his attention was drawn to the prognostic report. Suddenly blood was drumming in his ears. He blew away the flakes of snow that had settled on the page and read with horror: "best date for conception – 1st December, 1927". He squeezed his eyes shut as hard as he could and imagined Sophie waiting in their dining-room. She is determined and unapproachable, but a moment later her face lights up at the sight of the ruby necklace. She kisses her husband, skimming his strong neck with her hand . . .

Mock took the jeweller's business card from his silver card-holder and carefully read the home address. "Breslau, Drabitziusstrasse 4". Without shutting the window, he fired the engine and abruptly pulled away. A journey across the entire snow-covered city awaited him.

BRESLAU, THAT SAME DECEMBER 1ST, 1927
NINE O'CLOCK IN THE EVENING

Paul Sommé the jeweller found it hard to swallow the saliva that aggravated his swollen throat. He felt his fever mounting. At times like this, he found comfort in one activity alone: perusing his numismatic collection. So he lay wrapped in his navy-blue dressing gown with purple lapels, browsing through his collection of old coins. His expert eyes, sparkling with high fever and armed with a powerful magnifying glass, caressed seventeenth-century Danzig guldens, Silesian gshyvnas and Tsarist imperials. He imagined his ancestors hoarding stacks of gold in their money bags, then buying property, homes, farms, women and titles. Given surety by the generously rewarded sheriffs, provosts and other officers of the law, he imagined their satiated, peaceful sleep during the wars and pogroms in Poland and Russia. Policemen always awoke warm feelings in Sommé. Even now, laid out as he was with a bad cold and torn from pursuing his collector's passion by the sudden sound of the bell, he was happy to receive Criminal Counsellor Eberhard Mock's business card from the butler.

"Show him in," he said to his servant and, with relief, lay his shivering body on the soft pillows of his chaise-longue.

The sight of Mock's broad figure filled him with just as much pleasure as had his business card. He esteemed the Criminal Counsellor for two reasons: firstly, Mock was a policeman; secondly, he was the husband of a beautiful and capricious woman twenty years his junior, whose changeable emotions frequently encouraged her husband to pay a visit to the jewellers. He himself, older than his wife by more than thirty years, was well acquainted with the sulking, melancholy and migraines of women. Only this did he have in common with Mock. His response to these phenomena was different, however; unlike the Counsellor, he was wise, understanding and tolerant.

"Please do not justify yourself, Excellency." Despite his burning throat he would not let Mock get a word in edgeways. "I go to bed late. Besides, no visit of yours is ever inopportune. How can I be of help?"

"My dear Mr Sommé," Mock, as always, was overcome by the impression made on him by the Dutch masters hanging on the walls of the jeweller's office. "I'd like to buy that ruby necklace we spoke about. I absolutely have to have it today, but I can't pay you until tomorrow or the day after. I beg you to grant me this favour. I will certainly pay."

"I know I can trust you," the jeweller hesitated. His fever was distorting objects and perspective, and he thought there were two Mocks scanning his walls. "But I'm not very well. I have a high temperature . . . That's the main problem . . ."

Mock eyed the canvases and recalled the previous evening in Risse's office – and the samurai with a knife-point held to his eye.

"I would dearly like to grant you this favour, Excellency. I'm really not looking for excuses," Sommé's voice was breaking in agitation. His head fell back onto the hot, damp rut in his pillow. "We can call my doctor, Doctor Grünberg, right now – he can confirm that he's forbidden me to leave the house."

Seeing the change in Mock's face, Sommé quickly got up from his chaise-longue. He felt violently dizzy, and beads of sweat, occasioned both by his illness and the fear of losing a client, broke out all over his flushed face. He leaned heavily against the desk and whispered:

"But that's irrelevant. Please wait a moment. I'll be ready in a minute."

The jeweller slowly made for the door of his bedroom. He pulled an old-fashioned nightcap onto his wet, bald head.

"Mr Sommé," Mock held him back. "Could your wife not go to the shop with me? You really are sick. I wouldn't want to put you at risk."

"Ah, how considerate of you, Counsellor sir," the jeweller mustered unfeigned admiration. "But that would be impossible. My beloved Edith left this morning to go to an auction of old silver in Leipzig. During her absence and my illness, our trusted assistant is looking after the shop. But that's no good anyway. That is, the assistant can't help you. I'm the only one who knows the code for the safe where the necklace is kept. I'll just get dressed and we'll go."

Sommé went into the bedroom next to the office and slowly closed the door. Mock heard the distinctive rustle of a body sinking to the floor and the thud of a chair or stool hitting floorboards. He ran into the bedroom, and saw the jeweller lying on the floor in a faint. He rolled him onto his back and slapped him across one burning cheek. Sommé came to and smiled to his dreams. He thought he saw his beloved Edith, her hair flowing, during their last holiday in the Eulengebirge mountains. Mock, however, had an entirely different vision: Edith Sommé, decked with jewels from the display cases, her neck entwined with his rubies, lying in a swoon with her legs spread on the ottoman at the back of the jeweller's shop, and a handsome male, satiated with her body, yelling Reutter's song as loud as he could.

"There is nothing like a trusted assistant," he thought, leaving the delirious Sommé in the care of his butler.

Mock entered his apartment and looked about. He was surprised by the silence and emptiness. Apart from the dog, nobody greeted him, nobody was pleased to see him return, nobody was waiting for him. As usual, when the servants had the evening off. Marta had gone to visit relatives near Oppeln, and Adalbert, who was suffering from the same ailment as the jeweller, was stretched out in the servants' quarters. Mock removed his hat and coat and pushed down the handle of the bedroom door. Sophie was asleep, huddled under her eiderdown. Her arms were protecting her head as if warding off a blow, her fingers were wrapped around her thumbs. Mock had read somewhere that this unconscious configuration of a sleeping body signified uncertainty and helplessness. The tenderness he felt triggered a memory: Sophie and Eberhard at a station. He was leaving for Berlin to receive a medal for solving a difficult case, she was tenderly bidding him goodbye. A kiss and a request: "If you come back during the night, wake me up. You know how."

Mock could hear Sophie's low, debauched laughter even now. He heard it as he took a bath, as he closed the bedroom door and turned the key on the inside. It resonated in his ears as he lay down beside his wife and began to wake her in the way she so loved. Sophie sighed and gently moved away from her husband, but he stubbornly persisted with his endeavours. Soon she was wide awake, looking into his glazed eyes.

"Today's the day," he whispered. "The day we are to conceive our child."

"Do you believe in that rubbish?" she asked sleepily.

"Today's the day," he said again. "I'm sorry about last night. I had to help Erwin."

"I don't care," Sophie sulked, pushing away her husband's rapacious hands, "about Erwin or your astrological predictions. I don't feel well. Let me sleep in peace."

"Darling, tomorrow I'm going to give you a ruby necklace." Mock's breath burned her neck. She got up and sat on the couch by the window, tucking her silk nightdress under her. She looked at the bed and remembered the old man with his scratchy beard.

"Do you take me for a courtesan," Sophie stared at a point above Eberhard's head, "whose love can be bought with a necklace?"

"You know how I love it when you pretend to be a little whore," he smiled sensuously.

"You only talk about yourself. It's always 'I' and 'me'." Sophie's tone was lustful and provocative. "What 'I like', what 'interests me' and so on. You never ask me what I like, what I might like to do. The whole world has to jump to your attention."

"And what do you like most?" Mock went along with her encouraging smile.

Sophie sat beside her husband and stroked his strong neck with her hand.

"Pretending to be a little whore," she replied.

Mock grew wary. He could still hear her vulgar "You want to fuck?", and feel the touch of her delicate feet which, a few days earlier, had kicked him off the bed and onto the floor.

"So pretend you are one," he instructed dryly.

The little girl in white watched with horror as Baron von Hagenstahl slapped the red-headed harlot. "Am I to go on scattering the flowers?" she asked. Sophie felt exhausted. Staggering slightly, she approached the bed.

"I can't pretend to be a whore," she sighed, slipping under the eider-down, "because you haven't got anything to pay me with. You haven't got the necklace."

"I'll have it tomorrow," Mock said, nestling against his wife's back. "I can pay you as much as a high-class prostitute. With money."

"I'm an exclusive courtesan." Sophie held him back by his wrists and moved towards the wall. "I only accept expensive presents from my clients."

"Good," Mock panted. "You pretend you're a whore and I'll pretend to give you the necklace."

Sophie raised herself on one elbow and pulled her hair out of her face.

"Stop it!" she shouted. "Leave me alone! I've had enough of this game. I'm tired and I want to sleep. You could just as easily satisfy yourself now and pretend you're making love to me! Just pretend."

Mock panted even more heavily and pressed her to the bed with all his weight. The muscles in Sophie's face slackened and her cheeks shifted imperceptibly towards her glowing ears. With her tightly closed eyes she looked like a little girl pretending to be asleep but about to burst out laughing at any moment to show her father, who is leaning over her, what a wonderful joke she has played on him. Sophie was not a child, Mock not her father, and what was happening between them now in no way resembled an innocent game. Sophie was thinking about the little girl in white, her eyes swollen from crying, her fists clutching the rose petals, and her horror at the sight of females on heat. Mock was thinking about cosmograms, stars and the as yet unborn Herbert Mock riding a pony in South Park on a Sunday.

"Today is the day to conceive," he whispered. "You know a lot of prostitutes get raped."

"You bastard! You swine!" yelled Sophie. "You boor! Don't, or you'll regret it!"

Mock did. And later regretted it.

Mock regretted it greatly. He sat naked in the locked bedroom beside a cooling stove and pressed Sophie's nightdress to his face. The material was torn in several places. At his feet lay jasmine-scented writing paper covered with her rounded writing:

You bastard and scum,
   For the rape you have committed you'll pay before God. And now, in life, with the loss of your miserable reputation . . .

He laid his wife's nightdress on the tangled bedclothes and cast his eye about the room. He stared at the empty dressing table and at the open, bare wardrobe, whose hinges Adalbert had only recently oiled. He ran his tongue over his palate. It was not dry and rough. He had not touched a drink the night before. If he had got drunk, he would not be sitting by the stove now. His tongue would not be moving around his mouth searching for traces of alcohol. It would be compressed in the mouth of a hanging man.

You infertile impotent,
   You'll remember this date for a long time – December 1st, 1927. On this day I cease to write my diary, which was a desperate cry for the respect and dignity owed to a woman and a wife. I have described in detail the violence you have inflicted upon me . . .

He lay on the divan and, by the light of the bedside lamp, gazed at Sophie's few fair hairs as he wound them around his finger. His first morning without a wife. His first morning without a hangover.

He dragged himself from the divan to the floor. He lay on his stomach on the deep-pile carpet and with his arms gathered the mound of objects Sophie had built up like a funereal pyre. There were the furs, which, at his bidding, she had worn over her naked body, jewellery, perfumes and even silk stockings.

I don't need presents from you. All you are capable of is opening your wallet and buying forgiveness and love. But mine you can no longer afford.

You pitiful old alcoholic, you couldn't match up to a young woman like me. Your member is too small. But there are men in this city who are my equals. You haven't even the slightest idea how often and in what ways I experienced carnal ecstasy in the week you have crowned by raping me. You can't even imagine. Do you want to know? You'll soon find out from the diary I'm going to publish secretly, and which my friends will distribute throughout all the brothels in Germany. You have no idea what I am capable of. You'll find out from the diary how much life I sucked out of Robert, our former servant.

Mock buried his face in the pillow that Sophie had bitten the night before. During his police career, he had conducted four murder cases in which husbands had allegedly killed their wives. In three of them, the reason for the crime had been that the wives had ridiculed their husbands' sexual prowess. The deceased had made fun of the small size of their husbands' sceptres and had told them they had found satisfaction in the arms of other men. Mock had checked these stories. They were, with no exception, fictitious tales, incredible fantasies – the ultimate weapon sought by ill-treated wives. He remembered the insolent looks their previous butler, Robert, had thrown at Sophie. He remembered his wife's

107

perfume filling the servants' quarters, and the butler's oaths that it was the scent of a street-walker.

The Criminal Counsellor grasped his head. Were Sophie's threats entirely unfounded? Had she really written a diary about her "carnal ecstasy"? It would make perfect reading for brothelists, and what was described there would have to be what they wanted. Were these pornographic experiences real, or were they the invention of an aristocratic woman abused by her plebeian husband, of an artiste oppressed by a brutal philistine, of a woman ready for motherhood, fruitlessly ravished by an infertile male? There was only one person who knew the answer to the question, the man whose task it had been to note Sophie Mock's every move over the past week.

BRESLAU, THAT SAME DECEMBER 2ND, 1927
EIGHT O'CLOCK IN THE MORNING

Mock left Main Station by the rear exit. He passed the Administration of Iron Railways on his right and the frost-covered trees of Teichäcker Park on his left, then cut across Gustav-Freitag-Strasse. He stopped on the square in front of Elisabethgymnasium, bought some cigarettes at the kiosk there, and sat down on a bench glazed with ice. He had to take a break to think, had to link up causes to effects.

You'll never find me. At last I am free. Free from you and those stinking Silesian provinces. I'm leaving for ever.

His suspicions were confirmed. The ticket seller just finishing the night shift glanced at Sophie's photograph and recognized her as being the woman who had bought a ticket at about midnight for the night train to Berlin.

108

Mock drew the gaze of schoolboys hurrying to school; the woman selling newspapers and tobacco in the kiosk eyed him coquettishly; from a poster pillar he was pierced by the stare of a gloomy old man, below whom was the caption: "Spiritual father Prince Alexei von Orloff proves the imminent coming of the Antichrist. His portents: recurrence of crimes and cataclysms."

"He's right, that spiritual father," thought Mock. "Crimes and cataclysms are recurring. I've been left by a woman once more and Smolorz has started drinking again."

The thought of the Criminal Sergeant reminded him of the purpose of his expedition to a district he did not much like, behind Main Station. He walked along Malteserstrasse, passing Elisabethgymnasium and the red-brick communal school, and turned right into Lehmgrubenstrasse. He crossed at a diagonal, dodging the number 6 tram, and entered the gate of tenement 25 opposite the church of St Heinrich. On the fourth floor of the annexe lived Franziska Mirga, a young Gypsy from Czechoslovakia whose five-year-old son bore the beautiful Silesian name of Helmut Smolorz.

Opposite Franziska's lodgings, on a toilet with the door wide open, sat a corpulent old woman. Privacy, evidently, was not something she greatly prized. With her skirts arranged in waves at the foot of the pan, she held onto the doorframe with her arms and scrutinized the panting Mock. Before knocking on Franziska's door, he remembered the ancient adage about the candour of Gypsies, and decided to turn the old woman into his informer.

"Tell me, grandma," he shouted, holding his nose, "did anyone visit Miss Mirga last night?"

"But of course they did, of course they did." The old woman's eyes glistened. "All of them military men, and one civilian."

"And was there a general among them?"

"Of course there was. They all were. All of them military men and one civilian."

Nolens volens, Mock had to rely on the candour of Gypsies, questioned though it was by many. He knocked on the door with a force that shook the Advent wreath hanging there. In the gap above the door chain appeared the face of a young woman. When she saw the police identification, Franziska's expression became serious and she unfastened the chain. Mock found himself in a kitchen. On the stove stood a saucepan of milk and a kettle. Steam was settling on a child's clothes as they dried, on a small pile of neatly stacked firewood, on a bucket of coal and on walls covered with green gloss paint. Mock removed his hat and unbuttoned his coat.

"Are we going to talk here?" he asked, irritated.

Franziska opened the door to a room partitioned by a curtain depicting a sunset by the seaside, with boats bobbing on the waves. It was taken up almost entirely by a sideboard, a three-door wardrobe, a table and some chairs. On one of the chairs sat a small boy eating with relish from a bowl of semolina. If Kurt Smolorz ever wanted to disown his son, he would have to exchange heads with somebody.

The child gazed at Mock in horror. The policeman sat down and stroked his wiry, reddish hair. He knew he had found an informer. Hearing the mother rattling the stove lids, he asked quietly:

"Tell me, little Helmut, was Papa here yesterday?"

Franziska was on her guard. She took the milk off the stove, came into the room and looked at Mock with hatred. The boy had obviously eaten enough. He jumped off the chair without a word, and ran behind the curtain. Mock heard the sound of a body falling onto an eiderdown and smiled, remembering how little Eberhard had jumped from the stove onto the pile of eiderdowns on his parents' bed in their small house in Waldenburg.

Suddenly, the smile froze on his lips. Little Helmut had burst into tears, his howls intensifying and juddering. Franziska went behind the curtain and said something to her son in Czech. The boy kept on crying, but was no longer screaming. His mother repeated the same words over and over.

A year earlier, Mock had spent two weeks in Prague training police from the Criminal Department of the local Praesidium. The policemen had spoken fluent German with an Austrian accent, so Mock had learned hardly any Czech verbs, except one, which he had heard pronounced frequently with various endings. The word was *zabit*, meaning "to kill", and it was a form of this word, preceded by the negating *ne*, that he now heard from behind the curtain, accompanied by the internationally used diminutive "papa". Mock strained his philological brain. "Papa" could be either the subject of "to kill", or the object. In the first case, Franziska's sentence could be understood as meaning "Papa doesn't kill", "Papa didn't kill" or "Papa won't kill". In the second, "he isn't killing Papa", "he hasn't killed Papa" or "he won't kill Papa". Mock eliminated the first possibility – it was hard to imagine a mother saying "Papa won't kill" – and accepted the second. Franziska Mirga could only have reassured her son with "he won't kill Papa".

The child stopped crying and the woman emerged from behind the curtain, glaring at Mock in defiance.

"Was Kurt Smolorz here yesterday?" he repeated his question.

"No. He hasn't been here for a long time. He's probably with his wife."

"You're lying. He always comes to see you when he's drunk, and he was drunk yesterday. Tell me if he was here and where he is now."

Franziska said nothing. Mock felt extremely hot. Seven years ago, as an officer in the Vice Department, he had interrogated a prostitute who had refused to tell him where her pimp, suspected of human trafficking, could be found. Losing his patience, Mock's chief at the time had held her one-year-old child out of the window. Maternal love had superseded her love for her procurer.

Mock felt a small hammer banging in his skull. He pulled out his notebook and quickly wrote: "Tell me where he is or I'll tell the boy I'm going to kill his Papa" and gave it to the woman. By the fury on Franziska's face, he saw he had correctly deciphered the phrase she had used to reassure her son.

"I'm not going to tell you anything." She was frightened now.

Steam belched from the kettle. Mock stood up and made towards the curtain. He stopped in front of it and took a chequered handkerchief from his pocket to wipe his perspiring neck. Without another glance at Franziska, he turned into the kitchen and left the apartment.

The old woman sitting on the toilet waggled a finger at him. As he approached she whispered:

"They all were. All of them military men, even one general."

Mock felt like saying something unpleasant to her, but he had to spare his nerves. Today would be taken up wandering from one seedy haunt to another in search of the born-again alcoholic.

BRESLAU, THAT SAME DECEMBER 2ND, 1927
EIGHT O'CLOCK IN THE EVENING

Karl Urbanek had been working as a cloakroom attendant at the Café-Variété Wappenhof for four years, and every day at the start of his duty he prayed in thanksgiving to God for his good position. For an hour now he had been trying to send his daily quota of entreaties and muttered incantations towards the heavens, but had not yet managed to fulfil his norm. This time it was the bellboy, Jäger, who disturbed him. Just as the attendant was getting to his fifth Our Father, Jäger burst into the vestibule, skidding on the polished marble floor and performing what

112

looked like a dance step. Urbanek, annoyed, interrupted his prayers and opened his mouth to yell at the bellboy for using the floor as an ice-rink instead of carrying out his professional duties in a serious manner. The unfulfilled penitent Urbanek did not let his anger get the better of him, however; when he thought it over for a few moments, he realized that Jäger was not sliding on the polished tiles for pleasure. The torn collar of his Wappenhof uniform and the absence of his cap were proof that the bellboy had left his post on the pavement outside rather violently. And Urbanek had not the slightest doubt that Jäger's aggressor was the hefty fellow now hurling the boy's cap to the floor, while gallantly allowing a stocky, dark-haired man who was brushing snow off his hat, and a small man with a narrow, foxy face, through the revolving doors.

"I tried to explain to these gentlemen that there are no more seats for today's performance . . ." squeaked the boy, picking up his cap.

"So there's no table for me?" said the dark-haired man, staring fixedly at the cloakroom attendant. "Tell me, Urbanek, is it true that there's no table at this tingle-tangle for me and my friends?"

The attendant scrutinized the new arrivals for a moment, then a glimmer of recognition appeared in his eyes.

"But of course not!" he cried, looking sternly at Jäger. "Counsellor Mock and his friends are always our most welcome guests. Please forgive this idiot . . . He hasn't been here long and he doesn't appreciate his job . . . You shall have my company box immediately . . . Oh, it's so long since you've been here, Counsellor — it must be two years . . . "

Urbanek fussed over Mock and his companions and tried to take their coats, but clearly none of the three men intended to disrobe.

"You're right, Urbanek." Mock leaned amicably on the attendant's shoulder, enveloping him in a strong smell of alcohol. "I haven't been here for three years . . . But we don't need the box. I just wanted to ask you something . . ."

113

"I'm all ears, Counsellor." Urbanek returned to his position behind the counter and gestured to Jäger to take up his post on the pavement.

"Have you seen Criminal Sergeant Kurt Smolorz here today?" Mock asked.

"I don't know who he is."

"You don't know who he is? That's interesting." Mock studied the heavy curtain separating the vestibule from the auditorium. "I understand that your boss doesn't allow you to pass on information about your guests, but I'm well acquainted with your boss and I'm convinced he'll praise you for the assistance you're about to give me."

The curtain stirred. From beyond the thick material came muffled, lively music. Mock walked up to it and yanked it aside. The words of a song suddenly became quite clear, and they all recognized the famous hit about two inseparable friends that was then being sung in Berlin's theatres by Marlene Dietrich and Claire Waldoff. Behind the curtain stood a girl selling cigarettes. When she saw Mock she quickly hid something in her white apron and, disconcerted, approached the cloakroom counter. She was dressed like a chambermaid from a hotel whose owner skimps on the outfits of his female staff. While Mock, struck by the provocative length of her dress, was wondering what would happen if the girl leaned over without bending her knees, Urbanek gave her a fresh supply of cigarettes. The cold draught from the revolving doors had clearly done her no good, for she sniffed repeatedly through her red nose.

"How do you split it with her?" he asked the attendant when the girl had returned to the smoke-filled auditorium. "Fifty-fifty?"

"I don't know what you care to mean, Counsellor." Urbanek assumed an innocent expression.

"Do you think I can't guess what she's got hidden in her apron?" Mock smiled wryly. "Do you think I don't realize that you're selling your

114

own smokes on the side, then giving the girl her cut? How much is it? Enough for her to buy some cocoa?"

Silence descended. "God is clearly not siding with me today," thought Urbanek. "I have offended Him. It's because I didn't manage to thank Him today for my position." He remembered where he used to work: the cluttered counting-room at the printers, Böhn & Taussig, his accountant colleagues in aprons gnawed by moths, reading Marx's Das Kapital without fully understanding it. Later they would trumpet defiant slogans in smoky halls filled with the furious unemployed, whose consumptive children had nothing but the carpet horse in the yard to play with; alcoholics with untreated syphilis; and pick-pockets who used their stolen coins to buy favours from tubercular ladies of the night, whose sanitary arrangements consisted of nothing more than a brass basin and a chipped chamber pot. This whole crowd, absorbing the dark tautologies of demagogues like a sponge, was infiltrated by police agents on the lookout for weaknesses in potential collaborators. It was at one such meeting that Karl Urbanek had attracted the attention of an agent. Seduced in equal measure by money, promises and religious arguments, he quickly began to enrich his exacting accountant's mind with problems of fundaments, superstructure, production means and work, in the process of humanizing the ape. After several months of intensive study, Urbanek had found himself standing on an empty beer crate in the deserted warehouse of a river shipyard at An der Viehweide. His strong voice gushed with such a vehement hatred of capitalists and the bourgeoisie that his comrades listened to him ecstatically, and police agents began to wonder if his activism would not bring results contrary to those intended. Some weeks later, the agent who had recruited Urbanek congratulated himself on making the right decision. The new star of the communist firmament had won such favour with his comrades that after party meetings, in the back rooms of drinking dens, they revealed to him their clandestine intentions.

115

In 1925, Urbanek thwarted an attempt on the life of Captain Buth, chief of the municipal headquarters of the Stahlhelm, by betraying those who had taken part, and instigated a wave of arrests of members of the KPD,[†] Breslau branch, for belonging to a terrorist organization. Detonators, fuses, hand grenades and explosive materials with the mysterious names ammonit 5, romperit C and chloratit 3, came into the hands of the police. Thanks to the police, Urbanek was given the position of door attendant at Café-Variété as a reward for his work, and soon forgot about the counting-room that reeked of rat poison. Now, influenced by Mock's words, he caught a whiff of that stench again. For a moment he wondered whether he would have agreed to collaborate with the Criminal Counsellor had the latter not discovered his little secret with the cigarette girl. He glanced at Mock's stubborn, somewhat amused face and answered in the affirmative:

"What does he look like?" he asked.

"Medium height, red-haired, stocky." Mock concentrated, trying to bring Smolorz's distinguishing features to mind. "Wearing an old, crumpled hat. He would have been drunk, or at least a little inebriated."

"Yes, I saw a man like that today, at about six." Urbanek experienced platonic anamnesis for the second time that day. "He was with Mitzi."

"Which room does this Mitzi work in?" Mock pulled a crumpled cigarette from his pocket and tried to recreate its rightful form.

"She's with a client now," the attendant hesitated then added in a perfectly controlled, ingratiating tone, sweetening his response with a broad smile of large, uneven teeth: "My dear gentlemen, please enjoy our magnificent artistic programme. The Josephine Baker of Breslau will be performing in a moment. Topless. There's certainly something to feast your eyes on. When Mitzi's free, I'll send the bellboy to fetch you. Please, take my company box. The waiter will see you to it . . . Perhaps you would

† Kommunistiche Partei Deutschlands – German Communist party.

like to order some schnapps on the house? And Counsellor, please don't tell anyone about the cigarettes. We want to make a bit of money . . . The girl's saving up for a better future . . . She deserves a better future . . . Really . . ."

"She'll be lucky if she makes enough to pay the venereal specialist," muttered Mock, and he pulled the curtain aside. Urbanek looked at him blankly and returned to his prayers.

Mock and his two companions were taken to the company box by an obliging maître d', whose entire earnings must have gone on whisker-pomade. Without removing their hats or coats, the men began to study the clients at the variété. On stage danced two actresses with their dresses hitched high; first they embraced, then they bounded away from one another. Some of the clients were very animated and chimed in enthusiastically. One obese individual swayed from side to side, conducting with his huge cigar and singing with such passion that his golden watch chain almost snapped across his bloated belly. But he could not remember more than the first few words of the song: "*Wenn die beste Freundin mit 'ner besten Freundin . . .*"†

Waiters bustled about distributing rings of *weisswurst* and armfuls of bottles. The slicked maître d' flapped his stiffly starched napkin and stood before Mock a bottle of Silesian schnapps, a plate of steaming potatoes and a dish of duck-breast slices swimming in cranberry sauce. He skilfully served the men a couple of slices each and left with dance-like steps. The actresses received ovations and the audience puffed cigar smoke while Mock took to eating his duck, washing it down, all the while, with ice-cold schnapps. Zupitza, the Counsellor's heavily built companion, bravely kept him company, whereas Wirth, the short, foxy-faced man, did not touch a drop, being as he was a man of great imaginative capabilities: every time he smelled alcohol, there loomed before his eyes a certain tap-

† "When you're best friend with her best friend . . ."

117

room in Copenhagen where he had drunk too much and, instead of fleeing, had responded unnecessarily to the provocations of a band of Italian sailors. It was only thanks to his friend, the mute Zupitza, that he had survived. Every time he smelled schnapps, he would remember dens in the port where he and Zupitza had picked up extortion money from smugglers, and brothels where they had been welcomed with open arms on account of their generosity. Now, at his port enterprise on the River Oder, which was merely a cover for his criminal undertakings, he did not allow any of his employees to drink. So Zupitza was eagerly making the most of the opportunity to knock back one glass after another.

All of a sudden the lights went out and the beating of tam-tams resounded. The beating grew louder as spotlights came on one by one and swept the ceiling, a night sky painted with silver stars after the design of Berlin's Wintergarten. As if on command the spots swept across the stage. Their columns of light picked out palm trees and a dancer wearing nothing but a grass skirt, who skipped about frenetically. Her black-painted skin was soon covered in droplets of sweat. The jerky movements of her considerable breasts synchronized perfectly with the rhythm of her body, and became deeply embedded in the memories of Breslau's philistines. None of these men paid any attention to the tacky, pseudo-exotic accessories; in his mind every one of them was pressing the dancer against the palm tree, grinding his hips and raping her. All this was accompanied by the screech of monkeys coming from enormous gramophone trumpets positioned at the front of the stage.

The bellboy's whisper brought Mock back to reality. He waggled his finger and once more listened carefully. "Room 12", he memorized, and gave the sign to Wirth and Zupitza. They abandoned the box, leaving the duck growing cold, the schnapps growing warm, and the staid fathers of families aflame. As they approached the attendant's counter, Urbanek jumped out horrified and spread his arms in a gesture of apology.

118

"My sincerest apologies," he sobbed. "The bellboy informed you that Mitzi was free, but the client has just come out to pay for an extra hour. I couldn't turn him down – he's a very good client. He's drunk, and probably no match for fiery Mitzi. Gentlemen, please amuse yourselves a while longer, have another drink . . ."

Mock moved Urbanek aside and climbed the stairs leading to the rooms. The attendant took one look at Wirth and Zupitza and lost all desire to protest. Silence reigned in the red-carpeted corridor. Mock knocked energetically at the door to room 12.

"Occupied!" he heard a woman's voice.

He knocked again.

"Get lost, please! I've paid!" The client must have been an exceptionally polite man who, judging from his barely intelligible babbling, had evidently drunk too much.

At a sign from Mock, Zupitza backed away to the opposite wall, threw himself forward and rammed the door with his shoulder. There was a crash and some plaster crumbled, but the door did not give way. Zupitza did not need to renew his attack since Urbanek had run up and unlocked the door with a spare key. The sight they beheld was pitiful. An exceedingly drunk youth was pulling up his long johns while Mitzi, with her petticoat hitched up, sat on the edge of the iron bed, indifferently lighting up a cigarette in a long cigarette-holder. Seeing Mock, she wrapped the bedspread over her round hips. Mock stepped into the room and inhaled the smell of dust and sweat. He closed the door behind him, leaving Wirth and Zupitza in the corridor.

"Criminal police," he said somewhat quietly, realizing he did not have to threaten anyone with his authority. The boy had got tangled up in his trouser legs and was looking around helplessly. The Counsellor had taken part in many a brothel raid and was perfectly well acquainted with the embarrassed look of a client whose virility has let him down.

119

"What's up, Willy?" came shouts from outside the window. "Are you screwing so hard you're bringing the walls down?"

A burst of laughter followed, then hiccoughing and burping.

"My friends," the boy said, squeezing into shoes a little too small for him and with every instant growing more sober. "It was a present. They paid for the girl and I can't get it up. I've drunk too much."

"How old are you?" asked Mock, sitting on the bed next to Mitzi.

"Seventeen."

"Are you still at school?"

"No," the boy retorted, still swaying as he put on his jacket. "I'm apprenticed at a tailor's. I passed my craftsman's exam today. I haven't got any more money."

"And this was supposed to be a present for passing your exam?" Mock spat his cigarette end on the floor and looked at the boy. The boy nodded. "Today you were going to become a real man, is that it? If you can't get it up, your pals will laugh at you?"

The boy turned to stone and hid his face in his hands. Mitzi laughed out loud and glanced at Mock encouragingly, expecting him to do the same.

"Yell," Mock said in a low voice.

"What's that supposed to mean?" Mitzi's kohl eyebrows rode right up to her hairline in amazement. "What kind of shit are you giving me?"

"You're the piece of shit," whispered Mock, taking stock of her reddened nostrils. "And I'm the police. Yell as if this youngster was making you come no end."

This time Mitzi did not show the slightest surprise. She plucked out her cigarette from its holder and began a noisy performance. Moans and gasps tore from her throat. She kneeled on the bed and bounced up and down, without ceasing to emit passionate groans. The bedspread fell away from her full hips. Cries of approval reached them from the court-

120

yard. Mock closed his eyes and lay back on the tangled linen with Mitzi bouncing beside him. The bed rocked back and forth like the droschka in which he and Sophie had sped through Scheitniger Park one night. It was late summer. Sophie was wearing a light-green dress and he white tennis clothes. He was urging the cabby along, pressing handfuls of banknotes into his pocket. A strong, warm wind was blowing. Sophie, half reclining in the droschka, was grasping a bottle of champagne in her left hand, and heavy sheaves of hair whipped her drunken eyes. She moaned for the first time near the Japanese Garden. The coachman was uneasy, but did not look round. Sophie had no control over herself, nor did she wish to. The coachman clenched his teeth and whipped the horse furiously. The woman's throaty cries resounded in the empty pergola, bouncing off the stone arches and startling the animal who had never been lashed like that before. Sophie brought her lips to the neck of the bottle, the horse lurched a little to one side and what was left of the champagne gurgled in her throat. Drops of the noble drink trickled down to her windpipe and bronchial tubes. She stiffened and started to cough. Horrified, Mock fastened his trousers and began to blow air into her mouth. The last thing he remembered was the Centenary Hall and Sophie's stiffened body. He did not remember the journey to the hospital; he did not remember the swift resuscitation performed on his wife; he forgot what the droschka and the ill-treated horse looked like. All he could remember was the cabby, the old Jew who, grateful for the generous sum, and humiliated by Sophie's orgiastic cries, was wiping the froth off his horse.

Mock opened his eyes and signalled for Mitzi to stop. She gave one violent sob and fell silent. A cheer of approval rose from the courtyard.

"Get out of here," he said to the tailor's apprentice. "Don't stare at me like that, and don't thank me. Just get out . . . Leave the door open and tell my men to come in."

Wirth and Zupitza appeared in the room. Embarrassed by them, Mitzi covered her pudenda once more. Both men stood in the door and looked in amazement at the Counsellor still stretched out beside the prostitute, on bedclothes covered with cigarette burns. Without getting up, Mock turned towards Mitzi and asked:

"A drunk, red-haired gentleman came to see you today. What did he talk about, and where did he go?"

"I've had five clients and none of them had red hair," Mitzi said slowly.

Mock was overcome with boredom. He felt like a factory worker standing at the same machine for the thousandth time, for the thousandth time placing the same objects into a vice and squeezing them. How many times had he seen the impudent gaze of pimps or the fixed stare of bandits, the heavy eyelids of murderers, the restless eyes of thieves – and all of them saying: "Get lost, cop, I'm not going to tell you anything anyway!" At moments like these, Mock would arm himself with an iron bar, a truncheon or knuckle-dusters, remove his frock coat, roll up his sleeves, and don oversleeves and a rubber apron so as not to sully himself with blood. These preparations were not usually sufficient. He would then begin to persuade the interrogated parties with sentimental arguments. He would sit with them and, fondling his truncheon or knuckle-dusters, talk about their sick children, wives, fiancées, impoverished parents and imprisoned brothers. He would promise help from the police and freedom from their most pressing material worries. A few allowed themselves to be persuaded and, gazing gloomily into the iron sink – the only object of any interest in the interrogation room – would whisper their secrets and Mock, like a sensitive confessor, would talk to them for a long time and give his absolution. Many criminals, however, did not allow themselves to be deluded by sentimental arguments. So the resigned Criminal Counsellor would remove his executioner's outfit and detect flashes of triumph in the impudent eyes of the pimps, the staring eyes of bandits, and behind the heavy eyelids of the murderers. These soon vanished when Mock stood back from the interrogated parties and, in a barely audible whisper, presented his strongest arguments: colourful descriptions of their future life; epic tales of fratricidal wars between criminals; appalling prophecies of humiliation and rape that ended in vividly depicted deaths on rubbish heaps, or in the dark currents of the River Oder, with eyes being devoured by fish. When this failed to produce results, Mock would leave the room and hand over the instruments of torture to the burly officers who rarely took off their rubber aprons. After a few hours he would return to renew his alternating gentle and threatening arguments. He would observe desperate eyes lost within swollen bumps, and waited until the throats of those interrogated "filled" – as the Poet once said – "with sticky consent".

He was bored now because Mitzi would not be taken in by the usual "You're a whore and I'm a policeman", a simple statement which produced immediate results with most prostitutes. Mock had to move on to more advanced, grimmer forms of persuasion and for the thousandth time appeal to suppressed common sense. He looked into Mitzi's eyes again and detected stubbornness and amusement. This was how Sophie would look at him when he begged for a moment's love. His wife formed her lips in a similar way when she exhaled smoke; no doubt that was what she was doing at that moment, sitting in some seedy Berlin hotel, wrapping her slender hips in bedclothes full of cigarette burns.

Mock got up suddenly, grabbed Mitzi roughly by the shoulder and led her into the corridor, where he left her in Zupitza's care. He went back into the room and said to Wirth:

"Search this room thoroughly. Fiery Mitzi must surely put out her flames with snow."

It was a moment before Wirth understood what his police patron and protector wanted of him, at which point he began a thorough search. Mock stood by the window, watching the drunken youths as they shouted and patted the tailor's apprentice on the back. With their arms around each other, and slipping on the thick clumps of snow, they made their way across the courtyard towards the banks of the Oder. The sounds in the room also died away. Mock turned and saw, right in front of his nose, a tin for corn ointment held up in Wirth's crooked fingers. It was full of a white powder.

"Here it is – cocoa," lisped Wirth.

"Bring her in," Mock said.

Mitzi's eyes were now full of resignation. She sat on the bed with a sigh that was not in the least orgiastic. She was shaking with fear.

"You know what I'm going to do with you now? I'm going to pour the snow out of the window and lock you up for a long time. That'll be my good deed, to get you off cocaine." Mock felt the duck sit heavily in his stomach. "But maybe you don't want to be cured, maybe this stuff means a lot to you? Or maybe you're going to tell me something about that red-haired drunk who was here today. What did he say and where was he going, sweetheart?"

"He was here at about six. He had his way with me, then asked where Anna the Goldfish now works." Mitzi was less guarded and very much to the point. "I told him she's at Gabi Zelt's dive. He probably went there."

"Did he explain why he was looking for Anna the Goldfish?"

"Men like him don't tend to explain themselves."

Mock beckoned to Wirth and Zupitza, leaving Mitzi alone with her conscience. The sense of boredom receded. Instead he was bursting with pride at having such an efficient vice that nobody had been able to withstand: neither Urbanek nor Mitzi, nor – all those years ago – Wirth and Zupitza, who now, without asking questions, would accompany him on his odyssey through the dives of Breslau. As he ran down the stairs, he caught sight of Urbanek's frightened expression. He slowed his step. With every sudden movement he was reminded of the duck he had washed down with schnapps. It struck him that only one person had with-stood the workings of his vice, only one person had failed to find a place in his ordered and pedantic world.

"Have you got that cocoa?" he asked Wirth.

"Yes," he heard in response.

"Give it back to her," Mock said slowly. "Don't try to save the world. You're not much good at it."

A minute later, the three men were sitting in the car. Zupitza asked Wirth something in sign language. Wirth dismissed him with a wave of his hand and fired the engine.

"What does he want?" Mock indicated Zupitza with his eyes.

Wirth considered for a moment whether what he was about to say would undermine the Counsellor's authority, then translated Zupitza's question, trying to soften its bite.

"He asked why that door attendant and the whore were so cheeky at first, and weren't scared of you."

"Tell him they didn't know me. They were hiding behind their boss who's got good contacts in the police. They thought I wouldn't be able to jump out of line with him."

Wirth translated and Mock detected a smile of derision on the face of the thug.

"Now translate every word of mine accurately." Mock narrowed his eyes. "I know the manager of that brothel very well. On Saturdays and Tuesdays, I play bridge with him. The whore and the door attendant now know me well too. Does your Zupitza also want to get to know me well? If not, then he can save himself those smiles."

Wirth translated and Zupitza's face was transformed as he looked out at the empty, winter strand of the Ohlau on their left.

"But his girls are first class," Wirth said, trying to diffuse the atmo-sphere. "That Mitzi was quite, you know . . ."

125

"He knows his whores very well. He deals with them every day," said Mock as he tried to remember what Mitzi looked like.

BRESLAU, THAT SAME DECEMBER 2ND, 1927
TEN O'CLOCK IN THE EVENING

Trusch's bar in the Black Goat tenement opposite Liebchen's stove factory on Krullstrasse was named after its energetic manageress, "Gabi Zelt's dive". The tenement shutters were always closed, a circumstance which was dictated, above all, by a desire to maintain order and discretion. The owner had no need of new guests, and besides, he wanted to avoid the prying eyes of local children and wives seeking their husbands. The custom was regular: petty criminals, blind-drunk ex-policemen, young ladies from the upper classes in search of greater thrills, and more or less mysterious "kings of life". All shared a passion for the white powder, which, in carefully measured portions and wrapped in greaseproof paper, was carried by dealers in the lining of their hats. A hat indicated a dealer, therefore, and in the toilets these men would negotiate an average of ten transactions a day. This "snow" constituted the main trade in Gabi Zelt's bar. The former brothel madam bearing this name was but a figurehead who, for a considerable wage, lent her name to the establishment's real owner, the pharmacist Wilfried Helm, Breslau's biggest producer of cocaine. The activities in Gabi Zelt's bar were tolerated by the police; thanks to their informers who were a fixture there, they could on occasion lock away some cocaine dealer who worked independently of Helm, or some other criminal who had decided to spend his hard-earned money on "cement". But if the stool-pigeons were silent for too long, the drugs squad would ruthlessly raid the bar and catch the small fry of this demi-monde, and thus be able to close a few of their files with a good conscience. Gabi Zelt and Helm the pharmacist could also breathe more freely because the raids lent them credence in the eyes of the under-world.

Mock was well aware of all this but, as Deputy Chief of a different department, he did not interfere in the affairs of the "cement men", as the drugs police were called. So nobody at Gabi Zelt's would know him, and nobody should have been paying him any particular atten-tion. Here, however, Mock was mistaken. Shortly after they had made their way through the door with a sign advertising "DAS BESTE ALLER WELT, DER LETZTE SCHLUCK BEI GABI ZELT"† and sat on a long bench of roughly hewn planks, Mock was approached by an elegantly dres-sed man who then stroked his nose with a manicured finger. Although Mock recognized this sign, he was astounded – for the first time in his life he had been taken for a cocaine dealer. He was quick to guess why: he had forgotten to remove his hat, which he now did, sending the dandy off with a wave of his hand. The disappointed addict looked question-ingly at Wirth and Zupitza, but he found no hint of interest in their eyes.

There was another man wearing a hat, but he was so engrossed in cavorting with a stout woman that it was hard to imagine he had come to the bar for any other reason. He kept reaching into a large fish tank and pulling out fish. He would then approach his companion's cleavage and she would receive the thrashing creatures between mighty breasts unfet-tered by any bra. A moment later, the man would plunge his hand into the generous bust with a wild cry and extract the fish, to the weak applause of a few drunks and the rheumy-eyed mandolin player. The applause was weak because the woman had been acting out this charade for twenty years – regulars of all the seedy bars knew it only too well. Besides, this was how she had acquired her nickname, "Anna the Goldfish". This frol-icking "busty miracle" was no stranger to Mock either, and he recognized

† "The best thing in the world – the last swig at Gabi Zelt's".

127

the fishing enthusiast perfectly well as Criminal Sergeant Kurt Smolorz, born-again alcoholic.

Mock spat a mouthful of vile beer, somewhat reminiscent of petrol, onto the dirt floor, lit a cigarette and waited until Smolorz became aware of him. This happened very soon. On his way back to the fish tank, Smolorz glanced merrily at the three men watching him intently and lost all his jollity in an instant. Mock stood up, passed him without a word, and made for the toilets in the dark corridor cluttered with empty beer and schnapps crates, with a massive door at the end of it. Mock opened the door and found himself in a minuscule yard, as if at the bottom of a dark well whose sides consisted of the windowless gable walls of three other tenements. He tipped his head back and held his face up to the cloudy sky. A light, powdery snow was slowly falling. A moment later, Smolorz was at his side. Wirth and Zupitza had remained in the bar, having been told by the Counsellor that no-one was to witness his conversation with his subordinate. Mock placed his hands on Smolorz's shoulders and, despite the strong fumes of alcohol emanating from him, drew his face closer.

"I've had a heavy day today. My wife left me last night. My close associate, who was supposed to be following her, got drunk instead. The only person I trusted ignored my confidential instructions. Instead, he broke the grave oath of abstinence he had signed in church."

Mock could not put up with the smell of schnapps. He pulled back from Smolorz and stuck a cigarette in his sergeant's mouth. Smolorz staggered back and forth, and would have fallen had his back not found the support of a brick wall.

"My wife has been betraying me. My friend must know something about it, yet he doesn't want to come clean," Mock said. "But now he's going to tell me everything, including why he's started drinking."

Smolorz rubbed his fingers across his face and pulled away damp wisps of hair from his forehead, trying in vain to comb them back. His face was expressionless.

"I've had a heavy day today." Mock's voice became a whisper. "I had a certain Gypsy in my vice, a certain door attendant, a whore and a thug. I'm tired and bored with blackmailing people. Don't force me to do it. I'm going to feel terrible squeezing someone who is or was near to me. Spare me this, please . . ."

Smolorz knew well that Mock's whisper heralded a higher degree of interrogation, a levelling of irrefutable arguments. The reference to Franziska made him realize that Mock had such arguments to hand.

"Ye-es," he mumbled. "Orgies. Baron von Hagenstahl, Elisabeth Pflüger and your wife. They . . . with the Baron and with each other. Cocoa."

In difficult situations, Mock's mind sought support in what is permanent and indestructible. He would recall the best years of his youth: university; the old, grey-haired professors forever at odds with each other; the smell of soaking coats; seminars where discussions were held in Latin; entire pages of ancient poetry learned by heart. One section from Lucretius, which talks of the "flaming walls of the world", kept coming back to him. Now the walls surrounding the yard were in flames; the bricks on which he rested his hands were scorching, and the snowflakes landing on his head burned like drops of molten oil. "Lucretius wrote somewhere else about love as tragic and eternally lacking in fulfilment," Mock thought. "About lovers who bite each other so as to dream, a moment later, of biting again". He remembered the story of a Roman poet, one of the first *poètes maudits*, who was hopelessly in love, committing suicide at the age of forty-four. He thought of his own forty-four years, and of the small Walther gun weighing down the inside pocket of his jacket. The world was in flames and amidst the *flammantia moenia mundi*† stood the betrayed husband, a pitiful cuckold, a wretched and infertile manipulator.

† Flaming walls of the world.

129

"At the baths," Smolorz stammered, "the Baron's bodyguard caught me. Forced me to undress. The exercise hall. Climbing bars. They took a photograph of me there. Me, naked, prick in hand. Then, against the same bars, your wife, her mouth open. They said: 'Stop following us or Mock's going to get this photograph. A photo-collage. Of his wife and you . . .'"

The world was in flames, lovers bit off each other's lips, faithless wives betrayed their husbands at swimming baths, musical blondes with gentle, childish voices knelt before aristocrats, searching for excitement, and friends forgot their friendship. The world was in flames, and Lucretius, singer of fire, took a drug, supposedly to make him more attractive to his frigid chosen one, the cause of his madness. The world was in flames while the indifferent gods sat apathetic, idle and aimless in a luxurious realm between the worlds.

Mock pulled out his Walther and pressed it to Smolorz's hair, now plastered down with snow. He turned to face the wall. Mock let off the safety catch. In a wretched room, a little red-haired boy eats semolina. "Is he going to kill Papa?" he asks a young Gypsy in Czech. Mock put away his gun and sat down in the snow. He was drunk. He could feel the weight of the gun in his coat pocket. The dark well slowly filled with a carpet of snow. Smolorz waited for his punishment to be meted out while Mock lay there, pressing his face to the ground. After five minutes he stood up and told Smolorz to turn around. His subordinate shook with fear.

"I didn't do anything with her. It's a photo-collage," he croaked.

"Listen to me, Smolorz," Mock said, brushing the snow from his coat. "Stop drinking and keep tailing von Hagenstahl. My wife might get in touch with him. Even if the Baron notices you and carries out his threat, you don't have to worry. They'll just send me the photo-collage. I already know about it, and I won't do anything to you. Now sober up, and follow Baron von Hagenstahl's every move. That's all."

Smolorz finally managed to comb his hair with his fingers, buttoned

up his jacket, adjusted his crooked hat and went inside. In the dark corridor, Zupitza's mighty hand held him back. Wirth stepped out into the
courtyard and approached Mock.

"Shall we let him go?" he asked.

"Yes, you don't have to follow him. His conscience will do the job well
enough."

Wirth gave Zupitza the appropriate sign.

BRESLAU, FRIDAY, DECEMBER 9TH, 1927
SEVEN O'CLOCK IN THE MORNING

It snowed throughout Saturday and for half of Sunday. The city was
swathed in a white shroud that muffled every sound. Instead of the
clip-clop of hacks' hooves, Breslauers heard the faint whisper of sledges
gliding through the streets; instead of the clatter of women's shoes on
pavement, the crunch of snow; instead of the splashing of dirty water,
the dry crack of ice. Windowpanes were covered in blossoms of frost,
chimneys belched sooty smoke, skaters raced on the ice near the
Regierungsbezirk Schlesien building, servants used snow to clean
carpets, and carters smelled of booze. On Sunday afternoon it stopped
snowing. Frost bit hard. Light and thick layers of snow clumped together
in coarse clods. Their clean surfaces were cut by dog urine and stained
with horse excrement. In the alleys around Salzring, homeless people
chose spots on which to die, and criminals locked themselves in their
safe, warm, fetid caves between Neuweltgasse and Weissgerbergasse.
Newspapers told of the swindles of Willi Wang who, disguised as a
hussar, had robbed and infatuated maids and staid married women, and
of two ghastly and elaborate murders. Their perpetrator was of interest
only to journalists, and he already had several psychological profiles to
his name.

131

All this was unknown to the man the newspapers called "the star of Breslau's criminal police", or "the hound with an unerring instinct". This "genius of criminal detection" had been holding his head, shattered by a hangover, under a stream of icy water for the third time that morning, and now his servant, Adalbert, was drying his tangled hair and red nape with a coarse towel.

Without looking in the mirror, Mock ran a bone comb through his hair, just about managed to fasten his stiff collar, and went through to the dining-room where a jug of coffee was steaming, blackcurrant preserve oozed sweetly through the cheeky recesses of a Kaiser roll's crispy crust, and an egg yolk trembled temptingly in its slippery white membrane. But Mock had no appetite, and not because of the port which had doubtless tipped the balance of fluids in his stomach the previous night, but because of the presence of Criminal Director Mühlhaus. The latter was sitting at the table, greedily eyeing the breakfast and singlemindedly drilling into his blocked pipe with a small skewer. Mock greeted his chief and sat down opposite him. He poured himself and his guest some coffee. Then silence.

"I apologise for the intrusion at this time of the morning, Mock." Mühlhaus had finally managed to clean out his pipe and broke the silence. "I hope I haven't woken Frau Sophie."

Mock did not reply and spread the yolk, which tasted of iron, around his mouth.

"Smolorz did not turn up for work on Saturday," Mühlhaus continued. "Do you know why?"

Mock drank a mouthful of leaden coffee. Shreds of the crispy Kaiser roll pricked his gums like steel filings.

"Continue with your silence if you wish," Mühlhaus sighed as he got up from the chair. "Don't say a word, have a schnapps and remember the good old days . . . They're over. Never to return."

132

Mühlhaus straightened his bowler, stashed his pipe in its leather case and sluggishly left the table.

"Adalbert!" Mock shouted. "Breakfast for the Criminal Director!"

Then he took a huge gulp of coffee and experienced an odd harmony of tastes: dark-roasted coffee with the burned aftertaste of strong wine, traces of which unsettled his stomach.

"Nothing returns from the past," Mock glanced at Mühlhaus, who was once again making himself comfortable at the table. "That is the wisest tautology I've ever come across."

"Seneca captured it more aptly." Cutlery and plates clattered as Adalbert laid them down in front of Mühlhaus. "*Quod retro est, mors tenet.*"†

"Seneca was too wise to equate death with oblivion." Mock ran his tongue across his coarse palate.

"Perhaps." Mühlhaus dug a spoon into his egg exactly as he had dug the skewer into his pipe a moment earlier. The Kaiser roll crunched between his rotten teeth. "But you know that better than I do."

"Yes, I know. What has passed is not only in death's possession; it is also in the treasury of my memory." Mock lit a gold-tipped cigarette. Smoke swirled above the table. "And over memory, as over death, we have no control. Although that is not altogether so. In committing suicide, I choose one form of death, and in fighting I decide whether I am going to die with honour or not. Memory is stronger than death. Unlike death, it gives me no choice, and sends images from the past before my eyes against my will. I cannot wipe my memory clean unless I want to end up in a lunatic asylum . . ."

Mock paused and crushed his cigarette in the ashtray. Mühlhaus sensed the approach of the moment which would bring irreversible consequences. Either Mock would tell him everything and, in so doing, free

† What has passed is in death's dominion.

Mühlhaus from having to make any sort of decision, or he would say nothing and have to fill out a dreary form – the final document in his police personnel file.

"I request a month's unpaid leave, please, Criminal Director." Mock turned a cigar cutter in his fingers.

"And your reasons?" Mühlhaus finished eating and swallowed the rest of his coffee, tilting his head as abruptly as if he were drinking a shot of pure spirits.

There was silence. It was Mock's choice: either he would receive Mühlhaus' help, or he would be dismissed.

"I have to find my wife. She's left me. Run away. She's probably in Berlin." The Counsellor had made his choice.

Mühlhaus went to the window and waved his hand.

"Excellent breakfast," he said, lighting his pipe. "But now we have to go. Councillor Eduard Geissen has been murdered."

Mock was well acquainted with Geissen, a town councillor and a man of unimpeachable honesty who adored Wagner's operas above all, and ended each sitting of the Silesian Landtag with a dramatic appeal for the construction of a summer opera house.

"Where?" Mock swiftly fastened his amber cufflinks.

"In a brothel." Mühlhaus squeezed on his too-small bowler in front of the mirror.

"Which one?" Mock slipped his arms into the coat held out by Adalbert.

"On Burgfeld, near the old coach house." Mühlhaus opened the door, distributing a scented cloud of smoke.

"How?" Mock stroked Argos and made his way down the stairs.

"Someone hung him upside down." Mühlhaus' heels drummed on the wooden steps. "They put his leg through a noose made from piano wire and tied the other end to a chandelier. When his blood had flowed to his head, they severed his hip artery. Probably with a bayonet. He bled to death."

"Where was Geissen's whore?"

"Next to him. Butchered with the same bayonet," Mühlhaus said, allowing a bald man in a pince-nez through the door. The man glowered at Mock, and the Counsellor remembered the glint of those pince-nez from two occasions: once when Sophie had wrapped herself around his hips, and he had tried to grind her into the wall of the corridor, and again on that Thursday night, when he had raped his wife and she ran downstairs in a panic, clattering her heels. Now the eyes behind the pince-nez glinted with oppressive sleeplessness, scorn and derision. Mock, stunned by these recollections, stopped abruptly on the pavement.

"I have to find my wife."

A sledge pulled up at the curb beside them. The horse stank of stables, its driver of ill-digested moonshine. In the sledge sat a young man in a bowler, smoking a cigar. The horse thrashed its hoof against the frozen snow impatiently.

"Someone else will find her," Mühlhaus said, nodding towards the man in the sledge. "Someone she doesn't know."

"She knows everyone," Mock said. "All the men and all the women. But perhaps not this one. I haven't yet heard that she's had any dealings with queers."

Mühlhaus took Mock by the shoulder and pushed him gently towards the sledge. The young man smiled in greeting and tapped his finger in military style against the brim of his bowler. Mock saluted back.

"Let me introduce you, Counsellor," said Mühlhaus, "to Private Detective Mr Rainer Knüfer, from Berlin."

"Have you lived in Berlin for long?" Mock extended his hand to Detective Knüfer.

"Since birth." Knüfer swiftly squeezed Mock's right hand and passed him a business card. "I know the city as well as I do my own apartment. I can find every house-bug there."

Nobody laughed except Detective Knüfer. The sledge glided away. Snow crunched beneath its runners, and Mock's skull crunched in the vice of his hangover. Horses' hooves thumped at his temples, and snow, mixed with salt and sand, got in under his eyelids. Despite the biting cold, the Counsellor removed his hat, fanned himself with it and in one swift movement caught Knüfer by the throat.

"You can find every house-bug?" He peered at Knüfer with eyes of lead. "You son of a whore, my wife is not some house-bug which has wormed its way under your wallpaper."

Mühlhaus tugged him by the forearm. Mock collapsed on the rear seat of the sledge. Knüfer cleared his throat and threw away his cigar butt. An old woman selling oranges swore loudly as she searched for the butt among her frozen fruit. Mühlhaus held Mock by the arm, while Knüfer watched indifferently as a mongrel ran across Augustastrasse. Mock spread himself out comfortably and rubbed his red ears.

"I'll find your wife," Knüfer said dryly. "When I spoke of house-bugs, I had my own apartment in mind, of course, and not Berlin. Please forgive me."

"And vice versa," Mock retorted. "What do you need to know about my wife?"

"Everything. Most of my cases concern missing persons." He pulled a printed sheet of thick paper from his briefcase. "I've drawn up a special questionnaire. Some questions may be intimate and embarrassing, but you should still answer them, even if it's only with 'Don't know'. Please attach a recent photograph of your wife and have it delivered to me at Hotel Königshof on Claasenstrasse by two o'clock at the latest. Telephone me at a quarter past two, please. I may have some additional questions. The telephone number of the hotel is on the reverse of my business card. My train leaves for Berlin at three."

136

The sledge came to a halt, letting a peasant's cart pass.

"Now I bid you goodbye." Knüfer jumped down gracefully, gathered speed and, like a child, slid a long way across a frozen puddle on the corner near Spingarn's tobacconists, where street sellers usually set out their wares. Now, in their place, there were a few teenagers wearing caps full of holes, darned jumpers and woollen gloves. These novice thugs scratched the ice with their skates as they spun and danced. Knüfer came to a stop on the other side of the puddle, right next to a metal crate beneath which burned a small fire imprisoned in an iron grate. The detective reached into his coat pocket and the seller opened the lid of the crate, fished a fat frankfurter out of the boiling water and slipped it straight into Knüfer's hand.

"Shouldn't those boys be at school?" Mühlhaus asked, looking at his watch.

"I don't know. But I do know they prefer being on an ice-rink than under the eye of some tutor or alcoholic father." Mock took a woollen headband from his coat pocket and pulled it over his ears. "You knew about everything. Hence the brave detective summoned so speedily from Berlin. It happened only a few days ago. My wife ran off, and here we have this Knüfer . . . How did you know, sir?"

"Walls have ears, Mock," Mühlhaus answered after a moment's hesitation. "And the best ears belong to the walls of that tiny courtyard behind Gabi Zelt's bar."

"Thank you, sir. You're right, it is better that someone she doesn't know looks for her."

They stopped talking and squinted against the furious glare of the sun as it lit up icicles hanging from the roof of the investigative jail on Neue-Graupner-Strasse. Mock glanced through the questionnaire and took a sharpened pencil from his coat pocket. With swift movements, he dissected his unfaithful wife's character as if with a lancet, beginning with her external features:

137

"Age: 24; 166 cm; weight: about 60 kg; colour of hair: light blonde; colour of eyes: green; particular characteristics: prominent bust."

They drove into Nicolaivorstadt, long famed for its sanctuaries of Aphrodite. They passed the barracks on Schweidnitzer Stadtgraben, then Königsplatz, and found themselves between All Saints' Hospital and the Arsenal. Mock studied the questionnaire and, with a few strokes of his pencil, recounted Sophie's past: the old and impoverished Baron of Passau throws his fifth daughter into the air; this fifth daughter, a princess and the apple of her father's eye, prays in their private chapel, blonde plaits arranged in an elaborate crown; and there she is sitting on the veranda of a house smothered in Virginia creepers, snuggling into the fur of an enormous St Bernard.

"Place of birth: Passau; accent: slight, Bavarian; religion: Roman Catholic; religious commitment: vestigial, ceremonial; contact with family: none; family's residence: Passau, Munich; contact with friends: Philipp, Baron von Hagenstahl, aristocrat; Elisabeth Pflüger, violinist".

Mühlhaus and Mock walked into a dirty yard on Burgfeld. Mock, who until recently had worked in Department II, the Vice Department of the Breslau Police Praesidium, knew very well that the owner of this one-storeyed building, converted from a coach house, had gone to America for a spell. He also knew that the villa had been rented to a certain Hungarian who conducted various business transactions with Wirth and Zupitza. Above all, he spun a small fortune from a profession as ancient as the world itself.

In the doorway stood a uniformed man in a field-grey greatcoat. A Mauzer 08 protruded ominously from his unfastened holster. When he saw Mühlhaus and Mock, he saluted, two fingers to the peak of a shako decorated in the centre with a many-pointed star.

"Sergeant Krummheltz from the fifth district at your command."

"You're free to go, Krummheltz", said Mühlhaus. "And not a word about what you've seen here. The case is being taken over by the Murder Commission of the Police Praesidium".

"I don't talk much," Krummheltz replied in all seriousness.

"Very good." Mühlhaus extended his hand to Krummheltz and entered the building. Girls in petticoats, dressing gowns and curlers sat around on sofas and armchairs. In the exhausted, hollowed eyes of one, Mock detected a flash of recognition. Ehlers was standing on the stairs taking down their statements. In a weary voice, he repeated the same dry questions and received the same hopeless epiphorae: "I was asleep. I don't know", "I never asked. I don't know", "That's impossible. I don't know". "I don't know, I don't know" – Mock's mind wandered to the points in Knüfer's questionnaire. "Is she taciturn, or talkative, or impulsive, or well-balanced . . . I don't know anything about the person closest to me . . ."

Mühlhaus and Mock walked down a narrow corridor flanked by doors, trails of many a human humiliation. Mühlhaus pushed one open.

"I know, I know for sure." Mock fixed his eyes on the questions designed to expose his wife's complex mental universe. "She's not intelligent, she's jealous and deceitful . . . She's probably addicted to cocaine. She's worth loving and killing for. For many long years I never noticed she was a cocaine user . . . I didn't know her at all; all I knew was the concept I had of Sophie, not the living woman of blood and flesh who" – here a quotation came to mind – "'isn't a butterfly flitting in a pink mist and sometimes has to go to the bathroom'."

The bald crown of the pathologist, Doctor Lasarius, was glistening with sweat. In accordance with so-called police procedure, he had not even opened the curtains; the only thing he was allowed to touch were the corpses of the two who had been murdered. They were still warm. Holding a torch handle between his teeth, Lasarius was jotting down some comments in a notebook. Councillor Eduard Geissen's body was hanging from a chandelier that resembled a spider with wax-glued limbs. One of the deceased's legs had been tied to one such limb with piano wire. His hands were bound with the same, while his other leg hung at a peculiar angle, as if it had been dislocated at the hip. Stuffed into his mouth was a piece of material torn from a sheet, on his head a deep slash. His hairy back and buttocks were criss-crossed by blue threads of swellings. Mock took one look at the girl and surmised that these injuries had been inflicted by the whip she still clasped in her hand. He approached the dead prostitute. The protruding chin was somewhat familiar. He tried to remember where he had seen her before.

"Sexual deviation and possible perversion: bisexuality, dressing as a courtesan, jewellery worn on naked flesh, extensive foreplay before intercourse."

On the table stood an enormous gramophone player with a record still in place. The needle crackled as it traced small circles. The girl was sitting on a sofa, her legs and arms outspread. Her head had been almost completely severed, and her occipital bone rested on frail shoulder blades. Her eye sockets ran with brownish clots. A black streak of blood covered her eyes with a sticky film, stuck to her temples and encircled her shapely ears in narrow streams. This macabre headband rendered identification impossible.

"He chopped her head off and gouged out her eyes with a bayonet," said Lasarius, and began his detailed examination *par excellence*. "She had V.D. Didn't have intercourse before death. There are no signs of penetration."

"Past and present diseases not known," thought Mock.

After he had been tied to the chandelier, Geissen's blood had filled his cranium with a thick and viscous weight. The pressure had increased, his cheeks had grown purple, and the throbbing in his ears had intensified. The merciful bayonet, aimed at the groin artery, had cut short the suffer-

140

ing of this conservative councillor, advocate of strong paternal authority, champion of cheap, rented accommodation, and lover of opera.

"Political opinions and adherence to party: sympathy for the N.S.D.A.P.,[†] or rather, the primitive power of its members."

"They've been dead for two hours," said Mühlhaus. "I questioned the brothel madam. She doesn't know who the deceased is. His identity is known only to us – you two, Ehlers and myself. Oh, and Krummheltz, but he won't breathe a word . . . Krummheltz was on the night beat. Alone. He's the one who was summoned by our shaken madam. This is what we know: Geissen didn't come very often, but when he did come it was always at the same time of day, six in the morning, when most of the girls had sunk into heavy, well-earned sleep. He wanted to remain incognito. He always arranged to be with the same girl. By telephone. This one he was seeing for the first time. She was new here. He received her sweet lashes to the sound of opera." Mühlhaus looked at *Der Ring des Nibelungen* on the gramophone. "So we know what he liked. Opera. Both in the bedchamber and out."

"Interests other than sex: the music of Mahler; favourite objects and dishes: teddy bears, Berlin porcelain, coffee with an equal amount of milk, poppy-seed twists, Fach's cherry liqueur, Astoria cigarettes, strong men with a strong odour . . ." Mock thought on.

"At six in the morning," continued Mühlhaus, "there were no other clients in the brothel; all the girls – apart from this one here – were asleep. Including the madam. The only people on the move in this place were our lovers and the doorman, Franz Peruschka. One of his duties is to remind the guests when they've gone over their allotted time. Peruschka knocked on the door several times and, when no-one answered, went in, saw this romantic scene and woke the madam. Whereupon she ran hysterically

† Nationalsozialistische Deutsche Arbeiterpartei – National-Socialist German Workers' Party

141

into the street and saw Krummheltz doing his rounds. He phoned Ehlers, who was on night duty, and Ehlers tried without success to phone Counsellor Eberhard Mock. He didn't know you'd taken the phone off the hook. He phoned me. I arrived, examined the scene of the crime and went straight to your apartment. That's it."

"I've got a hangover today." Mock rubbed his swollen eyelids with his fingers. "Which is probably why I don't understand everything. There was one other person on the move in the brothel. The murderer. Or maybe not . . . Maybe there really were only three people."

"I don't understand."

"No, I don't understand *you*, Criminal Director. Geissen's hanging from a chandelier. A very strong man must have hung him there. Apart from the councillor, the only man – and a pretty strong man at that – was the doorman, Franz What's-his-name. My question is: is Franz What's-his-name being held at the station? Has he admitted his guilt? Has anyone even locked him up, Criminal Director? Where is he?"

"With his boss. Calming her down. He's very gentle with her. One can assume that their relationship is not merely professional. The madam has suffered a shock. Besides," – Mühlhaus spread himself out comfortably on the sofa right next to the murdered girl – "do you think I woke you up and brought you here out of spite? Just think about it. Is it normal for the chief, his deputy and one of three rank and file officers from the Murder Commission to visit the scene of the crime and conduct an investigation together? Or perhaps something like this has already happened in the past, hmm?"

"It happened last week," muttered Mock. "We met at Honnefelder's murder . . ."

Mühlhaus took a dark brown envelope from his briefcase and, using tweezers, gently extracted from it a page from a wall calendar dated December 9th, 1927.

142

"There was an apothecary's rubber band around Geissen's wrist," he said pointedly. "And this calendar page was held in place by it."

"Forgive me," Mock retorted. "But the doorman could have killed Geissen and pretended to be the 'calendar murderer'."

"Please don't drink any more, Eberhard." There was genuine concern in Mühlhaus' voice. "Alcohol doesn't do your imagination any favours – nice name by the way, 'calendar murderer' – it just kills any logic. The role played by the calendar in the Gelfrert-Honnefelder-Geissen cases is not known to any speculating newspapers, nor to anyone other than our men from the Murder Commission." Mühlhaus slapped his thigh with his palm. Mock could have sworn his chief had slapped the naked thigh of the dead girl instead. "And Franz Peruschka certainly didn't know about it."

"And why do you assume that the murderer of Gelfrert, Honnefelder and Geissen isn't Franz Peruschka?" asked Mock.

"From what Criminal Sergeant Krummheltz has told us, we know the madam was hysterical and, forgetting there was a telephone in the house, ran into the street. But before she got that far, she tripped on the drive and fell. The astonished Krummheltz, who was just passing, saw Peruschka run out after her. The doorman rushed to help the elderly lady and fainted. Please continue with your observations, Doctor Lasarius."

"Peruschka suffers from an acute form of agoraphobia." The pathologist stuck a finger into the deceased's mouth. "When he finds himself outside in an open space, he faints. He couldn't have killed Gelfrert and Honnefelder because he would have had to leave the house."

"Doctor," Mock stared pensively at Lasarius' thick neck. "Is it possible for this man to have been born in this building and then never left it?"

"He can only go out with his eyes closed. In cases of acute agoraphobia that's the only way, and it's not always effective at that."

"So if Peruschka was the murderer, he would've had to have an accomplice who could take him to Gelfrert and Honnefelder?"

"That's what it looks like," Lasarius said.

"How did you manage to arrive at a diagnosis so quickly? Surely agoraphobia is quite rare – I've never heard of it – and you're a physician, not a psychiatrist."

"I would never have arrived at it," – Lasarius glanced at his palms, cracked from formaline – "but when the doorman came to his senses, he showed me his recruitment papers, which describe him as being unfit for service due to mental illness. Like you, the military doctor didn't have the faintest idea of the existence of such an ailment, so he didn't give it a name – he just accurately described the symptoms. That's how I recognized it. The illness itself has been described in detail by Oppenheim and Hoch. Another dissertation on the subject was published recently, but I can't remember the name of its author . . ."

"Peruschka could have feigned the swoon," Mock muttered, unconvinced. "And secured himself an excellent alibi . . . There was no shortage of malingerers using false certificates during the war . . ."

"Don't exaggerate," Mühlhaus said with annoyance. "You think Peruschka faked it during the war so that, twelve years later, he would have an alibi for Geissen's murder? You're too distrustful."

"Shame it's only at work . . ." Mock lit a cigarette and blew an elegant smoke ring. "Clients pay by the hour at this brothel. How much time has passed since Geissen bled to death?" he asked Lasarius.

"When the iliac artery in the groin has been severed, a person bleeds to death in about five minutes," said the pathologist.

"So the murderer had," Mock continued, "ten minutes to stun them both, gag Geissen, hang him upside down, sever his artery and then slash the girl's throat. A veritable blitzkrieg. But this must have been executed after something like a quarter of an hour, when the client would have been so heated he would have been oblivious to this blessed world . . ."

"Does it really take that long?" Mühlhaus interrupted with a peevish smile.

" . . . meaning the murderer started work at a quarter past six, when Geissen had been at it for quarter of an hour, and then waited for the victim to bleed to death. Five minutes. Then he left."

"How?"

"The same way he came in – through the window."

"I've inspected the lawn meticulously. There were no tracks in the snow; it's hard, but not packed down. There's a small mound by the window to that room, but it's untouched."

"It could have been another client who'd slipped into the girl's room. There are usually a fair number here on a Sunday, and any one of them could have hidden himself without attracting the doorman's attention . . ."

"Maybe you're right, but how did he get out? Franz Peruschka claims not to have slept a wink." Mühlhaus got to his feet and fastened his coat. "Your theory, apart from the means of entry and exit, is credible. I haven't got a hangover today, yet there's something I don't understand either: why did the murderer wait for the victim to bleed to death? When he'd had his artery severed and been hung upside down, the man was going to die anyway. So why did the swine wait for Geissen to bleed to death? How did you arrive at that?"

"Bear this in mind." Mock held the calendar page with the tweezers. "If it's the same psychopath who killed Gelfrert and Honnefelder, then he has to behave in a similar manner. He attached the paper to the other two after they died. There can be no doubt about that. This time he also had to wait for his victim to die. Then he left, hid in the corridor, behind a curtain for example, and waited until Franz went to remind the client that his time was up. Any regular knows that's part of the doorman's job . . ."

"Is that so?" Mühlhaus pressed tobacco into his pipe.

145

"Yes, Criminal Director, the murderer has to be a regular at brothels. So he waited for the doorman to come and break into the room, then he quietly slipped out of the building."

"You're beginning to think sensibly, Mock." Mühlhaus looked at Lasarius. "Doctor, how long does a hangover last?"

"After port, a fair while," said Mock pensively.

BRESLAU, THAT SAME DECEMBER 9TH, 1927
NINE O'CLOCK IN THE MORNING

Mock merged into the crowd milling around the stalls on Neumarkt. He glanced at his watch. He still had an hour before his train left for Berlin. He wanted to spend it in the company of the bottle of dogberry schnapps that was pleasantly weighing down his right coat pocket.

All around, he heard cries of satisfaction and fierce bargaining. He leaned against the little wall surrounding the fountain in the square and, like the Neptune who hovered over it, observed the traders with irony. A fat forester, ruddy with cold and wearing a hat decorated with the emblem of von Maltzan's Militsch forests, extolled in Silesian German the Advent wreaths he was selling and collected orders for Christmas trees. At a neighbouring stall stood a formidable Silesian woman, her prominent backside wrapped in layers of striped aprons. She was arguing in Polish with her diminutive husband, who was smiling ingratiatingly at some servant girl and pressing a wicker basket containing a fine-looking goose into her hand. Next to them, a whiskered baker waved his arms and pointed at his spiralling pyramids of pastries snowed over with icing and blackened with poppy seeds.

Mock stroked the bottle of schnapps, loitered at the Silesian stall and listened with pleasure to the rustle of the Polish language. Sophie could imitate the Poles brilliantly. She did not do so willingly, however, claim-

146

ing her lips hurt from the effort of it. The Pole, paying no attention to his wife's reprimands, offered the goose to another client. The latter hesitated briefly and then bought the bird, asking the vendor to gut it. He lay the bird's head on a chopping block and, from under the awning, produced a military, non-commissioned officer's bayonet with ZUR ERINNERUNG AN MEINE DIENSTZEIT[†] engraved upon it.

"From the Franco-Prussian war. His grandfather's no doubt," thought Mock.

The body of the goose lost its invaluable crown. A bayonet chopped off the bird's head, a bayonet set loose a bloody waterfall from von Geissen's neck, a bayonet rolled the shapely skull of a brothel girl onto her frail shoulder blades, a bayonet severed her retinas, a bayonet drilled into the slippery mucus of her eye sockets. In a flash, Mock realized he did not even know the girl's name. He had not asked Mühlhaus for it.

The Counsellor lit a cigarette. He stood quite still among the stalls, and suddenly no longer heard all the bargaining and sales patter, as coarse as the blows of a flail. The murdered girl, slaughtered like an animal, was indeed a nameless body to him, one of the many filthy reservoirs into which the city's poor and wealthy relieve themselves of their frustrations, blindly sowing seeds from which nothing is ever born. Although Mock knew many prostitutes, he did not believe in the existence of "whores with hearts of gold" – he simply had not met any. He had often stroked their slender backs as they shook with sobs, assailed by genuine pain, but just as often he had seen how, beneath the alabaster skin, their muscles tensed during the acrobatics they performed with their clients. Snuggled into their breasts, he had often heard the fast and anguished beating of their hearts; but far more often those same breasts bounced teasingly in front of his face, while puckered lips and eyes squeezed shut in feigned ecstatic raptures.

† As a reminder of my military service.

147

Until now he had not seen many murdered prostitutes, but all had possessed names, thanks to which he could neatly place their files into the relevant compartment of his register, which Doctor Lasarius described as "containing unnatural – that is, not venereal – causes of death for the priestesses of Venus".

"This murdered girl was unworthy even of the company of those like her; even after death she has landed outside the pale of her dirty caste simply because I was not interested in her name," Mock thought. "And it's only because I'm chasing after another whore whose name is – yes indeed – the same as my own. That is the only reason I have robbed that butchered girl of the most basic right, of finding herself in the same file as all this city's filth."

In his mouth Mock tasted the bitterness of his conscience, and turned back. He did not go to the station from where the Berlin train was due to leave half an hour later; Rainer Knüfer could look for deceitful Sophie in the city of Marlene Dietrich by himself. Not far from the stall where the Silesian goose-vendor's bayonet had flashed in the bright winter sun, he threw away his ticket to the city on the Spree, and remained in the city on the Oder. He turned into Messerstrasse, tossed his half-empty bottle of schnapps to a beggar sitting outside the Three Roses tenement, and dragged himself towards the Police Praesidium – this gloomy, silent Criminal Counsellor cherished order in his files above all.

BRESLAU, THAT SAME DECEMBER 9TH, 1927
TEN O'CLOCK IN THE MORNING

All the officers from the Murder Commission were present in Mühlhaus' office; all, that is, except Smolorz. The group was complemented by Reinert and Kleinfeld, Mühlhaus' detectives for special assignments. Coffee and milk steamed in cups. Shafts of tobacco smoke swirled lazily in the sun.

148

"Any ideas?" Mühlhaus asked.

Everyone remained silent. Their heads were buzzing with Mock's disquisition. Means, place and time – only these are important. The victim is immaterial, incidental. That was Mock's theory, a theory with which no-one but he agreed. Tired from trying for half an hour to convince them – in vain; tired from thinking about Sophie, from remembering the bloody wound inflicted on the nameless whore; tired from the several generous swigs of dogberry schnapps, he looked at Reinert, Kleinfeld, Ehlers and Meinerer and read resignation and boredom in their eyes. This they shared with the stenographer, an old Jew by the name of Herman Lewin who, with hands folded on top of his belly, sat twiddling his thumbs at the speed of lightning. Mock poured himself another cup of hot milk and reached for the tray of chocolates that stood on a lace napkin. Mühlhaus' red, swollen eyelids were closed. Only the bands of smoke rising to the ceiling from his lidded pipe testified to the feverish workings of his brain.

"Do I have to call upon you one by one, gentlemen, to answer like schoolboys?" the chief opened his eyes and whispered ominously. "Counsellor Mock has presented you with his hypothesis. Do you all agree with it? Does nobody have any comments? Maybe you will be inspired when I repeat what the Mayor and the President of Police both said when they lost patience with us on hearing of Councillor Geissen's death. Reinert, what do you think about all this?"

"Don't be afraid, Reinert," said Mock, grimacing as he swallowed the thick, milky-chocolate suspension. "If you've got a different theory, go ahead and tell us. I'm not going to rant and rage."

"Yes, I do have a different theory," Reinert said emphatically. "So what if all the victims had different professions and were glaringly different in their education, interests and political views? There is something that brings people together irrespective of all that, and that is addictions: destructive

149

ones such as, for example, gambling, sexual deviation, alcohol, drugs, and milder ones, such as all sorts of hobbies. That is the path we must follow. Investigate the victims' past and ascertain what they had in common."

Reinert fell silent. Mock did not reveal the slightest inclination to disagree with him. He drank yet another cup of milk and watched the swift movements of the fountain pen with which the stenographer Lewin recorded Reinert's theory.

"Now I call upon you to give your hypothesis." Spittle gurgled in Mühlhaus' pipe as he fixed his eyes on Kleinfeld. "When everyone has presented his own point of view, I'll decide which path to follow."

"Gentlemen, let us take a moment to look at the dates of the murders and the crime scenes." Kleinfeld polished his pince-nez. "But not from Counsellor Mock's angle. The first corpse, walled in at the shoemaker's workshop, was the hardest to find. It was a real coincidence that the shoemaker was told about stinking eggs being bricked up in walls and that he smashed the wall down with a pick-axe. He might have waved it off and carried on working in the stench, or found another workshop. And the next craftsman to rent that hole might have done the same. The complaint brought to the owner of the tenement need not necessarily have led to the discovery of the corpse. The owner could have looked for something in the sewerage, and that would have been the end of the matter. In the end, some craftsman wouldn't have cared about the stench and would have gone on working quite happily, grateful to have a workshop in such an excellent location. To put it briefly, Gelfrert's body could have remained undiscovered. And what do you have to say, gentlemen, about Honnefelder and Geissen . . .?"

"That's it!" Reinert jumped, spilling a little coffee on his saucer. "Honnefelder was killed in his apartment. So he was certain to be found, but this might only have occurred once the stench of the corpse had become unbearable to his neighbours . . ."

150

"And Geissen?" Kleinfeld drummed his claw-like fingernails on the desk.

"Finding Geissen was an absolute certainty," Mock joined in the discussion. "And half an hour after the crime was committed at that – when the doorman knocked to remind the client his time was up . . ."

"So what we are seeing is something like a gradation," Kleinfeld acknowledged Mock's participation with noticeable satisfaction. "The first murder could have been discovered a very long time after it was committed or not at all, the second would certainly have been discovered, but only after a long time, the third would have been discovered after half an hour. How can we explain this gradual shortening of the time lapse?"

"Do you have any suggestions?" Mühlhaus tapped his pipe on a crystal ashtray to empty it.

"I do," Kleinfeld said tentatively. "The murderer was afraid we would-n't find the first victim – that's why he killed the second . . ."

"It's obvious," Mock cut him short. "He wants to draw our attention to the dates. If we hadn't found the victims, we wouldn't understand the murderer's message carried by the calendar pages."

"I think the murderer wants to get close to us," continued Kleinfeld, undeterred by Mock's ironic smile. "I once read an account in the Criminology Archive about serial murderers in America. Some of them subconsciously want to be caught and punished for their crimes. This applies particularly to criminals who had a very strict upbringing, and who have a strong sense of guilt, punishment and sin. It looks like the man we're after wants us to pick up his trail. But to be sure of this, we have to understand his mentality."

"But how can we understand the mentality of someone we don't know at all?" Meinerer, to Mock's scarcely concealed annoyance, was showing an interest in the case for the first time.

"We'll have to ask a psychiatrist who's had dealings with criminals to

151

give us a hypothesis, to attempt an expert opinion," said Kleinfeld slowly. "Let him write something like a report: what could the time lapses signify? Why does he murder so elaborately? And what could those calendar pages mean? There's never been a serial killer in Breslau before. Let's assemble copies of files on serial killers throughout Germany, for example Grossmann, Haarmann the butcher of Hanover, and others. Let our expert read them. Maybe he'll find similarities. That's all that occurs to me at this stage, Criminal Director."

"A fair amount, indeed" Mühlhaus remarked with a smile. "And what do the Counsellor's closest colleagues say?"

Ehlers' silent expression clearly proclaimed: "Nothing that Mock wouldn't say." Meinerer, on the other hand, said:

"I think we ought to check the dates bearing in mind the significance of numbers. Perhaps they have a symbolic meaning. A specialist in the Kabbala ought to be brought in on the case."

A drop of ink fell onto Lewin's shorthand notes. The old stenographer sighed, then spreading his arms and raising them to heaven, shouted: "I cannot bear to hear such nonsense! He" – pointing to Meinerer – "wants to take on a Kabbala specialist! Do you have any idea what the Kabbala is?"

"Did anybody ask you for your opinion, Lewin?" Meinerer asked coldly. "Concentrate on your duties."

"I'll tell you something," the stenographer laughed loudly – his forthright language made him a favourite with Mühlhaus – "I'll throw in another idea. Draw some lines on the map to join up the crime scenes. A mysterious sign is sure to appear. Perhaps the symbol of a sect . . . Shall we give it a go . . .?" He went to the map of Breslau on the wall.

"Yes, let's," Mock said seriously. "Ring 2 – the Griffins tenement, Burgfeld 4 and Taschenstrasse 23–24. Well, what are you waiting for, Lewin . . . Stick some pins in."

"Could it be possible that you got bottom marks in geometry at school, Counsellor?" Lewin responded in astonishment. "One way or another, it's going to form a triangle. Three points – three vertices."

Ignoring the stenographer's gabbling, Mock stood up, walked over to the map and stuck pins into the three crime scenes. They formed an obtuse triangle. Mock stared at the coloured pinheads for a moment, then took his coat and hat from the hat-stand and made towards the door.

"Where are you off to, Mock?" Mühlhaus growled. "The briefing's not over."

"My dear gentlemen, these buildings are all located within the perimeter of the Old Town moat," he said quietly, gazing at the map. A second later he was gone.

BRESLAU, THAT SAME DECEMBER 9TH, 1927
NOON

"Counsellor, so what if these buildings are located within the perimeter of the Old Town moat?" Leo Hartner, Director of the University Library, smiled faintly.

Mock rose from the newly upholstered, eighteenth-century green-plush armchair and began to pace Hartner's office feverishly. The thick purple carpet muffled his steps as he went to the window and gazed at the bare tree tops on Holteihöhe.

"Director, sir, I spent practically a whole day at the Construction Archives recently." Mock turned away from the window and leaned against the sill. "Then in the Evidence Archives looking for any trace of a crime which might have taken place in these buildings because, as I've told you . . ."

"I know, you've told me, 'what matters are the means, place and time,'" interrupted Hartner somewhat impatiently. "Not the victim . . ."

153

"Exactly . . ." Mock relieved the sill of his weight. "And I found nothing . . . Do you know why? Because the archives I visited only hold files from the nineteenth century, with very few earlier ones. The archivists informed me that most of the older files were inundated during the flood of 1854. The Municipal Archives, on the other hand, house files from an earlier date: criminal, construction, and all the others. So that something that is imperative to our case may have taken place in these buildings earlier, but for various reasons all trace of it has disappeared, or can only be found by a specialist reader of old documents."

"I still don't understand why you attach so much importance to the fact that these crimes were committed within the perimeter of the Old Town moat."

"My dear Director," Mock said, approaching the map of Breslau on the wall and studying the date at the bottom of it, "this beautiful map was produced in 1831, so it probably represents the town within boundaries that were established at the beginning of the nineteenth century. Am I mistaken?"

"No," said Hartner. He reached towards a shelf by his desk and took down a book, then opened it slowly and leafed through it carefully. Within a few minutes he had found the information he was looking for. "You're not mistaken. In 1808 the villages of Kletschenkau, Tschepin and Elbing, as well as the land alongside the Ohlau and what is known today as Ofenerstrasse, were added to our metropolis on the Oder. This map represents the city after these villages were annexed to it."

"When earlier, before 1808, had the town's territory been expanded?" Mock asked in the sharp tone of an interrogator.

Hartner paid no attention to the Counsellor's tone of voice and focussed his entire attention on the book. A moment later he had the answer.

"In 1327. The territory of the so-called New Town was added at that

154

time." Hartner approached Mock, took him by the arm, led him to the window and pointed to the high-rise Cheque Post Office building. "Meaning the area beyond Ohlau Ufer and Alexanderstrasse."

"And earlier still?" Mock stared at the eleven-storeyed skeleton of the Post Office building jutting out from behind the trees on Holteihöhe.

Hartner screwed up his nose, detecting alcohol on his guest, and went back to the map. Pointing at it with one hand, he held the book in the other. His glasses slipped to the tip of his nose and his short, greying hair bristled at the nape of his neck.

"In 1261, as Margraf writes in his work on the streets of Breslau," Hartner's eyes flitted from book to map, "these territories were officially added to the early town settlement on the Oder . . ."

The Director ran his finger over the map, tracing ellipses and irregular circles, some large and some smaller, which, with a little goodwill, could have been taken as having a common centre somewhere within Ring. Mock joined Hartner and slowly moved his finger along the blue snake of the Old Town moat.

"Is this the territory?"

"Yes, that's exactly what was added to the town in the thirteenth century."

"The territory within the moat, is that right?"

"Yes."

"So the territory bordered by the moat, within which the three murders were committed, is, apart from Dominsel, the oldest part of the city."

"That is correct."

"Do you understand now, sir?" Mock grabbed Hartner's finger tightly and drew squiggles with it on this area of the map. "Do you understand now? I sat in the archives looking for evidence of events which might have taken place exactly on the days and months indicated by the calendar pages found on the victims. But all these archives keep relatively new files, while the area in which the crimes were committed belongs to the oldest part of Breslau. And so this investigative path is not wrong, nor is it as fanciful as my chief and men would believe, but is simply a path . . ." Mock became thoughtful, searching for the right word.

"Along which you're groping a little," Hartner offered, moving away decisively from the map and thus reclaiming his finger. "Difficult, because the records are meagre and hard to decipher. Yielding few results and holding no prospect of success."

"Well put." Mock collapsed into the armchair, crossed his out-stretched legs and closed his eyes. He noticed with pleasure that he felt sleepy, which meant that all the Erinyes, all the whores – named and unnamed, dead and alive – were taking pity on him, all the vermin-infested, quartered and bloodless corpses, and his entire world, were mercifully allowing him to sleep. He fell into a torpor and yet felt a strange stabbing sensation, perhaps in his diaphragm, perhaps in his heart or stomach. It was a stabbing he cultivated at times, particularly when he awoke after a bout of drinking; his body, twisted by a hangover, would then demand sleep, but his mind would order "Get up, you've got piles of work to do today." Mock would then summon up some unpleasant image – his enraged chief; the hopelessness and tedium of police work; his subordinates' stupidity – and keep it fixed until he felt a piercing pain and an anxiety that stopped him sleeping. He would then lift his head, throbbing with the hangover, hold it under a stream of cold water, rub eau-de-cologne over his pale cheeks and swollen eyelids and then, wearing a somewhat too-small bowler hat and a tie fastened as tightly as a noose, he would enter the old, cold walls of the Police Praesidium. As he sat there now in the eighteenth-century armchair, Mock felt a similar anxiety, but, unlike on those mornings after he had been drinking, he could not identify its source. No enraged Mühlhaus, no Sophie wrapped

.in dirty bed-linen surrounded by cigarette ends, no waterfall of Geissen's noble blood appeared before him. Mock knew he had to recreate the circumstances that had set off his anxiety. He opened his eyes and glanced at Hartner, who appeared to have forgotten about his guest and was pensively turning the crank of a metal pencil-sharpener secured to his desk.

"Director, sir, would you please repeat what you just said," he croaked.

"I said," Hartner retorted, still sharpening pencils, "that you're groping in the dark, that you don't have many sources to help you, that those you do have might be difficult to decipher and interpret, and that I don't predict any success in this investigation."

"You've put it very well, Director, but please clarify what you mean when you say I 'don't have many sources'."

"If you're looking for something that happened in the past – in these places or even these buildings – then you have to find sources that hold the history of these places, meaning archival records," Hartner explained patiently. "You said yourself that the archive materials you've been studying go back no further than the beginning of the nineteenth century, whereas – as we established a moment ago – the history pertaining to the crime scenes could be much older, seeing as they are situated in the oldest part of the town. That's why I said the sources are meagre. There simply aren't very many files dating from the thirteenth to the end of the eighteenth century."

"If there are hardly any files," Mock said irritably, "where would I find information about these places or buildings? Where would you, as a historian, look for them?"

"My dear Counsellor." Hartner tried in vain to hide his impatience, "I am first and foremost a scholar of Semitic languages . . ."

"Stop bickering, Director." Mock had a great respect for Hartner's

157

modesty, a rarity among scholars who were not active lecturers and could not defend the fruits of their thoughts in the crossfire of student questioning. "As someone who has had a solid education in the Classics last century, a veritable *saeculum historicum*,† you know I consider you to be more of a polyhistor, a historian in Herodotus' sense of the word . . ."

"That's most kind." Hartner's impatience was waning. "I'll try to answer your question, but you'll have to be more precise about certain points. What do you mean by 'information about these places'? The small quantity of files does not relieve us of the task of studying them in depth. So first we have to look at the old files. Then we have to start the factual research, look in a factual or terminological index of a textbook, for example. But what are we to look for? Are you thinking of legends connected to these places? Or the owners of these places and their inhabitants? What are you looking for?"

"Until recently I thought I was searching the files for a crime which we were to be reminded of years later, on the very same day of the month as it had been committed. By killing innocent people, the murderer wants us to reopen an old investigation and find the original criminal. But there's nothing, not even a mention in our archival records about any crime committed in the first two places – I haven't checked the third yet. So the hypothesis of reminding us of something after all these years falls through."

"Yes . . ." Hartner interjected, dreaming of a lunch of meat loaf, red cabbage and potato dumplings, ". . . a crime intended to reopen an investigation into another committed years ago . . . That does, indeed, sound unlikely . . ."

Mock felt sleepiness and unidentified anxiety simultaneously. A moment later, his brain began to make connections. The anxiety was linked to a school building, to Sophie and to the words "recurrence" and

† Century of history.

158

"crime". He feverishly pondered whether he had been thinking about Sophie when walking or driving past some school. A few seconds later, an image came back to him from the day before: the announcement pillar near Elisabethgymnasium: *Spiritual father Prince Alexei von Orloff proves the imminent coming of the Antichrist.* "He's right, that spiritual father," Mock remembered thinking then. "*Crimes and cataclysms are recurring. I've been left by a woman once more and Smolorz has started drinking again.*"

Mock pictured himself leaving the flower shop. He had bought a copy of the *Breslauer Neueste Nachrichten* from a newspaper boy and his attention had been drawn to an unusual image on one of the announcement pages: a mandala, the wheel of change, encircled a gloomy old man with his finger raised upwards. "*Spiritual father, Prince Alexei von Orloff, proves that the end of the world is nigh. The next revolution of the Wheel of History is now taking place — crimes and cataclysms dating back centuries are recurring. We invite you to a lecture given by the sage from the Sepulchrum Mundi. Sunday, November 27th, Grünstrasse 14–16.*"

Mock heard Hartner's voice again: " . . . a crime intended to reopen an investigation into another committed years ago . . . That does, indeed, sound unlikely . . ." He glanced glumly at Hartner. Now Mock knew why he had come. In a split second, the Director realized that his dream of a longed-for lunch might not be fulfilled that day.

BRESLAU, THAT SAME DECEMBER 9TH, 1927
TWO O'CLOCK IN THE AFTERNOON

A pencil with a golden ferrule moved quickly across the lined pages of a notebook. Hartner was jotting down Mock's last instruction.

"Is that all?" he asked without enthusiasm, mentally relishing an exquisite meat loaf.

159

"Yes." Mock took out a similar notebook, the notebook of travellers and policemen: black, bound with a rubber band, with a pencil attached by a narrow, canvas strip. "There's one other thing I'd like to ask of you, Director. Please don't mention my name or position to your staff. Remaining incognito is the best option in a situation where . . ."

"There's no need to explain," Hartner said quietly, in his imagination chewing on a dumpling with crunchy crackling, covered with sauce and a tangle of red cabbage.

"And please understand," Mock said as he wrote the heading CALENDAR MURDERER in his notebook, "how awkward I feel handing instructions out to you."

"My dear Counsellor, after the 'four sailors' case, you can go on handing out instructions to me for the rest of your life."

"Yes." The pencil found its way between Mock's teeth. "And so you agree to my sitting in your study and working alongside you, be it till morning?"

"On one condition . . ."

"Yes?"

"That you allow me to invite you to lunch now . . . I will, of course, first give the appropriate instructions to my employees."

Mock smiled, nodded, stood up laboriously and sat at the neat, nineteenth-century davenport desk at which Hartner's secretary usually wrote down the Director's orders each morning. Hartner placed the telephone in front of him and opened the door to the front office.

"Miss Hamann," he addressed his secretary and indicated Mock. "The professor is an associate of mine, and a friend. Over the next few hours, perhaps days, we will be working together on a few scholarly issues. My study is his study and all his instructions are mine."

Miss Hamann nodded and smiled at Mock. The same smile as Sophie's, but a different hair colour. Mock dialled Meinerer's number and, before Hartner had closed the door, embraced Miss Hamann's slender waist and prominent bust with one glance. With the Director's melodious words "all his instructions" still ringing in his ears, he set his imagination to work, evoking immodest and wild scenes in which he and Miss Hamann were the key players.

"Meinerer," he muttered when he heard his subordinate's characteristic falsetto, "please come to the University Library on Sandstrasse. There'll be a cardboard file with the addressee's name on it waiting for you with Director Hartner's secretary, Miss Hamann. You're to take it to Hotel Königshof on Claasenstrasse. Irrespective of any tasks Mühlhaus may have given you, my order to follow Erwin still holds. My nephew should be finishing his classes in an hour. Is Reinert anywhere near you? No? Then please find him for me."

Quickly assured by Meinerer of his compliance, Mock waited for Reinert to come to the telephone.

"Please ask Doctor Smetana to come and see me," Hartner's loud baritone resounded through the door. "He's to bring the Register of Loans with him."

"Reinert, I'm glad you're there," Mock looked down at the notes he had made in his slanting writing. "Don't let Prince Alexei von Orloff out of your sight for a second. You don't know who he is? I haven't got time to explain to you now. You'll find something about him on every announcement pillar in town and in every newspaper, and certainly in the edition of the *Breslauer Neueste Nachrichten* that went out the day we found Gelfrert. You're to alternate with Kleinfeld."

"Specht, from the cataloguing department," Hartner's voice bellowed, "is to bring the catalogue boxes labelled 'Breslau', 'Criminology', and 'Silesia'. Alright, I'll repeat that: 'Breslau', 'Criminology', 'Silesia'. And please make an appointment for me to speak over the telephone to the Director of the Municipal Library, Theodor Stein. Yes, Doctor Theodor

161

Stein. In the afternoon, evening . . . it doesn't matter."

Mock dialled another number and soon managed to persuade a young man at the other end to interrupt Counsellor Domagalla's important meeting.

"Warm greetings to you, Herbert," he said when he heard the somewhat irritated voice of his bridge partner. "I'm conducting an important case just now. Yes, yes, I know I'm disturbing you, but the matter is very urgent. I'm going to have to look through the files of all the followers of sects your men have investigated. Apart from that I need to know everything there is to know about the Sepulchrum Mundi and its leader, Alexei von Orloff. Fine, note it down . . . You don't know how to spell Sepulchrum? What did you get in Latin? Just as I thought . . ."

"From the main reading room" – the Director's voice betrayed excitement – "they're to bring me the following books without delay: Barthesius' *Antiquitates Silesiacae* and *The Criminal World of Ancient Breslau* by Hagen."

Mock telephoned again but gave no more orders; instead, he listened to Mühlhaus' raised voice. At one point he held the receiver away from his ear, tapping a cigarette against the davenport with his free hand. When the voice fell silent for a moment, Mock put the cigarette between his lips and began a strange dialogue in which his own laconic statements were constantly interrupted by the angry and intricately constructed phrases of his chief.

"Yes, I know I behaved like a boor leaving the meeting like that . . . This is a new avenue . . . I'll explain everything tomorrow . . . Yes, I know, it's my last chance . . . I have abused your patience . . . I know . . . I'll be there tomorrow . . . At eight in the morning . . . Yes, certainly . . . Thank you, and I'm sorry . . ."

Mock replaced the receiver and once again thought fondly of Reinert and Kleinfeld. They had said nothing to Mühlhaus and had gone out to follow von Orloff. Hartner finished handing out instructions and re-entered his study carrying Mock's coat and hat. A moment later, both were making towards the door. Hartner let Mock go first and smiled radiantly at Miss Hamann. His dream of a meat loaf was to be fulfilled.

BRESLAU, THAT SAME DECEMBER 9TH, 1927
TEN O'CLOCK IN THE EVENING

Breslau was sinking under a soft down of snow. All was silent and still on Sandstrasse. From time to time a car growled, and once in a while sleigh bells tinkled. Even the screeching of the last trams gliding towards Neumarkt and the Post Office was muffled by the soft filter laid down by the blizzard. The windows of the Norbertan monastery glowed with friendly warmth. Mock watched all this from a window in the old Augustinian monastery on Sandinsel, where the University Library was located, and his mood was far from the joyous, festive expectation that seemed to dazzle the entire city. He was not interested in either Sandbrücke or Matthiasgymnasium, or the Museum of Mineralogy. He was interested in the windows, ablaze with Christmas trees, of the poor tenements huddled around the perimeter of Ritterplatz, where a work-worn father, waiting for his dinner, was putting aside his pipe of smoking, cheap tobacco to bounce the children sitting on his knees and yelling joyfully. Their wild cries did not annoy either father or mother who, with an apron tied around her waist, was standing a pot of her husband's soup on a hot stove – day after day the same barley soup with smoked bacon. Then satisfied burps, a kiss after supper, a mouth full of smoke; scolding the children and chasing them off to bathe in a steaming tub; small faces flushed with sleep; the husband's hands under the heavy eiderdown. Day after day the same – faith, hope and love.

Mock approached the door to Hartner's study and reached for the handle.

163

"In those rented houses," he thought, "in those smoky kitchens, behind the bug-infested wallpaper resides yet another virtue, a virtue which does not belong to the Gospels, which could not find a place in the sterile, five-room apartment on Rehdigerplatz. That virtue could not be lured there by force, flattery or expensive presents, and it would not remain there a moment longer. Not long after their wedding, it abandoned the ethereal wife and self-confident husband who could not express their needs to each other; she – because she didn't know how, he – because he didn't want to. It left them to themselves; her – haughtily silent, him – furiously thumping his square head against the walls. What is the name of that virtue that spurned the apartment on Rehdigerplatz?"

Mock opened the door, allowing the caretaker to pass with a heavy bucket of coal, and heard Hartner's voice:

"Yes, Director Stein, I do mean jotting down the book entries from the general catalogue; that is, compiling a factual catalogue of the following key subjects: Silesia – Criminology – Breslau. If you could find a cross-reference in any book that would be wonderful. If not, then I'd be very grateful if you could send me a list of the books to which at least one key word applies. And if I then decided to borrow the books . . . Yes? That's wonderful, thank you for kindly agreeing . . ."

Mock closed the study door and went to the bathroom. Passing the caretaker, he put an arm around him and whispered:

"Do you know what it's called, the virtue that didn't want to live with me?"

"No, no I don't," replied the owner of the ear so thickly covered with hair.

"Faithfulness," breathed Mock, and entered a cubicle. He locked himself in and scrupulously examined the small window beyond which a city of faithful wives, children smiling in sleep and work-worn fathers was falling into a slumber, a city where stoves belched warmth, and faithful dogs with wise eyes yelped for joy. In this city, a certain five-roomed apartment was an incongruent curiosum, a gloomy aberration.

"There, in all four corners of every room, lurks the evil demon of violence, the resigned demon of delusion and still one more . . ." thought Mock, undoing his belt, "still one more . . ." he repeated, executing a well-known act, old as the world and condemned by the Church, "the demon of death". When he had found the appropriate word, he slipped his head into the noose formed by his belt and secured it to the handle of the window, beyond which Breslau was becoming whiter than the snow that enveloped it.

WIESBADEN, TUESDAY, DECEMBER 13TH, 1927
ONE O'CLOCK IN THE AFTERNOON

Private Detective Rainer Knüfer got out of the carriage at Spa Park and walked through the black, leafless chestnut trees towards the casino. A gust of cold wind from the pond broke through the trees and soared upwards in spirals of powdery snow. Knüfer pulled down his hat, turned up the collar of his coat, briskly passed the stone flower-beds dusted with hoar-frost and burst into the brightly lit temple of gambling. A page leaped to his side, energetically brushed him down, happily accepted a few coins and ran off to the cloakroom with the client's coat and hat. Knüfer stood in the foyer looking around, admiring the white and brown chequerboard flooring, the stained-glass window above the entrance, the arched vault and the enormous statues that lined the walls. When he had contemplated all this splendour, he turned into the great gambling hall on his left. Standing in the doorway, he squinted in the merciless blaze of the chandeliers, which revealed every wrinkle around the gamblers' eyes aggravated by a lack of sleep and by their addiction, reflected off bald pates covered in droplets of sweat – a manifestation of their owners' loss

165

– highlighted the artificial blush on the cheeks of ageing aristocratic dames, and gleamed on the alabaster skin of young ladies whose habits were as frivolous as the multi-coloured ruffs of feathers in the bands encircling their immaculately cut and glossy hair. Knüfer's eyes rested for a moment or two on one of the younger ladies. He was not sure whether he had found the right person. According to the description given to him by Mock, Sophie's hair was long. The cut of this smiling woman's light-blonde hair was fashionably short and sporting. Other aspects of the description tallied. Her breasts, which heaved against the silk of her dress and rose delightfully when she lifted her arms suddenly and joyfully, corresponded to Mock's accurate description: "prominent bust with an almost visible firmness". Her voice cut through the stuffy air of the hall with a silvery hue and could easily be described as "pearly" (Mock's description again). With difficulty he tore his eyes away from the blonde and peered into the card-room next door. When he was satisfied that none of the other ladies present fitted the description drawn up by the Criminal Counsellor, he sat down at an empty roulette table near to where an old, chubby croupier was standing at his post and, placing a few fifty-mark chips on the red, he began to weigh up the problem: if this is Sophie Mock, why is she being so noisy? By the time the croupier had pushed a doubled column of chips towards him, Knüfer had already found two explanations. Firstly, the blonde was not denying herself champagne, and secondly, her shouts of joy and raised arms were a response to the gambling successes of a small man with sorrowful, melancholic eyes. Knüfer decided to play an even-money bet. He placed all his chips on red again and quickly memorized the features of the short man on whose shoulder the blonde had just laid her head, tenderly grasping the place where other men usually have biceps. The player was not much taller than the gaming table. He tossed his chips nonchalantly and they landed in a gentle arch on the coarse, green baize, invariably finding a place on one of the thirty-six squares.

"He doesn't think at all," the chubby croupier whispered to Knüfer. "He surrenders to chance. He throws a few chips at random and generally lands them spot on. If a chip falls on, say, twenty-two red, he bets either on evens or on red. He never plays *en plein*, or even a six line . . ."

"And what happens," Knüfer divided his considerable column into two and again placed both on red, "if a chip falls on a line between two squares? For example, between eighteen red and seventeen black? Where does he place his bet?"

"A larger part of the chip," the croupier spun the wheel, "always falls on one or the other. The line between two squares never cuts a chip exactly in half."

"So he has no method whatsoever." Knüfer looked on dispassionately as the ball bounced and settled in the twenty-nine red slot.

"That's right." The croupier pushed four columns of chips towards Knüfer. "He isn't superstitious like other players; he doesn't believe in some magical sequencing of numbers, or in attracting opposites; doesn't wear copper jewellery when Saturn is in opposition to Mars, or play *va banque* on twelve. Or *les voisins du zéro* at the beginning of the month. He believes, so to speak, in the determinism of chance."

"Who is he?" Knüfer placed everything once again on red.

"This is the first time you've been here, isn't it, sir?" The croupier spun the wheel of disappointed hopes. "He's a well-known player, very famous . . ."

Dear Elisabeth,

I've been in Wiesbaden since Friday and am keeping Bernard von Finkelstein company. He's a film director at the U.F.A., and was well known at the beginning of the twenties under the pseudonym Bodo von Finckl. After this short piece of information about my present stay, I give up. There's so much I'd like to write to you about

that I don't know where to start. Maybe with my leaving Breslau?
No, no, and thrice no! I don't even want to think about that town
where I met with such base behaviour. Not on your part, of course,
darling; everything that brought us together was so pure and so
good!

I'll just tell you what I'm doing here in Wiesbaden, and at whose
side I now find myself. I met von Finckl five years ago in Berlin, when
I was trying to get a minor part in Fritz Lang's film Der müde Tod.†
I must have made a great impression on von Finckl because he
invited me to dinner the day we met, and revealed to me the most
hidden recesses of his soul. He turned out to be a timid man who,
despite his wealth and elevated position in the art world, yearns
above all for love, clear as crystal and full of rapture. He asked me
at the time to fulfil a certain eccentric, intimate desire of his and
when I refused – somewhat indignantly and yet, I must admit, also
very intrigued – he begged my forgiveness and swore to entrust me
with the part for which I was auditioning. I then met him another
couple of times and, despite his desperate and feverish insistence,
allowed him only to kiss my slippers – which he did with great joy,
bestowing on me in this way his reverence and adoration. Von Finckl
was a true gentleman, and he charmed me with culture and, above
all, a love of art. I might even have married him had not my late
Papa – who by then had found me in Berlin after a long search –
become entangled in the whole affair; he called von Finckl a stink-
ing Jew and then took me back to Passau where a certain Bavarian
landowner was also seeking my hand in marriage. However, I didn't
end up as a Bavarian Hausfrau, but in the company of a certain
painter – oh, this love of mine for art! – made my way to Breslau
where I quickly found myself in fashionable society.

† Der müde Tod – Destiny.

But going back to von Finckl. When I arrived in Berlin a few days ago he was already waiting for me at the station, alarmed by my telephone call in the night (luckily, I never throw my old address books away, as you know) – I called him the very night Eberhard raped me. Von Finckl hadn't changed one bit: he was still sad, misunderstood by others, full of complexes and bizarre, dark needs. I realized that, in tying myself to him, I would have to satisfy his desires and decided to do so on the very first day. Don't ask me what they were; maybe I'll whisper them in your ear one day. Suffice it to say that von Finckl is prepared to give up his life for me. How easy it is to make someone happy! He has become confident and claims that – with me at his side – he could face any challenge. He wants to make a fortune so he can finance a new film, and with me in the starring role! After analysing all the chance coincidences that led me to him and allowed him to achieve his greatest happiness, Bodo has come to the conclusion that there exists a higher determinism of chance, and has come here with me to Wiesbaden to make the money he needs and to prove his theory. And just imagine – he's winning all the time . . .

"Really? That's the famous von Finckl?" Knüfer gathered into an ebony casket the mound of chips he had won after the croupier called twenty-three red. He lit his first cigar of the day. "And what's your name?"

"Richter, honourable sir . . ."

"Tell me, Richter, why are you telling me this? After all, casino employees aren't allowed to talk to guests! Otherwise croupiers could come to all sorts of arrangements with players . . ."

"It's all the same to me. I'm going to lose my job anyway . . ."

"Why?"

"Every croupier is assigned to one table, and one table only." Richter spun the wheel from force of habit even though Knüfer had not shown any desire to continue playing but, puffing smoke from his cigar, was trying to stuff the casket into the pocket of his jacket. "My table is regarded as being unlucky so nobody plays here. If nobody plays, I don't get any tips and it's the tips I live off because our wages are . . . I apologize, I wasn't trying to wheedle anything out of you, sir . . ."

"As of today, your table is no longer unlucky. After all, I've just won a great deal here." Knüfer counted out ten chips and slipped them into the croupier's tailcoat pocket. "If you want more, much more, report to me everything that blonde does with her little fancy man."

He patted Richter on the shoulder and left the room, followed by the eyes of the other players, the blonde woman and her short companion appearing to show the most interest in his recent activities.

WIESBADEN, THAT SAME DECEMBER 13TH, 1927
FIVE O'CLOCK IN THE AFTERNOON

Knüfer placed a photograph of Sophie near the telephone and cast his eyes over the room. Wherever he looked – be it at the wall covered in pale-blue wallpaper with little roses, or at the ceiling speckled with dead flies, or at the screen that separated the iron bed from the washbasin – he saw her face disappearing in the reversed, black, white and half-tones of a negative.

Knüfer felt a vague unease and reached for the telephone receiver bouncing on its hook. He held it to his ear and heard the telephonist's Hessian dialect informing him that he had just been connected to number 6381 in Breslau. A moment later he heard the calm voice of subscriber 6381 who, with lengthy pauses between words, emitted what sounded like puffs on a pipe.

"Good afternoon, Criminal Director." Knüfer, pressing the receiver

170

tube to his ear, brought his head closer to the mouthpiece. "I've found her. She's in Wiesbaden under the name of Isabelle Lebetseyder, in the company of a Bernard Finkelstein. Yes, I do know a little about him. How did I find out? I've got associates in Berlin and the telegraph is swift. Finkelstein was a popular film director at the beginning of the twenties . . . Really, I assure you! Does the name Bodo von Finckl mean anything to you? Of course, it's the same man. He was famous for a while then got into some sort of trouble. He had a poor record with the Berlin police, Vice Department, for being a notorious gambler. Suspected of making pornographic films. He's playing very hard here in Wiesbaden and winning heaps of money. Sophie Mock, alias Isabelle Lebetseyder, is clearly his good muse."

"Listen to me carefully now." Knüfer heard the crackle of a match and could almost smell the aroma of Austria tobacco. "You're going to have to isolate the woman."

The voice fell silent. Knüfer said nothing either.

"Don't you understand?" Saliva gurgled in the pipe. "You're to abduct her and hide her for a month or two. Until further notice. Expenses are of no importance."

"I understand you perfectly, Director Mühlhaus," Knüfer said, and replaced the receiver.

WIESBADEN, THAT SAME DECEMBER 13TH, 1927
SEVEN O'CLOCK IN THE EVENING

Croupier Richter happily slid the enormous pile of chips towards von Finckl's immaculate white shirt-front. The film director was expressionless as he screwed a Turkish cigarette into a long, ivory cigarette-holder and passed it to his fair-haired companion. Sophie accepted it thoughtfully, then slowly raised her eyelids. The green flame in her eyes licked

171

at the men gathered around the table. Several snow-white cuffs emerged from the sleeves of dinner jackets, and paraffin lighters hissed between manicured fingers. Sophie wrapped her hand, clad in a lace glove, around another with plump, red fingers, in which a glittering cone that clicked alight with a bluish flame was barely visible. The owner of the fingers was so moved by her touch that he felt hardly any pain from the heated metal.

At Richter's table no-one was playing but von Finckl. It was the only occupied table in the casino. All the others were empty since the guests who usually sat at them now surrounded Richter's. The croupier lived his great day radiantly, blessing the moment when Knüfer's chips had first hit the red and black board printed on green baize. This had been the start of Knüfer's splendid run, which was the talk of all present, and now Bodo von Finckl had been drawn to the table, who, for the past several hours had been telling guests and casino employees that the ill-fame attached to the table, which so discouraged players, was a foolish superstition, invented, as Richter claimed, by envious fellow croupiers.

The huge crowd thickened around the table and left the croupier, the player and the blonde goddess of gambling practically no room to breathe.

"*S'il vous plaît*," called Richter. "*Mesdames, messieurs, faites vos jeux.*"

Von Finckl counted out twenty ten-mark chips and pushed the column towards Sophie who, to the indignation of the few ladies watching the game, made a sign of benediction over them. Von Finckl then tossed one chip towards the board. Most of it covered twenty-eight red. On von Finckl's instructions, Sophie then placed the two-hundred-mark column on twenty-eight and the rest of the chips, five similar columns, on red. The audience gasped; this was the first time von Finckl had not placed an even-money bet.

172

"*Rien ne va plus.*" Richter spun the wheel. The clanking of the ball skipping in the squares and the faint hiss of the wheel sliding in its cylinder resounded in the deathly silence. After a while, the wheel came to a standstill. A murmur of admiration billowed through the crowd. Sophie threw both her arms in the air, revealing depilated armpits. Nineteen red had come up. The column standing on twenty-eight made its way towards Richter, while twice as many chips as had stood on red were pushed towards von Finckl. The latter reverently kissed his companion's hand and tossed another chip, once again setting the determinism of chance in motion. After being "blessed", the chip landed on the line between squares nineteen red and even. Sophie, von Finckl and Richter leaned over the table and a vault of heads and shoulders closed above them. The player got to his feet, took a breath of air and looked at the spectators who moved away unwillingly.

"Perhaps you could all step back and allow me to make a decision," he said in a calm voice and looked at Sophie expectantly: "What do you think, madame?"

"Probably *pair.*" Sophie glanced uncertainly at von Finckl. "No . . . I don't know myself . . ."

The player took the chip between two fingers and slipped it into Richter's tailcoat pocket. Then he carefully chose another one, let a spell be cast over it and tossed it up. The greater part of it landed on six black. Von Finckl then placed a thousand marks on six black and ten thousand on black. Richter uttered the French incantation and the ball began its dance among the wooden divisions of the wheel. Von Finckl closed his eyes and pictured his childhood in Będzin, in the wooden cottage reeking of onions that also served his father as a tailor's workshop, his eight siblings as a field of constant battles, and numerous bedbugs as a comfortable haven. He no longer heard the rattling of the ball but the clatter of an old Singer sewing machine; he did not hear the moan of disappointment from the people surrounding him but the yelling of the tailor's displeased client; he did not sense Sophie's fear but his mother's anxiety as they faced another day of hunger. Von Finckl did not open his eyes when he heard the rustle of chips being moved away, when Sophie dug her fingers into his shoulder, when the scraping of his former supporters' shoes reached his ears, and when suddenly other tables came to life with French phrases and his own croupier chanted a funereal "*Les jeux sont faites.*" He opened his eyes only when he felt the cold touch of glass against his hand. Opposite him sat a distinguished, grey-haired man delicately holding a glass of champagne like those that now stood in front of von Finckl and Sophie.

"Claus von Stietencrott, manager of the casino," he smiled. "Please allow me to express my admiration. I have never yet met a player whose every bet was a *va banque.*"

"Thank you," said von Finckl in a shaky voice, afraid to look at Sophie. "I am honoured by your admiration."

"No, the honour is mine." Von Stietencrott made a swift movement and two glasses tinkled musically. "After such a loss you haven't said: 'What good is your admiration to me!' or 'Go to hell!', but have reacted like a true gentleman. We treat gentlemen with great respect in our casino and, when fortune ceases to be kind to them, we always offer a loan of whatever sum they desire without their having to leave anything with us on security. Would you like such a loan?"

BRESLAU, THAT SAME DECEMBER 13TH, 1927
ELEVEN O'CLOCK IN THE EVENING

Elisabeth Pflüger was just coming to the end of Erik Satie's third *Gnossienne* and her white piano had begun to patter with the sound of falling rain when the chambermaid entered the parlour, informing her of

174

an urgent telephone call from Wiesbaden, and asking where Miss Pflüger wished to take it. Elisabeth wished to take it in the parlour and, crossing her shapely legs on the chaise-longue, asked the chambermaid in an irritated voice who had the gall to disturb her at such a late hour. When told, she suppressed her anger and held the receiver to her ear. After a series of sobs, snivels and assurances of love and friendship, she listened to her friend's request for help and advice.

"I beg you, Elisabeth, tell me what to do . . . He's lost everything . . ."

"That von Finckl you wrote to me about? A messenger picked up your letter from the Wiesbaden train today and delivered it to me . . ."

"Yes, von Finckl. The casino manager suggested a loan without security, but he refused and asked for the bills of exchange and cheques he had with him to be exchanged for chips. When his request was granted, he lost everything. He hasn't got anything to pay the hotel with. He then accepted the offer made by the casino manager, but the offer had changed . . . Now it's a different kind of loan, and the security's supposed to be me . . ."

A man's hand pressed down the telephone cradle. Elisabeth gazed through her gathering tears at Baron von Hagenstahl and was relieved that she did not have to listen to her friend's weeping any longer.

"There's nothing you can do," the Baron said quietly. "Only I can help her now. I know what it means to hold a beautiful young woman as security in a casino. *Va banque.*"

WIESBADEN, THAT SAME DECEMBER 13TH, 1927
MIDNIGHT

"Von Stietencrott gave von Finckl a thousand marks for his bills of exchange and cheques," Richter spoke quietly, casting nervous glances about the park that surrounded the casino. "Von Finckl played *va banque*

175

as usual, and lost. Then the boss offered a loan, but with a warranty. That warranty is to be Miss Isabelle Lebetseyder. The boss has valued her at three thousand marks. That's the sort of loan it is."

"I don't understand anything, Richter," Knüfer said, shivering with cold. "They're going to play for Miss Lebetseyder?"

"Yes." Richter pulled his hat down over his eyes. "And tomorrow even, at my table. At midnight. Von Finckl is placing his lover on one side of the scales, and on the other, von Stietencrott has put three thousand marks. If the film director wins, he gets chips for that sum; if the boss wins, Miss Lebetseyder has to stay on in our casino for some time. There's only the one game – black and red. Nothing else. One game. *Va banque.*"

Knüfer felt his legs shaking.

"It's cold in this park," he growled. "Let's go and get something to drink, damn it. Lead the way, Richter."

The croupier adjusted his gloves and hurried away across the park. Knüfer set off after him. By night Wiesbaden was decorated with festive lanterns and, despite it being Advent, the Ente wine bar in Hotel Nassauer Hof pulsated with life. Beneath the statue of Emperor Frederick, a couple were kissing passionately, their lips chapping in the frost. A moustachioed police sergeant was giving the directions to Emperor Frederick's baths to an inebriated man. Richter took Knüfer by the arm and pulled him through one of the doors into Hankäs mit Musik, a homely bar smelling of onions and cheese. They sat in a dark corner and the croupier ordered two tankards of hot *äppelwoi.*

"Tell me, Richter," Knüfer said, placing a ten-mark note on the table. "If von Finckl loses, how long will Miss Lebetseyder have to stay at the casino and what will she have to do there?"

"If I told you . . ." Richter put his hand over the note. "What I'm *going* to tell you," he corrected himself, "could cost me my job . . . But what the hell! You've brought me luck . . . We've got another casino . . . an unofficial one . . . in the basement . . . That's where seriously rich clients gamble. The croupiers are beautiful, naked women. If a player wins a very high sum – its value would depend on the player's skill and addiction – he gets the croupier who served him as a gift for the night. You've no idea how lust can blind those men. They lose piles of gold, they hardly ever manage to win a girl, and yet they still keep coming . . . They'd play like maniacs to win Miss Lebetseyder. You just have to take one look at her. Our boss knows what he's doing . . ."

"How long would Miss Lebetseyder have to work in this secret casino?" Knüfer repeated his question.

"Two months is mandatory. Any extension would be up to our blonde Venus."

"And when did you say the game was to take place?"

"Tomorrow at midnight. The boss wants to notify a few journalists he's acquainted with, as well as the regular clients of our unofficial casino who'll be all too willing to cast an eye over the goods. I imagine he'll invite you too, after the decent amount you won at my table."

"There's something you haven't taken into account." Knüfer tried to hide the trembling of his hand as he tipped back the apple wine spiced with cloves and cinnamon. "The girl might not agree. And von Finckl might not lose."

"I don't think so," retorted Richter. He drew a grubby curtain, which, if it had been in one piece, would have separated their table from the rest of the room. "I've seen many losers in the casino who have treated the game as their one and only possibility of getting any money. Most of them didn't say who they were, and were about as genuine as this 'aristocratic' film director who anyone can see is a Jew, and that pseudo-Austrian with the Bavarian accent. Losers will do anything for another chance."

"Thank you, Richter." Knüfer threw yet another note on the table. He made to leave but the croupier caught him by the sleeve. He was very strong for his age. Clearly his muscles had not been developed merely by spinning a roulette wheel.

"They'll do anything and lose everything," he looked intently at Knüfer. "Every single one. Without exception. Just remember that."

With a silver spoon, Rainer Knüfer scooped up a heap of red caviar and garnished a square of coarse, dark, wholemeal bread with it. He then twisted half a lemon, cut lengthwise and set in an upturned cup, into a cone of crystal glass. The cup filled with juice, a few drops of which cut the bland taste of the caviar. Knüfer washed this morsel down with champagne and once again pulled out his invitation, handwritten by the manager:

I have the honour of inviting you, Esteemed Gentleman,
to a special game at midnight on December 14th, to be held in
the main hall of the casino. Following the game, you are invited to
a reception, which will take place in the basement of our casino.
This invitation applies only to the respected Rainer Knüfer
– with no companions.

With my respects,
Claus von Stietencrott
Manager

Knüfer scanned Käfer's Bistro, the casino restaurant, and a violent shudder ran through him. His mother used to explain this unpleasant sensation as "death looking you in the eye". Now the hope of an easy life was looking him in the eye: Knüfer eating his dinner on silvery-white tablecloths every day, sitting on these soft seats of cherry-coloured leather; Knüfer slicing a roasted suckling pig using a knife with an engraved crest, then replacing the knife on a silver knife-rest and handing the girl next to him a piece of pink meat in a crunchy coating of bread-crumbs; the girl's fair hair, in the golden halo of the spidery chandeliers, sharply contrasting with the plush cherry curtains; a waiter bowing from the waist and, in the background, a rainbow of drinks arranged on trian-gular napkins, sparkling on the enormous mahogany bar; Knüfer looking at the girl one more time and wondering who she could be . . .

The detective shook his head and found himself alone with his dreams. He folded the invitation carefully, slipped a ten-mark note under the white, starched napkin, and went to the casino hall. At the entrance to the main hall, a man with moulting blond hair and a pointed goatee was showing the doorman an invitation identical to the one that nestled in Knüfer's dinner jacket. The doorman bowed and his white-gloved hand gestured to the man to enter. A moment later, Knüfer also found him-self in the main room of the casino. He quickly counted thirty-eight men already present, all of whom were wearing tailcoats or dinner jackets, with their shirt-fronts diffusing a snowy brilliance. Croupier Richter silently spun the wheel as the guests adjusted their top hats, re-tied silk scarves around their necks and tapped their canes – some to conceal their embarrassment, others to draw attention to themselves, but most to express their impatience. Minutes passed. Knüfer's eyes wandered over the cream walls, lit up in the electric brightness of the chandeliers, and found relief in the calm, rough, green baize that covered the tables. The murmur of impatience swelled, then, a little later, turned into a roar of greeting and a fawning hum of approval. Into the hall walked Sophie, followed by the manager, von Stietencrott, and Bodo von Finckl. Sophie was wearing a long, tight dress of black satin with elbow-length gloves of

179

the same colour and material. Knüfer drew near to her and thought he could detect traces of recent tears in her pale green eyes. Von Finckl's eyes were unmoved and his tiny yellow teeth gnawed at his upper lip. Von Stietencrott adjusted his monocle, raised both his arms and began his speech.

"Ladies and gentlemen, I have the honour this evening of welcoming you to this special game – the only one of its kind and the second in the history of our casino. I welcome, above all, the central figure of today's celebration, Madame Isabelle Lebetseyder." Here von Stietencrott tipped his top hat and bowed deeply to Sophie. "I welcome the representatives of our Hessian nobility, Count Adrian von Knobloch and Count Hermann von und zum Stein, as well as men of letters: the excellent journalists of our daily newspaper *Wiesbaden Woche* and, above all, the well-known author Markus Wielandt, who has kindly agreed – *mutatis mutandis* – to describe this occasion in his new novel, which is still *in statu nascendi*. And, last but not least, I welcome all the gentlemen present here, both those who come regularly and guests who are new to our establishment."

Applause thundered and von Stietencrott bowed profusely.

"My dear ladies and gentlemen, I will now present you with the rules of today's game and with the rest of this evening's programme. In a moment, we shall play a special and unique *va banque*: Bodo von Finckl versus the Wiesbaden casino, represented by myself. The honourable von Finckl will be so kind as to be the first to bet on red or black, or on even or odd. I, of course, will have to bet on the opposite square from that upon which Mr von Finckl has placed his bet. Should he win, my honourable opponent will have the debt he owes the casino annulled, the value of which is, and will remain, known only to myself and him. Should he lose, Madame Isabelle Lebetseyder will be employed in our casino for a minimum of two months. The conditions of her employment and remuneration, as well as of her resignation from the post, are known to

Madame Lebetseyder. The roulette will spin only once. The placing of secondary bets between yourselves is not forbidden. These will be taken by croupier Paul Richter, present here. One per cent of these secondary bets will go to the casino. When the game *va banque* has ended, you are invited to the basement where a reception will be held, and you will be able to play the kind of roulette that is not generally accessible to our casino regulars." Von Stietencrott filled his lungs with air and asked in a pompous tone. "Would Madame Lebetseyder and Mr von Finckl like to confirm, in front of witnesses, that what I have just said corresponds to the truth?" When both responded with a resounding "yes", von Stietencrott gave the sign to Richter. The latter had set out a laboratory pair of scales and now placed a ball on one of the weighing pans, and on the other, a small weight. When he found them to be perfectly balanced he stood to attention and shouted:

"*Mesdames, messieurs, s'ils vous plaît, faites vos jeux.* I shall also accept secondary bets."

Von Finckl pulled up a high, heavy chair for Sophie, occupied a seat at the table opposite the manager, took a golden Tsarist imperial coin from his pocket and held it out to his companion for her blessing. The soft mounds of her breasts moved agitatedly in her large décolleté as a gloved finger made the sign of the cross. Von Finckl tossed the coin above the betting table. The coin spun and rolled past the board. Von Finckl squeezed his eyes shut and with one thought triggered a series of associations: eight children in a damp room belonging to Bendzin's tailor, Finkelsztejn, who sewed kittels for the poor; their parents, a quick-tempered consumptive and a caring mouse in a crooked wig; a couple of stinking goats who spent the winter with the rest of the household; the May 1st parade in Bendzin and sheets of blood-red flags; the red face of Schai Brodski as he hugged the new treasurer of the Jewish Bund, Bernard Finkelsztejn, and then, four months later, opening the party cash-box and finding the pile of gold imperials missing; the red shawl of a high-class whore in a hotel in Lodsch; the red blood of workers on the cobblestones of Bęndzin, the red blood of the Bund members, whose contributions had brought him a fortune in the Grand Hotel casino in Lodsch. Von Finckl opened his eyes and said:

"I place my bet on red."

"No!" shouted Sophie. "You're to place it on even. This game is being played for me, so I should have something to say in all this too."

A murmur of admiration spread through the men gathered there. They placed bets against each other. A hefty bearded man with a Slav accent and appearance slipped a roll of notes into Richter's hand.

"Even! She has a hunch, that *krasavitza*,"† he bellowed.

"General Basedov knows what he's doing," said the blond man with the goatee to Knüfer, and tossed Richter a hundred marks. "Even!"

"Red," Knüfer said, throwing down fifty marks.

There was great confusion. Men crowded around the table shouting, although none of them dared touch Sophie. Richter noted everything down and tossed the ball into the wheel.

"*Les jeux sont faites. Rien ne va plus!*"

"Of course you accept Madame von Lebetseyder's decision?" von Stietencrott looked inquiringly at von Finckl.

"*Ce que femme veut, Dieu le veut.*"‡

"Mr Richter, please begin!"

The ball fell in with the rotation of the wheel and commenced its dance. It stopped in the pocket marked zero, then – as if ejected by an invisible spring – rolled out and settled in the pocket marked twenty-nine red. The wheel stopped and Richter announced the result. Von Finckl closed his eyes and saw the colours of the casino spin: pale brown, green

† Beauty (Russian).
‡ A woman's will is God's will.

182

and gold. He got up from the table and went into the hall. Sophie burst into tears and ran after him. Knüfer cashed in a hundred marks and discreetly approached the door of the room, where von Stietencrott stood accepting congratulations.

"They might just as well," said Knüfer to himself, "congratulate a shark for having torn a tuna fish to pieces."

"That *krasavitza* missed the mark," roared General Basedov as he too entered the hall. "*Vot sud'ba* . . ."

The *krasavitza* was standing beside von Finckl and stroking him on the cheek. The eminent film director bit his lip and immersed himself in memories of Będzin. Knüfer detected a questioning tone in Sophie's voice. He drew closer and heard von Finckl's reply:

"Yes, I will."

"Always, and despite whatever happens now?" Sobs distorted Sophie's voice.

"I'll go to Berlin and wait for you there. When two months have passed, I'll go to Zoologischer Garten Station every day to wait for the evening train from Wiesbaden. Every day I'll have a bouquet of roses for you." Von Finckl took his coat and hat from the bellboy, kissed Sophie on the forehead and calmly made his way out into the frosty park, a cemetery of frozen chestnut tree stumps. Sophie tried to follow him, but came across the massive figure of a doorman.

"As far as I know, madame," said the Cerberus, "you ought to be at work."

BRESLAU, THURSDAY, DECEMBER 15TH, 1927
ONE O'CLOCK IN THE MORNING

Mühlhaus went to the crystal mirror in his bathroom and opened his mouth wide. His upper left canine was very loose. He pressed it back hard with his thumb and extracted it from his gum, then flicked his fingers and the tooth fell into the washbasin. Mühlhaus tasted blood. He sucked at it, not without some pleasure, and set to work on the upper first incisor. A moment later he held it in his fingers and examined the brownish stains of plaque against the light. The tooth hit the porcelain of the washbasin, tinkling loudly. The tooth tinkled, the washbasin tinkled, the telephone tinkled. Mühlhaus yelled and sat up in bed.

"Maybe it's Jakob?" the terrified eyes of his wife glistened in the dark.

Mühlhaus put his index finger into his mouth and was relieved to find that the poor condition of his teeth had not deteriorated overnight. He then picked up the receiver and said nothing. The person at the other end of the line, on the other hand, was exceptionally talkative.

"I need money, Criminal Director. Two thousand. That's how much I need to pay the boys in Wiesbaden. They've got a car and they'll help me get her to Berlin. I can keep her in a hideaway there."

"Hold on," muttered Mühlhaus. "One minute."

He put on his dressing gown and slippers and, running the tip of his tongue over his intact canine, shuffled into the hall. He sat down heavily in the armchair and pressed the receiver of the other phone to his ear.

"Explain something to me, Knüfer." Mühlhaus was still a little sleepy. "Why do you need the two thousand so urgently?"

"The boys from Wiesbaden are gamblers – they lost a huge amount in the casino today. They got a loan from the casino boss and have to have the money by tomorrow . . ."

"They'll go back to the casino and lose it again, you idiot," growled Mühlhaus. "They'll lose and not go anywhere with you. And Mrs Sophie Mock will fly off to another spa . . ."

"If they don't pay the boss five thousand by midday tomorrow, they won't be able to show their faces in Wiesbaden. And they live off this town and casino. For them that money means 'to be or not to be'. I've got to let them know immediately if they can have it by tomorrow."

"Listen to me, Knüfer," Mühlhaus said, no longer sleepy. "It's one o'clock in the morning and your story is exhausting me like a market vendor's yapping. You'll get the money – I'll send it *poste restante*. Every casino has a good postal counter. You'll have it by tomorrow. You say these boys lost a lot. I tell you, if you're lying to me, you're not just going to lose a lot like them – you're going to lose everything."

Mühlhaus replaced the receiver and padded back to the bedroom. He lay down next to his wife and sensed that she was not asleep.

"Who was that? Jakob?" she asked anxiously.

"The dentist," murmured Mühlhaus, and then a black, dull drowsiness deprived him of any desire to crack more equally apposite jokes.

WIESBADEN, THAT SAME DECEMBER 15TH, 1927
A QUARTER PAST ONE IN THE MORNING

Knüfer wiped the sweat from his brow, replaced the receiver and descended the marble stairs to the secret casino. As he went through the heavy oak door screened by a purple curtain, his head spun at the sight of naked, smiling women pushing columns of chips across the fiery-red silk that covered the tables. Knüfer had visited many a brothel in his time, some of them incredibly expensive and exclusive, in which he had celebrated the conclusion of various profitable and complex assignations, but he had never seen so many beautiful women at once. He noted moreover that it was not their naked bodies, but their smiles that made him so uneasy and excited. In their lips, parted to reveal moist pearls of teeth, lay encouragement and promise, to be bought with money and honour.

The men in the room threw down mountains of chips to reach the limit that would turn this promise into a reality, suggesting that the price they

185

paid was well worth it. Only von Stietencrott and the male employees distributing champagne and snacks played no part in this fight, but merely handed out cash and bills of exchange for chips. This he did now when Knüfer handed him a bill for the sum of two thousand marks. Inviting him to play, von Stietencrott indicated the table at which General Basedov and another dozen or so flushed addicts were gaming for the fair-haired beauty. Sophie was making mistakes, but no-one at the table held it against her. Besides, her errors were set right by a dark-haired croupier who was initiating her that evening into the mysteries of the profession. She differed from Sophie not only by the colour of her hair; she was not completely naked but wore a very short, white, starched apron, which highlighted her olive complexion.

Knüfer pushed his way through to Sophie's new place of work and lit a cigarette, keenly observing what was happening at the table. He soon grasped that Sophie would be a bonus prize for the player who won five thousand marks. Every thousand marks was represented by a little elephant of green jade. General Basedov had three such elephants in front of him, the blond man with the goatee two, and the remaining players, none. All were playing in a very similar way, and rather safely. They would place one hundred marks on specific numbers and lose again and again. In this way they did not lose very much, and still kept open the option of playing *va banque*. This last move was played more often than not by those who had no elephants. When there was one pile of chips left in front of them, they would place it on red or black to win a second pile, and place single chips on specific numbers. This was rather boring but not enough to deform Sophie's beautiful smile with yawns.

Knüfer made five small piles of chips worth three hundred marks each and shook his head when the dark-haired croupier offered to exchange them for elephants. At the command *"faites vos jeux"*, which Sophie pronounced with an impeccable accent, as if she had spent her entire life

186

in Monte Carlo, Knüfer placed everything on red. The move did not impress his fellow players, nor did it influence their own tactics. The ball rattled and the detective closed his eyes. When he opened them he saw Sophie's smile. The new croupier was pushing towards him his five stacks along with five additional ones. Her heavy breasts swayed above the table and Knüfer could have sworn her nipples rubbed against the shiny silk. He stood up, nodded to the waiter and drank two glasses of champagne, one after the other.

"How much do you have to win for the bonus prize?" he asked the player next to him, who turned out to be the man with the goatee.

"Five," was the reply. Knüfer put everything on black.

"Careful," sang the dark-haired croupier. "You're staking everything on a win, sir. Should this man win, gentlemen, the game at this table may come to an end — that is, if he decides to take the bonus prize immediately. Is that what you think will happen, Mr . . ."

"Knüfer. I don't know what's going to happen," his voice was hoarse. "I'm not going to say anything in case I prevent it from happening."

Basedov and the man with the goatee, apparently the only players who could afford it, bet — on red and black, odd and even — a sum that, if they won, would give them six thousand marks each. Knüfer closed his eyes and tried to numb his sense of hearing. He could not, however, do so entirely; the tremendous applause that broke out at the table was still audible. He opened his eyes and got his reward: the most beautiful smile he had ever seen in his life. Unfortunately, a similar smile was bestowed on the man with the goatee. Knüfer looked at the ball. It rested in the pocket two black.

"Mr Knüfer and Mr Wlossok have won six thousand marks each as Mr Knüfer bet on black and Mr Wlossok on even," roared the voice of von Stietencrott, who had appeared at Sophie's table along with most of the guests in the secret casino. "Only these two gentlemen may continue to play on, and whoever has the advantage – be it only one mark – is entitled to the bonus prize in the form of Madame Lebetseyder's favours."

Knüfer, thinking of Sophie's hardened nipples on the purple silk, placed everything on red. Wlossok also bet six thousand marks on even. Knüfer closed his eyes once more and a moment later heard applause. Sophie was smiling radiantly. At Wlossok.

WIESBADEN, FRIDAY, DECEMBER 16TH, 1927
HALF PAST SEVEN IN THE EVENING

Knüfer suppressed a yawn and scratched his head, which was heavy with nicotine. Although he had slept for more than thirteen hours, with only brief periods of wakefulness, he felt short of sleep, haggard and over-full after the meal he had just eaten, after yesterday's champagne, after the furiously erotic dream he had had and the strong sense of frustration that had been eating away at him ever since Wlossok had won Sophie and left the secret casino with her at five in the morning, his pockets full of chips. Knüfer had then drunk a bottle of champagne and dragged himself to his room at Hotel Nassauer Hof, supported under the arm by the caring Richter. He now glanced at his watch and established that the allocated fourteen hours that Wlossok spent with Sophie, which he himself had been denied by the "roulette goddess", had passed. Knüfer stood in front of the small hanging mirror behind the folding screen, washed his face in a basin of cold water and slicked down his hair, which stuck out here and there. He then shaved, put on a shirt-front and dinner jacket and, sucking the finger he had pricked on a cufflink, went down to the casino in order to cash the money from Mühlhaus.

He collected two thousand marks from the postal counter and entered the main hall, showing the doorman his invitation from the day before.

"I'm for the secret casino," he whispered.

188

"Very good, sir." The uniformed official pulled back the plush curtain behind which lay the entrance to hell.

Knüfer raised his hand in greeting and descended the broad, winding stairs. A moment later, he found himself within windowless walls, amongst tables of purple silk and extremely beautiful, naked sirens who lured him with their shaking hips, swaying breasts and French refrain. But the one he could not stop thinking about was not among them. Knüfer lit a cigar and waited. Then he heard Mühlhaus' voice ringing in his heavy head: *I tell you, if you're lying to me, you're not just going to lose a lot like them – you're going to lose everything.*

Like all gamblers, Knüfer was superstitious. He took Sophie's absence at the table and Mühlhaus' voice booming in his skull as warnings. He should not repeat the game with the money he had just received from Mühlhaus because he had lost that sum once already, the day before, and had written out a bill of exchange for it. So he would have to give it back to von Stietencrott, rent a room in Wiesbaden, and not leave town for two months so that he could keep a discreet eye on Sophie. Thanks to a fortunate coincidence, Mühlhaus' instructions had been obeyed and von Stietencrott had effectively "isolated" Sophie for two months. Fate had done Knüfer's work for him and he should have been jumping for joy to be able to spend his winter holiday peacefully and happily in Wiesbaden, but this momentary joy was wrecked by a grating voice that kept repeating: *I tell you, if you're lying to me, you're not just going to lose a lot like them – you're going to lose everything.*

"You're going to lose everything if you lose sight of Sophie even for a second," added Knüfer, and abandoned the secret casino and its naked croupiers' siren song.

Von Stietencrott struggled to contain his mounting rage. With furious, bloodshot eyes he glared at Markus Wielandt, who was smiling ironically as he exhaled columns of cigarette smoke through his nostrils, and forced himself to adopt a polite tone:

"My dear Mr Wielandt, you have already explained it to me. You're a writer and you want to describe Miss Lebetseyder's mental state the day after – as you put it – 'she was consumed as an additional reward in erotic roulette'. I'm pleased you approach your work so seriously, but Miss Lebetseyder is indisposed just at the moment and doesn't wish to see anyone."

"They must really have been at it," Wielandt remarked, "if she can't stand at a table twenty-four hours later."

Von Stietencrott was spared an attack of apoplexy by the ringing of the telephone. The casino manager picked up the receiver, listened for a moment and yelled:

"Bring me that receptionist!"

The door opened and into the room filled with Biedermeier furniture, ferns and palms burst three powerfully built doormen and a short receptionist wearing the Hotel Nassauer Hof uniform.

"Name?" von Stietencrott shouted, aiming his fat index finger at the receptionist's chest.

"Zeissmann, Helmut Zeissmann," said the man, trying not to look his boss in the eye. He was clearly suffering from Parkinson's disease.

"Tell me, Zeissmann." The manager grabbed the receptionist by his frail shoulders. "Tell me everything."

"Mr Knüfer came to see me half an hour ago," Zeissmann said, immobilized by the vice of his boss' hands and burned by the sparks fired from behind the monocle, "and asked whether Mr Wlossok was in his room. I told him the truth, that he had just returned. Mr Knüfer then went up, and he's still there."

"You know that I'm looking for Knüfer for not redeeming a bill of exchange?"

"Yes, I do." Zeissmann finally found the courage to raise his shaking head and watery eyes to von Stietencrott's face, which was purple with anger. "I was told that five minutes ago. That's why I immediately called the doormen. Two of them are standing outside Wlossok's door right now."

"You act with lightning speed, Zeissmann," the monocle flashed with satisfaction. "You'll receive an appropriate bonus. And now tell me everything about Madame Lebetseyder and Wlossok. How many times have you seen her today?"

"Two," Zeissmann said, relaxing, and he patted his trouser pockets with his hands as if looking for something. Wielandt the writer handed him a cigarette. "Twice. Once at about five in the morning. She went into her room with Mr Wlossok. At about twelve, Mr Wlossok phoned and asked me to check the times of trains to Breslau. I looked them up and called him back. Three hours later, at about three o'clock, Madame Lebetseyder left the hotel. She seemed to be going for a walk in the park. At about five, Mr Wlossok called for some dinner, which I took up to him personally."

"Couldn't a more junior member of staff have done that?" There was no irony in von Stietencrott's voice.

"Do you know, sir," Zeissmann smiled from ear to ear, "I preferred to do so myself, to emphasize our respect for guests who make large winnings."

"You were more concerned to get a tip," muttered von Stietencrott. "Go on, go on."

"I brought him dinner at five. He was alone. He didn't go out after

191

that. Half an hour ago, Knüfer went up to see him. Shortly after that, Mr Wlossok called and asked for some cigarettes. Again I saw to the request myself. Mr Wlossok was in a heated discussion with Mr Knüfer about something. I then returned to reception and the casino steward, Mr Hechs, called me to say that Mr Knüfer was wanted by the manager. I immediately informed the guards and since then they've been standing outside Wlossok's room awaiting further instructions."

"Thank you, Zeissmann." Von Stietencrott revealed a set of teeth that were about as authentic as the "von" in front of his name. "I won't forget this. And now, everyone apart from Mr Wielandt – out!"

When the office was empty, the manager collapsed into his armchair and raised his eyebrows.

"Any questions, my dear Mr Wielandt?"

"Yes." The writer was clearly worried about something. His face reflected the astonishment of a primary school pupil who has been told to conjugate all the basic forms of the Greek verb *gignomai*. "Did none of your men follow Madame Lebetseyder? Is all you know what the receptionist has told you? Did you let her leave, just like that, to go for a walk? Maybe she's no longer in Wiesbaden? Aren't you worried about such a beautiful croupier? Any man would wager his wife's dowry to have her!"

"My dear Mr Wielandt," von Stietencrott smiled. "Have you fallen in love with Madame Lebetseyder? Are you worried you'll never see her again?" He took a cigar from an ebony box, snipped it with clippers and pushed the box along the shining surface of the desk towards the writer. "If I was as foolish as you think, I wouldn't have been running this casino for the past twenty years. Let me tell you something very interesting– you must give me your word of honour not to use it in your book." Von Stietencrott scrutinized the writer who, hand on heart, gave his word of honour. "In the agreement signed by that whore and her pimp, it states as clear as day that if she flies the coop, that director from the burned-out theatre is going to have to work for me instead. And my bodyguard is following his every step. I'm not letting him go . . ."

"And?" Wielandt laughed out loud, making a mental note to jot down von Stietencrott's linguistic metamorphosis from elegant man of fashion who drops foreign quotations into his speech to vulgar lout. "Is von Finckl going to lie naked on the roulette table and push stacks of chips with a spatula? What a worthy substitute for Lebetseyder!"

"My good fellow, the only thing those two are going to have in common is working in the secret casino. That Jew is going to make me more money than his lady."

"As a naked croupier?" Wielandt asked once more. But then he became serious, and took no offence when he heard von Stietencrott whisper:

"As my sharper, you imbecile."

WIESBADEN, THAT SAME DECEMBER 16TH, 1927
HALF PAST NINE IN THE EVENING

Von Stietencrott and Wielandt walked along the corridor to Wlossok's room. They wore neither coats nor hats, even though Hotel Nassauer Hof was on the other side of the street. Behind them, two doormen tossed their bellies rhythmically, while Zeissmann the receptionist skipped along. A cloud of cigar smoke wafted into the open mouths of the doormen and encircled Zeissmann's trembling head.

"Now you'll see," von Stietencrott said, as a column of ash fell from his cigar onto the red carpet, "how I deal with bastards who don't repay me."

They stopped at the door to the room and von Stietencrott thumped his fist on it several times. The door was not locked, and the manager and writer entered. On the floor Wlossok and Knüfer lay prone, their blue faces turned up towards the new arrivals. A film covered their staring eyes and their tensed Adam's apples almost burst through the skin of their necks.

"*Scheisse*, someone's screwed their heads round a hundred and eighty degrees," muttered one of the doormen.

Von Stietencrott approached Knüfer's corpse and turned it onto its back. The heavy head spun on the limp rope of the neck. Von Stietencrott reached into the inside pocket of the dead man's dinner jacket and pulled out a wad of notes.

"What are you doing?" yelled Wielandt. "We mustn't touch anything. We've got to call the police."

"I can't touch my own money?" The manager extinguished his cigar in some sauce left on a plate on the table. "The rest is the business of the police, and yours too. Yes, yours . . ." Von Stietencrott patted Wielandt on his chubby cheek. "As you can see, there's never a lack of material for writers in my casino."

"What have they got in their mouths?" asked one of the doormen, bending over the bodies.

"Scraps of paper," replied the other. "They look like pages from a calendar."

BRESLAU, MONDAY, DECEMBER 19TH, 1927
SIX O'CLOCK IN THE MORNING

Breslau was cloaked in swollen skeins of grey cloud from which fell large, sticky flakes of snow. Viktor Ziesch, assistant to the administrator of St Georg Hospital on Mehlgasse, removed his stiff, peaked cap, fanned himself with it, unbuttoned his greatcoat and leaned on his snow shovel. Ziesch was of a reflective nature and enjoyed above all those moments of reverie that would suddenly overcome him, directing him to stop work and meditate on the world around him and its inhabitants. It seemed to

Ziesch that his eyes could penetrate the walls of the rented tenement on Mehlgasse and see the people living within: Slotosch the barber finds it hard to wake up and regretfully leaves the safe haven of his eiderdown, dunks his head in a basin of cold water, slicks down what hair might be standing on end and turns up his moustache, and then sets off for his establishment on the corner near the Registry Office; the seamstress, Mrs Wiedemann, slides her leg from beneath her nightdress and with her toes pushes a full chamber pot towards the old servant stoking up the kitchen stove; in a moment the bar owner, Scholz, is going to come down and chide the caretaker, Hanuschka, for not having shovelled away the snow outside his place; the caretaker is not cleaning the sign of the inn because he is hacking away at the crystallized edges of old mounds of snow with his shovel and chasing away a stray dog that, searching for something to eat, pokes its muzzle through the cellar window and puts its front paws up on the rims of the cast-iron buckets of ash that the caretaker has taken out into the street. Ziesch looks up at the hospital and sees a distinguished, bearded man opening a window. Ziesch can almost smell the aromatic clouds of Austria tobacco coming from the sickroom and wonders whether he should not tell the management about the smoker. But he meets the man's watchful eye and discards the thought: "What's it got to do with me!" The man turns back towards the patient's bed and sees that he is no longer asleep.

"So you're awake, Mock. You've been sleeping for twenty hours. And even longer before that. Two whole weeks in a coma. Can you talk?"

Mock nodded and realized his head was held in something stiff. He then felt a stinging tear through the skin on his chin. He closed his eyes and tried to ride out the shooting pain.

"Your skin is badly and quite deeply flayed," Mock heard Mühlhaus' grating voice. "The buckle of your belt tore into your chin. Apart from that, you've suffered a crack of the cervical vertebra. You're immobilized in a corset. That's all. You'll survive," a tone of joyfulness sounded in Mühlhaus' voice. "I welcome you back to this vale of tears."

The events of the preceding few days passed before Mock's eyes in slow motion: a maggot burrowing into the corpse's eye in the shoemaker's workshop, Honnefelder hacked to pieces, the throbbing dryness of a hangover, Sophie's rape, her escape, the nameless prostitute with a severed head, the blue swellings on Councillor Geissen's hairy back, the investigation conducted together with Director Hartner, "forget about that whore, get on with your work and don't think about her!", happy families in modest, happy homes, Breslau turning white, becoming whiter than snow, *Asperges me, Domine, hyssopo, et mundabor; lavabis me, et super nivem dealbabor.*†

"You were saved by the University Library caretaker, one Josef Maron," continued Mühlhaus. "He didn't feel like being your Charon," he sniggered.

"I forgot to give him the obol." Mock closed his eyes and fell asleep. But he slept only for a moment, during which the slow rhythm of recent events passing before his eyes gained in strength. He turned onto his side with difficulty and spurted vomit onto the granite-patterned hospital linoleum.

BRESLAU, THAT SAME DECEMBER 19TH, 1927
TWO O'CLOCK IN THE AFTERNOON

Mock awoke again later that day and immediately sat up in bed. Blood rushed to his head, a piercing pain tore through his neck and his scraped chin rubbed painfully against the rough edge of his corset. He fell back on the pillow and let the sweat trickle down his brow. Slowly extending his arm, he pressed the button by the bed and a moment later saw a Borromäerinner sister enter his room.

† Sprinkle me with hyssop and I shall be cleansed, wash me and I shall be whiter than snow.

"Is the man who came to see me this morning," he managed to whisper, "still around somewhere?"

"He's been around for a few days." The sister lowered her eyes modestly. "He hasn't left you for a moment. Other than to go to the bathroom or to smoke. He'll be here shortly. Is there anything else?"

Mock wanted to shake his head but remembered his fractured cervical vertebra. So he said nothing and the sister dispersed into the whiteness of the hospital interior. In her stead appeared Mühlhaus, warming his hands on his hot pipe.

"Ah, you're awake again!" he said. "I hope you're not going to react with the same degree of revulsion at this subsequent return to reality."

"What is there to return to?" snorted Mock and closed his eyes. He then saw an entirely different image: night, Mühlhaus asleep on an iron hospital chair, ash from his pipe scattered over his waistcoat.

"Thank you, sir," he said, opening his eyes, "for being with me. It's like keeping watch over the deceased. The last respects . . ."

"Yes, I'm keeping watch over you," said Mühlhaus slowly. "As a friend and as your superior. Besides, the one's tied up with the other. The superior wants you to come back to work. The friend believes work will cure you."

Mock looked at the article standing in the corner of the room, a brass frame with two supporting rings. The lower one held a water jug, the upper a basin. Above the basin was a small pole with a mirror. The washstand was intricately decorated with violin keys; the metalworker must have been a music lover. On the rim of the basin were the remnants of some shaving foam, flecked with black specks of redundant growth. Mock touched his chin and felt that it was smooth.

"Who shaves me here?" he whispered.

"I do," answered Mühlhaus. "I ought to be a barber. Your flayed chin would have been quite a challenge for any professional."

"Why? Why are you taking care of me? I'm not going back. What for?" murmured Mock.

"Am I to reply as your superior or friend?"

"It makes no difference."

"You'll go back to your wife and your work."

Taking no notice of the pain, Mock sat up, got out of bed and grabbed the corset with both hands, trying to pull it over his head. His feet searched for his shoes and his arms struggled to free themselves from the sleeves of his nightshirt. But within moments he could no longer ignore the pain. He collapsed onto his bed and glared at Mühlhaus. Somewhat alarmed by his subordinate's behaviour, Mühlhaus remembered the doctor's instructions not to annoy the patient and decided to come clean.

"Listen, Mock," he began, feverishly stuffing tobacco into his pipe. "I spoke to Knüfer four days ago. He's found your wife in Wiesbaden and today – or tomorrow at the latest – she's going to be in Berlin. There, Knüfer's going to bring her to a certain apartment where some friends of his are going to watch her day and night. She'll have everything she needs. As soon as you've wrapped up the calendar murderer's case, you can pick her up in Berlin and it'll all be over. Your theory of crimes repeating themselves is convincing."

"And what now, Mühlhaus?" Mock had never addressed his boss in this way. "You've got me in a checkmate, haven't you? 'Find the "calendar murderer", Mock, and I'll tell you where your wife is,'" he aped Mühlhaus' grating voice. He sat up suddenly once more. "Now listen to me carefully. This job and that monster who's killing alcoholics, Hitlerites and corrupt politicians can go to hell. All I'm interested in is my wife. I'm going to get up, get dressed and go to Berlin. I'm going to find Knüfer in his lair and he's going to tell me where Sophie is. Understand? That's exactly what I'm going to do right now."

"You forget," Mühlhaus said, clutching at straws, "that another girl was murdered too. A whore, who for a couple of pfennigs did anything scum like Geissen desired. She was only nineteen, and before dying of syphilis she could still have had a bit of a life . . ."

"What do I care about some nameless whore." Mock rang for the sister again. "There's no way even of putting her in our files. I'm going to fetch a different whore . . . And I'm going to change her . . . Never again . . ."

"And what are you going to do, damn it, when you've found her?" yelled Mühlhaus.

"Put my arms around her," replied Mock calmly, "and ask her for . . ."

The sister appeared and began to protest as the patient informed her of his intention to leave the hospital. Mock's bass voice was spliced by the sister's hysterical soprano. In all this commotion, Mühlhaus tried to pin down one thought, which gave him no peace; it was to be a counter-argument to something Mock had said, something he had been quite wrong about, or had not taken into account. It was not about Mock putting his arms around Sophie to hug or strangle her, it was something he had said earlier, something that did not tally with the truth. Yes, now he remembered.

"Quiet, damn it! Can you shut up for a moment, please, sister!" yelled Mühlhaus, and with relief he watched the flutter of the starched apron disappear out of the door. "What makes you think that whore didn't have a name? She's been identified by her father who was worried she hadn't turned up for work which he, incidentally, had found for her. Quite a bastard, eh? His own daughter's pimp," he shot the words out with the speed of a machine gun. "She'd been working in the brothel for just three days and her colleagues knew her only by her nickname. Her father identified her the day before yesterday. You have to find whoever murdered that girl . . . You're the one most involved in the case . . . You've got some new ideas . . . That victim wasn't Hitlerite scum or some drunken musician . . . She was just an ordinary girl forced into prostitution by her own father!"

"Her father, you say?" Mock was still sitting on the bed. "What was her name? Tell me!"

"Rosemarie Bombosch."

At this, Mock fell silent. Mühlhaus was out of breath, searching for some matches. A scratch on sand-paper and the pipe sparked alight. A doctor stood in the doorway and opened his mouth to chide Mühlhaus for smoking, but before he could say anything Mock announced: "Thank you, Doctor, for your care, but I'm leaving. I'm discharging myself!"

"You can't!" the young doctor raised his voice. "You've got to stay here for another few days at least . . . From a doctor's point of view, nothing is so urgent that . . ."

"There are things more urgent than a doctor's point of view!"

"And what, my gracious man, can be more important than decisions about a patient's health?" the doctor looked ironically at Mock as he wriggled helplessly in the stiff corset.

"I have to enter a name in a police file," said Mock. He got up from the bed and, staggering, went over to the window. Looking out he met the eye of Viktor Ziesch who, struck by a sudden attack of contemplation of the world and its inhabitants, had stopped shovelling snow yet again that day.

BRESLAU, THAT SAME DECEMBER 19TH, 1927
FOUR O'CLOCK IN THE AFTERNOON

Heinrich Mühlhaus took down from a shelf a small, square, ancient publication. Weighing it in his hand for a moment, he examined the library ladder at the top of which were two hooks secured to an iron pipe that ran along the bookshelf some three metres above the ground. Mühlhaus took a sudden interest in the number of rungs and started to count them. He could not finish this task, however, because the upper part of the ladder was almost entirely concealed by the baggy storeman's overalls worn by his subordinate, Eberhard Mock. Constantly adjusting his outfit, slipping his hand beneath the surgical corset and scratching his neck imprisoned therein, the Criminal Counsellor began in a quiet, croaky voice to give his briefing in the University Library storeroom. Director Hartner sat at librarian Smetana's desk – the latter had finished work unexpectedly early that day – and watched uneasily as the police officers rolled cigarettes between their fingers, pulled out matches and then, remembering that smoking was forbidden, stashed them nervously in their pockets. He looked at the map of Breslau displayed on the wooden stand and at the three red pins stuck into the heart of the town, encircled by the moat, then looked irritably at Mühlhaus who was leafing intently through a small, ancient publication. He did not feel at ease in this particular position in the storeroom, whose far wall adjoined the church of Maria auf dem Sande. All the librarians and storemen avoided this spot because of a persistent icy draught, and because of the risk of the same books constantly falling from the upper shelves.

"No doubt you are surprised, gentlemen," Mock began, "that today's briefing is being held in such an unusual place, and late in the afternoon at that, at a time when you normally finish work. This can only be explained by the high degree of confidentiality attached to the investigation we are conducting. Since I've suffered an accident and my throat has been damaged, I'll speak briefly and, in a moment, hand the voice over to you. I suspect that the murders of Gelfrert, Honnefelder and Geissen, committed by the 'calendar murderer', have something to do with the area in which their bodies were found. The link may go far back in time. Hence my research in the library and archives – in which Director Hartner has proved to be of inestimable help. And now, to the point," Mock sat on the penultimate rung of the ladder and coughed dryly. "You will now, gentlemen, sum up your assignments in the context of what I've just said. Reinert?"

"Together with Kleinfeld and Ehlers, I'm tailing Alexei von Orloff," Reinert threw a glance at the colleagues he had just mentioned, who were standing nearby. "We don't quite know why. It's difficult for me to sum anything up because I've no idea how this assignment fits into the context you have spoken of, sir."

"I'll help you," Mock muttered. "What does von Orloff have to say at his séances?"

"That the end of the world is nigh," answered Reinert.

"What proof has he got?"

"He claims some predictions are coming true," said Kleinfeld, "and gives an account of them. I've jotted down the examples he quotes from the various sacred books. Admittedly, he cites fragments of the Five Books of Moses in his own translation . . ."

"And does his 'proof' touch on anything that might interest our Murder Commission?" Mock waved his hand as if wanting to chase away Kleinfeld's words.

Silence descended. The storeroom was in semi-darkness, illuminated only by the weak light of some lamps that burned here and there. The policemen resembled conspirators, or participants in some secret mystery. Mock's overalls were draped over the rungs of the ladder like the cloak of a priest.

"Yes," Kleinfeld wheezed, with notes of tobacco in his voice. "Von Orloff also mentioned 'criminal' proof. Apparently old crimes are being repeated . . . Crimes committed long ago . . ."

"How long ago?"

"Ages ago," Ehlers said, slapping his bald skull as if he had remembered something.

"Are these crimes being repeated in Breslau? What does our guru say?"

"Yes. In Breslau, Berlin, the whole of Europe and the whole world," Reinert clearly felt unwell in the cold storeroom, where the skeletons of monks lay at rest in crypts under the stone floor. "The guru claims crimes are being repeated everywhere, which means that the end of the world is nigh . . ."

"Well remembered, Reinert," Mock spoke ever more quietly. "Murders were committed in Breslau long ago which are now being repeated or renewed, as von Orloff claims. Breslau was very small in ages past and lay within the perimeter of the Old Town moat. And now, gentlemen, look at the map . . . Gelfrert, Honnefelder and Geissen were killed within the territory delineated by the moat . . . Now do you understand my hypothesis?"

"Yes," Mühlhaus replaced the old volume. "Except that we don't know for certain whether or not the murders of these three people had their prototypes in past ages . . ."

"That's mine and Doctor Hartner's task," Mock said as he got off the ladder and stroked the stack of books and boxes of index cards on Smetana's desk. "You're to keep on von Orloff's heels, and try to discover whether the guru isn't trying to hasten the end of the world himself by re-enacting past crimes."

"Forgive me, Counsellor," Kleinfeld modestly lowered his eyes. "But that is neither your task nor Doctor Hartner's . . . It is von Orloff's. If he wants to draw people to his sect, he's the one who has to prove that crimes are being repeated . . . And he's already done so in his presentations. People asked him exactly which crimes are being repeated, and he gave examples of murders in various parts of Europe . . ."

"In Germany too?" asked Mock.

"Yes. In Wiesbaden," Kleinfeld said.

"And in Breslau?" Mock desperately tried to reject the thoughts of Sophie that her country of birth had invoked.

"He didn't say anything about Breslau at the lecture I attended."

"And what about you two, did you hear him say anything about Breslau?" Mock turned to Reinert and Ehlers.

"You can't remember what he said?" Mühlhaus raised his voice. "So why did you go along then?"

"If you will permit me, sir," Mock said in a conciliatory spirit. "They're sure to have noted everything down neatly in their reports, am I right?"

Reinert and Ehlers nodded.

"Then bring me your reports!" There was excitement in Mock's voice. "In a flash, damn it! On top of that, check when von Orloff first began to be active in Breslau . . ."

"We know everything already," Reinert said, looking anxiously around the library dungeon as he buttoned his coat and put on his hat. "We've not a minute to lose. We know our assignments . . ."

"And what's Meinerer's assignment?" Mühlhaus looked at Mock with interest.

"I've detailed him to special tasks," Mock replied calmly. "He's going to help me in a survey of what is stocked in the library."

Mühlhaus nodded to the three policemen, and they made towards the exit, leaving Mock, Hartner and Meinerer in the dark cellar.

"One moment!" Mock shouted and went after Mühlhaus. "Please answer me one question." He held his chief back by the sleeve. "Why, after my attempted suicide, did you allow Ehlers, Reinert and Kleinfeld to continue the tasks I'd given them? After all, I allocated those tasks without consulting you . . . Lunatics commit suicide . . . Why did you allow them to follow the instructions of a lunatic?"

Mühlhaus looked at Mock and then at his subordinates as they left the library catacombs only too willingly. When he heard their footsteps resonating at the top of the stairs, he leaned towards Mock:

"People who commit suicide aren't lunatics – they're usually right," he said, and left the storeroom.

BRESLAU, THAT SAME DECEMBER 19TH, 1927
FIVE O'CLOCK IN THE AFTERNOON

The palm leaves in Hartner's study swayed gently in the wafts of cigar smoke. The Director of the library and the police officer, clad in his surgical corset, silently watched the caretaker and Meinerer bring stacks of books from the storeroom and arrange them on the davenport and the Director's desk.

"Thank you, Meinerer," Mock broke the silence. "You're free to go for today. But the same task awaits you tomorrow . . ."

"Couldn't we have met here?" Meinerer placed a large box with copies of index cards on the davenport with a thud. "Aren't the conditions here good enough for a briefing? Did we have to go down to that cellar? And why am I the only one lugging all this? What am I, some sort of caretaker?"

Mock gazed at his subordinate for a long time. Pain pierced his neck and bored its way down between his shoulder blades. He could not swallow or move his head; all he could do was continue to stare into Meinerer's small eyes and, after the latter had left, telephone Herbert Domagalla and suggest a new employee for the Vice Department, "the young and ambitious Gustav Meinerer".

"We had to meet there," whispered Mock, then thought he was being a little too understanding with Meinerer. Immediately he changed his tone. "And now shut up and go home . . . Since you don't know any Latin, your help reading *Antiquitates Silesiacae* won't be of much use to me. That's all. Adieu!"

"Incidentally," Hartner got up, crossed his hands behind his back and closed the door behind Meinerer, who left without a word of farewell, "I wanted to ask you the same question, my dear Counsellor. Why did we meet in the storeroom?"

"There's nobody in the storeroom apart from ghosts." Mock slotted his cigar between his gums and his cheek. "And if they listened to our conversation and heard about our confidential investigation, they wouldn't pose a threat. They're not the ones who murdered or left calendar pages at the crime scenes . . . Human beings did that – historians, scholars who know how to find out about events and facts from the past, who can also read old books and chronicles. There are a great many of them in this very institution of which you are director. Both scholars and staff . . . All of them could be suspects, which is why it's best that no-one knows about our briefing . . ."

Mock was exhausted by this long statement. He panted loudly and touched his flayed chin with a finger. He felt prickles of beard growth breaking through the skin.

"Surely you're not saying," Hartner tried to conceal his indignation, "that one of my men could . . ."

"We've known each other for too long, Director," Mock said quietly. "You don't have to pretend to me that you're full of righteous indignation. Besides, I've had enough of this discussion . . . Let's get to work . . . We have to make a list of all the murders committed in old Breslau because this von Orloff or some other believer in the end of the world might replicate them, and innocent people will die . . ."

"If there are any innocent people in this town," remarked Hartner dryly, and began to daydream of cold chicken in mayonnaise. He sank into an armchair, adjusted his pince-nez and buried himself in *Antiquitates Silesiacae* by Barthesius. On his desk lay a notebook and a well-sharpened pencil. Mock sat down at the davenport and began to read *The Criminal World of Ancient Breslau* by Hagen, starting with the subject index. Next to the word "crimes" were references to a fair number of pages. The first of these was page 112, where a quarrel was described between several thugs who could not come to an agreement as to how to share their loot, and ended their dispute with a bloodbath in the Green Stag inn on Reuscherstrasse. Mock continued his meanderings through the stinking world of old Breslau: he came across tanners who drowned a travelling salesman in the Weisse Ohle when they were drunk; desecrators of graves defecating among tombstones; soldiers of the Austrian garrison, diseased with syphilis, who duelled feverishly in Oswitzer Wald; Jewish plunderers who robbed their fellow Jews at a fair; Polish peasants who landed up in the dark cells of the Town Hall, known as "bird cages", for disturbing the peace at night. All these seemed like innocent games to Mock, the pranks of jesters, the pageants of clowns. Nothing bore a resemblance to the film-covered eyes of the walled-in musician, the torn tendons of the quartered locksmith, the blue, swollen head of the senator hanging by his leg or the cleanly severed Adam's apple of the young prostitute. Mock rubbed his eyes and returned to the index. Discouraged, he ran his eyes over the various subject entries and thought about his apartment, which he had not been to for two weeks. He decided to note that there was nothing in Hagen's monograph that could add anything new to the case. Out of philological habit, he decided to write down the exact bibliographic address of the book. He reached towards Hartner's desk and took the first card to hand from a considerable pile. It was a blank order slip from the Municipal Library which had found itself among the boxes of index cards. One glance at it was enough for Mock to smell the stale odour of cherry liqueur that had permeated Gelfrert's room. The smell had permeated everything then, even the thin piece of paper that Ehlers had held in his tweezers as they sat in the car sharing their first impressions of their visit to Gelfrert's lodgings. *"We found a request form from the Municipal Library."* Ehlers held a piece of

printed paper under Mock's nose. "September 10th, Gelfrert returned a
book . . ."

Mock did not even attempt to remember the title of the book. He had
no intention of exploiting his memory unnecessarily. He approached
Hartner's desk and dialled the number of the Police Praesidium, where
the telephonist connected him to Ehlers. Some time elapsed before Ehlers
found Gelfrert's file on Mock's table. He quickly satisfied his boss' curiosity. Without replacing the receiver, Mock glanced at the book Hartner
was studying and read its title out loud.

"*Antiquitates Silesiacae* by Barthesius?"

"That's it. That's the book," he heard Ehlers say. "And Counsellor, I've
found the files from the Vice Department on your desk, the ones that
relate to religious sects . . ."

"Bring them to me with your report." Mock replaced the receiver and
smiled at Hartner. "If that Domagalla was as quick at bridge . . ."

BRESLAU, THAT SAME DECEMBER 19TH, 1927
TEN O'CLOCK IN THE EVENING

Mock finished summing up the results of his five-hour search. Hartner
poured some Kupferhammer sour cherry schnapps into two large glasses
and handed one to Mock.

"You were right. Let's drink to the knowledge we've acquired."

"We know a good deal about the crimes that charlatan talks about in
his sermons." Mock went to the window and stared out at the Oder's dark
mass. He thought he could hear ice-floats grating against the buttresses
of Sandbrücke. "We do not, however, know how to deal with him.
Whether to lock him up or wait for him to make a move. I'm one hundred
per cent sure our Russian prince has an unshakeable alibi. But I'm not
sure about many of the lesser issues. For example, how can the Municipal

Library possibly loan eighteenth-century publications like the *Antiquitates Silesiacae* to ordinary readers . . ."

"I'm sorry!" shouted Hartner and poured the contents of his glass into his empty stomach. "I forgot to tell you . . . You were engrossed in reading your subordinates' reports when caretaker Maron brought me a message given to him by Theodor Stein's messenger from the Municipal Library. Director Stein explained that some readers representing an institution are allowed to borrow old publications if they leave a large deposit."

"That's nice," muttered Mock. "But what deposit could an alcoholic like Gelfrert afford? What institution did he represent?"

"Director Stein has answered the second question. Gelfrert was Secretary of the Society of Devotees of the Silesian Fatherland."

"It's good of Director Stein to look into that for us."

"Not only did he look into it." Hartner, worked up, poured yet another glass down his throat. "He also sent me a list of members belonging to that society – he is, as it happens, its president – and an extract from the Register of Loans . . ."

"Did he indeed? I'm listening, Doctor. Please go on . . ."

"It looks as if eight readers borrowed Barthesius' work before Gelfrert. They all have unusual names . . ."

"In what way are they unusual?"

"In that they're the names of historical figures."

"I'd be glad if you'd tell me them."

"My dear Counsellor, you can even see their faces. They all appear in the Leopold Lecture Theatre at our alma mater . . ."

"I don't understand," Mock rotated his glass and observed the drops of schnapps trickling down the curved sides. "I'm rather unwell today, rather sad, rather tired . . . Please speak clearly."

"Some reader or readers borrowed Barthesius' *Antiquitates Silesiacae* to browse through in the reading room, and instead of entering their own names in the register, wrote down the names of eminent scholars and benefactors of our university whose portraits can be found in the Leopold Lecture Theatre. Unless they really were the names of the readers . . . Unless Franz Wentzl, Peter Canisius, Johann Carmer and Carl von Hoym visited the Municipal Library's reading room last year . . ." Hartner joined Mock at the window and stared for a minute at the small number of black birds perched on a fast-moving ice floe. "You'll have a lot to report to President of Police Kleibömer if Mühlhaus has managed to arrange a meeting for you. Come on, let's drink to the end of a good day – we've managed to settle so much . . ."

"I think the two of us are going to report this to the Mayor. We've finally got the swine," Mock said quietly, then shook the Director's hand and, without touching his schnapps, left the study.

BRESLAU, TUESDAY, DECEMBER 20TH, 1927
EIGHT O'CLOCK IN THE MORNING

Mock's servants, Adalbert Goczoll and his wife Marta, were dressed in their Sunday best in order to celebrate – as Adalbert told Mock when he woke him – their employer's happy return to health. The old butler had squeezed into a somewhat worn tailcoat and pulled on a pair of gloves, while his wife had wrapped herself in a dozen Silesian aprons. They served breakfast in silence and Mock, irritable from lack of sleep, also remained silent as he filled his protesting belly with apple strudel. Marta was delighted with her master's appetite, Adalbert with his own pocket, which now contained their wages for the month, and Mock with the ascetic look of the apartment, which the day before had been stripped of anything that might remind him of Sophie. The Counsellor swallowed his last sips of coffee and went into the hall. He put on his ankle boots using an amber shoehorn, took his hat and coat from Adalbert, and stood in

210

front of the mirror for a long while, pressing and smoothing the brim of his hat to give it its rightful appearance. Under his arm he slipped a brief-case he had borrowed from his servant, now filled with documents and a cake that Marta had made, and left the apartment, passing a huge sack that contained, amongst other items, a briefcase given to him once by Sophie. A sledge ordered by Adalbert was already waiting outside the tenement, its cabby talking to a newspaper vendor who was stamping his hole-ridden shoes on the icy pavement. Beneath the crumpled peak of his cap, the boy's face was green and pale. Mock took a copy of the *Breslauer Neueste Nachrichten* and in return gave him a five-mark coin and Marta's cake. Brushing off the boy's thanks, he climbed into the sledge and col-lapsed onto the hard seat. The piercing pain in his neck reminded him momentarily of the existence of deceitful wives, and of caretakers and surgeons who save lives. The coachman smoothed his impressive whiskers and cracked his whip as vigorously as if he wanted to chase away all the sorrows of the world. Hidden by his newspaper, Mock looked for any mention of crimes, the city's history and Russian aristocrats, instead of which he found mention of the Sepulchrum Mundi meeting planned for that day, negotiations concerning mutual trade between Germany and Poland, and hunger in China. The coachman disturbed him just as he was jotting down the details of von Orloff's lecture. They had stopped outside Palais Hatzfeld, where the headquarters of Regierungsbezirk Schlesien were located. Mock reached into his pocket, handed the cabby the same amount as he had given the newspaper boy a quarter of an hour earlier, and waited for his change. As he handed over the coins, sticky with grease, the cabby reproached Mock from between his broken teeth:

"That boy, you gave him such a good tip . . . It's cold, sir, and I'm a long way from home . . ."

Overcoming his disgust, the Counsellor leaned towards the cabby and whispered:

"That boy is bound to drink it all away, and you, would you invest it in anything?"

"In what, sir?" the walrus whiskers waggled.

"A new pair of stockings and garters for your daughter," Mock yelled back through the snow as he entered the palace.

Mühlhaus was standing in the lobby and, seeing Mock, glanced at his watch.

"You're punctual," he said by way of a greeting. "And what about that Hartner of yours?"

"He's usually late in a calculated and consistent manner. Always five minutes. But today he's going to be on time."

They fell silent. They both knew that the leader of the Silesian provincial government, von Schroetter, would have more understanding for Geissen's weaknesses than for Leo Hartner's aristocratic lack of punctuality. But Mock was right. Neither Hartner nor von Schroetter's secretary were late. The sleek official descended to the lobby and ceremoniously invited them up to the government leader's office. They passed busy employees – agitated secretaries and personages of greater or lesser importance, searching vainly for happiness in the Silesian provincial capital. Von Schroetter's office was arranged with Danzig furniture. The government leader greeted them no less ceremoniously than his assistant and, justifying himself with a sitting of the Silesian Landtag, requested that they come to the point as quickly as possible. Mühlhaus took this to heart and asked Mock to present the "calendar murderer" case.

"Government Leader, sir." Mock omitted the title "Excellency". "There is a murderer at work in our city who leaves pages from a calendar at the crime scenes, and a leader of a sect, a certain Alexei von Orloff, who heralds the approach of the end of the world. The latter supports his assertions with various predictions, according to which the end of the world is preceded by terrible crimes. These crimes are a repetition of crimes committed far back in time – people are being murdered in similar circumstances. Three murders – three examples of age-old crimes . . ."

Government Leader von Schroetter opened a round box from which protruded the tips of cigars. They each lit one, apart from Mühlhaus.

"Von Orloff provides proof of his theory in his lectures." Mock blew a smoke ring. "He claims that three murders from long ago have been replicated recently. All the details he provides have been noted by my men . . . Now I'm going to ask our expert, Doctor Leo Hartner, to carry on for me. I have a sore throat and can't talk for very long . . ."

"Excellency," Hartner began, glancing at Mock's notes. "Gentlemen. The first case recounted by von Orloff is that of the 'sinner's bell'. You've heard of it?" Even though every child in Germany was acquainted with the story, Hartner would not allow anyone to stop his flow. "The story's been told by Wilhelm Müller in his famous poem 'Der Glockenguss zu Breslau'.† The apprentice to a certain bell founder in fourteenth-century Breslau disobeyed his master and made a cast of a bell for the cathedral of Maria Magdalena without following his instructions. The master was so infuriated that he killed his apprentice . . ."

"Von Orloff," Mock broke in, "states that according to the most recent historical research, the apprentice was walled in alive by the bell founder in the Griffins tenement on Ring. This happened on September 12th," he glanced at Reinert's notes, "in 1342. And now let us return to the present. On November 28th, in the Griffins tenement, we found the body of Emil Gelfrert, a musician who worked at the Concert Hall. He was walled in alive. To his waistcoat was pinned a page from a calendar dated September 12th, 1927. The police pathologist, Doctor Lasarius, has confirmed that Gelfrert's death took place some time in August or September. In the fourteenth century, a bell founder's apprentice – that is,

† 'The Casting of the Bell in Breslau'.

someone who listens to and analyses the sound of a bell – and a few months ago, someone who works with sound."

"And what about Councillor Geissen?" choked von Schroetter.

"Let us proceed chronologically." Mock ignored the question. "One day later, on November 29th, we found the quartered body of an unemployed man, Berthold Honnefelder. On the table lay a calendar with the date of November 17th marked. We didn't have to ask Doctor Lasarius when that death occurred . . ."

"This happened at Taschenstrasse 23–24." Hartner adored lecturing and the Government Leader was a most appreciative listener, since he was bursting with curiosity. "In 1546, in more or less the same place, a certain boltsmith known as Tromba was quartered just where the town fortifications used to be, beyond Ohlauer Tor. We know neither the perpetrator nor the motive. I discovered all this in Barthesius' work, *Antiquitates Silesiacae*. The worst thing is that the murderer seems to be playing games with us. Honnefelder lived at the house of the Golden Bell-Cast . . ."

A dreadful silence descended.

"A boltsmith then – and now an unemployed locksmith, Berthold Honnefelder," Mock broke the silence, somewhat irritated by the ambitions of Doctor Hartner, who was stepping boldly into police territory. "The third victim was known to you, sir, and you are aware of the circumstances of that murder. Councillor Geissen and a prostitute, Rosemarie Bombosch, were murdered in exactly the same way as the Austrian Emperor Albert the Second's chamberlain nearly five hundred years ago. The Emperor had chosen Breslau as his base for expeditions against the Polish King, Kazimierz Jagiellończyk, in his battle for the Czech throne. His chamberlain . . ."

" . . . went, according to Barthesius," Hartner interrupted Mock, considering the past to be his domain, "on December 9th to a certain brothel in Nicolaivorstadt, where he was killed and robbed. The prostitute he was with didn't survive either. Unfortunately, Barthesius gives no details of the crime . . ."

"On December 9th," concluded Mock, "Councillor Geissen was murdered in the arms of a prostitute. This was at Burgfeld 4, that is, in Nicolaivorstadt."

At these last words, the Government Leader flushed and reached for the case containing his fountain pen. He opened and closed the case several times, and his visitors caught a glimpse of a dedication engraved on it. The flush spread slowly across von Schroetter's bald head and grew in intensity.

"What, in fact, are you doing here?" he yelled suddenly and leaped to his feet. "Have you come here to ask my permission to arrest some Russky marquis?" With a chubby fist he thumped the desk with all his might. "Why isn't that swine already locked up in your station at Schuhbrücke? Are you waiting for more crimes to be committed?"

"With all respect," Mühlhaus now joined in for the first time, "please kindly note, Your Excellency, that these crimes are being reported in newspapers that von Orloff is bound to read. He presents his proof at the lectures only after a crime has been committed, that is, as Counsellor Mock and Doctor Hartner ascertained in the reading room yesterday, after the appropriate paragraphs have appeared in the press. Consequently, we have absolutely no reason to arrest him. No judge is going to sentence a man simply because some murders prove useful to him as he argues the end of the world. At present this is nothing more than a trail leading us to von Orloff and throwing a shadow of suspicion over him or somebody else from his sect."

"Yes . . ." von Schroetter sat down at his desk and extinguished his cigar in the ashtray, staring for a moment at the crumbled leaves, which resembled the wings of a squashed, monstrous insect. "You're right . . .

There are no grounds for the arrest of von Orloff, but somehow we've got . . ."

"Allow me, Your Excellency." Mühlhaus filled his mouth with the taste of his beloved tobacco for the first time that day. "There is one way out. We must find out the time and place of the next murder. In that way we'll spare the next victim and set a trap for the murderer."

"How do you intend to do that?" asked von Schroetter, raising a cup to his lips.

"The murders," Hartner once more assumed a didactic tone, "are being committed in chronological order. Unfortunately, this chronology applies only to the day's date. So the crime models could have occurred in any century. The first took place in the Middle Ages, the second during the Renaissance, and the third in the Baroque period. So all available sources must now be studied to uncover murders that were committed after . . ." he hesitated. "What date is it today? Yes, from December 20th onwards . . . Paying attention to the date and not the year . . ."

"Who is to do this?" inquired von Schroetter.

"That's what we've come to see you about, Excellency," answered Mühlhaus. "A team of experts must now be assembled to begin research- ing the archives as swiftly as possible."

"What skills do these people need?" The Government Leader relaxed in finding himself in the role of organizer once again. "And how many of them should there be?"

"They have to know Latin," said Hartner. "They have to be able to read manuscripts and old publications, and work tenaciously day and night – for which they will be paid appropriately. If we want to find the date of the next crime as quickly as possible and spare any prospective victim . . . we would need quite a number of people . . ."

"Apart from that they must be beyond any suspicion," added Mock. "We cannot entrust someone with this task who might themselves be the

216

murderer. We mustn't forget that it's someone for whom the archives hold no secrets. And these are the people among whom we will be looking for our experts."

"Exactly," von Schroetter said, taking a blank sheet of paper and noting something down. "And who is going to draw up this team?"

"The man who will lead it," Mühlhaus replied. "Doctor Hartner."

BRESLAU, THAT SAME DECEMBER 20TH, 1927
HALF PAST NINE IN THE MORNING

Mühlhaus and Mock parted with Hartner outside the door of the clerk's office who, on the instructions of the Government Leader, was to write out an appropriate contract for the newly appointed head of this team of experts. They went down to the main hall in silence, left Palais Hatzfeld, and set off towards the Police Praesidium. Snow settled on the brims of their hats.

"There's one thing that interests me." With his palm Mühlhaus rubbed his ears, frostbitten in trenches on the Russian front on the Chvina. "Are these crimes only being replicated in Breslau? And if so, how does von Orloff explain this? Why does the end of the world have to take place right here in our town?"

"No." Mock observed two men clad in greatcoats load balls of frozen horse manure onto a cart. "Not only in Breslau, but in Wiesbaden too. I've got to telephone someone there. But it's a good question. We'll have to ask von Orloff."

"He might tell you the crimes are being committed by Satan, or by an exterminating angel heralding the end of the world."

"If the end of the world really is to come about, then it should have been an actual bell founder's apprentice living in the Griffins tenement. As it is we have a strange substitute, a drunken musician transported to

217

the Griffins tenement by some dark angel . . . This angel reminds me of a schoolboy who cheats at exams, even though he's perfectly capable of answering the questions himself . . ."

BRESLAU, THAT SAME DECEMBER 20TH, 1927
THREE O'CLOCK IN THE AFTERNOON

The usual lunchtime bustle reigned in Schweidnitzer Keller. Baker women stood in their usual spots at the entrance, selling bread rolls and sausages. Waiters dressed in cassocks as if from centuries gone by rushed around like busy bees, carrying trays of plates, jugs, glasses and tankards above their heads. Some bore large wooden trays with wine cups the size of two Silesian quarts. These were filled with "white" or "dark sheep", as the products of the Keller's brewery had been called since time immemorial. Their ankle-length aprons and the napkins thrown neatly over their arms glowed white in the dim light of the restaurant. On the walls gleamed squares of wood panelling. At one of the tables, under the insignia of student associations, shone the white cuffs of a shirt: a man was assiduously reading some documents, tilting back his head from time to time – as far as his surgical corset permitted – and staring at the ceiling. He looked as if he was trying to learn something by heart. He raised his tankard to drink the last drops of his beer. The head waiter, whose eyes had hardly left him, immediately sent a junior waiter to this peruser of documents to ask if there was anything else Criminal Counsellor Mock wished. Mock did wish something else. He wished another Fabian beer. This request was swiftly fulfilled by the waiter, who was speechless at the thought of talking to a famous police officer. The hero of Breslau took a long draught of the beer and looked once more at the list of members belonging to Breslau's occult societies, prepared for him by Domagalla. Next to the names of those listed was no more than a short note: their age, their profession, and whether or not they were mentioned in any police files. Similar details appeared on another list prepared by the Director of the Municipal Library, Theodor Stein. Those people listed by Stein, however, were distinguished by an entirely different, far safer and more down to earth passion: they were devotees of Silesia and Breslau. Mock's suspicious nature did not allow him to put aside any of the lists, and he kept sowing questions such as: "Why did the forty-five-year-old house-wife, Christel Buschhorn, get involved in the Rosicrucian movement?", or "How did roaming the cobbled streets of Breslau and studying the town inspire the thirty-eight-year-old postman, Paul Fink, to join the Society of Devotees of the Silesian Fatherland?"

Hartner approached the alcove and greeted Mock, interrupting his musings on the causes of human motivation.

"I've already got twelve men together, mainly school professors," he said happily, accepting a menu from the waiter. "Nobody has declined. They were probably tempted by the generous remuneration. Von Schroetter has allowed me to recruit only eight, so I had to invent some sort of criteria to help me make the selection. I told them all to submit a description of their scholarly work and a bibliography. The decision is now yours, Counsellor. A starter of *kesselwurst* for me, followed by veal cutlet with egg and anchovy," he said to the waiter who stood by politely, waiting for Mock's order.

"And you, sir . . ."

"Ye-es . . ." murmured the Counsellor. "For me, cod in mustard butter and eel in aspic with baked potatoes. Yes, that's all." He looked at Hartner. "You're right, now it's down to me. I'll veto them, and if the result is unfavourable, we won't waste the Mayor's money. But, but . . . I'm assuming, quite unnecessarily, that there's someone we aren't going to take on board. Personally, I can't imagine what could disqualify the docile teachers you've gathered . . . Unless . . ."

219

Mock scanned Hartner's list and then, engrossed in the bibliographies, became immune to all distractions. He did not see the starters placed in front of him by the waiter, did not smell the tobacco, did not hear the clatter of cutlery or the hiss of beer being poured from barrels. All he could see were two names that appeared on both of the lists in front of him; in those names, occultism was linked to a sentiment for the Silesian Fatherland, complex human motivations became straightforward and clear, and human aims unambiguous and murderous.

"Listen, Doctor Hartner," Mock said, regaining control of his senses. "You remember that, apart from Gelfrert, there were eight men who borrowed Barthesius' *Antiquitates Silesiacae* from the Municipal Library. They were the *viri Leopoldini*:† Urban Papst – Pope Urban VIII, that is – Franz Wentzl, Peter Canisius, Johann Carmer, Carl von Hoym. And now we have an interesting candidate for our team: Professor Erich Hockermann, a member of the Society of Devotees of the Silesian Fatherland and author of a monograph on famous men whose portraits can be admired in the Leopold Lecture Theatre. (It's a good thing you asked the candidates to prepare a bibliography of their works!) The names of these men appear in the Register of Loans. Why are they there? They could have come from the pen of someone who's thinking about them, or studying them. And who could be studying them more thoroughly than the author of a monograph about them?" All at once Mock felt a stabbing pain in his neck, an itchy throat and the pressure of his corset. "I believe Hockermann read Barthesius in the reading room, not at home, and then signed himself in using the names of 'Leopold's men'. If Hockermann had wanted to borrow Barthesius to take home, he could have done so far more easily than Gelfrert just by signing his own name. He is, after all, a professor at a secondary school! There is only one explanation: he didn't want anyone to know he was studying this ancient publication." Mock

† Leopold's men.

glanced regretfully at his cod as it grew cool, and continued his deductions in a whisper. "And as for this employee of the Municipal Archives, Wilhelm Diehlsen, we don't have to strain ourselves too much to consider him suspicious. According to Domagalla's list, he's a member of the occult organization the Breslau Society of Parapsychic Research."

Mock paused and started on his cod, which was now almost cold.

"And what are we going to do with them?" Hartner stared at Mock in bewilderment. "Not accept them on our team?"

"Oh, we'll accept them alright" – thick globs of eel in aspic dissolved in Mock's mouth – "so as to observe their skills carefully. My men aren't going to let them out of their sight. Nor any of your other experts. If they've got anything to do with the crimes, they'll try to deceive us, give us a different date so we can't lie in wait for anyone. Somebody is going to have to check their results every day, slowly and accurately . . . In secret, out of the team's normal working hours . . . And we're coming up to Christmas . . ."

"My wife's going to Poland today, to spend Christmas with her parents," Hartner said with a smile, lighting a postprandial cigarette. "I'm to join them on Christmas Eve. Another beer for me," he told the waiter dancing up to the table. "You too?"

"No." Mock thought he was hearing a stranger's voice. "Two are enough for today. Besides, I'm going to a lecture – I can't turn up drunk."

BRESLAU, THAT SAME DECEMBER 20TH, 1927
SIX O'CLOCK IN THE EVENING

The white-painted lecture hall in the Monistic Community of Breslau's building on Grünstrasse was too small to hold all the listeners who either believed in or doubted the imminent coming of the Apocalypse. The former applauded the lecturer who was just stepping up to the lectern; the latter pouted their lips contemptuously or whistled. Mock, although he firmly identified with the opponents of the Apocalypse, clapped with measured enthusiasm and studied the people around him. The majority were women of a certain age, angry and sullen, incessantly repeating the words "such is the truth", and asserting their aversion to everything that might burst through the corset of their principles and conventions. The small number of men, generally in their retirement, laughed out loud as they mentally levelled accusations at the lecturer that they had formulated long in advance. There were also a few present who betrayed signs of mental illness. A young man huddled in the fur collar of a worn, checked coat kept standing up and raising his hand and, since nobody gave him the opportunity to speak, would sit down again violently in his chair, curling up and hunching his narrow, rounded shoulders, and cutting himself off from the rest of the audience with a wall of furious glances. A grey-haired man with especially Semitic features sat next to Mock, browsing through notes coded in a complicated system of symbols and peering affectionately at his neighbour in the hope of attracting his admiration. When Mock maintained his stony expression, the man began to snort scornfully and tried to interest his neighbour on the other side – a plump, old woman whose multi-tiered hairstyle was crowned with a hat the size of a sailing boat – in his mysterious notes. In the corner, next to a stove belching heat, two schoolboys tussled in threadbare uniforms, rings of dried, salty sweat visible under their arms. Mock felt he stood out from von Orloff's audience and feverishly racked his brains for ways to disguise himself. Fortunately, all eyes were fixed on Prince Alexei himself.

The speaker raised his arms to calm the clapping, whistling audience. The protruding, tangled bristles of a grey beard encircled his round and flat countenance. Small, sharp eyes with Mongolian folds scanned the faces of the crowd. Slowly. From one listener to another. As they glided across Mock's face, the latter bared his teeth in an enthusiastic smile. The man sitting beside him sensed a brotherly soul in his neighbour and leaned over to say something. Mock listened to him understandingly and nodded his clear approval. Any further expressions of fellowship from the Counsellor were interrupted by a mighty shout. The voice of the prophet reverberated in the hall.

"Yes, my brothers," boomed a deep bass. "The end is nigh. The Lord's wrath will inundate us all and only the just will survive the flood."

The lady with the sailing boat on her head raised her short finger and nodded in agreement, while the young man in the fur collar spun around and blessed everyone.

"A revolution of the Wheel of Life and Death is taking place and the mandala of incarnations is coming to its end," von Orloff continued in a calmer voice. "History is repeating itself. The history of evil, murder and despair. The history of slaughter, corruption and sodomy. Oh, Sodom," roared the speaker. "Be cursed and die . . ."

Mock's neighbour was filling the pages of his notebook with strange signs, the schoolboys were making faces at each other as if to say "told you so", and Mock wondered whether von Orloff had prepared his performance or was improvising. The string of associations would rather suggest the latter: from sodomy the speaker had moved on to Sodom.

"Oh, Sodom," a theatrical whisper filled the air, "the chosen ones will leave you, the chosen ones will not look back at you. With joy they will welcome the waves of sulphur that will burn away your vile bodies. Brothers!" yelled von Orloff. "Be with the chosen ones."

The modulation of the speaker's voice caused one wrinkled old woman, who had been jostling with the schoolboys for a place beside the stove, to wake up and burst into rapid sobs.

"Brothers," von Orloff raised his finger, a gesture repeated by a large number of the ladies gathered in the hall. "All over the world, crime is triumphant. But crime is revealing its former face, crime is telling us: 'I've been here already, I've been committed before, many ages ago.'" The speaker fell silent and sought understanding in the eyes of his listeners. "Yes, my brothers, old crimes, hidden in chronicles of the past, are being renewed in Sodom . . . And these are the oldest crimes, the cruellest, inhuman . . . Because only they can move the inhabitants of Sodom to conversion . . . Yesterday, in Buenos Aires, a child's torn-off leg was found on a rubbish heap. A hundred years ago, a Spanish marquis tore apart an illegitimate child borne by his daughter . . ."

"Where was that?" Mock felt rotten breath on his ear.

"In Argentine," he replied rather loudly, expelling the words with a hiss.

"Yes, my dear sir," von Orloff roared at Mock. "In Buenos Aires, Argentine. But dreadful murders, murders from the past, are being committed here too. A man was walled in alive in the very heart of our town, another quartered not far from here, another still drained of blood and hung upside down . . . All these murders have already taken place once . . . a very long time ago . . . Do you want proof, sir?"

Mock's neighbour, thinking that the speaker was addressing him, jumped up delightedly and shouted:

"Yes, yes! I want proof!"

"Sit down! Keep quiet! We know the proof! It's irrefutable!" the crowd began to bawl.

Von Orloff stood silent. The break in his oratory had a disciplinary effect on his listeners.

"Yet there is deliverance for us." His narrow lips, concealed beneath a coarse moustache, were stretched in a broad smile. "A holy man is coming to us . . . He will save us . . . It is not I – I am but his prophet; I announce his coming and the funeral of the world, the eternal grave of the world, *sepulchrum mundi* . . . I am not worthy to tie the strap of his sandal . . .

He will save us and take us with him to the seventh heaven . . . Brothers, be among the chosen ones!"

"When is he coming?" The question shouted out by the man in the fur collar contained no curiosity. It contained longing. Mock smiled inwardly, expecting an elusive response. It turned out, however, to be very concrete.

"The holy man will be conceived in four days' time, on Christmas Eve. The eve of Christ's birth is the day of the new saviour's conception. The birth of the old saviour will empower those who are to beget the new. Christ was conceived of a modest virgin, and God was his father through the intermediary of the Holy Spirit . . . He came into the world in a place intended for animals, in utter degradation . . . The new prophet will be begotten in even greater degradation . . . For here is the holy book of prophecies, *Sepulchrum Mundi*. Listen to what the Master says in his conversation with the Disciple in Book III." Von Orloff opened a large book bound in white leather and began to read from it. "'Master,' asked the Disciple, 'why must the saviour be conceived of a Babylonian harlot?' 'Verily, I say, God is closest to you when you sin . . . His power is then greatest because it is entirely focussed on you, to turn you away from sin. That is why the new saviour will be conceived in sin, of a sinful woman, of a Babylonian harlot, because only in this way will God's power rest upon him.' So speaks the book of prophecies."

When the elder finished reading he collapsed onto a chair behind him. From where he sat, Mock could discern beads of sweat forming on von Orloff's Mongolian folds. A tall youth who had been selling tickets before the lecture now approached the pulpit.

"Ladies and gentlemen," he said, "the Prince is ready for your questions. Please don't hesitate to ask. This is your last chance. The next lecture will not take place until Saturday. The Count is going away on a lecture tour to Berlin and won't be back in Breslau until that day, Christmas Eve."

225

The young man in the moth-eaten, fur-collared coat raised his hand yet again that afternoon. Von Orloff nodded at him.

"I have a question." The young man threw distrustful glances at his neighbours. "Who is going to impregnate the harlot?"

"*Spiritus flat ubi vult*,"† von Orloff replied thoughtfully.

BRESLAU, WEDNESDAY, DECEMBER 21ST, 1927
THREE O'CLOCK IN THE AFTERNOON

"*Spiritus flat ubi vult*," Mühlhaus scowled as Mock finished telling him about von Orloff's lecture. "That was his answer you say . . ."

There was silence. As he observed the Criminal Director, Hartner realized that this unthinking repetition of the Latin sentence, the sudden brooding and the closing of the eyes suggested that the police chief had been overcome by intellectual languor after a satisfying lunch. Unlike Hartner, the police officers sitting in Mühlhaus' office were used to their chief's inconsequent remarks, and to repetitions that might appear thoughtless, had these not betrayed the feverish workings of a mind that, by and large, came up with pertinent ideas, a simple and inspiring summation of facts, or a new hypothesis. That was not the case this time – Mühlhaus had no ideas at all. Hartner felt an annoying itch in his lower back and recognized it to be a burning impatience. He decided to relish the knowledge he had acquired that day, and the ignorance of those present.

"What do you think about all this, Mock?" asked Mühlhaus.

"The whores are going to be rather busy on Christmas Eve. All the followers of Sepulchrum Mundi are going to be seeking out the Babylonian harlot."

"You can spare us the feeble jokes," Mühlhaus drawled quietly – lunch

† The spirit blows where it wills.

226

had deprived him of any desire to respond more energetically – "and tell us something that might interest us."

"I received a short report on von Orloff and the Sepulchrum Mundi from Criminal Counsellor Domagalla," Mock obeyed his chief. "It contains the guru's life story and some very brief information about his activities in Breslau, where he's been for about a year. Shall I read it out to you?"

Mühlhaus closed his eyes to express his consent, and with his small skewer began to drill through the carbonized tobacco that blocked the shank of his pipe. Reinert rested his heavy head on his hand, squashing a chubby cheek. Ehlers rolled a cigarette and Kleinfeld made sucking noises in an effort to probe a rotten tooth with his tongue. From outside came the joyful cries of children. Mock walked up to the window and saw a sleigh attached to a large sledge, a coachman, and a malnourished hack that had just raised its tail to leave a memento on the dirty snow covering Ursulinenstrasse. A little, laughing girl left her group and toddled over to the coachman. Her cheeks were tinged with blood-red stains. Mock turned away, not wanting to know whether it was blood on the child's cheeks or an ordinary flush, whether the coachman was the girl's perverted neighbour or her father who, in a few years' time, would sell her into the bondage of some brothel madam. Mock did not want to know anything about the empty, cold linen of his marital bed, and his servants' desperate efforts to avoid the subject of their mistress; he was interested in nothing but the apocalypse foretold by the Russian aristocrat.

"We have the employees of the Ministry of Foreign Affairs to thank for this report, which was put together at the request of Criminal Counsellor Herbert Domagalla. Unfortunately, all they have at their disposal is a biography written by our guru himself. Count Alexei Konstantinovich Orloff was born in 1857 on the Zolotoye Selo estate near Kishyniev, and comes from a wealthy, aristocratic family. He finished cadet school in St

Petersburg in 1875 and began his military service in the Caucasus. In 1879, after the war with the Turks, he unexpectedly abandoned his military career and entered a spiritual seminary in Tbilisi. He was expelled from there in 1881 for – as he writes – 'a lack of humility and for his intellectual independence'. He spent the next ten years in Moscow, where he published a novel, *Plague*, as well as numerous philosophical pamphlets and magazine articles. One can assume that he lived off his rich family." Mock paused and looked intently at the sleepy listeners. "He was particularly proud of one of these articles, and Domagalla has had it translated into German to enclose with his report. I read it yesterday. It is, *sit venia verbo*,† a terrifying religious apotheosis of evil and degradation." Mock swallowed with revulsion. "Every criminal ought to read it and commit murder, happy in the knowledge that, at the moment of the murder, he is in all but tangible contact with God himself . . ."

This description of von Orloff's thesis made no great impression on anyone except Hartner. Mühlhaus was ploughing in his pipe with his skewer, Reinert was dozing, Ehlers smoked and Kleinfeld, with masochistic pleasure, was drawing new waves of subtle pain from his tooth. Hartner bit his tongue and shivered.

"Von Orloff left for Warsaw in 1890," Mock continued, "where he undertook his own private war with Catholicism. He published lampoons on the papacy and theological polemics on the Catholic concept of sin. Von Orloff appended one of these to his biography, and we also have a translation of it at our disposal. In it he claims there is no escaping sin, that sin cannot be eradicated, that we have to live with sin, and even cherish it. Our guru was probably an agent of the Okhrana, the Tsar's secret police, because in 1905 he was shot by Polish freedom fighters. He was seriously wounded and, as he writes, only hospitalization in Germany saved his life. That year he found himself in Breslau, in

† If I may use the words.

Bethanien Hospital. He was then discharged for convalescence, travelled across Europe and returned in 1914 to Breslau. At the outbreak of war, he was interned here as a Russian citizen and locked up in the prison on Kletschkauerstrasse. He left prison a year later, founded the Sepulchrum Mundi sect in Breslau and, as he claims, conducted research into the philosophy of history." Mock paused and tapped a cigarette against his silver cigarette-case. "Well, so much for his life story. Now for the reports from Domagalla's men. The officers in Department II of the Police Praesidium took an interest in von Orloff after he came into close contact with Breslau's Society of Parapsychic Research, which Domagalla suspected – listen to this! – of procuring orphanage children for wealthy perverts. This was never proven, but von Orloff still ended up on our files. Up until September of this year, nothing more was heard of him, but since October he has been extremely active. He's been giving two lectures a week, during which he works himself extremely hard. That is everything in Domagalla's report. As to what took place at yesterday's holy service of the Sepulchrum Mundi, I've already told you."

Mock lit a cigarette for the first time since leaving the hospital. The fragrant smoke of the Halpaus drifted down into his lungs and filled his head with a light, pleasant confusion. He looked at the bored expressions of his colleagues and then, feeling a prickling in his throat and a stabbing pain in his spine, sat down in his chair.

"That is all, gentlemen," Mühlhaus broke the silence. "We can go home. Oh, I'm sorry Doctor Hartner . . . I see you have something to add . . ."

"Yes." Hartner pulled a neat pile of cards fastened with a paper clip from his yellow, pigskin briefcase. He spoke very slowly, savouring the anticipated outburst of knowledge, questions and admiration. "In the space of one day, the commission I am leading arrived at an interesting conclusion. As you know, gentlemen, the last murder was committed on

229

December 9th. I told my team, therefore, to look for a crime committed between December 9th and the end of the year." Like every armchair scholar, Hartner suffered from a galling lack of listeners, and decided to hold their attention by means of retardation. "As Counsellor Mock has stated, the most recent murder differed from the others in that, in all certainty, it had to be discovered . . . I no longer quite remember your reasoning . . ."

"Well," Mock said, extinguishing his cigarette, "the first crime could quite easily have gone undiscovered if the shoemaker in whose workshop Gelfrert had been walled up had had a weaker sense of smell. The neighbours would have found Honnefelder after two or three weeks, when the corpse's stench would have begun to penetrate beyond the walls and closed doors of the room. Geissen had to be discovered very quickly, either by the caretaker or by another client entering Rosemarie Bombosch's room. The murderer is shortening the time span between the crime being committed and its discovery . . . If this isn't mere coincidence then the next murder will be committed practically before our very eyes . . . If only we knew when and where it is to take place . . ."

"And we do know," Hartner said, dragging out the syllables and relishing the sight of flushed cheeks, shining eyes and trembling hands. "We do know. The next murder will take place on Christmas Eve. And it will be committed at Antonienstrasse 27. We even have the time – half past seven. In that tenement on that same day at that time in 1757, two people were killed . . ."

BRESLAU, SATURDAY DECEMBER 24TH, 1757,
TEN O'CLOCK IN THE EVENING

The town was wrapped in smoke from hearths and dying fires. It wound its way over roofs and was sent back down chimneys by a gusting wind.

Prussian mercenaries, who had three days earlier conquered the town, were still drinking in the inns and bawdy houses. The wind forced the hat of a Prussian foot soldier down over his eyes as he watched, in the glow of torchlight, a merchant seated up on the box of a large wagon. Candles in the windows of the factory next to Nicolai Tor threw flickering reflections onto the two men and the sergeant who, armed with a spontoon, had now approached them. The sergeant nodded to his men who were sheltering from the gale behind a low stone wall by the round tower, and motioned to the merchant to proceed, receiving in return a small barrel of honey and a casket of alum. The merchant's wagon rolled into the narrow Nicolaistrasse, the horse's hooves squelching through the slush and horse manure. The candles on a Christmas tree decorated with apples shimmered in the window of the corner house. A dog lying outside the house growled at the merchant, and then put all his energy into scratching at the door and whimpering. The tired horse pulled the wagon along the embankments, then turned into Antonienstrasse and stopped at the back of the Franciscan monastery, beside a small, wooden house where not a single light was burning. The Town Hall flautist sounded for supper. The merchant climbed down from his wagon and went into the yard. On wooden frames in the neglected garden hung lengths of felt, stiff with frost. He approached the small servant's room and peered in through the window. Two apprentice weavers were sitting drinking weak beer, with a basket of bread rolls in front of them. The merchant anxiously retraced his steps to enter at the front of the house. In the entrance hall, he inhaled the smell of prunes. He leaned against the small barrel of beer standing outside the door to the room and felt a wave of drowsiness. He opened the door and found himself in his familiar, warm world of many varied scents. From the stove drifted the aroma of gingerbread cake; from a pigpen in the corner came the stench of animal excrement; from the barrel dug into the dust floor, the pleasant smell of salted meat. The stove was lit but, because its little door had been closed, the fire gave out only a dim light. The merchant sat down at the table and another of his senses came into play: he heard the scratching of a mouse, the banging of wooden shutters, the moaning of a woman in the next room, the rustle of a weasel's paws on straw, and the rustle of straw in the mattress, the grating of forces unknown in the beams sunk in the wall, the familiar throaty cries of ecstasy coming from the woman, the hiss of the fire in the stove, the panting of a man and the squeaking of bedboards beneath them. The merchant quietly went outside to his wagon, stroked the horse's muzzle, threw aside the caparison that covered the cart and groped about in search of something among the sacks of salt, barrels of honey and little bales of Ghent cloth. He found a small chest of medicines. He returned to the room and sat down by the stove. His feet were numb with cold. From the chest he took a syringe and a bottle of liquid from which he filled the syringe completely. He then approached the door to the side room and, by the sounds that came from within, soon recognized the approach of those final moments when lovers feverishly reach the point of climax. The merchant entered the room and stroked the face of the baby asleep in its cot. Then he focussed his entire attention on the amorous scene. In the feeble light of the Christmas Eve star he made out an enormous backside bouncing up and down between a pair of legs spread wide. On the floor lay a uniform braided with cord and a tall hat with two plumes. The outfit revealed the man to be a Prussian hussar. The merchant regained control of his feet at once; he no longer felt cold. He bounded onto the bed and sat on the man's back. With one hand he pressed down on the man's neck, with the other he plunged the syringe into his buttock, pumping in its entire contents. The hussar threw off the merchant, leaped from the bed and reached for his sword. Then he started to choke. The woman stared in horror at her husband, the syringe in his hand, and sensed the inevitable approach.

232

Barasch Brothers department store was bursting at the seams. It was mostly filled with children running around frenetically, paying no heed to the trickles of sweat running down from under their caps. In the enormous two-storeyed hall encircled by two galleries, metre-long metal arrows hung from the glass ceiling and pointed towards the toy stalls. They moved up and down on springs activated by men employed temporarily for the Christmas and New Year period. So the children knew perfectly well how to find the smiling Father Christmases who, demonstrating the allure of the goods on sale, set colourful tops spinning wildly, carefully mounted the rocking horses, rummaged through armies of lead soldiers, stuck dummies into the mouths of unwilling dolls, set porcelain lions upon tortoise-shell giraffes, made wound-up strongmen lift weights, and ran trains incessantly along the same electric route.

Mock unbuttoned his coat, removed his hat, smoothed his unruly waves of hair and sat down on a quilted seat made of two concentric cylinders. Leaning back comfortably, he began to wonder why he had come. All he knew was that he had been drawn there by an irrepressible urge that had emerged from his earlier ruminations, but realized, to his horror, that he could not remember what they were. To reconstruct this chain of associations, he would have to go back to Hartner's story. He remembered his efforts to justify the actions of the merchant's unfaithful wife: she sinned, and therefore she was human, extremely human! Bah! Alexei von Orloff would claim that, at the moment of sinning, she was closer to God! And how would that Russian sage judge her husband's actions? In killing her, he too was committing a sin! Which of them was closer to God? The one whose sin was the greater?

Mock recalled his violent reaction to this perverse axiology of sin, and his attack of rage when he had passed Sommé the jeweller's. "Isn't it better to get rid of the sin," he thought at the time, "and forget it rather than dwell upon it?" The notion of rejecting sin provoked another thought – little Eberhard's First Confession in the vast Schutzengel church in Waldenburg, his father's work-worn hand shaking his when he apologized to his parents for his sins. He did not really know what he was apologizing for – he did not feel that he had any sins, even regretted not having any, and thought he was deceiving his father. Eberhard Mock could still feel the hard pressure of shoemaker Johannes Mock's hand as he watched the children tearing themselves away from their parents and running around under the huge neon sign, GEBR. BARASCH. Now he knew why he had come to the department store. He stood up, made his way to the alcohol counter and bought a square bottle of Schirdewan schnapps, which his brother Franz adored.

"The next crime won't be committed for another three days," he thought as he passed a string quartet playing the Christmas carol "*O, Tannenbaum*"† on the ground floor. "So I've got plenty of time. All my men have got a bit of time before Christmas Eve. So I can get happily drunk – and anyway, why should I get morbidly drunk?"

BRESLAU, THAT SAME DECEMBER 21ST, 1927
HALF PAST FOUR IN THE AFTERNOON

Mock just about managed to climb to the fourth floor of the tenement on Nicolaistrasse and, panting loudly, knocked hard on one of the four doors. It was opened by Irmgard, who then turned away and sat on a stool like an automaton. Stove lids rattled. Mock looked into the anxious eyes of his sister-in-law, and walked past her to enter the room. Railway engineer Franz Mock was sitting at the table in a collarless shirt. Strong, black tea ate into the enamel mug in front of him. The muscles of his forearms

† "O, Christmas Tree"

tensed as the index fingers and thumbs of both hands gripped a lined sheet of paper covered in even handwriting. Eberhard stood the schnapps on the table and, without removing his coat or hat, reached for the letter. Franz gripped it even harder and began to read in a strong, hard voice:

Dear Mama,

I'm leaving your house for ever. It was more of a prison than a home for me, more a gloomy dungeon than a peaceful haven. And in that dungeon I was kicked around by a raging tyrant. He didn't even try to understand me and had only a coarse notion of a world in which every poet has to be a Jew or a homosexual, and where life grants a prescription for success only to railway engineers. I'm giving up school and I'm going to live with a woman with whom I wish to spend the rest of my days. Don't look for me. I love you and uncle Eberhard. Keep well, and farewell for ever.

Yours,

Erwin

When Franz finished reading the letter, he raised his head and stared at his brother. In his eyes lurked the certainty of his impending judgement.

"He thinks of you as his father," he hissed through clenched teeth. "You got what you wanted, eh, you filthy swine? You brought my son up for me. You couldn't produce one of your own with that useless prick of yours, so you made it your business to bring mine up instead . . ."

Eberhard fastened his coat, turned up his collar, pulled his hat down on his head and left the room. A few seconds later he returned for the square bottle of Schirdewan schnapps, his older brother Franz's favourite.

It was loud and crowded in the Silesia pastry shop on Ohlauerstrasse. Wrapped in a fog of cigarette smoke, waitresses in navy-blue dresses and lace collars slalomed between the bar and the marble tables, the misted mirrors, the noisy shopkeepers, the office workers stuffing themselves with strudels, and unhappy schoolboys who blackened paper napkins with the sorrows of love, delaying the moment when they would have to settle their bills for as long as they could.

One of these "sorrowing Werthers" was racking his brain for a metaphor that might most appropriately render − in a rather Expressionistic style − Catullus' *"Odi et amo"*,† when a shadow fell on his napkin of tangled emotions. The boy looked up and recognized Mr Eberhard Mock, the uncle of his friend Erwin. In different circumstances such a meeting would have given him enormous pleasure. Now, however, the sight of the Criminal Counsellor greatly embarrassed the schoolboy, just as it had when, at a few meetings a year earlier, Mock had helped Erwin and his friends understand Livius' tortuous style; just as it had when, after several free private lessons, they had invited the Counsellor to this very same café and listened to his police tales. Without a word, Mock sat down next to the schoolboy and smiled. From his coat pocket he extracted a cigarette-case and ordered coffee and apple cake from a waitress. The schoolboy did not say anything either and wondered how he could prolong this silence indefinitely. He knew why the Criminal Counsellor had come.

"Tell me, Briesskorn," Mock pushed the cigarette-case towards the young man, "where can I find Erwin?"

"He's probably at home." Without looking at Mock, the youth fished out a cigarette from under the elasticated band.

† "I hate and yet I love". Poem 85.

Mock knew Briesskorn was lying, that this was another schoolboy's joke like the one he had cracked when – according to Erwin – their Latin teacher, Piechotta, had asked him where the predicate was in a particular sentence, and he had answered that it was between the first word in the sentence and the full stop. Mock was certain Briesskorn was lying because Erwin's uncle would have looked for him at home first, and not in this steam bath full of cakes, coffee and thick, warming liqueurs; anybody in on the secret of Erwin's absconding would have known this, and so in saying: "He's probably at home," the schoolboy had in fact meant: "I know where he is, but I'm not going to tell you."

"My dear Mr Briesskorn," Mock bored into his interlocutor with his eyes, "did you know that Professor Piechotta was a colleague of mine when we were students? A good colleague at that, almost a close friend. We went through a lot together, and drank many a beer during our students' union meetings. Many a time did we sweat together in our pews as Professor Eduard Norden glared at us, picking out a new victim to analyse the metre in one of Plautus' choruses . . . Yes . . ." He cut the apple cake with his spoon. "We were good friends, like you and my nephew Erwin; we were loyal to each other, neither of us would have betrayed the other . . . But if Ferdinand Piechotta's relative or friend had been looking for him in those distant days in order to speak to him, to prevent some foolish act, then I'd have broken my word to Piechotta . . ."

"Do you, Counsellor sir, imagine that I'm going to be persuaded to betray my friend by such an interesting proposal?" Briesskorn was twirling a second cigarette in his long fingers. "I know Piechotta hates me, and he would sooner break with you than stop tormenting me . . ."

"You insult me." Mock finished his coffee and, getting up from the table, carefully felt for the bottle in his coat pocket. "You doubt my word . . . You're not stupid – you've understood my proposal correctly. But you think I want to deceive you, that I'm a petty swindler, a shady cheat, right? Young man, do you know the meaning of friendship between men?"

"Erwin is at Inge Gänserich's," said Briesskorn and crushed the unlit cigarette in his fingers. The pale Georgia tobacco crumbled onto the marble surface of the table.

"Thank you, sir." Mock offered his hand. The schoolboy grabbed it and held on to it tightly.

"A man's word and friendship between men are without doubt the surest things in the world," said Briesskorn. "I believe you, Counsellor sir . . . The fact that I have revealed Erwin's whereabouts to you doesn't mean our friendship will die . . ."

"The surest thing in the world," Mock turned his hat in his fingers, "is death. Write that to your Lotte."

BRESLAU, THAT SAME DECEMBER 21ST, 1927
HALF PAST FIVE IN THE AFTERNOON

Mock did not need to ask anyone who Inge Gänserich was, nor where she lived. He knew the annexe at Gartenstrasse 35, behind Hartmann's haberdashery, perfectly well. This, he remembered from his files, was where the famous painter who had arrived in the Silesian capital ten years earlier now lived. At first she had tried her luck as a model. She was notorious for the fact that, if she agreed to pose for an artist, it explicitly meant she had consented to share a bed with him. Her consent was not granted very often, however, and to a large extent depended on what she would be paid. It was therefore no surprise that beautiful, mysterious and taciturn Inge became a model and muse to only the wealthiest of painters. To one of these, a certain Arno Gänserich, a painter of surrealist underwater seascapes, Inge had given her consent twice: once shortly after he had been introduced to her, and then at the altar. After a grand wedding, the young couple had lived at Gartenstrasse 35 and, to the horror and fury of their quiet and industrious neighbours, had continued with their wedding celebrations most nights for over a year. This was where Mock had seen Inge for the first time when, in 1920, he had been called in by his boss at the time, the Chief of Police of the fifth district, to quell a wild, drunken orgy organized by the newly married couple. The painterly passion of the guests at the party had made Mock's life a misery. He had roundly cursed the artistic talents of the men and women who, intoxicated with morphine, had tipped out pots of paint and mixed it together with their naked bodies, using the floor as a palette. Mock had grabbed Inge and covered her with a blanket, and then began the difficult struggle of leading her out of the apartment. Even today, as he passed Hartmann's haberdashery, he could feel her teeth in his hand, still see her pour over his suit of expensive, Polish Bielsko wool a pot of blue oil paint otherwise used by her husband in his attempts to depict the melancholy of an underwater-scape. Mock also remembered, as if from a distance and in slow motion, how he had raised his fist above Inge's shapely head and struck her a blow.

He cast aside these memories of violence against the arrested woman, and turned his thoughts to what fate had in store for Inge some time later. He remembered another summons, an autumn night and the armchair in which Arno Gänserich had ended his own life, just after he had discovered his wife with her slender thighs wrapped around the shaved head of a strongman from Busch Circus.

Mock paused on the landing and opened the window. Despite the cold, he felt sweat trickle down the inside of his surgical corset. Children were skidding around in the small yard by the light of a gas lamp. Their joyful cries startled a flock of crows who were besieging the lids of rubbish bins, and mingled with two more rasping sounds. The first of these came from a knife-grinder who had set up his pedal-powered machine in the yard, and was sharpening knives destined to sink into the soft bellies of Christmas Eve carp. The second rasping came from the water pump, where a little girl in a darned coat was swinging off its handle to fill her bucket, the heels of her over-large shoes clopping on the packed snow in time with the screech of the rusty mechanism. From the old, roofless shack at the very end of the yard there rose a thin trickle of smoke. Two children dressed as American Indians had dug four stakes into the dirt floor and hung a patched blanket over them to construct a wigwam, in the centre of which burned a campfire. A moment later Mock heard the wild cries of redskins coming from the wigwam.

He made his way upstairs, trying to remember more about Inge: opening nights of exhibitions, during which her perfect body would be wrapped in nothing but a sheet of velvet cloth; her lovers, representatives of every profession; her eroticized paintings, which disturbed the sleep of tranquil Breslauers, and her thick file in the archives of the Vice Department. All this Mock now meticulously gathered from the recesses of his mind to be used as a weapon against his crafty opponent. Someone was standing on the landing outside Inge's door. With one hand the Counsellor reached for his gun, with the other flicked on his cigarette lighter. The tiny flame illuminated the corridor. Mock put away his old Walther and offered his free hand to the man.

"Good, Meinerer," he panted. "You're where you should be."

Meinerer held out his hand without a word. In the silence of the winter afternoon, in the semi-darkness of the stairway, they could hear the moans of a woman that not even the cries of the Indians outside could drown out. The sounds were coming from beyond Inge Gänserich's door, and to them was added the dreadful squeaking of bed springs.

"Is that my nephew?" asked Mock. He did not wait for a reply and looked at Meinerer with concern. "You're tired. Take tomorrow off. Come and see me the day after tomorrow at eight, for a briefing . . . You've carried out your assignment well. We're closing Erwin Mock's case. As

240

of now, you'll be on the 'calendar murderer' case with us."

Meinerer turned without a word and went down the stairs. Mock smiled at the thought of his nephew and listened again. Minutes passed; the light in the stairwell went on and off as shabbily dressed inhabitants of the tenement passed by. One of them, an old railwayman, asked Mock what was he doing there, but a police identification card soon satisfied his curiosity. A woman's voice called her children in for supper, the shouting in the yard died down, Inge's moans died down, and the pump, the knife-grinding machine and the bed on which Erwin Mock had been proving his manhood no longer squeaked.

Mock pressed the doorbell and waited. A long time. A very long time. Eventually the door opened a little and Mock beheld a face that came to him in his dreams sometimes as Erinyes, as pangs of conscience. Inge knew who her latest lover's uncle was, and so Mock's visit could not have been a mistake. She opened the door wide and turned back into what he remembered was the only room in the apartment, leaving the Counsellor alone in the dark hall. Mock looked around and, to his surprise, did not see any easels. He breathed in but did not detect the smell of paint. His surprise was even greater when he found nothing amongst the mess to point to the profession of the mistress of the house. Erwin sat on the squeaky bed in silence, wrapped in a sheet that was gradually growing damp with his sweat.

"How nice it is here, Mrs Gänserich," said Mock, sitting down at a table strewn with cigarette ends on which he barely found room for his elbows. "Could you leave us alone for a minute, please?"

"No," Erwin said firmly. "She's to stay."

"Fine." Mock removed his coat and hat. For lack of anywhere to put them, he slung the coat over his shoulders and put the hat on his knee. "Then I'll be brief. I have a favour to ask of you. Don't give up school. You're a first-class pupil. You've got your final exams in a few months. Get them over with and then study German, philosophy or anything else your father doesn't agree to . . ."

"But you don't agree to it either, Uncle. At dinner three or four weeks ago you said . . ."

"I said what I said," Mock grew annoyed. "And I regret it. But it wasn't what I really thought at all. I wanted to tell you that when I went to fetch you from the casino, but you were too drunk."

"The words 'I'm sorry' come hard to you," said Inge. Mock gazed at her for a moment and struggled with fury, admiration and a desire to humiliate the artist. In the end, admiration won out. Inge was simply too beautiful with her dark hair loose. The mature male smelled warm bed-linen, a hot body, and sensed total satisfaction. He smiled at her and turned once more to Erwin.

"Finish school and pass your exams. If you don't want to live with your father, come and live with me. Sophie is very fond of you." He walked over to his nephew and patted him on the neck. "I'm sorry." He stood the bottle of schnapps on the table. "Let's all drink and make up."

Erwin turned to the window to hide his emotion. Inge put a handkerchief to her mouth and began to cough; and in her eyes, fixed on Mock, tears appeared. He stared back at her, but he was not thinking about her. He was thinking about what he had said: "Sophie is very fond of you"; about a reunion with his wife: they are together again, Erwin is staying with them, sleeping in Mock's study, Erwin studies for his exams, Sophie goes to see him in her husband's study . . .

"You have to apologize to her too, Uncle," Erwin said.

Silence. Then a terrifying howl resounded in the yard. Boots thudded on packed snow. Somebody had tripped or slipped on the ice and fallen heavily. Mock rushed to the window and strained his eyes. He saw nothing in the dim gaslight apart from a crowd gathered around the shack. He made for the door. The floorboards in the hallway boomed under his feet. The wooden stairs boomed. He ran out into the yard and raced across the ice, plunging into the crowd and pushing his way through. People allowed them to pass in stony silence. Mock shoved aside the last man barring his way into the shack. The latter turned furiously towards him. Mock recognized him as the old railwayman whom he had frightened with his identification. On the dirt floor of the shack lay the tattered blanket that had been used as a wigwam. From under it, in a pair of torn tights, protruded legs that were as thin as a stick. Fresh blood-stains covered the tights and a pair of shoes that were clearly too large. The rest of the body was concealed by the blanket, and next to it lay a bucket and some scattered chocolates.

Mock leaned against the wall of the shack and opened his mouth to catch snowflakes. The old railwayman came up to him and spat in his face.

"Where were you," he asked, "when he was murdering the child?"

Twenty uniformed policemen in shakoes and belted greatcoats burst into the yard, led by a senior officer with a sword at his side. The police-men surrounded the people and the shack. The crowd stood in silence looking at the whiskered faces of these guardians of law and order, at their holsters and tall caps. Mock was still leaning against the wall, feeling the damp flakes of snow tickle him at the top of his surgical corset. He did not approach the policemen, did not show his identification. He did not want to be one of them; he wanted to be a railwayman, a tailor, a travel-ling salesman.

Meinerer entered the yard with several armed police and a man lug-ging a camera tripod. He crossed the yard diagonally towards a corner from which emanated the unmistakeable smell of a cesspit. There, small toilet windows that were painted over in white stretched up the entire height of the building. The entrance to the lowest toilet was up a few steps straight from the yard.

"I locked him in there," Meinerer pointed his finger at the door unnecessarily.

The policemen accompanying Meinerer marched off in the direction he was pointing, while the remainder unfastened their holsters and eyed the crowd with hostility; it had begun to stir threateningly.

"Kill the son of a whore! People, kill that son of a whore!" roared the railwayman, and he threw himself at the nearest policeman. The latter drew his gun and fired into the air. The crowd obediently stopped dead. Mock felt a shudder run through his entire body and closed his eyes. All the corpses he had seen appeared before him: Counsellor Geissen offered him a cigar; Gelfrert blew into his French horn; Honnefelder shouted "Sieg heil"; Rosemarie Bombosch revealed her thin thighs to him with an alluring smile. And here, in this gloomy shack, he was visited by his father, who set out his tools and impaled a shoe on his shoemaker's last. Then the old blanket that had been a wigwam moved and the little girl crawled out from beneath it to join the other phantoms. A hand-knitted scarf was wound tightly around her neck and in her side there was a well-sharpened knife.

Mock covered the girl's remains again and reached for his gun. He no longer wanted to be a craftsman or a travelling salesman. Nor did he want to be a guardian of the law. He wanted to be an executioner.

He pulled his police identification card from his pocket, squeezed through the crowd and ran towards the toilet. Two policemen were dragging out a man who was handcuffed to the pedal-powered knife-grinding machine. The man was numb with cold and his blue lips were moving as if in prayer. His clothes – a workman's apron and overalls – were covered in blood. The policemen kicked him to the ground. The knife-grinding machine struck him on the temple.

Meinerer stood over the fettered murderer. The photographer released the shutter. A column of magnesium drifted upwards. Holding aloft his gun and identification, Mock ran towards the murderer. The policemen obediently let him through. The Counsellor knelt and placed the gun to the man's bloody temple. Magnesium cracked. Everyone looked on. In a fleeting vision, Mock saw himself being thrown out of the police. He released the safety catch on his gun. He saw himself again as the accused in court, and then in prison where all those whom he had put behind bars now awaited him with joy. He began to recite to himself Horace's "*Odi profanum vulgus*".† After the first verse, he put the gun away in his pocket. He knew nothing, he felt nothing – apart from the old railway-man's spittle, which was turning to ice on his cheek.

BRESLAU, THURSDAY, DECEMBER 22ND, 1927
EIGHT O'CLOCK IN THE MORNING

A special Christmas edition of the *Breslauer Neueste Nachrichten*, dated December 22nd, 1927, p.1 – interview with Police President Wilhelm Kleibömer:

What happened yesterday at Gartenstrasse 35?
Kleibömer: A Criminal Sergeant, whose name I cannot divulge, was taking part in an investigation in the building when he saw the knife-grinder leave the yard. He was trying to escape in a great hurry, dragging the knife-grinding machine behind him. The detective's attention was drawn to the bloodstains on the knife-grinder's apron. He apprehended him and locked him in the toilet on the ground floor of a neighbouring building. He then discovered, in a shack in the yard, the corpse of little Gretchen Kauschnitz. Afraid of mob law on the part of the inhabitants of the building, he brought

---

† "I loathe the unenlightened crowd".

245

in a considerable police force and, with their protection, arrested the man *lege artis.*

Somebody tried to hinder the arrest.

K.: Is that a question or a statement?

The press have a photograph of a high-ranking police officer holding a gun to the murderer's head. Did he want to take the law into his own hands?

K.: Indeed, one of my men did behave in such a manner. In view of the vile nature of the crime, an instinctive reaction like this can be understood. Fortunately, he came to his senses and left judgement to the judiciary.

Is the murderer, Fritz Roberth, a sexual pervert?

K.: Yes. He's a paedophile. He has already served a prison sentence for such a crime.

Was the victim raped?

K.: No.

Has Roberth confessed to being guilty?

K.: Not yet, but he will when we present him with the evidence. His fingerprints were found on the newly sharpened knife and the victim's blood was on his apron.

Has that been so quickly ascertained?

K.: Diligent men can achieve a great deal in one night. And our technicians are diligent.

Is Roberth mentally ill?

K.: It is hard for me to judge. I am not a psychiatrist.

What will his sentence be if it turns out that he is mentally ill?

K.: He will undergo treatment.

And if he is cured?

K.: He will be released.

Do you consider that to be just?

K.: I will not comment on the rulings of the penal code. I am not a legislator and I doubt that I shall ever be one.

But you do have an opinion on the matter?

K.: I do, but I am not going to tell you what it is. You are not interviewing me as a private individual, but as the Police President of Breslau.

The majority of lawyers, doctors, psychologists and philosophers state that a man is guilty when he knowingly commits a crime. If illness forces a man to commit a crime, then he himself is not guilty. Can illness be condemned to death?

K.: I do not belong to any of the professions you have mentioned.

Thank you, sir, for the conversation.

Mock put the newspaper aside and stared for a long time at his father's portrait hanging on the wall. The artisan shoemaker was clenching his teeth and looking intently at the photographer. Mock posed a very difficult question to his father, and immediately he received a reply. It was what he had expected.

BRESLAU, THAT SAME DECEMBER 22ND, 1927
NINE O'CLOCK IN THE MORNING

Alfred Sommerbrodt was relishing his breakfast of two fried eggs and watching his wife as she busied herself in the kitchen. With equal pleasure, he admired the well-scrubbed kitchen and his police uniform hanging on the peg by the kitchen door, which was also the entrance door of their small dwelling behind Stangen bicycle shop on Trebnitzerstrasse. Sommerbrodt was pleased that in a short while he would dress in his uniform, his greatcoat and shako, fasten to his belt the truncheon that now sat on top of the electricity metre, and take up his position on

Trebnitzerplatz to direct the traffic, as he did every day. His wife was far less pleased.

"They can't leave you in peace, even so close to Christmas," she said angrily.

"Darling, today, just before Christmas, people will be very jumpy out there," said Sommerbrodt, and he fell to thinking. He drank his ersatz coffee and patted his plump wife, wondering if he still had time to pay her the honours before he left. A knock on the door dispelled any such erotic whims. His wife opened and at the same time, shoved forcibly, sat down on the table. The decrepit piece of furniture rocked dangerously, and the mug of coffee jumped and spilled over Sommerbrodt's shirt. The policeman threw himself furiously at the two arrivals, but the barrel of a Walther soon made him abandon his aggressive intentions. The faces of both men were masked with handkerchiefs. One of them produced a pair of handcuffs and gestured to Mrs Sommerbrodt to come closer. He then secured her to the pipe that held the electricity metre to the wall. With a wave of the gun, the policeman was instructed to approach. His initial hesitation soon dissolved when a second Walther appeared in the hand of the other man. A moment later Sommerbrodt was kneeling next to his wife, secured to the same pipe. The first intruder pushed two chairs towards them and then sat down on the table, gaily swinging his legs. The second man undressed down to his underwear, and put on the uniform jacket and shako. He then yanked Sommerbrodt's trousers off and pulled them up over his own thin hips. When he had fastened the belt and truncheon, he went out of the door. The man who stayed behind threw some wood into the fire and stood an enormous kettle on the stove.

A large, brand-new Horch 303 pulled up outside the investigative jail on Schuhbrücke and three men climbed out. They went through the gloomy gate, showed the guard their identification and made their way up to the first floor and the duty officer's room.

"Which of you is Professor Nieswand?" asked the duty officer.

"I am," replied the grey-haired man wearing a brightly coloured tie.

"I see I'm not the only one to be on duty just before Christmas," smiled the duty officer. "If some madman were to get it into his head to . . ."

"These are sick men, not mad men," remarked the professor dryly.

"And you, sirs, must be President Wilhelm Kleibömer's trusted men," the duty officer's voice gave Nieswand to know that he had not been greatly impressed by this remark. "To protect the prisoner during transportation, is that right? The orders, please."

The two other men nodded, and one of them took an envelope from the inside pocket of his jacket and handed it to the duty officer. The latter opened it and read under his breath:

"Confidential instructions concerning the transportation of the prisoner Fritz Roberth for psychiatric examination . . . aha, good . . . good . . . signed, phew . . . President Kleibömer himself."

The duty officer stowed the instructions in his desk drawer and reached for the telephone.

"Essmüller here," he growled. "Bring Roberth to exit C immediately. That's right. Take special precautions. Professor Nieswand will wait for you there – he's taking the prisoner for examination in his own consulting room on Einbaumstrasse." He gazed thoughtfully at the men in the room. "The prisoner is yours until eight."

249

BRESLAU, THAT SAME DECEMBER 22ND,
HALF PAST TWO IN THE AFTERNOON

There was a great deal of traffic in the city. It had not snowed since the previous day and the roads were icy. Not only did the cars skid, but the sledges and droschkas too. Breslauers squeezed into over-crowded trams and discussed the high prices of Christmas shopping.

The eight-cylinder Horch was not able to make use of its considerable power and drove very slowly, like all the other cars that day. It was stuffy inside. All the passengers, apart from the handcuffed prisoner, kept wiping down the steamed-up windows. They came to a halt at the crossroads next to Oder Station. The Horch waited behind a huge lorry with an advertisement for Wrigley's Chewing Gum painted on its tarpaulin. A similar lorry stood behind the Horch. The traffic policeman gave a signal and the vehicles began to move. When the second lorry had passed the crossroads, the policeman unexpectedly changed the direction of the traffic. Several cars jammed on their brakes, and a driver in a checked cap stuck his head out of the window and glared at the policeman with anything but goodwill. The two lorries drove beneath the viaduct with the Horch between them. There was no other vehicle in sight; all had already disappeared towards Rosenthalerbrücke. The first lorry came to a halt and from it leaped ten men armed with Mausers. The same number of similarly armed men appeared from the second lorry and stood behind the car. No-one inside made the slightest move. No-one said a word. A pock-marked giant walked over to the Horch, opened the door and grabbed the driver by the collar of his uniform. A moment later the driver found himself on the cobbles, where the other passengers soon joined him. All, apart from the prisoner, stood in front of the car. The armed men pointed towards the back door of the first lorry, and they crowded in. A train clattered across the viaduct. A short, smartly dressed man with a long foxy face approached the car, accompanied by an older man in a railwayman's cap. The railwayman leaned into the car, looked the prisoner over and nodded to the little dandy. Nobody said a word. Only the prisoner began to howl; his howling was lost amid the clattering of the train.

BRESLAU, THAT SAME DECEMBER 22ND, 1927
EIGHT O'CLOCK IN THE EVENING

There were only two people waiting at the tram stop on Zwingerplatz. Both had their collars turned up and their hats pulled down over their eyes. The taller of the two traced zigzags in the snow and bent towards the shorter man who was whispering something to him on tiptoes. The snow fell at a slant through the blurred boundary between the black sky and the glow of a gaslight. The taller man listened to the other's brief report without a word.

"Yes, just as you said, Counsellor. We let the two cops and the nutcase quack go after two hours, when it was all over . . ."

"And what about the traffic policeman?"

"I went to his place with my men and we set him and his wife free. Right after the operation . . ."

"Was he very battered?"

"Their hands had gone a bit numb. Apart from that, they were fine."

"Wirth, you're to go and see him now," the taller man said, taking a wad of notes from his inside pocket and handing it to his companion, "and leave him these few marks. Give him the money but don't say anything." He drew the symbol of infinity in the snow. "You've done well."

"Don't you want to know what they did to that swine, Counsellor?"

"They? They were but tools in my hands."

Wirth pocketed the money and looked at the Counsellor intently.

"The tools slipped out of your control a bit, Counsellor."

251

The Counsellor shook hands with Wirth and set off towards the Municipal Theatre, whose hazy lights were diffused in the snowy mist. Huge posters on the columns outside urged people to come and see Wagner's *Tannhäuser*, the proceeds of which were to go towards various charitable causes. A few late spectators were climbing out of sledges and cars, disseminating various scents purchased at perfume counters. The Counsellor bought a ticket for the stalls and entered the bright foyer decorated with Baroque gilding. The mighty sounds of the overture, despite its force, had managed to enrapture the stout cloakroom assistant. After clearing his throat for half a minute, Mock shook the man by the shoulder and brought him back to earth. He left his snow-covered outer garments in the cloakroom and, tapping his cane, ascended the stairs to the first floor. There he found box number 12 and gently pressed down on the handle. The horns were conveying a seascape. In the box was Criminal Director Mühlhaus, who started when the Counsellor sat down next to him. The splashing of naiads was now represented by racing violins.

"Nobody will hear us here, Mock," said Mühlhaus, and took a deep breath as if about to sing *"Naht euch dem Strande"* along with the chorus of mermaids. "You know that today Hänscher from Department IV was looking at the photograph of you holding a gun to Roberth's head? You know you're the one they chiefly suspect of organizing the lynch mob that attacked that unfortunate schizophrenic man?"

The violins sawed away mercilessly, and with surgical precision. The sound of trumpets mingled with the deep blackness of the double basses. Then Venus commenced her seduction of Tannhäuser.

"Thank you for the warning," said Mock.

"Warnings are for things that can be avoided. But I've already received orders from President Kleibömer to suspend you from service until Department IV has completed its investigation into the lynching of

Roberth, of which Hänscher suspects you. This isn't a warning – this is the end of your career."

"It would be the end if Department IV could prove I had something to do with the lynching. But I'll ignite their hopes by telling them I'm pleased about Roberth's tragic demise."

"So you don't deny having something to do with all this. You only doubt that evidence will be found against you. Now you've confessed to me!" shouted Mühlhaus, but his voice chimed in with Tannhäuser's aria *"Dir töne Lob"*. "God damn it, that man might have been innocent! He wasn't the one who committed the murder – it was his illness! Can you not understand that, you idiot?"

"If that were so . . ." Mock's quiet voice was clearly audible under Venus' unhappy response to her rejection by Tannhäuser, "then he was seriously ill, terminally ill even. Is it surprising that a man who is terminally ill should die? His illness killed others, and now it has killed him too."

Mühlhaus said nothing as Venus continued to reproach her ungrateful lover.

BRESLAU, THAT SAME DECEMBER 22ND, 1927
HALF PAST NINE IN THE EVENING

Breslau's high society milled around in the foyer, puffing smoke, wafting assorted perfumes and sweating profusely. Ladies scythed with their peacock feathers and revelled in this gathering, a foretaste of the New Year's Ball that was so eagerly anticipated. Gentlemen idly discussed the approaching holiday, improved business and increases in expenditure. The birdlike chirping of young women complemented the thoughtful frowns on the cloudy brows of young men, intended to convey their mature reflections on the particular interpretation of Wagner they had been watching.

253

Mock took an Ariston from his cigarette-case, broke it in half and twisted it into his cigarette-holder. At that moment, a yellow flame shot up from somebody's hand and licked the torn tip of his cigarette.

"Good evening, Doctor Hartner." Mock inhaled. "Thank you for the light. I didn't know you liked Wagner."

"We have to talk in a quiet place." Leo Hartner's grey hair bristled in involuntary warning. There was something peculiar about his behaviour.

Mock nodded, dived into the crowd of music lovers engrossed in discussion, and with gentle taps of his hands began to plough his way through to the other side. Hartner followed close behind. Mock went out to the corridor and made for a door bearing a golden triangle. A short, old man was having difficulty trickling into the urinal. The Counsellor occupied one of the cubicles, closed the toilet seat and sat down. As he smoked his cigarette, he heard similar sounds coming from the neighbouring cubicle. The gong resounded and, although it was very loud, it did not drown out the sigh of relief emitted by the old man. The door slammed shut at last. Mock and Hartner stood next to each other, critically eyeing their reflections in the wide mirror. Mock checked in all the cubicles and then blocked the door to the gentlemen's room with his cane.

"The murderer is among my team of experts," Hartner said quietly.

"Go on," Mock said, anticipating what was coming next: a series of questions and answers, the doctor's application of the Socratic Method, resistant to all pressure.

"Who in my team is suspect, and why?" Hartner did not disappoint. "Diehlsen." The Counsellor blew into his cigarette-holder and the cigarette hit the mirror with a shower of sparks. "Since he works in the Municipal Archives and is a member of the Breslau Society of Parapsychic Research. And Hockermann, who read the same book as Gelfrert and signed himself into the Register of Loans using the names of the famous men from our Leopold Lecture Theatre . . . That's right. What period does my men's investigation deal with? . . . The period is limited to two, perhaps three centuries . . . But that is not the point. I have asked the wrong question. What dates, or what days of the year are we looking at? From the date of the last murder, meaning December 9th, to the end of the year . . . Yes, to find the date of the next murder as soon as possible. And what have we ascertained? . . . That the next murder will take place on Christmas Eve, at Antonienstrasse 27. We're going to be there and we're going to catch the cad. You even gave us the time of day! . . . I'm afraid the murder's going to take place sooner," Hartner was about to prove his theory. "Yesterday evening I was telephoned by the archivist at the Municipal Archives. Every day after work, my men return any files or books they have been studying that day. The archivist comes to fetch them personally from our offices on Neumarkt. It so happens that one file, number 4536, went missing. This item is most certainly the report of a trial because the files numbered 4500–4555 are all trial reports. One of the experts had stolen it."

"You should have detained your men the moment the theft was discovered, then telephoned the police and thoroughly searched them," Mock said.

"I'd have done so had the archivist discovered it sooner. He didn't, however, go through the files at our offices. He only made the discovery when he was putting the files away back at the archives."

Mock went to a washbasin, turned on the tap and put his head under a stream of water. After a while he stood upright and savoured the cold rivulets trickling down inside his corset. He approached Hartner slowly and gripped him by the shoulders.

"We've got him, Hartner," he shouted, and laughed savagely. "We've got him at last! It's one of your men! All we have to do is follow them . . . And if that doesn't work, I'll interrogate each of them appropriately . . . And Diehlsen and Hockermann most thoroughly of all."

"The files have to deal with to the period after December 19th," Hartner said slowly. "Meaning the murder would have to take place some time between December 19th and 24th. You're the one who came up with this chronology – the successive murders have been discovered sooner on each occasion. So we have to expect a murder now, and you'll find the body on the same day. The same day as appears on the calendar page. You can't find a body with a page dated, say, December 12th tomorrow, on December 23rd," Hartner laughed heartily. "Yes, now I understand your excitement. As of yesterday, all my experts – especially Hockermann and Diehlsen – are being shadowed by a guardian angel from your department. The murderer will be caught red-handed."

Mock said nothing. On the afternoon of the day before, when he had learned that the next murder was due to take place on Christmas Eve, he had relieved all his men of their task of tailing the suspects. He now left the toilets, said goodbye to Hartner and ran down to the cloakroom. He woke the stout cloakroom assistant for the second time that evening and put his coat on. As he put on his hat, he felt something pressing on the side of his head. From behind the inner ribbon of his hat he extracted a small, rectangular Salem cigarette-box. He knew he had been behaving strangely lately: he had tried to hang himself in a toilet; he had not been drinking; he had fawned upon a youngster asking for forgiveness, and he had taken justice into his own hands. But never in his life had he bought menthol cigarettes. He pulled on his gloves, shook the box and heard something rattle inside it. He opened it and took out a small, white business card: "Doctor Adolf Pinzhoffer, solicitor, Tiergartenstrasse 32, tel. 34 21". He turned it over and read the meticulously handwritten words: "I've done it again. Steam baths on Zwingerstrasse".

At this time of day the only men who frequented the public baths on Zwingerstrasse were those who were hungry for each other's company. They stood around the walls, some wrapped in towels, some half-dressed; others who were ready to leave fanned themselves with bowler hats damp from sweat. Nobody was able to leave the establishment, however, since the exit was being blocked by a fat, uniformed policeman who took up the entire breadth of the narrow corridor leading to the bathrooms. Counsellor Mock just about managed to squeeze past him and advanced slowly towards the bathhouse attendant, who was pointing through an open door.

Doctor Adolf Pinzhoffer was tightly bound from his neck to his toes with coarse rope, as if someone had squeezed him into a cocoon of cord. The cocoon had clearly been started at the neck since the end of the cord, which had been wound between his feet several times, was secured to the shower arm with a series of complicated knots. Doctor Adolf Pinzhoffer's body was held in the vertical position by another rope tied to his legs, while his head was immersed up to his neck in a chipped bucket and encircled by a gently swirling wreath of floating hair. The bucket stood in the bathtub directly below the shower head, from which gushed extremely hot water. It ran down the body, heating it to redness *par excellence*, and filling both bucket and bath. In the bucket, tied to the victim's neck, floated a small jar containing a scrap of paper.

Mock was not especially surprised by this last discovery. He approached the bath and, through the steam rising from the scalded skin, saw that it was almost full – the outlet had been stopped with a plug. He turned off the water and looked at the attendant, who was swallowing hard.

"How long has the water been running into the bath? How long does it take to overflow?"

257

"How should I know?" stammered the attendant, trying not to vomit. "It must be about twenty minutes, half an hour . . ."

Mock sat on the edge of a bath in his hat and coat and stared at the floor tiles. He listened to the technicians in the next-door bathroom safeguarding evidence and positioning metal signs beside any vital details. He heard the crack of magnesium and the clattering of hundreds of pairs of feet up and down the corridor. Suddenly, into this apparently chaotic racket, there crept a suggestion of order and hierarchy. Heavy, slow steps in metal-capped shoes reverberated, silencing all other noises with their ceremonious echo. This was accompanied by the ominous wheezing of diseased bronchi. The majestic footsteps came to a halt outside the bathroom in which Mock sat.

"*Grüss Gott*, Mock," the deep voice corresponded to the sound of the shoes. "That's what they say in my beloved Munich."

"Good evening, Police President, sir," Mock said, standing up from the bath.

Wilhelm Kleibömer was in evening wear, obviously on his way home from the opera. His eyes swept across the room and he shuddered at the sight of a cockroach scurrying along the bottom of the wall.

"You're surprised to see me here, Mock," he squashed the insect against the wall with the tip of his shoe, "when I should be sleeping. Well, you've been keeping me awake at night recently. But not for much longer. To the end of the year. Only to the end of the year."

Mock did not utter a single word. He took off his coat and slung it over his shoulder.

"You've got until the end of the year," wheezed a high-pitched, asthmatic intake of breath. "If you haven't caught the 'calendar murderer' by

258

the end of the year, your position will be taken by Gustav Meinerer. The hero who arrested that paedophile. Breslau needs heroes like him. Not Don Quixotes, Mock. Not Don Quixotes."

BRESLAU, FRIDAY, DECEMBER 23RD, 1927
TWO O'CLOCK IN THE MORNING

The candle standing in the middle of the round table illuminated only the attentive faces and tightly closed eyes of those who sat around it. They raised their outstretched hands above the table surface, with thumbs touching and little fingers meeting those of their neighbours. On the table stood a perfectly still porcelain saucer. An elderly lady suddenly opened her eyes and shouted:

"Spirit, make your presence felt!"

The candle went out. The people assembled were struck with terror. But it was not a spirit. The door had opened suddenly, creating a draught to which the weak flame succumbed. There was a click. The click of a light switch. The merciless glare of electricity removed all concentration from the faces of those seated at the table, and revealed wrinkles and bags under their eyes. It was just as unforgiving for the two unshaven men who now stood in the doorway, with the horrified housekeeper shuffling from one foot to the other beside them.

"Criminal police," yawned one of the new arrivals. "Which of you gentlemen is the owner of this apartment, Professor Erich Hockermann?"

BRESLAU, THAT SAME DECEMBER 23RD, 1927
TWO O'CLOCK IN THE MORNING

A black Adler approached the building at the corner, Zwingerstrasse 4, with its sign showing SCHIFFKE'S ORPHANAGE and, skidding a little on

259

the packed snow, parked at an angle that was almost perpendicular to the road. Two men climbed out of it while another two remained inside, one of whom was clearly short of space between the window and his neighbour's massive shoulder. The former two approached the door and thumped loudly. No sound came from within. One of the men took a few steps back and looked up as lights came on in the windows. The other turned his back to the door and kicked it three times with his heel. In the little barred window appeared the frightened face of an elderly woman wearing a bonnet. The man closest to the door held his identification card up to the window. It worked like a key.

"How could you," cursed the woman whose attire showed she had not been asleep. "This is an orphanage. You're waking our children!"

"Is Wilhelm Diehlsen here?" came the curt question.

"Yes. He is," the woman answered. "He's helping Pastor Fohdorff decorate the Christmas trees."

The men entered the building, betraying no surprise.

BRESLAU, THAT SAME DECEMBER 23RD, 1927
A QUARTER PAST TWO IN THE MORNING

The Adler stopped on Ofenerstrasse — deserted at this time of night — outside an iron gate with a tin sign that read WIRTH & CO. ~ TRANSPORT AND DISPATCH. A bolt shot back and a moment later the iron gates stood open. The Adler turned into a small, cobbled yard where the driver stopped for a few seconds, then drove on, turning left behind a tall, brick wall and coming to a standstill in front of a two-storeyed building which appeared to be some kind of warehouse. To the two handcuffed passengers climbing out of the Adler, the building resembled a prison.

One of the larger storerooms in the warehouse belonging to the company Wirth & Co. was rarely used. Usually it stood cold and empty, which did not particularly surprise any of the company workers. Even if they were eaten up by curiosity as to what their boss and his inseparable bodyguard might be using it for, nobody dared to ask. They valued their well-paid jobs too highly, and the principle of asking no questions had been instilled in them by long years spent in the clink.

On this particular winter morning, the day before Christmas Eve, the storeroom was not empty: there were six people present. Kleinfeld, Ehlers and Meinerer wore rubber aprons, and knuckle-dusters gleamed on their fingers. They were sitting on upturned crates, stamping their feet on the oily floor against the cold, smoking cigarettes and watching as Mock circled the two handcuffed men. These men were stripped down to their long johns. In the sub-zero temperatures, this had a terrible effect on their circulation, and after he had been walking around them for half an hour Mock sensed a change in the prisoners' attitudes. Diehlsen was shivering and kept on bending his neck to blow on his wrists where the handcuffs had left a dark mark. The Counsellor was certain he was ready to talk, but he could not say the same for Hockermann. Unlike his fellow prisoner, the school professor had been observing the policeman all along without blinking. A derisive smile kept appearing on his face, which was blue with cold. This was not, however, what aggravated Mock the most. He could not understand why Hockermann was not shivering, but for the time being he kept his anger in check. He knew he would need it later.

"My dear gentlemen," he said gently, "I know you're cold. So I suggest a little warm-up."

He stopped his rounds and went to one corner of the room. He raised his arm and touched a rail protruding from the wall, belonging to a hand gantry that ran between two opposite walls. Mock winced and hung his hat on a rusty window handle. He then took off his coat, carefully turning it inside out so as not to get it dirty, and threw it over the rail. Having safeguarded his garment, he jumped nimbly and caught hold of the rail. He hung there for a while, then pulled himself up five times until the veins bulged on his forehead. Mock's men stifled a laugh, unlike Hockermann who gave full vent to his mirth. Mock began to laugh too.

"I'm a bit past it, Professor Hockermann," he said brightly. "Once, I could do twenty pull-ups. During the war I had to clamber out of a dry well in which I'd hidden to escape the Cossacks. And do you know what? I managed it. There was no other way out."

Mock came up to the prisoners and squatted next to them. He carefully felt their necks and shoulders like a slave-trader. He was not happy with the result.

"You have no other way out either," he said quietly. "It's below zero, and you're only wearing underpants. You'll freeze to death. Unless you do what I've just done, but many more of them."

The prisoners said nothing but bewilderment appeared in their eyes.

"Yes, yes. You'll warm up if each of you does twenty pull-ups. And then I'll take you back to your warm cell. It stinks a bit, but it's warm." He laughed out loud. "No-one's ever died yet from a stink, eh? Well? Are you ready?"

"You must be mad." Hockermann's voice was serious. "How dare you hold us here? What are you, a sadist?"

Mock stood and walked over to the rail. He put on his coat, then took to reshaping the brim of his hat.

"Let's go," he said to his men. "Christmas Eve tomorrow. We'll go and have a stiff drink and give these gentlemen until this evening to think it over. Then we'll meet here again."

"Officer, sir!" shouted Diehlsen. His round belly protruded a little over the cord of his long johns. His narrow shoulders slumped, and there appeared to be no biceps in his arms. "I can't do twenty pull-ups, but I don't want to die from the cold!"

"*Ut desint vires tamen est laudanda voluntas*,"† Mock said.

"Alright," Diehlsen's teeth chattered. "I'll try."

"Meinerer, undo his handcuffs!"

Once the handcuffs were removed, Diehlsen rubbed his hands and wrists for a long time. Then he began to spring up and down, slapping his belly and back.

"Ready?" asked Mock.

Diehlsen nodded and approached the rail. He jumped up and for a moment his hands gripped the rusty tee-bar. But only for a moment. Then he fell. He hissed with pain, rubbing his leg, and then limped back to the rail. He attempted to jump but only bobbed pathetically.

"I can't – I've sprained my ankle," he sobbed.

Mock went over to the prisoner, put his hands around his waist and lifted him up. Despite the cold, Diehlsen's body was covered in sweat.

"Grab it," said Mock, shaking his head in disgust. "Right now!"

Diehlsen grasped the rail and tried to pull himself up. He wriggled his legs as if trying to find support. Using a handkerchief, Mock wiped Diehlsen's sweat off his own face with revulsion. He walked up to the prisoner and studied his meagre muscles. Diehlsen was slowly pulling himself up and dropping again. As his chin neared the bar, he let go and collapsed to the ground. Howling with pain, he knelt and clutched his injured ankle.

"I can't," he whispered.

"You see, Diehlsen," Mock flung his handkerchief into a corner of the room. "Ovid was right. I praise your will to fight and, as a reward, I'm sending you to a normal police cell. There we'll be able to have a long chat

† Although there is no strength, the will itself is worthy of praise.

263

about the criminal history of our town. Yes, there in the warmth you're going to spend Christmas." He glanced at his men. "Did you hear that, Ehlers?"

Ehlers nodded, removed his rubber apron, slipped the knuckle-dusters into his pocket, and threw Diehlsen his clothes.

"Get dressed," he growled. "You're coming with me."

Mock turned to Hockermann.

"You're probably stronger than your colleague," he said. "Show me what you can do and you too will find yourself in a detention cell."

"I won't allow myself to be humiliated, you son of a bitch," Hockermann said in a steady tone of voice. No emotion, no chattering of teeth.

Mock stared him in the eye for a few moments, then turned to the two remaining policemen.

"Let's leave him to think about his manners. It's shameful that a school professor should use such language."

Mock walked out of the storeroom and into a gloomy corridor whose darkness was barely broken by a dirty skylight. Kleinfeld and Meinerer followed him. Seeing them, a man got up from his chair outside the door and started flapping at his sides with his arms.

"Cold, ain't it," he said.

"Watch him carefully," Mock said, handing the man a few coins. "And here's something for a bottle to warm yourself. Your boss won't forget about you either."

"That's not why . . . Just something to say . . ."

"It doesn't matter. Go in and take a look at him from time to time, and don't let him fall asleep or lose consciousness."

They climbed into the Adler. Mock, turning on the engine, caught sight of his colleagues' bewildered expressions in the rear-view mirror. The car slowly made its way across the courtyard.

"What are you two staring at? Do you always have to wallop someone when they call you a son of a bitch?"

"It's not that," said Kleinfeld after a moment's silence. "But why did you tell them to do pull-ups?"

Mock braked at the barrier between Wirth's warehouses and Ofenerstrasse.

"What's up with you?" Mock drove off abruptly onto the snow-covered road and went into a slight skid. He stopped the car in the middle of the road and, ignoring a tram-driver's furious bells, examined the faces of his subordinates. "Is Christmas all you're thinking about now? Honnefelder, Geissen and that last one . . . well . . . what's his name? Pinzhoffer . . . Yes, Pinzhoffer. They were murdered by somebody who is extremely strong. Only someone who's strong can quarter a man, or hang a man by his leg from a lamp or shower. Someone who's able to pull himself up on a tee-bar twenty times. Don't you agree?"

BRESLAU, THAT SAME DECEMBER 23RD, 1927
NOON

Mock was now sitting at the round table at which the participants in the spiritual séance had formed a magic circle the night before. Cardboard files tied with ribbons lay scattered on the floor around him, and on chairs and shelves and every other possible surface. Various Kabbalistic and occult symbols had been drawn on these files, and on some appeared the signs of planets and the zodiac, or short Hebrew captions. The files were stuffed with yellowed pages of notes or small index cards covered with beautiful Sütterline handwriting, with a summary of their contents written at the top of each in red ink. Mock pulled a pair of rarely used pince-nez from his pocket, polished them, and listened absorbedly to the sounds coming from other rooms, which Kleinfeld, Ehlers, Meinerer and

265

Reinert – who had recently joined them – were searching centimetre by centimetre. He shook his head and began to go through the notes and cards once again. All of it standard research material relating to the history of Breslau. A couple of questions gave Mock no peace: why had Hockermann coded the captions on the files if what they contained was no secret? Why had he not organized the material in the conventional way, by writing what each file contained on its cover and spine? The only explanation he could think of was that the scholar was an eccentric. Having worked through these obsessive thoughts, Mock immersed himself in reading. He waded through notes about Polish cattle markets in fourteenth-century Elbing, about the unrest among seasonal workers in the fifteenth century, about the first Protestant Masses celebrated by Father Jan Hess, about the desecration of the Włostowic family grave by a drunken mob in 1529, until he felt his sleepless night demand its due. He closed his eyes and saw the scene with the tee-bar exercises in the cold warehouse. Shaking off a growing drowsiness, he tied the ribbons of the tenth file he had looked through that day, and with bloodshot eyes skimmed over the stacks piled on the floor and all around. He stood up and started to count them, but soon grew impatient and simplified his method as much as possible, estimating each batch of ten files. Moments later he knew: that there were approximately four hundred files. He sighed, glanced down at the notes in front of him and learned that, in eighteenth-century Breslau, prisoners were employed to clean the town.

BRESLAU, THAT SAME DECEMBER 23RD, 1927
FOUR O'CLOCK IN THE AFTERNOON

Mock still had ten files to look through. He untied the ribbons despondently, opened yet another box covered with curved Hebrew letters, and prepared himself for a fascinating account of the problems encountered by the administrator of Mochbor village, near Breslau, who did not want to pay the municipal authority tax on fish caught in the River Lohe. Whenever he was coming towards the end of some tedious task, all kinds of subjective and objective obstacles would crop up unexpectedly, making it impossible for him to complete it. The obstacle that now prevented him from reaching for the next file was of an objective nature: drowsiness assailed his head, heavily and determinedly. It was, as usual, preceded by a visual recollection of an event that had occurred recently. Mock saw his men leaving Hockermann's apartment and heard his own voice say: "Go now. After all, it is Christmas. I'll go through the files myself." He saw their grateful faces and heard Kleinfeld's attempts to protest: "I'll stay and help you, Counsellor. I don't celebrate Christmas and I was good at Latin in school. I can read all this." His own laughter rang in his ears: "And what is the word for murder in Latin?" "Homicidium, I think . . ." Kleinfeld did not reflect for long. Mock lay his arm on a file and then rested his head on it.

Homicidium – the word echoed in his head. He blinked and experienced a new sensory incentive. Not only could he hear the word now, he could also see it when he blinked. He opened his eyes. At a distance of five centimetres from his pupils was a yellowed card of thick, woven paper, and on it, in old handwriting, was written *Homicidium Gnosi Dni Raphaelis Thomae in balneario pedibus suspensi die prima post festivitatem S. Thomae Apostoli AD MDCLXXXV*. Above the Latin text appeared a stamp with four numbers – 4536.

"The murder of Raphael Thomae," he muttered to himself. "What are the abbreviations *Gnosi* and *Dni*? And so 'The murder of one Raphael Thomae, hung up by his legs in the public baths two days before Christmas Eve in 1685.'"

Mock felt blood rush to his brain. He stood up suddenly, knocking over the heavy chair. He hurried around the table and into the hall.

Grabbing the receiver of the Bakelite telephone, he dialled Hartner's number.

"What was the number of the file stolen by one of the experts?" he shouted. Moments passed. "Repeat that, please," he said when Hartner finally answered. "Yes, I'm taking it down . . . 4536."

BRESLAU, THAT SAME DECEMBER 23RD, 1927
HALF PAST FOUR IN THE AFTERNOON

The Adler rolled slowly into the courtyard of Wirth & Co. Transport and Dispatch. Mock climbed out to see its owner standing on the ramp, frantically shouting something, waving his hand and opening the door to the counting-room. Mock stood in the glazed office for a moment, shaking the wet snow off his coat and hat.

"Mr Mock," Wirth was clearly perplexed. "My man doesn't know what to do with your naked fellow. You told him he wasn't to leave the warehouse. But he called in my man, grabbed onto a pipe and pulled himself up twenty times . . ."

"In handcuffs?" Mock interrupted.

"Yes, in handcuffs. Then he wanted to be taken back to the cell where he'd been locked up first. My man tried to brush him off, but he bellowed so loudly he had to be given a clout across the face. Even then he leaped up to the pipe and started pulling himself up again. Like an ape, Mr Mock. And then he yelled to be taken to that other cell, because that's what you'd promised. Said he'd done twenty pull-ups . . . He got another clout, but that didn't work. He's yelling again. He's some sort of lunatic, Mr Mock . . ."

"See what men do, Wirth," Mock laughed, "to secure themselves better conditions? He can pull himself up on a tee-bar wearing handcuffs. That's nice. See how much he wants to get to a warm cell? Such determi-

268

nation must be rewarded. Lock him up in that cell, throw him some wood and coal, let him get the stove going and spend Christmas in the warmth." He pulled a creased banknote from his pocket. "Buy him some bread and sausage with this. The cheapest. I'll come and interrogate him properly after Christmas."

"And who's to watch over him? My men have families, you know . . ."

"I know, Wirth. They have families and they are exemplary citizens," Mock stroked the seventeenth-century document in his breast pocket. "Nobody's going to watch him. And I'll hold on to the key." He patted Wirth affectionately on the shoulder. "Happy Christmas, Wirth! Tomorrow's Christmas Eve."

BRESLAU, THAT SAME DECEMBER 23RD, 1927
FIVE O'CLOCK IN THE AFTERNOON

A terrible mess reigned in Inge Gänserich's apartment. Dresses, petticoats and stockings were strewn over two screens that stood in the middle of the room. Dirty plates with remnants of food towered on the table, while rows of empty wine bottles stood under it and on the sideboard. Dusty newspapers and magazines lay on the windowsill, above which hung a curtain held up by only one hook. In the centre of the room, next to the stove against which someone had smashed a guitar, stood the iron bed in which Erwin Mock was asleep.

His uncle closed the front door and looked around in disgust. He approached the sleeping youth and shook him hard by the shoulder. Erwin opened his eyes and closed them again, pulling the coverless eiderdown over his head. Mock noticed the sour reek of digested wine coming from his nephew. He sat in the armchair, having first thrown aside its lumpy, shapeless cover, pulled a flick-knife from his pocket, opened it and scratched his neck with it under the corset. He then rolled a cigarette of blond, Georgia tobacco, lit it and stared at the shape of Erwin's body wrapped in the eiderdown. The boy began to wriggle about, until finally he poked out his dishevelled head.

"Forgive me for receiving you like this but . . ." he said with difficulty, as if unable to squeeze the words through his parched throat, "we had a party last night, which went on until morning . . ."

"Where's Inge?" Mock interrupted him.

"In the studio," replied Erwin. "Working . . ."

Mock thought about his empty apartment without Sophie, and without Adalbert or Marta who had gone to see their family near Striegau, and even without the dog, Argos, which they had magnanimously taken with them so as to spare the Counsellor any trouble. Mock imagined the following day's Christmas Eve dinner: he alone at the head of the huge table, cutting slices of roast goose; lighting candles on the Christmas tree; drunk, and singing carols so loudly that Doctor Fritz Patschkowsky from above has to thump the floor with his walking stick; staring at the telephone, a bottle of schnapps in his hand. He did not want his predictions to come true. He longed to be able to place a piece of carp on Erwin's plate, drink schnapps and sing carols with him. Which was why he had to suppress his fury at his nephew's drunkenness, at this pigsty in which he lived – which successive lovers of Breslau's femme fatale used to clean – at his two-day truancy from school, and at his failure to find himself, which was something nobody could help him with.

"I am inviting you . . . both of you . . ." Mock corrected himself, "to join me for Christmas Eve dinner. Families ought to spend Christmas together . . ."

Erwin sat up in bed, scanned the table and reached for a glass with a little water in it. Contrary to Mock's expectation, he did not drink, but poured it onto his palm and slicked down his hair, which was sticking out in all directions.

270

"Thank you very much, Uncle," he tried not to mumble, "but I'm going to spend Christmas with Inge. And she won't come to yours, Uncle. Unless you apologize to her for what happened in the past . . . Forgive me, Uncle . . . I have to go to the toilet on the landing . . ."

Erwin wrapped himself in a threadbare dressing gown – Mock guessed it to be a trophy passed on to subsequent lovers of the seductive artist – and staggered out of the room. The Counsellor went to the window and threw it wide open. He listened with some surprise to the patter of rain in the gutters as it cut across the snow-covered roofs, causing small avalanches and icicle daggers to break off. He heard Erwin's footsteps and turned around.

"The day before yesterday, I suggested that you come and live with me; today I am inviting you to spend Christmas Eve with me," said Mock slowly. "The day before yesterday we were interrupted by a paedophile. Today you try to cut the conversation short yourself. You told me to apologize to Inge, and went to the toilet. You didn't wait for my reply; you didn't want to know what it was because you thought I'd take offence and leave. You'd have a clear conscience and be able to spend Christmas Eve drinking wine in this filthy tip, this disgusting shakedown . . ." Mock stuck his cigarette into a plate of disintegrating herring. "You can always count on me, but can I count on you?"

Erwin got up and approached his uncle. He wanted to put his arms around him, but held back. Tears glistened in his eyes. He glanced over Mock's shoulder and his tears immediately dried. Mock turned and saw Inge. She stood there without a hat and her black hair, wet with rain, was wrapped around her face. She stared at them, beautiful, scornful and drunk.

"Apologize to her, Uncle, apologize," Erwin whispered.

"Apologies," Mock said, fastening his coat, "must be preceded by a request for forgiveness. What are apologies worth if they are not accepted.

271

They only humiliate the one who apologizes. And I'm not going to ask her to forgive me." Mock kissed Erwin on both cheeks. "Happy Christmas, Erwin," he said, and then turned to Inge. "Happy Christmas, dear lady."

Hearing no response from Inge, he left the apartment and paused in the dark corridor. He stroked the bottle of Franz's favourite schnapps in his pocket. He knew how he would be spending Christmas Eve.

BRESLAU, SATURDAY, DECEMBER 24TH, 1927
FOUR O'CLOCK IN THE AFTERNOON

Mock stood in front of the bathroom mirror and glared in annoyance at the surgical corset that prevented him from wearing a bow tie. Helpless, dressed in a dinner jacket that had been immaculately pressed by his servant, he fiddled around at his neck trying to fasten to his shirt the largest available collar, which, because of the corset, kept bursting open and sticking out. Mock spat angrily into the washbasin and flung the collar onto the tiled floor. He turned on the hot water and rinsed the shaving lather off his razor. Steam settled on the mirror, filled the air and stopped his breath. He turned off the tap and left the bathroom.

The large table in the parlour was laid with a white tablecloth. On it stood only an ashtray, a pot of coffee and a platter with honey cake. Mock did not fetch any of the dishes Marta had prepared for him from the larder. He was not hungry; the previous night spent at the chessboard with a bottle of schnapps had taken away his appetite. He was not pleased they had found the serial killer. He was not pleased he had granted himself a day off. All that pleased him were the frost, which had frozen the puddles just before dawn, and the snow, which had spread a fluffy covering over the slippery black ice.

Bored and indifferent, he sat at the head of the table. "*Stille Nacht*", which always made him sad, drifted from the radio. The thought of a solitary Christmas Eve dinner had not yet struck him with its full force. He stared at the telephone, still believing it would ring. He thought about the beautiful, feminine hands picking up a receiver somewhere far away, and hesitantly placing it back on its cradle. He thought about words of forgiveness, a plea for forgiveness carried along the telephone wires, breaking through the crackling and unearthly whistling.

But the telephone did not ring. Mock went to his study and took out the chessboard and Überbrandt's book, *Chess Traps*. He set up the pieces and began to play out the Schmidt versus Hartlaub game of 1899. But then he remembered that he had played it out the previous night, and that it did not present any more puzzles for him. He swiped his arm over the board and the pieces scattered across the floor.

He stood and walked around the table. He went to the Christmas tree and lit all the candles. He sat down, poured himself some coffee and picked at the cake with his fork. A short while later he fetched from his study the last few of the files he had taken from Hockermann's house. He opened them and made an effort to go through their contents. He could not say what he had found in them, but instinctively felt that they contained nothing important. As he leafed through them he could feel Hockermann's ironic eyes upon him, as well as those of Inge as he had tried to explain to Erwin that forgiveness is a prelude to apology. He held onto the thought feverishly, then got up and paced around the table, cup in hand.

"I can't ask Inge for forgiveness. But can I ask Sophie?"

He looked at the telephone, approached it, returned to the table, lit a cigarette and sat down again. Then he leaped up, grabbed the receiver and almost blindly dialled Mühlhaus' number.

"Good afternoon, Criminal Director," he said when he heard a puff on a pipe and a drawn out "hello". "I'd like to wish you and your whole family all the best for Christmas."

"Thank you, and the same to you," Mock heard, and imagined his chief's eyes long fixed on the empty place at the table where his son, Jakob, had sat for many years.

"Criminal Director," Mock said, feeling a pressure in his diaphragm, "I'd like to wish my wife a happy Christmas. Could you please give me Knüfer's number in Berlin?"

"Of course, hold on a moment . . . Here, I've got it: 5436. Ask him to call me. I'd completely forgotten about him – I haven't heard . . ."

Mock thanked him and hung up. The pressure in his diaphragm increased as he asked the telephonist to dial Berlin 5436. He replaced the receiver and waited to be connected. Minutes passed. He sat and smoked. Wax dripped from the candles on the tree. Mock glued his eyes to the telephone. After a quarter of an hour the receiver jumped on its cradle with a shrill ringing. He waited. He picked up after the third ring. The voice on the other end belonged to an elderly woman who was either crying or drunk.

"Good afternoon, Madame," Mock shouted into the receiver, "I'm a friend of Rainer Knüfer. I'd like to wish him a happy Christmas. Can I speak to him please?"

"No, you can't." The woman was obviously crying. "He's dead. He never came back from Wiesbaden. He was murdered there. Last Friday. Somebody wrung his neck. Broke his spine . . ."

The woman began to sob loudly and hung up. Mock was puzzled by this information. On a piece of paper he wrote "December 24th – Saturday". He worked out that "last Friday" would have been December 16th. Everything began to fall into place. With shaking hands he untied the file in which Hockermann kept his bills and expenses. Among them was a train ticket for the Wiesbaden–Breslau line, dated December 16th. Mock cried out with delight.

"Now I've got another bit of evidence against you, you son of a whore."

He then analysed the information about Knüfer from a different angle. Half a minute's conversation was all that had been needed; he did not have to ask anything else. The last man to have seen Sophie was dead. His joy evaporated.

"Sophie's guardian angel is dead," he thought. "And she has vanished too. No Sophie, no pain."

The telephone rang again. Mock picked up and heard a familiar voice in the receiver:

"It's about your wife. Something's very wrong."

"Something's wrong with her? Is she alive?" Mock yelled.

"She is, but she's involved in something evil. In the cellar of Briegerstrasse 4."

"Who is that, damn it?"

"Kurt Smolorz."

BRESLAU, THAT SAME, DECEMBER 24TH, 1927
FIVE O'CLOCK IN THE AFTERNOON

The building at Briegerstrasse 4 was destined for renovation. The stairs were at risk of collapsing, the roof leaked, the sewerage was forever getting blocked, and the neglected chimneys caused soot to surge into the wretched two-room dwellings. Having made up his mind to repair the building, its owner had rehoused its inhabitants at his own expense, and in this way so depleted himself financially that he decided not to begin the work until after New Year. In the meantime he had surrendered the building to the rats, and to local rascals who stripped the windows of glass with unbridled joy.

On that Christmas Eve there were neither rascals nor a caretaker at the property, so Mock had no trouble getting to the dark gate. In one hand he held his Walther, in the other a torch. He did not, however, switch it on, allowing his eyes to accustom themselves to the darkness. This they did readily and on his left-hand side he made out the cellar entrance. The door squeaked a little. He slowly went down the stairs. Now he had to switch on his torch. The bright shaft of light drew shattered and unhinged storeroom doors from the semi-darkness of the cellar corridor. He entered one of the rooms; his nostrils were assaulted by the smell of rotting potatoes, mouldy preserves and sweat. Human sweat.

Mock swept his torch around and pinpointed the source of the smell: on the ground sat a bound man. The torchlight revealed hands cuffed behind a back, a gag, and beads of sweat on a bald, shaven head covered in bleeding gashes and bruises inflicted by heavy blows.

"It's Moritz Strzelczyk," Mock heard Smolorz whisper. "The man who kicked me in the swimming baths. Baron von Hagenstahl's bodyguard. Now's my chance for revenge. I caught him unawares."

"Where's Sophie?" Mock pointed the light at Strzelczyk and Smolorz in turn. His subordinate proved a lamentable sight: his eyes were barely visible in their swollen sockets, his nose was probably broken, and his clothes were torn and devoid of buttons.

"Let's go," Smolorz muttered.

They made their way along the dark corridor towards a flickering glow. They heard a shuffling of feet. A moment later they were standing at the entrance to a side corridor lit up by paraffin lamps. Smolorz was proceeding with a fair amount of noise. Mock held him back and put a finger to his lips.

"They can't hear much," Smolorz said. "I was on my way back after I'd called you. Strzelczyk attacked me just here. There was a fight. They didn't hear anything then. And Strzelczyk was yelling his head off."

They reached the corridor and peered into it. It was not a typical corridor, more a small cellar hallway closed on three sides by doors to storerooms. On the floor lay scattered rags that probably served as bedclothes for homeless people, and empty bottles of wine, beer and cheap toiletries. In the centre of the room stood a Christmas tree and a stable with a crib, little sugar lambs strewn around it. Next to the stable was a stool covered with a white napkin, on which lay three half-full syringes and, next to them, a pharmaceutical jar containing what appeared to be the same suspension. Amidst all these objects two figures bobbed up and down. Baron von Hagenstahl was leaning against a wall, and kept collapsing involuntarily into a squatting position; swaying from side to side, he would push himself up slowly, and then a moment later his knees would give way again. Alexei von Orloff was stark naked. He too was leaning against the wall in a similar position to von Hagenstahl, but, unlike the Baron's, his eyes were not hazy. Behind the Christmas tree squatted Sophie, urinating on the dirt floor. Having completed her bodily function, she emerged and, stretching her lips into an unnatural smile, lay down beneath the tree on a pile of rags. Mock closed his eyes; it seemed that her smile had been directed at him.

"The holy man will be conceived in four days' time, on Christmas Eve. The day of Christ's birth is the day of the new saviour's conception. The birth of the old saviour will empower those who are to beget the new. Christ was conceived of a modest virgin, and God was his father through the intermediary of the Holy Spirit . . . He came into the world in a place intended for animals, in utter degradation . . . The new prophet will be begotten in even greater degradation . . . in sin, of a sinful woman, of a Babylonian harlot . . ."

Mock opened his eyes. Von Orloff had lain down next to Sophie and had begun to clamber on top of her. From half-open lips a trail of spit trickled down to his protruding beard. Mock appeared in the light cast by the paraffin lamps, a gun in his right hand. The Baron, uneasy, shook his head, grabbed a syringe and made towards him. He did not get very far – a heavy blow from Smolorz threw him against the wall and he collapsed to his knees. Smolorz set his leg into action. The Baron's head flew back violently, then returned to its former position, sinking with his body onto the heap of empty bottles a moment later.

Seeing Mock advancing towards him, von Orloff scrambled to his feet and made for the nearest storeroom door. A bullet hit him in the buttock and came out the other side. Smolorz saw a fountain of blood spurt from von Orloff's groin. Mock fired two more shots but missed his target; the bullets ricocheted off the wall with a hiss. The guru burst into the storeroom and reached into the pocket of a coat hanging there. Mock kicked him with such force that a pain shot up his leg and neck. The tip of his shoe hit von Orloff in his wounded buttock. The old man howled, fell onto the coat and tore it from its hook. Mock leaped at him, held the gun to his temple and pulled the trigger. The dry crack of the firing-pin reverberated in the musty air. Von Orloff pulled a small Sauer from his pocket and fired blindly. Mock felt a wetness near his ear and kicked out again. His hobnailed shoe struck von Orloff in the temple. The battered head rolled on its neck as if it were going to fall off, then twisted violently and one temple hit a huge stone, which was permeated with the stench of pickled cabbage. The leader of the sect churned up the earthen floor with his feet, then stopped moving.

Mock left the small room and made for the exit. He did not even glance at Sophie, who stood frozen and helpless next to the crib. Lighting his way with the torch, he found the staircase and emerged at the gate to the building. Drops of blood flowed from his ear onto the collar and shoulders of his pale fleece coat. He pressed a handkerchief to the wound. A moment later he detected the smell of Bergmann Privat cigarettes, Smolorz's favourite brand.

"Will you forgive me?" Smolorz said as the smoke from his cigarette mingled with the vapour of his breath. "I lied to you . . . I had — with her — a . . . It's not a photo-collage . . ."

"Shut up and listen carefully," Mock said. "Here's the key to Wirth's warehouse on Ofenerstrasse. Handcuff her and the Baron, take them there in the Adler and put them in the cell below the counting-room. There's one man there already. Kick Strzelczyk in the arse and get rid of him somewhere on the way. Then dump the old man's body on Hollandwiesen. Once you've done all that, come and find me. I'll be walking down Klosterstrasse towards Ofenerstrasse. I could do with a walk."

Mock set off towards the gap in the fence through which he had entered the property.

"Oh," he turned towards Smolorz, "I forgive you for lying and running away from me. You still kept following the Baron, and thanks to that we're here. Anyway, how could I be angry with someone just for screwing a Babylonian harlot?"

BRESLAU, THAT SAME DECEMBER 24TH, 1927
SIX O'CLOCK IN THE EVENING

Mock walked slowly along Klosterstrasse. A sledge approached from the opposite direction and passed him, jingling and flashing with the coloured lights of lanterns attached to the coachman's box. Mock contemplated the people sitting in the sledge. A little girl in a check coat was clutching a package wrapped in white paper and tied with a red ribbon. She had been given a present. Sophie had squatted to urinate on the dirt floor of the cellar. Then she lay on the heap of rags under the Christmas tree, distributing smiles in every direction. Like Christmas presents. Mock had been given a present too.

Clutching his head, he turned left into Margareten Damm just before the Bethanien Hospital. Staggering a little, he scraped his pale coat along the rough brick wall, entered a small yard and leaned against a carpet horse. Christmas Eve windows decorated with boughs of spruce glittered.

279

Some low stairs led up to a dwelling whose windows were not shuttered. From there drifted the music of a carol:

> *O du fröhliche, o du selige,*
> *Gnadenbringende Weihnachtszeit!*
> *Welt ging verloren,*
> *Christ ist geboren,*
> *Freue, freue dich, o Christenheit!*
>
> *O du fröhliche, o du selige . . .*

Mock stood on the steps and observed the singers. Two whiskered men raised their tankards of beer above their heads and swayed from side to side, setting in motion all those gathered around the table. Their stout wives were laughing, revealing the gaps in their teeth. A grandmother took the last of the chocolates from the Advent calendar. The children were either singing with their parents or running around the table at such speed that they almost knocked over the Christmas tree. The fair head and beaming face of a four-year-old boy peered out from under the table. In his hand he held a man's shoe. These people were happy and singing because it was their right. They had finished their work. Mock did not have that right. He never finished work. Even now, when he had delivered the city of a serial killer. The evidence he had against Hockermann would be ridiculed by any lawyer. "A school professor writing a history of the town has an index card from the archives amongst his files. He stole it because he needed it for his research. That does not mean he murdered Pinzhoffer. He visited an old aunt in Wiesbaden to wish her a happy Christmas. That does not mean he murdered Knüfer. Even if he is not your typical school professor, even if he can easily manage twenty pull-ups on a tee-bar in a deserted warehouse when he is frozen and handcuffed."

Hockermann would be set free, and Mock would lose his job for sadistically torturing a prisoner.

He went back down the stairs and left the yard where carols rang out in the safe glow of Christmas trees. Out on the street he felt nauseous; pressing his palms against a wall he deposited a steaming pile of honey cake on the powdery snow. He wiped his mouth and walked on. He passed by the Bethanien Hospital and Websky's villa. "I wonder what that lunatic professor feels like now, locked up in a cell with a degenerate and a Babylonian harlot? Did he really wring Knüfer's neck and drown Pinzhoffer in a bucket of water?" Mock slapped himself gently on the cheek. "Of course, the final proof will be this evening. The crime won't take place because the murderer is locked up in Wirth's cell below the counting-room, and therefore can't commit it. He can do no wrong today, and tomorrow or the day after he'll confess to everything. Today, all they'll die of in this town is overindulgence and old age."

Slipping, he walked slowly. Suddenly he saw a flat stretch of packed snow. He gathered speed like a child, spread his arms and skidded with the momentum. At the end of the skid, the sole of his left shoe caught on a small ridge and lost contact with the smooth surface for an instant. That was enough. Mock lost his balance and wheeled his arms violently. A moment later he felt his surgical corset crack, and was dazed by a stabbing pain in his neck. He lay on the ground, waiting patiently for the pain to subside, and gazed up at the starry sky. "And maybe the new prophet's star is somewhere up there among those stars? And what if someone commits murder on Antonienstrasse? What if two lovers are caught *in flagrante* by a jealous husband, and are poisoned?" He tried to stand, but only managed to get onto all fours. "I've got to be there. On Antonienstrasse. With all those people. Watch every door, check identification and question everyone who goes through the gate." With great difficulty he got to his feet, panting heavily, and lifted his head towards the festive windows. "The only person I could go to is Kleinfeld, the Jew; all the others are at home with their families. Celebrating. Why should I drag them away from their wives and children? To freeze to death standing about in some tenement for no good reason? The murderer is locked up in Wirth's cellar, after all. And I'll go to Antonienstrasse with Smolorz. That'll do. The town is safe."

A couple staggered out of an entranceway above which hung a sign: B. BREWING FAHRRADSCHLOSSEREI. The hugely fat man was leaning his entire weight on the shoulder of a slim woman. As they passed Mock, the woman gave him a happy look. Her companion noticed this, pushed her aside and thundered incoherently:

"You whore you, why are you looking at this prick? You've had as many pricks up your arse as there are rivets in Kaiserbrücke, and still you want more!" He took a swing but missed the horrified woman, who had run a few steps ahead. "You shit!" he yelled, hurrying after his companion.

"What's got into you, Friedrich?" said the trembling woman, stopping every now and then, but whenever Friedrich drew near, waving his fists, she would dodge away again. "I didn't even look at him."

Friedrich slipped and flopped heavily onto his backside; there was a loud crack. The man lay in the snow and howled. The flaps of his overcoat fell away to reveal his left leg and a lump that arched above the knee. The woman disappeared. Mock quickened his step and left Friedrich howling there alone with an open fracture to his thigh.

"If that drunk knew the end of the world was going to take place in Breslau, and that the last crime would be the murder of an unfaithful wife and her lover, he could end his madness once and for all. He could bring his wife to Antonienstrasse 27, put a fictitious or real lover with her and stab both of them with a poisoned dagger. Even if she were innocent, out of her mind with drugs, like Sophie. Like Sophie . . ."

282

"Don't you want to know what they did to that swine, Counsellor?"

"They? They were but tools in my hands."

Mock was dazzled by the lights of a car coming from the opposite direction, and stiffened in the sudden glare. Then he took off his coat and threw it on the frozen prism next to the curb. He knelt in the snow, tipped back his hat and began to rub crystals of ice into his cheeks.

"I've gone mad, but I'm going to do it!" he shouted out loud. Nobody heard his shrill declaration. The contented people of Breslau were sitting at copiously laid tables, enjoying the holy peace of Christmas.

BRESLAU, THAT SAME DECEMBER 24TH, 1927
A QUARTER PAST SIX IN THE EVENING

A stocky, red-haired man without a hat got out of the Adler. He ran over to the dark-haired man kneeling in the snow, grabbed him under the arms and pulled him to his feet. The dark-haired man put on his hat and a pair of gloves, and climbed into passenger seat of the car.

"We're going back to where we've just come from."

The Adler moved off, turned left into Webskystrasse and left again into Brockauerstrasse. It stopped at the corner of Briegerstrasse, by Linke's bar. The man in the pale coat with the bloodstain eating into its collar got out of the car. He once again found the gap in the fence that surrounded the derelict building and entered the grounds of the property. Lighting his way with his torch, he went through the gate and down to the cellar. Moments later he was standing beside the crib, the Christmas tree, and the stool with the syringes and the pharmaceutical jar of colourless liquid, once known as the most miraculous medicine in God's pharmacy. The man drew some liquid from the jar into the two syringes. He looked around and his eyes fell on an old medicine chest standing in the corner next to von Orloff's coat. He opened the small chest and paused as several

283

black spiders scurried out of it. He then stowed the syringes and the jar inside. His footsteps echoed in the cellar, then out into the yard and onto the pavement. The car sank on its suspension as the man with the medicine chest jumped inside.

"Now for the prisoners," he said to the driver, "and then we'll all go to Antonienstrasse 27. Is that clear?"

The Adler pulled away.

BRESLAU, THAT SAME DECEMBER 24TH, 1927
HALF PAST SEVEN IN THE EVENING

Meinerer stood on the empty, dark staircase, staring at the door of the last dwelling in the garret. From below came the sound of families having their Christmas Eve dinner; the clatter of cutlery, the hiss of gas escaping from beer bottles, the drawn-out syllables of carols. The only door from which no such sound issued was the one Meinerer stood outside. There, silence had descended not long before. There, his beloved had stopped playing the piano. The voice of the man who was her lover had also fallen silent. Meinerer approached the door and put his ear to it. He could hear whispers and muffled laughter. Leaning his back against the doorframe, he slid down and sat on the floor. He listened, clutching his head in his hands. Whispers reached him from behind the door, whispers reached him from below, grew clearer, became strangely familiar, filled his skull, hissed in his temples, drilled into his jaw. The whispers became voices, playful voices, lustful, raised, tender; his daughters' voices full of reproach as he left them during dinner on this Christmas Eve; the sweet voices of his lovers, who always abandoned him on winter evenings; Mock's bellowing, which humiliated him. All these merged and then Meinerer heard only a swish as he lost consciousness.

The air in the Adler was stuffy. The three people sitting in the back seat gave off a strong odour that was familiar to both Mock and Smolorz. This was the sweat of fear, of people being interrogated. Similar to the stench that emanates from the accused in a courtroom. This was the odour of people being led to their death. Mock stopped the car outside the tenement at Antonienstrasse 27. He opened the small chest and passed it to Smolorz.

"Take the syringes, Smolorz, and get Hockermann's fingerprints on them," he said as he got out of the car.

Smolorz reached into the chest and felt round, smooth shapes and round, rough ones. He presumed the first to be the syringes, the second torches. He turned around to look at the gagged and bound prisoners. The Baron was shaking and his eyes bulged; Sophie, wrapped in a blanket they had found in Wirth's warehouse, sat quietly with lowered eyes; Hockermann tensed his muscles and the lines on his face contracted and relaxed. Smolorz grabbed him by the shoulder and forced him round to face Sophie. Hockermann's sweating forehead landed on her chest. Smolorz pressed his gloves firmly over his fingers, then reached for the syringes with his left hand, and, with his right, for the prisoner's hands tied behind his back. After a few unsuccessful attempts he squeezed the man's blue, swollen fingers around the syringes. As he was doing so he saw Hockermann's gag grow damp, then wet.

"Oh shit!" Smolorz groaned. "He's spewed up, the son of a bitch. Now he'll probably go and choke . . ."

Smolorz threw the syringes into the box and tore the gag from Hockermann's mouth. He was wrong. Epileptic froth bloomed from the prisoner's mouth. Hockermann doubled over, rested his head on Sophie's knees, stiffened and began to shake. The inside of the windows covered over with condensation. Mock, seeing the car rock on its suspension, opened the door on Hockermann's side and dragged him out into the snow.

"Shut the door," he shouted to Smolorz, not wanting to see Sophie's eyes fixed on him.

Smolorz did as he was told and raced up to Mock, who was trying to shove his own wallet into the prisoner's mouth to prevent him biting his tongue. All of a sudden Hockermann opened his eyes and began to laugh.

"The last murder before the coming of the prophet is being committed right now," he said quietly to Mock. "There, there! He's coming!" he yelled, and he suddenly lurched with all his strength towards the tenement.

"Oh shit," sighed Smolorz, and shoved the gag back into Hockermann's mouth. He grabbed him under the arms, opened the car door and, just about managing to keep his own balance, pushed the body inside.

Over the light, powdery snow came a sound that was familiar to them all. The clock on the Town Hall chimed twice. Mock froze.

"Half past seven!" he shouted to Smolorz. "That's when the merchant killed them! Let's go! We'll check all the apartments! Starting at the top." The policemen burst into the building and switched on the light in the entrance hall. Their heavy, snow-covered boots clattered on the wooden stairs. Various sounds reached them from behind the doors as they passed, some joyful, some less so. Sounds of life. Mock put his ear to each door and breathed a sigh of relief. When they got to the top floor, they paused.

"There's only the attic up there," Smolorz said, pointing.

Mock started to climb. Light refracted on the landings and half-landings, with only feeble remnants reaching the garret. Mock moved cautiously, feeling for each stair with the tip of his shoe. When he got to the top, he was in complete darkness. He lifted one foot and waggled it in the air, feeling for the next stair. Suddenly, he heard a muffled groan. He took a gun from one coat pocket, and from the other a cigarette lighter. He looked down and saw that his foot was resting on somebody's stomach. Bending over, he made out Meinerer's pale face in the flickering light of the gas flame. He stepped over him and approached the door. No sound came from within.

"They're in there," he heard Meinerer say. "She and her lover."

Mock grabbed hold of the handle. The door was locked. He stepped back and leaned against the rickety banister, pushed himself off and charged at the door. A loud crash resonated through the entire tenement. Mock felt plaster and pieces of rubble fall down the back of his cracked corset. He nodded to Smolorz, who then resumed the onslaught with his shoulder. Rubble poured onto the floorboards. Somewhere below somebody stepped out onto the landing. Smolorz charged again and fell inside the apartment, together with the door and some lumps of brick. Mock slipped his hand through the doorway and ran it up and down the wall near the doorframe. He felt the light switch. He pressed the small switch down and jumped aside as the electricity blazed. Nothing happened. Smolorz remained on the floor, motionless; Mock stood out in the corridor next to Meinerer, who was still prostrate. Both peered into the dwelling. There was one large room whose focal point was a piano. On the piano stood two bottles of wine and some half-empty plates of food. Around the walls and next to the divan stood wooden stands. Mock felt his corset tighten. The stands had a name he could not remember. One corner of the room was divided from the rest by two screens. Mock had seen screens like that somewhere else recently . . . His memory was clearly playing up on him. Smolorz clambered to his feet, crouched and charged into the room. Nothing happened; nobody fired. Mock stepped tentatively into the dwelling and edged towards the screens. He grabbed one of them and clapped it together like an accordion. Behind the screen was a semi-

287

circular sink. Under it lay two naked bodies. Those of a man and a woman. Blood trickled from small, round puncture wounds. The heads were obscured in the shadow cast by the sink. Mock did not approach the bodies, but sat on the divan and closed his eyes. He had just remembered what those frames were called. He pressed his red, swollen eyelids to stop the flow of hot tears. There was a stinging, bitter taste in his throat. He could not catch his breath. He now knew perfectly well that those frames were called "easels", and that they usually stood in an artist's studio.

BRESLAU, TUESDAY, DECEMBER 27TH, 1927
NINE O'CLOCK IN THE MORNING

Magnesium flashed on the first floor of the Police Praesidium building on Schuhbrücke, and columns of smoke drifted towards the ceiling. Journalists thronged and hollered in the briefing room. Heinrich Mühlhaus sat behind the wide table, calmly puffing away at his pipe. Ernst von Stetten, Mock's secretary, pointed at the journalists in turn to give each of them the voice.

"Is it true that the lovers were poisoned with a drug?"

"It is."

"What was Counsellor Mock doing there at the time?"

"The murdered man is . . . was his nephew. Counsellor Mock went to visit him to wish him a happy Christmas."

"That's strange . . . an uncle visiting his nephew . . . Shouldn't it be the other way round?"

"I have no idea. *Savoir vivre* isn't my speciality."

"What was the motive?"

"The perpetrator killed out of jealousy. He was a spurned lover."

"The murdered woman had left him for Counsellor Mock's nephew?"

"Yes."

"A thirty-year-old woman has a nineteen-year-old lover?"

"*Had*, my good man. And may I congratulate you on your good memory. I mentioned the victims' ages five minutes ago. You're a bright lad."

"How did Mock arrest the perpetrator?"

"He found him mourning over the woman's corpse."

"How did the perpetrator, a policeman, come to know Inge, a princess of the demi-monde?"

"Police work often involves contact with the demi-monde."

"How is the perpetrator linked to the 'calendar murderer'?"

"The perpetrator impersonated the 'calendar murderer'."

"Who is the 'calendar murderer'?"

"Erich Hockermann. This morning he confessed to having committed five murders in Breslau and one in Wiesbaden."

"Why did he commit them? What was his motive?"

"He was a fanatical follower of von Orloff and a well-known occultist. He claimed to be the hand of God, God's scourge . . . Someone who is preparing the world for Christ's Second Coming . . . With his knowledge of history he had no difficulty finding accounts of old crimes in files, and then replicating them . . ."

Mühlhaus stood and left the room while von Stetten politely thanked the journalists for attending.

NEW YORK, MONDAY, NOVEMBER 21ST, 1960
FIVE O'CLOCK IN THE MORNING

Anwaldt got to his feet and went to the map on the wall. He ran his finger over it and found himself for a moment in the snow-covered town, a town of slender church steeples, a town wrapped in factory smoke, a town now called by a different name, which lies in a different country.

"You didn't tell me, Eberhard," Anwaldt said, turning away from the map and sitting in the armchair once more, "what you did with your wife . . ."

From the window came the barking of a dog and the splash of paws in a puddle.

"I set her free," Mock said. "I let her carry on sinning with the Baron. Not long after that, I divorced her. *Per procura*. She didn't take any money from me and went away somewhere."

The gurgling of the drip cut the night's silence. Mock stared at Anwaldt in silence.

"It's an unusual and tragic story." Anwaldt rubbed his sleepy eyes. "But why does your confession depend on it? Oh, I think I understand . . . You've never confessed the sin to anyone . . . And you wanted to tell me about it first . . . I see . . ."

"You don't see anything at all," Mock wheezed. "Firstly, I've already confessed this sin, and secondly, I'm brave enough to make my confession on my deathbed without having to rehearse in front of you."

A beam of light drifted across the ceiling and wall. For a moment, Anwaldt's face was lit up in its glow.

"The murder of my Erwin and Inge Gänserich was not committed by Meinerer," Mock chose his words carefully. "It was the work of a devil, an evil spirit, or whatever you wish to call it." Mock reached for his cigarette-case and turned it in his fingers. "It wasn't Meinerer. He never went into Inge's studio. He'd been lurking outside and claimed to have heard voices . . . Our forensic pathologist, Doctor Lasarius, undertook a chemical analysis of the poison that killed Erwin. It contained a compound that . . ."

The clock in the tower of the Lutheran church on Kaiserstrasse struck one. Its chime travelled far in the sunny air and penetrated the windowpane of the laboratory at the Institute of Forensic Medicine on Maxstrasse, where Lasarius and Mock were sitting in white gowns.

"It's opium," said Lasarius, shaking the test tube. "Once considered a miraculous cure. In the case of your nephew and his lover, it became a lethal poison. They were injected with ten cubic centimetres of opium dissolved in water."

Doctor Lasarius lowered his pince-nez to the tip of his horizontally furrowed nose – which had earned him the nickname 'Anteater' among his students – and patiently acknowledged Mock's blank expression.

"They choked. That's how opium and morphine work when they get into the lungs via the blood. But something worries me. The opium in your nephew's blood is very peculiar."

Mock gazed at the test tubes, the retorts, Bunsen burners, at this whole ordered world of science where – will wonders never cease? – there was a place for the sensitive young poet, Erwin Mock.

"Excellent!" Mock felt his fury rise. "My nephew's body was a catalyst that isolated or released your 'peculiar' opium! Write a thesis on it, why don't you, but spare my sister-in-law!"

"The problem, my dear Counsellor," Lasarius smiled sorrowfully, "lies in the fact that this opium is extremely impure."

"I don't understand," Mock slowly calmed down.

"As you doubtless know, opium is a product from which morphine was derived at the beginning of the nineteenth century. Every gram of opium contains some morphine. The opium in poor Erwin's body does too, but there's very little of it. Why? Because it contains a vast number of other substances, which are usually removed during the purification process.

Someone pumped the deceased full of opium that had not been purified. But where did he get it from?"

"Why are you telling me all this?" Mock jiggled his leg incessantly.

"Opium is not very popular on Breslau's black market, or even in Germany as a whole." Lasarius tapped the test tube with a fingernail discoloured by acid. "Drug addicts prefer to inject themselves with morphine, which is cheaper and stronger. Your nephew's murderer must have brought the opium in from far away . . . But from where? After all, even in China it goes through a purification process . . . It's all rather puzzling . . ."

"Meaning the bastard must have produced it himself," muttered Mock. "There's no other way . . ."

"There is." Lasarius grew pensive. "This opium could be old. Very old . . ."

"How old?" Mock asked.

"You know," Lasarius said, enjoying the sun on his bald skull as it slanted through the window, "I'm not a historian but I seem to remember that sometime in the middle of the nineteenth century, England and France waged so-called opium wars with China. After these wars, the quality of the drug was much improved. It contained about twenty alkaloids, not thirty or forty like the one found in Erwin's body. This may sound a little far-fetched, but maybe the opium that caused Erwin's death could have been produced before 1850?"

NEW YORK, MONDAY, NOVEMBER 21ST, 1960
A QUARTER PAST FIVE IN THE MORNING

Mock heaved himself up in bed and pointed at the map.

"In that city, on Christmas Eve in 1927," he shouted, "there was a manifestation of evil. Do you understand, Herbert? I released that evil, evoked it with my own. The one I wanted to inflict on that unhappy, drugged woman. The Devil appeared in the city of Breslau, and it was I who summoned him there."

Mock collapsed back onto the pillows, breathing heavily. Gnarled fingers picked at the sheets.

"I confessed it, Herbert," said Mock. "It wasn't giving me any peace and I had to tell somebody about it. Somebody who battles with the Devil." He coughed dryly. "This was at the beginning of the thirties. My confessor had only one piece of advice. That I should forgive all those who had hurt me, on whom I'd wanted to enact my revenge. Meaning Baron von Hagenstahl and Sophie . . ."

"And what happened – did you forgive them?"

"The Baron – yes, but Sophie disappeared somewhere and I divorced her *per procura.*"

"Listen, Eberhard," Anwaldt said, slapping his thigh with the newspaper. "I have to . . ."

"You don't have to do anything except one thing." Mock writhed with the pain that cut through his shins eaten away by the tumour. "You have to promise me you'll find Sophie and give her this letter." He handed a long, white envelope to Anwaldt. "It's my forgiveness. I forgive her everything. You promise to find her and give it to her?"

"I do," Anwaldt replied, staring at the envelope.

Mock pushed himself up to embrace Anwaldt, but abandoned the idea. He remembered that his body now gave out a similar odour to that which had emanated from Hockermann and the Baron all those years ago, in the old Adler on the market square of a town that no longer exists.

"Thank you," he said with a smile. "Now go and call the priest. I can die . . ."

Anwaldt shook the sick man's hand and left the room. He went downstairs and passed Father Cupaiuolo, napping in an armchair. He put on

293

his hat and left the house. He made his way slowly towards the nearest subway station. At the corner he caught sight of an enormous dustcart crushing rubbish. He pulled the previous day's *Süddeutsche Zeitung* from his pocket and reread the news of the death of one of Berlin's most famous theatrical actresses, Sophie von Finckl. Beneath the obituary appeared an interview with the well-known violinist, Elisabeth Körner, a close friend of the deceased. In the interview Mrs Körner revealed Sophie's secret for the first time: she had been married before to Eberhard Mock, high-ranking officer of the Breslau Police. Anwaldt read through everything one more time and thought about forgiveness. Then he threw the newspaper into the grinding maw of the dustcart and walked down the concrete stairs.